*Praise for the award-winning
Cotten Stone mystery Series*

THE GRAIL CONSPIRACY

ForeWord Magazine's 2005 Book of the Year for Best Mystery

"Gripping!"—*Mystery Scene* Magazine

"Spellbinding!"—Book Sense

"A thriller … *The Da Vinci Code* meets *Jurassic Park*."—*ForeWord*

"This page-turner is bound to show up … at public libraries across the country."—*Library Journal*

"Religion and science battle through a spectacular hold-your-breath conclusion when the Holy Grail supplies the blood of Christ to the forces of evil."
—M. Diane Vogt, author of *Six Bills* and other Willa Carson novels

"If you liked *The Da Vinci Code*, run out and buy this book!"
—Nancy J. Cohen, author of *Died Blond*

"From a dig in the deserts of Iraq to the inner sanctum of the Knights Templar, this multi-layered tale is a gripping blend of modern science, ancient ritual, and page-turning suspense."
—Christine Kling, author of *Surface Tension* and *Cross Current*

THE LAST SECRET

"Fascinating and breathless. Sholes and Moore are true storytellers, with unerring eyes and the souls of artists. You'll love this one!"
—Gayle Lynds, *New York Times* best-selling author of *The Last Spymaster*

"A great book makes you think when you're done. I'll be thinking about *The Last Secret* for years to come."

—Nelson Erlick, author of *The Xeno Solution* and *GermLine*

"Demonic possession, strange suicides, and Biblical prophecy collide in Sholes and Moore's *The Last Secret*, an intelligent religious thriller with bite. Once again, Cotten Stone proves herself to be a heroine for the new millennium. Insightful, engrossing…but more importantly, a suspenseful thriller from first page to last!"

—James Rollins, *New York Times* best-selling author of *Black Order*

THE HADES PROJECT

"An exceptional novel, a dark labyrinth of suspense, international intrigue, and apocalyptic horror."

—Douglas Preston, *New York Times* best-selling author of *The Codex* and co-author of *The Book of the Dead*

HADES
THE
PROJECT

A COTTEN STONE MYSTERY

HADES
THE
PROJECT

LYNN SHOLES AND JOE MOORE

MIDNIGHT INK
WOODBURY, MINNESOTA

First Edition
First Printing, 2007

Book design by Donna Burch
Cover design by Kevin R. Brown
Editing by Connie Hill

Midnight Ink, an imprint of Llewellyn Publications

Library of Congress Cataloging-in-Publication Data
Sholes, Lynn, 1945–.
    The Hades Project / Lynn Sholes and Joe Moore. — 1st ed.
        p.   cm. — (Cotten Stone mystery ; 3)
    ISBN-13: 978-0-7387-0930-7
    1. Stone, Cotten (Fictitious character)—Fiction.   2. Women journalists—Fiction.   3. Good and evil—Fiction.   I. Moore, Joe, 1948– .   II. Title.
PS3619.H646H33   2007
813'.6—dc22   2007013605

Midnight Ink
Llewellyn Publications
2143 Wooddale Drive, Dept. 978-0-7387-0930-7
Woodbury, MN 55125-2989, U.S.A.
www.midnightinkbooks.com

Printed in the United States of America

ACKNOWLEDGMENTS

The authors wish to thank the following for their assistance in adding a sense of realism to this work of fiction.

Dr. Seth Lloyd, PhD
Professor, Department of Mechanical Engineering
Massachusetts Institute of Technology

Cary E. Moore
Special Agent, Office of Special Investigations
United States Air Force

Jimmy Young
Former Officer, United States Secret Service

Jim McCormick
President, CENCORE, Inc.

> *"The descent to Hades is the same from every place."*
> —Anaxagoras, Greek philosopher, 500–428 BC

"The descent to Hades is the same from every place."
—Anaxagoras, Greek philosopher, 500–428 BC

IN THE BEGINNING

AFTER LOSING THE GREAT Battle of Heaven, Lucifer, the Son of the Dawn, and his rebel angels were driven from Paradise—cast out for all eternity into a world of darkness. Obsessed with hatred and vengeance, Lucifer, now known as Satan, plotted his first act of revenge against God—the temptation of Adam and Eve.

Seeing that Man was vulnerable, and armed with the knowledge that all humans could be tempted, Satan began his battle to prevent souls from entering the Kingdom of Heaven. With each passing Age of Man, he devised ever more elaborate methods of tricking the naïve human psyche into repeating Adam's original sin. To do so, Satan's Brotherhood of the Fallen and their offspring, the Nephilim, roamed the earth in search of prey, building their ever-increasing list of souls that were damned forever to the same darkness from which Evil thrived.

There was one who shared their blood, but not their condemnation. She alone stood in the way of Satan's ultimate goal: to claim all the souls on Earth to his Dark Empire. He had the ability to tempt Man, but she had the will to stop him.

She was Cotten Stone, the offspring of the only forgiven Fallen Angel. God formed a covenant with her father, Furmiel, the Angel of the Eleventh Hour. For his repentance, God granted Furmiel mortality, and he was given two daughters—twins. Because Furmiel could never return to Paradise, God took one of the daughters at birth to fill her father's ranks in Heaven, but the second daughter was to live on Earth. She was therefore called upon by God to fight in His name.

Cotten Stone had discovered her legacy by coming face-to-face with the Son of the Dawn. His hatred of her grew stronger with every confrontation. She had foiled his plan to bring about an unholy Second Coming, and when she understood that God had given Man free will, the ability to create his own reality, she had thwarted Lucifer's attempt to have Man commit the ultimate sin against God—suicide. Deciphering a message inscribed by the hand of God on an ancient crystal tablet, she led those who would choose to live in goodness to a new world of peace and joy.

Unselfishly, Cotten Stone then returned to the old world to continue to fight against her eternal enemy—a world where good and evil were forever at war.

With each new battle that she fought, the End of Days grew closer.

Now two armies were forming: the Ruby, led by the Great Deceiver; and the Indigo, led by the daughter of an angel. Soon, Cotten Stone would again be tested as another battle loomed against the Forces of Evil.

THREAT LEVEL

RIZBEN MACE STOOD IN the center of the pentagram carved in the stone floor, its five points striking out like the blades of an ancient weapon. Six black-robed children knelt before him, their faces hidden beneath hoods.

Clothed in a ruby-red robe, Mace held a golden cup in one hand and a jewel-encrusted dagger in the other. He said, "I call upon Samael, the Guardian of the Gate."

In unison, the children intoned, "Samael."

Responding to the incantation, a finger of high vapor clouds drifted across the moon that shone down like a pale spotlight.

Candles flickered in the night air, their flames protected by high walls as they cast an orange glow upon the ancient rite. Dark figures, cloaked in black and torches in hand, ringed the courtyard.

"I call upon Azazel, the Guardian of the Flame," Mace said, "the Spark in the Eye of the Great Darkness."

Again, the small voices spoke, "Azazel."

At the word, the torches brightened.

"I call upon the Light of the Air, the Son of the Dawn."

"Son of the Dawn," the children repeated.

A hot breath of wind swooped down and furled the robes about the forms of the shadowy figures.

Mace held the dagger and the golden cup in outstretched hands. The flames reflected off the polished metal making it appear as if fire burned from within. He brought the cup to his lips and sipped. The wine warmed him. He had waited with anticipation for the ceremony—the initiation—the official presentation of these young warriors to Lucifer, the Son of the Dawn. They were the offspring of the Fallen Angels, the latest Nephilim soldiers in the ranks of the Ruby Army amassing in preparation for the Final Conflict. A wave of pride rippled through his veins as he held up the cup for all to see.

"In the name of your mighty sword and the flowing lifeblood that gives you the power to conquer, enter into the minds, hearts, and souls of these young warriors, and fill them with your terrible and crushing strength."

Mace raised his arms high and the children stood, forming a single line. Each in turn kissed the blade of the dagger and took a sip from the chalice. When all had done so, they returned to their places and pulled back their hoods revealing their young faces.

Mace opened his arms in a sweeping gesture. "Oh, great Son of the Dawn, behold, the newest soldiers of your vanquishing Ruby Army."

———

Mace walked out of the building and down the three levels of narrow steps onto the sidewalk. It was always such a jarring transition, he thought, going from the medieval courtyard hidden deep in the heart of the building out into the harsh glare of the Washington, D.C., streetlights, and from his ceremonial robe back into a suit.

He reached in his pocket and took his cell phone off vibrate. The text message earlier during the ceremony had forced him to rush through the ancient ritual. He wouldn't want to have to explain to anyone what kept him.

Standing on the sidewalk, he glanced to his right at the sphinx-like granite lion guarding the entrance. It had a woman's head with a cobra entwining her neck. Its matching sister stood guard to his left. His limousine waited at curbside, an FBI agent holding the door open. A black Suburban with a forest of rooftop antennae sat poised like a timber wolf in front of the limo. Two police cruisers, one at the front of the small caravan, the other at the rear, were at the ready, their blue and red strobes casting a hypnotic glow on the tall bronze temple entrance behind him.

Mace slipped into the back of the limo, and the heavy, armored door shut with a bank-vault thud. Immediately, the caravan pulled away—sirens screaming, engines racing. The acceleration pushed him into the deep leather seat as he glanced at his watch. A few minutes past 11:00 PM.

"What do we have?" Mace asked his advisor, who sat opposite him.

"About an hour ago, we received word of a significant increase in cyber intrusions on a global scale. The Internet is down in parts of Asia and Africa, and it's spreading across Europe. Three-quarters of our worldwide monitoring stations are experiencing simultaneous attacks, and over four hundred thousand servers have been infected and shut down."

"Is it just the Internet?"

"So far."

"What are the source addresses?" Mace asked.

"Mostly from China—a few in Malaysia."

"Random targets or a focused assault?"

"It looks random. But it's huge."

"Has anyone notified POTUS?" Mace asked.

"Not yet."

"Make the call." Mace rubbed his face. He could still smell the smoke from the torches and taste the faint sweetness of the wine on his lips. "I'm going to recommend raising the threat level to orange for specific infrastructures. No reason to get the general public in an uproar."

"I agree, sir." The advisor picked up one of several phones from the communications console and pushed a speed-dial number labeled POTUS. In a moment he said, "The Secretary of Homeland Security is calling for the President."

THE TOMB

Cotten Stone stared at the massive columns inside Assumption Cathedral and marveled at the sacred murals ringing each one. The church was one of the oldest structures within the walls of the Kremlin.

"Nothing is by chance in a Russian cathedral, Ms. Stone," said the president of the Russian Federation in stiff English. "The columns support the ceiling, and the saints support the church. That is why the saints are painted on the columns." He motioned toward the lofty recesses overhead.

"Breathtaking, Mr. President," Cotten said, shifting her gaze upward to the splendor of the centuries-old artwork.

Accompanying Cotten and the president were a small camera and sound crew from Satellite News Network, and a handful of Presidential Security Service agents. Bathed in the glare of the camera floodlight, the two strolled through the building—each footfall and word echoing until dying away among the hallowed shadows. It was after hours, and Assumption Cathedral was empty of tourists.

They paused in front of the iconostasis, a collection of sixty-nine painted icons that stretched from floor to ceiling.

"The history of the Bible from the Old Testament to the Last Judgment is illustrated here." The president extended his right arm in a sweeping motion. "So, now I believe that we have seen all there is."

"Well, Mr. President, I can't thank you enough for sharing the amazing splendor of these magnificent churches with our SNN viewers."

"This is the heritage of Mother Russia," he said. "We are proud to share it."

"And you should be." Cotten reached to shake his hand just as a deafening boom rocked the inside of Assumption Cathedral—the blast so intense it knocked her to the floor. Instantly, the chandeliers went out, throwing the interior of the cavernous church into darkness. A spatter of emergency lights flickered around the perimeter of the church.

Cotten raised her head, dazed. She saw the SNN cameraman on the floor—his camera-mounted floodlight shattered. Small bursts of light sparked from a number of locations in the church—muzzle flashes. The weapons must have been silenced, for she only heard the sickening thuds as their bullets found the soft flesh of those around her. Her cameraman cried out, but the darkness kept Cotten from knowing how badly he was wounded. "Are you hit?" she called. But there was no reply.

The PSS agents shouted orders, drew their guns, and returned fire.

Another concussion grenade a few yards away made the cathedral shudder—so violent, Cotten expected the ceiling to collapse and the sacred columns to crumble.

The president's strong hand gripped her arm, pulling her to her feet. "This way! Keep low!"

"What the hell's going on? Who's shooting at us?"

"Could be Chechen rebels. Assassins."

Bullets impacted the marble, spewing up shards of stone that bit her legs as he shoved her behind one of the enormous columns. Beside him were two PSS agents, guns blazing.

She looked over her shoulder in time to see her soundman rise off the floor to follow her, only to be struck down by a barrage of bullets. Her cameraman lay motionless in a crumpled heap. Nearby were the bodies of three Russian security officers.

One of the two PSS agents turned to his commander-in-chief and spoke quickly—his Russian sounding like a recording played at double speed. The second agent fired a volley of shots toward their attackers.

"Keep your head down!" The four broke into a run, sprinting across the open space to the next column.

They crouched behind the thick pillar as a hail of bullets flaked away the five-hundred-year-old masterpiece above their heads.

Another concussion grenade exploded—a supernova in the darkness, the shockwave reverberating in Cotten's bones.

The lead agent tried his radio. No response.

The president turned to Cotten. "We've lost communication, and they've blocked our exits."

"How do we get out?" A torrent of bullets slammed into the column, raining down more slivers of ancient artwork.

"We are going to pray with the tsar," he said, then instructed the agents.

Before Cotten could ask for an explanation, they were running toward a far corner of the cathedral.

Bathed in the strange shadow-world produced by the minimal emergency lighting, Cotten saw a small structure perhaps twenty feet high surrounded by a metal railing. The base of the structure was about ten feet square. With its pointed spires, it reminded her of a miniature pagoda-like cathedral—its white surface decoratively and intricately carved.

As they rushed toward it, the president shouted over his shoulder, "Ivan the Terrible's praying seat."

The two agents began cover fire while Cotten and the president scrambled over the metal railing.

"This way," he said, guiding her to the narrow space behind the Tsar's Praying Seat and the wall. There, he opened a gate and led her into the miniature cathedral. She saw the single chair where the tsar had once presided during high mass. The president pushed the chair aside, revealing a trapdoor in the floor.

One of the agents who accompanied them slumped, holding his neck as blood gushed from between his fingers. A second later, bullets hit the other agent, throwing him against the railing—the back of his head was now a mass of blood and tissue. With a thump, his gun bounced onto the floor beside the praying seat.

The president flipped the trapdoor open. As it slammed against the wooden floor, he sank to his knees—a bullet striking his arm. "Get the pistol," he ordered Cotten, his words strained.

With bullets chipping away at the ornate structure and wood splintering around her, she grabbed the dead agent's gun. When she turned back, the president was already in the hole.

"Hurry!" he yelled.

Cotten sat on the edge of the opening and felt with her foot for the first step of the stairs while the air around her buzzed with bullets and debris. Her toe found it, and she dropped down.

After a dozen or so steps, she came to a platform.

The president leaned against the wall. He moaned and said, "Find the light switch."

Cotten ran her hand along the cold stone locating a small, round switch mounted on the wall. Flicking it caused a bulb below the platform to glow. She saw stairs leading downward.

The president sagged and reached out to her.

"Lean on my back," Cotten said, tucking the agent's pistol inside the belt of her skirt. When she felt his weight against her, she started cautiously down the tight passageway, bracing herself on each side with her arms as she supported him.

At the bottom of the stairs, a narrow tunnel led into darkness. This time, she quickly found the next light switch. It turned on a string of bulbs running along the center of the tunnel's ceiling.

"Go!" he said.

She looked back at the president and saw that the arm of his jacket was dark red, soaked in blood. His face contorted in pain, his eyes half closed.

Bullets, fired from the trapdoor opening, slammed into the platform halfway down the stairs, raining shavings of chewed-up wood.

Cotten led the president through the tunnel until it finally widened and split into two passages.

"Which way?" She ducked as bullets struck the wall near her.

The president's words were weak, almost whispered. "Stay left."

With a trace more room to maneuver, she draped his arm around her shoulder, ran hers around his waist, and started through the tunnel.

Footsteps echoed from behind.

Ahead, the tunnel opened into a series of large drainage pipes and more passages.

"Mr. President. Which one?"

He raised his head. "Always stay left."

The footfalls grew louder. Maybe they didn't know she had a gun, Cotten thought. She could buy a few seconds, perhaps a minute, if she fired several shots. Yanking the pistol from her belt, she glared at it and prayed that when she pulled the trigger, bullets would come out. The Russian agent could have emptied the gun before going down. "Just do it, Cotten," she said.

"Yes," the president whispered.

Cotten peered around the corner. Like alien creatures, figures in black combat gear rushed single file down the narrow tunnel. They wore helmets, thick body armor, and each face was covered by a strange apparatus—night vision devices, she assumed. Pointing the pistol at the lead rebel, she pulled the trigger.

The sound was deafening in the hard-rock walls of the tunnel. The recoil jolted her arm up. Immediately, she readied to fire again. This time she steadied the gun with both hands and braced for the kick.

Again and again she fired.

The first rebel fell—whether she had killed him or not, she didn't know, but she had hit him. A second and then a third rebel, dropped. The crack of more gunfire came from farther back, sending sharp-edged rock fragments and wooden splinters flying.

"Can you keep going?"

The president nodded. The assassins would keep coming, she knew, but maybe not as fast. If they didn't know when she would stop and fire at them again in the tight confines of the passage, they would be more cautious, and that would give her a slight advantage.

As she and the Russian president rounded a corner, a set of stone steps angled up the wall.

"Up, up!" he said.

Laboring, Cotten shoved him from behind as they climbed to a stone platform. Facing them was a large door, black and old.

Reaching out, the president pushed, but the door didn't budge.

"Together," she said. "On the count of three."

He blinked and nodded.

"One, two, three." Cotten threw her shoulder into the door. With a loud metal shriek, it gave.

They stumbled into what appeared to be a storeroom. A flick of a switch turned on an overhead light. By the looks of it, Cotten figured the room had not been used in a long time—perhaps decades. But someone had made certain the light was maintained. An escape route for just such an occasion?

"Quick, bar the door," he said.

Cotten saw the heavy sliding latch. She shoved it into the locked position.

"Now what?" she said.

He gestured to another door on the opposite wall. "There."

Cotten grabbed its handle and pushed. When it swung forward, she saw a hallway, this one made of what looked like black marble—floor, ceiling, walls—all dark and shiny. The lighting was indirect, soft, and modern. As she closed the door behind them, she heard pounding on the tunnel entrance door. The rebels were blocked. But for how long?

"Go!" He pointed to the end of the short hall.

A few steps later they entered a spacious room. It, too, was coal black and softly lit. The walls bore large lightning bolt designs, and a thick red carpet covered the floor. In the center sat a long glass-enclosed display. Smaller at the bottom and flaring out at the top, the display had thick glass walls supported by a metal framework. Eerily, it seemed to glow.

It took Cotten only seconds to realize what she gazed upon.

A sarcophagus.

There before her, laying in repose and protected behind the glass, was the body of a man. His face waxen, his head resting on a white pillow. He wore a black suit, a white shirt with a collar, and a tie. The right hand was clenched.

"Is that—?" Cotten asked.

"Yes," the president said with great effort. He motioned to follow the path around the display bier. On the opposite side, a wide hallway led to the formal entrance.

"Are we locked in?" she asked.

"The doors are designed to open from the inside in case of an emergency." He leaned against the wall and pushed a large red button mounted beside the doors. With a great rush of air and a

14

loud whoosh, they swung open. Immediately, alarms and klaxons screamed as red strobes flashed overhead.

Bursting into the chill of the Moscow night, Cotten stared upon a surreal scene—a sea of police and military vehicles racing across Red Square. They were headed in the direction of the Savior Tower entrance to the Kremlin, responding to the rebel attack, but attracted by the sirens and strobes coming from the mausoleum, many slowed and changed direction.

"Over here!" Cotten shouted, waving. "Help us!"

Suddenly, the president's weight seemed to double, his legs folded, and he collapsed. Cotten wilted beside him on the cold cobblestones outside Lenin's Tomb.

AFTERMATH

"THE RUSSIANS ARE CALLING you a national hero," said Ted Casselman, SNN news director.

"So I've heard," Cotten replied into her cell phone. She stared at the Moscow River from her tenth-floor room at the Rossiya Hotel, twenty hours after the Chechen rebel attack. As she watched a tour boat glide along the river, she pictured Ted Casselman—her boss, friend, and mentor. The forty-eight-year-old black man had been like a father to her since she started at the Satellite News Network more than seven years ago. Some serious health problems had slowed Ted down, but he still ran the news department with the force of a general and the heart of a teddy bear. Ted was always the one to pick her up each time she fell and push her to ever greater heights when she hesitated. Without Ted's guidance and support, her career as a successful network correspondent would never have gotten off the ground.

"The image of you standing next to the president of Russia in his hospital room has shown up on the front page of every newspaper in the world."

Cotten watched the tour boat disappear around a bend. "My heart aches so for the crew, especially those killed. I just met those guys a few minutes before the video shoot. Hardly had time to learn their names."

"Our Moscow bureau says the cameraman will survive. He's pretty bad off, but thank God, he'll pull through. The soundman was from Minsk. They're flying his body home tomorrow. We're taking care of all the arrangements."

Cotten shook her head. "I still can't forget the sounds—the screams, bodies hitting the floor, bullets striking flesh and stone. It was like every sound seemed to echo forever."

There was a long pause. Then Ted said, "I've seen all the reports and interviews, including yours. The government is keeping tight-lipped about everything. Do they really know how the rebels got in?"

"I heard they've already arrested six top officers in the Russian military—sympathizers who helped the assassins get fake IDs, everything. It's a mess. Everyone in the Kremlin is looking over their shoulders."

"If this had happened back in the bad old days, those traitors would have been dragged out and shot."

"That's still a good possibility."

"The rebels picked a perfect time for an assassination attempt," Ted said. "The ideal situation—small crew, little security, empty church."

17

"This was all well planned, Ted. Ironically, the president told me that nothing happens by chance in a Russian church. Boy, was he right."

"What's the damage to the building?" Ted asked.

"A disaster. The curator estimates years before they can think about reopening. But even when they do, almost nothing in the cathedral is replaceable. Treasures accumulated over centuries are destroyed."

"How are your injuries?"

Cotten glanced down at the bandages on her legs and arm. "What does it say about combat pay in my contract?"

"You don't have a contract."

"Then I guess I'll live."

"The conspirators must not be too pleased with you. Do you feel safe?"

"The government emptied this floor of the hotel and stationed two large, serious-looking Russian men outside my door."

"I'm impressed."

"Hey, when you save the president's life, you get to hang out with guys carrying machine guns."

Ted gave an uneasy laugh. Then he said, "John called."

"Yeah, he rang my cell, but I was live on the air with the BBC." She formed an image of John Tyler—his smile, his eyes—the bluest she had ever seen. Probably the only man she had ever truly loved. *You always want what you can never have, Cotten Stone.*

Cardinal John Tyler was director of the Venatori, the ultra-covert intelligence agency of the Vatican—and the most important person in her life. They had met years ago when she was a rookie reporter and he was a priest on leave-of-absence from his duties but not his vows. Together, they uncovered and stopped an attempt to clone Christ. The plot became known in the media as the Grail conspiracy.

"I plan to call him just as soon as I can get a moment's peace and gather my thoughts."

"I assured him that you were fine, just a bit banged up. He said he's been following all the reports. Anyway, I'm sure the Russians have already fully briefed the Vatican. He's worried about you, Cotten."

"I know," she said, closing her eyes. "Ted, I'm completely spent. I've got to get some sleep before my flight tomorrow."

"I won't keep you a minute longer, kiddo. Just take it easy and get back to us safe."

"Deal."

"Oh, by the way. Before I forget, someone else called for you—I mean besides the mountain of media requests for interviews."

"Who?"

"Said she was an old friend from your hometown. Saw you on the news and had to get in touch right away. Something about her daughter."

"Did you get her name?"

Cotten heard a rustle of paper through the phone.

"Here it is. Jordan, Lindsay Jordan. I told her where you were staying. Hope you don't mind. It sounded legit."

"No, that's fine. I haven't heard from Lindsay in ages."

"Okay, kiddo. Get some rest. We can't wait to get you home."

"Same here. Thanks, Ted."

Cotten pushed the button to end the call. She would wait to contact John when she could think clearly. Right now, all she wanted was a good night's rest.

She watched the last rays of the sunset fade and the blanket of city lights come alive across the capital of Russia.

Lindsay Jordan? Her closest friend from childhood through high school. Why would she be calling after so many years?

TERA

THE SOUND OF THE crickets reminded Lindsay Jordan that she'd left the window open. It was careless. Too careless. She closed it and tested the brass lock.

Earlier, just before nightfall, Tera, her eight-year-old daughter, had been staring out the window. Lindsay opened it for her. "What are you thinking about so hard, Tera?" Her daughter's response rocked Lindsay, catching her so off balance that she had forgotten about the open window until now.

Lindsay checked the dead bolt on the front door before pacing her living room. She glared at the telephone, trying to decide whether or not to make the call. How was she going to explain without sounding like she was crazy?

"Damn you," she said, lifting a picture of her husband from the end table beside the sofa. Then she clutched it to her chest. Sometimes she not only grieved for him, but she was angry with him for dying and leaving her and their daughter alone.

Lindsay put the framed photo back on the table before padding down the hall, following the soft glow of the nightlight. Quietly, she opened the door to her daughter's room and peeked in.

Tera slept soundly, curled under a pink coverlet printed with ballerinas striking elegant poses. Tendrils of Tera's blond hair spread out on the pink pillowcase. Her favorite stuffed animal rested just below her chin.

How precious Tera is, Lindsay thought.

She stared at her only child for several more minutes until the fear inside her built to such a staggering panic that she was afraid she would cry out and wake Tera. Lindsay closed the door and returned to the living room.

Again, she looked at the phone.

———

Cotten Stone fumbled in the dark hotel room for the ringing telephone on the nightstand.

"Hello," she said, her voice whispery and gravelly with sleep. She squinted at the red numbers on the clock radio. 5:19 AM. The faint sound of a siren drifted up from the Russian streets below.

"Cotten, I don't know who else to turn to. You've got to help me. Please. I'm desperate."

"Who is this?" Cotten said.

"It's Lindsay." When there was no response, she said, "Lindsay Jordan, from back home."

Remembering Ted's comment about her calling, Cotten suddenly recognized the voice. "Lindsay? It's five in the morning . . . what's wrong?"

"I'm sorry to call like this. I phoned SNN earlier and they finally put me through to your boss. He told me where you were staying. Sorry I woke you. I wasn't sure what time it was there, Cotten, but ... oh, God, I don't know how to explain."

Cotten sat up and switched on the lamp. "Slow down. It's okay that you called. Are you all right?"

"It's Tera."

"Has something happened to her?"

"Not yet." A moment of dead time passed before Lindsay said, "Tera is . . . different, Cotten. I've known it since she was just a baby. Special. I know that's what every mother says, but Tera really is. I can't explain it all to you on the phone. I need you to come here. See Tera. Then you'll understand."

"Lindsay, what's going on? What's this all about?" Cotten pushed up against the headboard, completely puzzled.

"You have to trust me." Lindsay heaved out a sigh. "You won't believe me if I tell you. You've got to see for yourself."

They used to remember each other's birthday, but over time, even the exchange of Christmas cards faded. So why the sudden frantic call, now?

"Lindsay, I'm flying home tomorrow." She looked at the clock. "I mean today. Maybe after I get this Moscow story squared away, I'll give you a call. I've wanted to come to Kentucky to do a piece on thoroughbred racing anyway, so I could come by to see you and Tera in a couple of weeks—"

"No." Lindsay's voice was sharp. "You can't wait that long. I'm going to lose her, Cotten. I'm certain of it. She's had these dreams—nightmares. I say they're nightmares, even though they don't frighten her. But when she tells me about them, it scares the hell out of me." Lindsay's voice cracked. "I wish I could explain better."

"Dreams are just that, Lindsay."

"There's much more than that. It's not just the dreams."

Cotten raked back her hair. What was wrong with her friend? She had heard that Lindsay's husband died—a fall from the barn roof he was repairing. Someone, she couldn't remember who, sent her the local newspaper clipping and obituary. Maybe Lindsay hadn't recovered—maybe she'd become a little out of touch with reality.

"Lindsay? Are you there?"

"I'm here. Cotten, I don't want you to think I'm nuts or that Tera is a freak—but she sees things, knows things. I don't under-stand, but I believe Tera does. And I think you will. That's why I'm calling. Please, Cotten, you've got to help us."

"Lindsay, if you don't have any clue what Tera's *dreams* mean, why would you think—"

"Because of who you are, Cotten. The stories in the news over the years—all the religious stuff you've covered and been involved with. You're the only one who will understand. Just believe me, please."

"I do, Lindsay. I do. Tell you what. Let me give you my cell number. That way if anything changes, you can call me no matter where I am."

"Hang on," Lindsay said.

Cotten waited for her friend to get a pencil and paper then gave the number. "Leave a message on my voice mail if I don't answer. I'll get back to you as soon as I can."

"I promise I won't pester you." Lindsay's voice cracked and there was a moment of silence as if she had to stop herself from crying before she could speak again. "Cotten, today Tera was staring out the window, and when I asked her what she was thinking about, she looked right in my eyes and said, 'Momma, they're coming for me.'"

PROBE

A SECRET SERVICE AGENT ushered Rizben Mace into the Oval Office. The outer-office staff had gone for the night. "Good evening, Mr. President," Mace said with a respectful nod as the door closed behind him.

"Rizben, come in and make yourself comfortable." The president motioned to an empty wingback chair. He wore a jogging outfit—and his brown hair was tousled and lacked the expert styling normally seen when he made public appearances. "Your call gave me a good excuse to take a break from the nightly treadmill."

Philip Miller, National Security Advisor, occupied a second chair. Dressed in a tuxedo, he gave Mace a forced smile, obviously annoyed that he had been pulled away from some official Washington function.

Small gathering, Mace thought, glancing at the two empty couches facing each other in the middle of the room. The couches were separated enough to display most of the Great Seal of the Presidency embroidered in the carpet.

Mace acknowledged Miller with a cordial handshake. "Phil, how are the kids?"

"Hopefully sound asleep by now," Miller said, glancing at his watch. The Harvard Law School graduate had been the only opposing voice in the cabinet when the president appointed Mace to direct Homeland Security. Mace knew that Miller still held a grudge from years ago when he'd backed Miller's opponent in the Arkansas governor's race. It would be more than a grudge if Miller knew the reason he had done so.

The president sat behind the historic Resolute Desk, built from the timbers of the HMS *Resolute*. It had been a gift from Queen Victoria to Rutherford B. Hayes in 1880 and was used by every president since then except Johnson, Nixon, and Ford. "Gentlemen, thanks for coming at such a late hour." He turned to Mace with a slight lift of his hand. "Rizben, bring us up to date."

"Mr. President, as previously reported, significant portions of the Internet were brought down this evening by attacks from primarily Chinese and Malaysian sources. Since the first call to you tonight, we have confirmed that over a million servers across Asia, Africa, Europe, and India have crashed. The word got out quickly, so the damage is starting to subside as everyone still online takes preventative action, but from a commercial standpoint, the attack has already caused considerable damage."

The president removed his glasses and pinched the bridge of his nose. "How much?" he asked.

"Too soon to tell, Mr. President," Mace said, "but preliminary estimates are approaching the multibillion dollar mark."

"Is there any evidence that specific organizations were targeted?"

"Actually, no, sir," said Mace. "It looks like some sort of a flood attack that was meant to disrupt service. So far, we have not received any reports of loss of data."

"Maybe we're getting all revved up over nothing," Miller said. "Could it have just been malicious hackers?"

"Crackers," Mace corrected. "Criminal hackers."

"Sorry, crackers," Miller said with an appeasing wave.

"Again, it's too soon to tell." Mace spoke slowly with a deliberateness he knew Miller wouldn't miss.

"And you're recommending raising the threat level?" the president said.

"Yes, sir, but only for selective infrastructure"

"Isn't this a bit of an overreaction?" asked Miller. "I mean, just because a bunch of Europeans can't log on to their favorite porn sites for a few hours—does that warrant scaring the hell out of the nation?"

"I wish it were that simple, Phil," Mace said. "The fact is we still have to consider the possibility that events like this could be the first wave of a cyber-terrorism attack. This could easily have been a probing action to see our reaction and gauge vulnerabilities."

"But the damage to our infrastructure was minimal, correct?" the president asked.

"So far," Mace said.

"This is the same argument we keep going over, time and again," Miller said to Mace. "I just can't believe that terrorism is going to come from the Internet. Terrorists don't want to see some guy denied access to his AOL account. They want the shock factor of jet airliners crashing into buildings, subways filled with toxic gas, and dead bodies scattered in the streets. Hell, how about trying to assassinate the president of Russia inside the fucking Kremlin, for God's sake. That's terrorism." He turned to the president. "Their objective is to terrorize, not piss off. We'll be justifiably accused of crying wolf over this. Corporations and agencies in this country are doing a hell of a good job hardening access to their assets. We need to reserve adjusting the national threat level to real threats, not what happened tonight."

"You're right, Phil," Mace said. "Striking at the heart of America with physical attacks does create the most impact, but that doesn't mean we have to ignore more subtle probes into our virtual heartland. The true damage can take place without shedding one drop of blood or blowing up a plane."

There was a silence that settled over the Oval Office, broken a moment later by a slight squeak of the president's chair as he leaned back. "I tend to agree with Phil," he said. "Rizben, send out an official alert bulletin to all private and public organizations that would be vulnerable to this sort of intrusion. Advise them of what happened and suggest they review all security procedures involving cyber attacks." He gave Mace a patronizing smile. "Let's keep a sharp eye on this one, but not get our knickers in a knot." He stood. "Thanks again, gentlemen. Keep me informed of any new developments."

The three men shook hands. Miller led the way out of the Oval Office, Mace behind. Beyond earshot of the president, Miller turned. "Sorry, Rizben, but we can't be trigger-happy, can we?"

"No, we can't," Mace said with a nod. He stopped and pulled his cell phone from his pocket. Looking at the caller ID, he said, "Got to take this, Phil."

Miller waved over his shoulder as he rounded a corner.

Rizben glanced around, making sure he was alone before pushing the talk button. "Pastor Albrecht, do you have the girl?"

"No. She and her mother disappeared."

"But she definitely identified you?" Rizben said.

"Yes."

"Then we have a problem."

"Actually, there's an even bigger problem."

Rizben switched ears. He had been riding high on the predictable response from the president and Miller, and didn't want anything spoiling it. Now this. "And what would that be?"

"Cotten Stone just showed up."

LORETTO

Cotten's drive from the Louisville airport to Loretto, Kentucky, brought with it a flood of memories. The ribbon of road threaded through the countryside, embraced by the gently rolling land of expansive horse farms and the more modest hay, soybean, and tobacco farms. Cotten's roots were buried deep in this soil, even though she had created another life very different in New York with SNN—a galaxy that glittered and spun in all directions, so unlike the universe of her childhood that she had put behind her. With much effort she had even discarded the southern accent so it only put in an appearance when she got excited.

Cotten turned off Highway 49 onto a series of back roads until finally steering into Lindsay Jordan's long dirt driveway. The house sat in the middle of what had once been five hundred and twenty lucrative acres of tobacco fields, a crop that had supported the Jordan family for generations. But Lindsay's farm hadn't grown tobacco in twenty years, yielding to soybeans.

Closer, Cotten noticed that the house seemed in disrepair. Weeds spiked through the grass to knee height. A slat in the porch rail hung loose, jutting out at an angle. She glimpsed the barn from which Neil Jordan fell on a stormy, summer afternoon.

Neil Jordan. Wow. She and Lindsay had both had crushes on him. He was definitely the catch of their high school class—good looking, smart, first string on the varsity football team, voted *Most Likely to Succeed.* Lindsay had wound up with him. Pregnant. They got married a week after graduation, and Neil went to work with Lindsay's family on the farm—his *Most Likely to Succeed* plowed under with the next crop. Two months later, Lindsay miscarried. It was another nine years before Tera was born. *Strange how life takes everyone on a different path*, Cotten thought, parking the car in front of the house.

At the front door, Cotten heard a mewing sound. She looked down between the cracks of the wooden porch. A mother cat with a litter of kittens stared up.

"Hey, kitty, kitty," Cotten said softly, before returning her attention to the door. She rapped it with her knuckles. "Lindsay?"

Cotten waited a moment before knocking again, this time louder. "Lindsay, it's me, Cotten. Hello."

Still no answer. She made her way around to the rear of the house and climbed the wood steps to the back porch. The screen door twanged shut behind her. "Hello."

To her right was a metal storage cabinet, and stacked beside it were five cases of canning jars. To her left were cans of spray paint, a hand trowel, and a jug of Roundup sitting atop an old maple dresser.

Cotten stood at the back door of the house, its white paint peeling away.

"Lindsay? Anybody home?"

She turned the tarnished brass knob, but the door was locked. Cotten pressed her forehead onto the window and butted her hand against the glass, but the window was draped from the inside. She tried to get a glimpse by looking sideways at the edge of the window, thinking maybe there was a gap between the drape and the glass. No luck.

Cotten glanced around. The place had not been cared for—it looked almost deserted.

And there was no car. Unless it was in the barn.

Something brushed her leg, and Cotten jumped, flailing backward into the storage cabinet. The metal doors rattled and clanged, flapping open in unison with a high-pitched screech.

Cotten spotted the cat springing off the porch, hair on end. A pair of pruning shears latently clattered onto the floor.

The damn cat, she thought, then laughed at herself. Poor thing was looking for affection, and she had scared the living daylights out of it.

Cotten picked up the shears and cleared a space for them on a shelf inside the storage cabinet. As she did, she saw a faded blue and red box of Diamond kitchen matches. When they were kids the spare key had been kept in that box. She wondered if . . .

Cotten slid open the box and wriggled her forefinger through the thin layer of matches. Bingo. She plucked the key from the box and tried it in the lock. The door opened.

Before going inside, Cotten closed the match box and put it back inside the cabinet, but she slipped the key into her jeans pocket.

She entered the kitchen. It was uncomfortably warm and musty, as if fresh air had not circulated in a long time, and there was an awful smell that made her want to gag, forcing her to breathe through her mouth.

A piece of an old quilt was nailed over the window and sealed on the edges with duct tape. Lindsay obviously didn't want anyone to see in or out. Cotten found the light switch. The fluorescent bulbs strobed before emitting a steady light.

The deep porcelain sink held a couple of food-crusted dishes. Cotten turned on the faucet. It choked and sputtered but finally water came streaming out, rusty and cloudy before clearing. She turned it off after filling the sink.

"Lindsay, are you here?" she called, pushing the swinging door that led from the kitchen to the dining room. As she moved through the house, she turned on the lights, becoming more nervous with each room. It was so dark with the sun blocked out.

The smell grew worse, and she heard the buzzing of insects. Flies.

As Cotten moved into the living room, she saw that all the windows were covered, just like the one in the kitchen. Quilts, bedspreads, and sheets had been nailed and taped over every opening.

And the damn stench was horrid. What the hell had gone on here? She started imagining finding a body—Lindsay's body. Perhaps there had been an accident. Or worse. And where was Tera? She slowed her steps, realizing that when she discovered the source of the stench, she would probably find the answers.

Cotten crept cautiously down the hall and came to a halt in front of the utility closet. When she cracked the door open, the rank air seemed to congeal and overwhelm her. She covered her mouth and gagged.

PAINTINGS

COTTEN REELED BACKWARD AS swollen black trash bags tumbled from the utility closet. A rupture in one bag spewed its guts—a dark red sauce coating wormy threads of old spaghetti, the decomposing remains of a zucchini, chicken bones, banana peel, and other more unrecognizable contents. A putrid gelatinous puddle formed on the gray linoleum.

"Jesus," Cotten said, getting a full complement of the dreadful stench. Why had Lindsay been storing her garbage in the closet?

Cotten shoved the bags back with her foot just enough to allow passage down the hall. The door stood open to the first room. Tera's bedroom, she thought, seeing the ballerina-print coverlet as she turned on the overhead light. Instantly her eyes were drawn to the walls. Paintings, beautiful paintings, covered the walls. Unframed canvases of portraits and landscapes, surreal visions of light and shadow, haunting depths of color, stunning and amazing works of art.

Cotten stood in front of a portrait that was probably five feet high by four feet wide. It showed a breathtaking picture of an angelic child, her blonde hair tumbling to her shoulders, clear blue eyes that seemed to transcend the canvas and look right into the viewer's soul. She was surrounded with a halo of soft, deep blue light. Was this Tera? Cotten turned in a slow circle, taking in the dozens of paintings covering the walls.

Dazed by the magnificent artwork, Cotten sat on the bed and noticed a journal on the nightstand. Even though she felt as if she were violating Tera's privacy, she couldn't resist seeing what it contained. Opening the cover, Cotten read the first page:

The Glaze
Burns the stains from the water
The soul of the swan finds solace
Transcending the perfect hour
To swirl in the glory
Of the mysteries

She shook her head. This was not normal reading for an eight-year-old and certainly not the writing of one. If Lindsay had written it for her daughter, what was she thinking?

Cotten turned the page and leaned against the headboard as she read,

I asked you,
Come with me
The weeping Selene draped me in ebony
And cast my tears onto a cloth of obsidian
I asked you,
Come with me

On page 3, she read,

The stillness stole the rhythm
Silence crashed on the shore
But above the mighty river
Soar, soar, soar

Can you feel the light as it touches your mind
Hear the roar of the whisper
Across the twinkling edge
Soar, soar, soar

Cotten fanned the pages with her thumb. *Incredible.* Page after page of poetry written in a beautiful, flowing hand. Mature and controlled, not the handwriting of a child.

She set the journal back on the nightstand before continuing her search of the house. A bathroom separated Tera's bedroom from what looked to be Lindsay's. Cotten turn on the ceiling light along with the lamp on the dresser and another on the nightstand.

Unlike Tera's bed, Lindsay's was unmade. The quilt lay rumpled on the floor at the foot of the bed, the pillows askew. But like Tera's and every other room, the windows were covered and sealed tight.

There were paintings here, too, gracing every wall—some fanciful and others astonishingly realistic. Cotten moved close to one and ran her finger over the face of a brown-skinned child whose large dark eyes peered up at a star-filled sky. Like the one in Tera's room, the child was surrounded by a soft, cerulean glow. She touched a painting of a white horse, mane blowing in the wind as it stood atop a hillcrest against a brilliant blue sky.

Cotten wondered when Lindsay had started to paint. Maybe after Neil's passing, she thought. Perhaps it had become her therapy. None of the paintings were signed. Instead, each bore a simple blue slash at the bottom—a mark reminding Cotten of a thunderbolt.

She looked about, thinking that Lindsay could certainly sell her work, and wondered if her friend had tried. If Lindsay hadn't made the connections she needed out here in the middle of the Kentucky farmland, Cotten would get her in touch with someone in New York. Cotten had little knowledge of the art world, but she did know that these paintings were beautiful, moving, and probably valuable. She would ask the SNN art critic to have a chat with Lindsay.

She moved in front of the dresser again and lifted a photograph—Neil with his arm around Lindsay, who was holding a baby. Tera, she assumed.

So, where were Lindsay and Tera, and what was that desperate call all about? Cotten explored the rest of the house and found nothing unusual other than the covered windows. The other rooms had a painting or two hanging on the walls, but nothing like the collection in the mother's and daughter's rooms.

A stack of mail sat on the coffee table in front of the couch in the living room. Cotten plunked herself down and picked up the envelopes. Junk mail, gas bill, the typical pre-approved credit card offers, *People* magazine, MasterCard statement.

Cotten tossed the mail back on the table. That's when she caught a glimpse of the blinking light on the phone. She leaned over to the end table and pressed the button on the phone to play back the message.

Hello, Lindsay. This is Pastor Albrecht. I just wanted to say that there's no harm done. I understand your daughter is still under a great deal of stress with the death of her father and all. Sometimes things get the best of young girls that make them go a little . . . Lindsay, no one feels worse than me about the outburst at church. I came by to visit but you and Tera were not home. I'll try again.

The date—four days ago.

Outburst? Cotten glanced around the dark room at the covered window. What the hell was going on here?

CONNECTION

COTTEN SAT ON LINDSAY Jordan's couch. The message on the phone distressed her. What kind of outburst was this guy, Pastor Albrecht, talking about? And why were Lindsay and Tera living like this, sealed up in a house full of clutter and garbage? In her call to Cotten, Lindsay truly feared for her daughter.

Cotten wondered if she should call the authorities. But what would she tell them? That Lindsay was a messy housekeeper? That she left bags of rotting garbage around and had some kind of compulsive fear of direct sunshine and fresh air? Her daughter had an outburst at Sunday service?

It had been a week since Lindsay's middle-of-the-night plea. What if something had happened to them and she was too late?

No reason to take chances. After calling information for the non-emergency number, she dialed.

"Sheriff's office." The female voice sounded young and bored. Cotten thought she heard the smack of chewing gum.

"I'd like to report a missing person—two missing persons," Cotten said.

"Your name?"

"Cotten Stone."

"What is your location?"

She gave the address for the Jordan farm.

"Hold please," the girl said.

A few moments later, a man came on the line. "I don't suppose this is *the* Cotten Stone? Furmiel and Martha Stone's daughter? World-famous news correspondent?"

"I'm not so sure about the famous part," Cotten said.

"Ms. Stone, this is Sheriff Maddox. I can't tell you how proud we are of you around here. Not only do my wife and I watch you on SNN all the time, but when we saw what happened over there in Russia, well, we're just so proud. And if I might add, you sure have grown up to be a mighty pretty young lady."

"Thank you, Sheriff." She remembered Maddox. He had investigated her father's death—Furmiel Stone's suicide.

"So what's this about missing persons?"

"I'm out here at Lindsay Jordan's place. She and her daughter appear to be missing."

Maddox gave a loud, heavy sigh.

"What's the matter?" Cotten asked.

"Well, how should I put this? She tends to get a bee in her bonnet now and then, takes Tera and leaves for a few days. Just picks up and goes on the spur of the moment. I think she simply needs to get away from Loretto sometimes, even if it's for just a day or two. Lindsay once told me she felt like she was living underwater in the deep end of a swimming pool. I believe taking these little mini-vacations is the way she comes up for air."

"I'm not sure that she's gone on vacation this time. I got a phone call from her. That's why I'm here. She sounded upset and scared. She begged me to come."

"I'm sure she's just overreacting to what happened at church the other Sunday."

"What did happen?"

"It's a bit embarrassing, Cotten—may I call you Cotten?"

"Of course."

"I wasn't there, mind you, but apparently a couple of Sundays ago was the first time Lindsay had taken Tera to church in a long time. The girl didn't like being there because that was where she last saw her father after he was killed. Tragic accident, you know. That's where they had the funeral. We have a new pastor at the church, a Reverend Albrecht. It was the first time Tera had met him. Well, as soon as she laid eyes on the pastor, she just went berserk and started calling him evil and the devil and such. I heard that it was awful. She was screaming and yelling. Poor thing had to be sedated by the doc. Lindsay took her home and they haven't been heard from since."

Cotten realized the sheriff had placed his hand over the receiver for a moment to give an order to what she figured was a deputy.

"Sorry, Cotten," he said, "we've got a minor fender-bender out on five-twenty-seven. Where was I? Anyway, I think that Lindsay has been battling some real demons since Neil passed. And what's worse, I think it has taken a toll on Tera. She's a sweet little girl, but not like any other eight-year-old I know."

"What do you mean?"

42

"Always claiming to see things—ghosts, spirits, visions. I believe she just wants attention. Can't blame her, I suppose."

As Cotten listened, she tried to push away the haunting question of why Lindsay had chosen to contact *her* in the first place. Now she was confident that her friend not only needed to be found, but it sounded like she could use professional help—for her and Tera.

"I'm sorry to hear all this," Cotten said. "When Lindsay called me a week ago, she did say that Tera was having unusual dreams. But Lindsay seemed so scared—frightened that she was going to lose her daughter. She sounded desperate."

"When you get right down to it, Lindsay is in a pitiful state. Though a lot of folks have offered to help, she refuses. I'm sure she'll be back in a couple of days. If she doesn't show up soon, I'll look into it. Meanwhile, I'll call around and see if I can find out anything else."

"Thanks, Sheriff Maddox. I hope you're right and that I have reason to be a little embarrassed over bothering you with this. I would appreciate it if you'd get back to me with any information. Anything at all." Cotten gave him her cell phone number.

"You bet," he said, then chuckled. "I still don't believe it. A real celebrity right here in Loretto. Stop by and say hello. Everybody would really get a kick out of meeting you."

"I will, Sheriff."

Cotten hung up. She felt empty. And gloomy. Her friend was obviously suffering, and there was probably nothing she could do about it.

Something still bothered her, though. Maybe she was just being overly cautious—the news reporter always coming out. Question everything. After all, doing just that is what got her the senior news correspondent position at SNN.

She wasn't ready to call it quits, yet. Instead, she would dig just a little deeper.

Cotten decided to start with a thorough search of the house, hoping that whatever she found would convince her to either go home or stick around and investigate further.

She headed down the hall and entered Tera's room again. In many ways it was a typical girl's bedroom except for all of her mother's paintings. There was a large collection of books on the shelves along one wall. Cotten scanned the titles: *Evidence of God*; *Experiencing Prayer*; *Peace on Earth;* Billy Graham's *The Journey*; *The Power of Intention*, by Dr. Wayne W. Dyer; *The Isaiah Effect,* by Gregg Braden. Not the usual reading for a kid Tera's age.

On another shelf were what appeared to be Tera's school books. Cotten brushed the books with her fingertips recalling Lindsay's phone call. *Because of who you are, Cotten. The stories in the news over the years—all the religious stuff you've covered and been involved with. You're the only one who will understand.*

Cotten took a deep breath.

She continued through the house, exploring cubbies and nooks, drawers and cabinets. In the kitchen, beneath the dinette, she found a stack of teacher's manuals that matched Tera's texts. There were also folders with tabs marked math, reading, and spelling. Lindsay was home-schooling her daughter. Why had she chosen that route rather than sending her to public school?

Cotten fanned herself with an empty folder. Even though it was early fall and the weather cooling off, the day was unusually warm.

With the windows closed and covered, the air inside smothered her. Not to mention the stench of spoiled garbage.

Cotten sensed the walls closing in and likened it to what a claustrophobic must feel in a crowded elevator. She made her way back to the living room, snatched the blanket off the front window and slid up the bottom pane. Then she unlatched the front door, helping it coast back until it hit the stop on the wall. A fresh breeze blew through. The screen door whined as Cotten stepped onto the porch. The sun washed away the cloying darkness of the house and she let the pureness of the day stream over her.

After clearing her head, Cotten strode to Lindsay's bedroom where she rifled through drawers and closet—all of which were in disarray. It struck her that the rooms looked like they might have been searched before she arrived. Maybe somebody else was anxious to uncover clues to where Lindsay and Tera had gone.

On top of the dresser was a framed photograph that caught Cotten's attention. As she lifted it, a wave of familiarity swept through her—a sensation akin to déjà vu.

Cotten touched her finger to the face in the picture—a little girl whose wispy blonde hair tumbled around her shoulders. Her blue eyes, like her mother's, were clear and wide as she smiled at the camera. She held a calico kitten to her cheek, seeming to relish the softness of the fur. The girl looked to be seven or eight. It had to be a recent photo of Tera.

Cotten felt herself well up with emotion. Not because she was concerned for the child, but because of some unexplained connection—like she knew more about Tera than she realized. Almost as if a distant memory was just on the verge of recall.

Stunned, Cotten set the picture on the dresser and backed away. She parked herself on the side of the bed, trying to rationalize an explanation for what just happened. Never had she experienced anything so unexpectedly stirring. Lindsay was right, there was something unique about Tera, and Cotten was determined to find out what had happened to them.

At the foot of the bed was an antique trunk. She lifted the lid, and the unmistakable sharp scent of cedar permeated the room. Cotten removed a crocheted throw blanket, and beneath it discovered pencil drawings—detailed, beautiful drawings. She sorted through them, overcome with wonder at Lindsay's talent. There were also small paintings with the same dramatic detail as those on the walls. Each bore the tiny blue thunderbolt signature.

Reams of poetry filled a shoebox. Cotten read several before replacing the lid. Next, she found a scrapbook. Fastened in corner mounts on every page were black and white photographs. It had to be Lindsay's mother's album. Near the back were some faded color photos, as if bathed in yellow light. One was of Cotten and Lindsay in high school. She wanted to take time to muse over them, but not now.

There was a folded piece of paper shoved under the picture—a corner sticking out. Out of curiosity, Cotten removed it only to freeze. Her name was written on top.

Carefully unfolding the note, she read:

Dear Cotten. If you are reading this, then it is too late. We have gone into hiding. Tera told me that a guardian angel would come to protect us. I know that must be you. She said they are hunting us and they will stop at nothing to keep you from finding her first. They are pure evil, Cotten. Please pray for us. Lindsay and Tera.

Despite the warm, stale air, Cotten felt a chill run through her. Desperation flowed from Lindsay's words. As if someone were watching, Cotten glanced around the room, then folded the note and placed it in her pocket.

She knew it was time to make the call.

DEVIN

"DOES DOLPHIN STADIUM HAVE a Code Adam?" Alan Olsen asked.

"No, sir," the Miami-Dade police officer said. The cop led the way into the men's room. As he entered, he keyed his shoulder mic. "Unit forty. Possible missing child. Standby."

"How can you not have an emergency alert?" Alan felt his face start to burn with frustration. "You know how many kids come to these games? How could you not . . ."

"Unit forty, possible missing child. Ten-four," replied the thin, metallic voice from the police radio.

"I've already checked in here," Alan said. "Devin came in, but I never saw him come out."

"Start Me Up" by the Rolling Stones blared from the giant stadium speakers. The Dolphins and Jets were ready for the second-half kickoff.

The officer moved along the line of stalls. After confirming there were no children in any, he said, "Let me see your tickets."

Alan reached into his pocket, then handed the officer the stubs.

"Have you gone back to see if your son is at your seats?"

"Yes. I did that, too." Heat built inside Alan, and the pressure in his head thudded. "I've done all that. Can't you alert stadium security?"

"Let's have a look just to make sure. Kids do this all the time. Wander off, then wind up back in their seat wondering where their parents are. First, let's see if he's there."

"But if something is wrong, we're wasting . . ." There was no sense finishing the sentence. Alan could tell he was being ignored. Maybe the police dealt with this all the time, but he didn't, and he wanted to see some sense of urgency in the cop's attitude. Besides, the policeman didn't understand about Devin.

"Listen," Alan said. "We're wasting precious time. If we find him, then no harm done, but if he's in trouble . . ."

The officer headed up the tunnel ramp with Alan a pace behind. Turning onto the steep steps leading upward, Alan's gaze focused on their empty seats. No Devin. His gut tensed, forcing air out of his lungs in an unexpected rush. He was close to panicking—something he never did. It wasn't part of his nature.

The deafening roar heralded the kickoff. Alan and the officer climbed the steps until they stood beside the two empty seats.

"Take a good look around and see if you spot him," the officer shouted into Alan's ear. "He might be in the wrong seat."

Damn the cheap seats, Alan thought. He could easily afford a corporate skybox, but he wanted Devin to experience the game like most other kids his age. *Please don't let it prove to be a mistake*, he prayed.

He scanned the nearby crowd while the officer spoke into the shoulder mic, but the crowd was too noisy for Alan to hear what he was saying. He hoped it was finally the call to alert the security staff.

He followed the officer down the steps and back through the tunnel. A few moments later, they entered the Miami-Dade Metro Police Substation on the ground floor of the stadium. The space was compact with a small waiting room and a few chairs. The officer showed Alan into a second room where another officer sat behind a desk. "This is Sergeant Carillo. He'll take it from here. Show him your ID, then give him a full description of your son."

"Can we make this fast?" Alan said. "Devin is missing and nobody's looking for him."

"Don't worry, Mr. Olsen," Carillo said. "Parents get separated from their children here all the time. We'll find your son."

Alan removed his driver's license from his wallet and handed it to the sergeant.

"This your correct address?" the sergeant asked, making a few notes on a pad.

Alan nodded, clasping his hands together to still the shaking and contain the anger. The delay was becoming unbearable.

Returning the license, Carillo took a brief look at Alan and said, "Have a seat. Can you give me a description of your son?"

Pulling the chair out, Alan felt his jaw clench as the wood legs scraped the floor. Sitting, he said, "His name is Devin. He's eight, about four-six, four-seven. Sixty pounds. Blond hair, blue eyes. He was wearing jeans, a yellow T-shirt and a Dolphins jacket. Oh, and a Dolphins cap."

Carillo busily scribbled on a pad of paper, not even looking up when he asked the next question. "When did you see him last?"

"During halftime, we went to get a snack. Devin said he had to use the bathroom, but the lines were a mile long." Alan wiped the sweat from his face with his hand. "He has a bladder control problem and has to urinate often—at least once an hour."

"You want something to drink?"

"No!" Alan took a deep breath. "Sorry. No, I don't need anything to drink."

"Okay, what else?"

"We went to the front of the line and I asked this guy if Devin could please cut in line ahead of him. The poor kid was standing there with his legs twisted like a pretzel and a look of agony on his face." Alan wiped his brow again. "The guy took pity on Devin and let him by."

"What did you do?"

"The concourse was packed. I walked over to the outside stadium wall and waited."

"How long?"

"Eight, maybe ten minutes."

"That's a long time for a kid to take a piss." Carillo finally looked up and locked on Alan's eyes.

"I realize that. That's why I'm so upset."

The cop made a few more notes. "Did you just hang around there or did you wander around, maybe leave and come back?"

"I never moved."

"Did you talk to anyone?"

"No. Well, yes. Some guy struck up a conversation with me about football statistics. I found him a bit overbearing and boring. I mean, I'm not that big of a football fan."

"Then why did you come to the game?"

"Devin loves the Dolphins. He can rattle off all the players' stats. This was his first NFL game."

The officer tore the page from the pad and stood. "Anything else you can tell me before I call this in?"

Alan hesitated. There was more, a lot more. But probably the guy wouldn't understand or believe him. "No, nothing else," Alan said.

THE BARN

COTTEN RETRIEVED HER PURSE from the rental and pulled her cell phone out of its side pocket. She checked her watch—12:30 PM in Kentucky, 6:30 PM in Rome. Leaning against the car, she scrolled through her phone list to the private Vatican number for Cardinal John Tyler. After getting his voice mail, she dialed his cell.

"*Ciao*," came the response after a half-dozen rings.

"John. You're working late."

"Actually, I'm in Washington for a security conference. We're winding everything up this afternoon. Hang on a second."

Cotten heard the mumble of background voices diminish as John found a quieter location.

"I was just thinking about you."

"Really?" she said. "We must have ESP." She shifted her weight to her other foot. His words flooded her with warm memories and a deep yearning. *I've always wanted what I could never have.* "It's great to hear your voice."

"How are your wounds healing?" John asked.

"Not everybody can brag about being shot by Chechen rebels."

"That's not funny. Ted told me you're investigating a story in Kentucky? How's it going?"

"What is it they say, fair to middling?"

"I don't hear that colloquialism around the Vatican very often. But I believe it means less than terrific. What's going on?"

Cotten started with Lindsay's call, a description of the farmhouse, Lindsay's paintings and poetry, Sheriff Maddox's comments, the outburst at church, what happened to her when Cotten saw and touched Tera's picture, and ending with the note in the scrapbook. "Pretty suspicious, isn't it?"

"It's all suspicious. What part in particular?"

"All of the above, but mostly what happened when I touched her photo."

"Knowing you like I do, nothing would surprise me. Your connection with Tera tells me there's something else going on there, something deeper than the sheriff's explanation."

"It was as if I felt whole—complete—like she was an extension of me."

"Any idea why?"

"Not yet."

"What are you going to do?"

Cotten scanned the area around the farmhouse. There was a barn nearby. "I've got a few more things here to check out. Then I'll head back to town and start asking around to see if anyone knows anything. If it turns out that they really are in danger, I'll find a way to get them some protection."

"I had planned on flying back to the Vatican in the morning. What if I delay that a few days and come to Kentucky?"

"You sure you can take the time? I mean, I'd love to see yo, but I really don't have much to go on here."

"Your comment about the connection to the girl concerns me."

"How so?"

"Things have been unusually quiet for a long time. Too quiet. This could be the start of another round with our old friends."

"That occurred to me, too." Cotten closed her eyes, thankful that John would be by her side if their concerns proved true. Actually, even if there were nothing to worry about, she'd be happy to be near him again. She touched the mouthpiece of the phone as if it might magically bring him closer. "How about I pick you up in Louisville? It's a nice drive between there and Loretto."

"I'll call you back with my flight info."

Before she had a chance to stop them, the next words tumbled out. "I miss you."

There was a pause. "Same here." She heard him take a deep breath. "I'll call you in an hour or two."

Cotten flipped the phone closed and tossed it on the front seat of her car. The battery was almost dead, and that would remind her to plug it into the car charger.

She wandered down the hard-packed clay path toward the barn. Lindsay's cat sat off to the side at a respectable distance, still leery of Cotten's intentions.

Like the house, the outside of the barn was in critical need of repair and a fresh coat of paint. Farm tools lay scattered in thin, overgrown grass. Weeds grew between the logs in a stack of firewood.

Bees buzzed about a patch of purple wildflowers near the corner of the old structure. An ancient oak provided shade.

How could Lindsay be so artistically talented and yet live in such shambles? Perhaps the paintings and poetry were her distractions from a crumbling life—maybe they had become obsessions to help get through the days . . . and nights.

Cotten stood in front of the barn doors. She would take a quick look inside before heading back to town. The heavy latch scraped and groaned—both of the twelve-foot-high doors swung open lazily. The aroma of turpentine and oil paint flowed out.

When Cotten's eyes adjusted to the dim interior, she marveled at what she saw.

Overhead, suspended from rafters, hung dozens of paintings in many sizes. They weren't just beautiful works of art—there was something spiritually and mystically inspired about them. The barn walls were also covered with paintings and drawings. And scattered about were racks of blank canvases along with boxes of oils, acrylics, charcoal, brushes, and palettes. The entire barn had been converted to an art studio. The smells of hay and earth were replaced with linseed oil and gesso.

An unfinished painting drew Cotten to the rear of the barn. It was a portrait of a man. Unlike the other beautiful images, his face was contorted, his eyes filled with hate and rage. Outlining his body was a pale, red glow.

Cotten wandered through the barn, looking at all the stunning art. She stopped in front of another painting, this one of a child who looked just like the girl in the photo—blonde, ice blue eyes, delicate features—sitting on a cliff at sunset, cupping a brilliant ball of light in her palms. Like the painting of the girl in Tera's room, she was surrounded by the familiar soft, deep violet-blue glow. It took Cotten's breath.

But it wasn't just the painting that had caused the reaction—it was the easel—the small easel—one suitable for a child.

WINDBREAKER

"Mr. Olsen," Sergeant Carillo said, "we now have over sixty security officers looking for your son. If you'll have a seat in the waiting area, I'll call you just as soon as he's located."

"Thanks," Alan said, rising. He had started to tell the officer about Devin's . . . talents. But he decided they didn't need to know that in order to find the boy. If need be, he would go into detail with the police later. Chances were it wouldn't ever come to that.

Alan sat in the small police substation lobby and watched the officer behind the glass enclosure talk to someone who had lost his wallet. The constant muffled roar of the stadium crowd rumbled in the background.

Devin was his only child. He'd lost his wife six years ago when a drunk driver ran a stop sign as she was going to pick up their son from daycare. From that moment, the boy became Alan's entire world. If something happened to Devin today, he would never forgive himself.

The door opened and an officer led a teenager past Alan into the next room. There was blood on the young man's shirt. A fight, Alan thought.

With sixty officers looking for Devin, they would have to find him soon. Even though Dolphin Stadium was huge, it was a contained area with controlled exits. He couldn't stay lost for long.

And then there was the other possibility—one that Alan kept pushing back in the shadows of his thoughts.

What if someone had kidnapped Devin?

"Mr. Olsen?"

Alan looked up as a man in a dark green golf shirt and Dockers slacks stood in the doorway. A gold badge was attached to his belt, as was a small automatic in a black holster.

Alan stood. "Have you found Devin?"

"I'm Lieutenant Martinez. Metro-Dade."

Alan shook his hand. "My son?"

"Sir, please come with me."

Alan felt his stomach twist as he followed the detective out onto the concourse. Twenty paces later, they stepped into an elevator. Alan felt it drop just like that knot in his gut. When the doors opened, they were in the underbelly of the stadium.

Martinez led Alan along a well-lit corridor to a door labeled *No Admittance*. The detective slid a card through a security lock mechanism and the door clicked open. He opened the first door they came to in the hallway and motioned Alan into a dark room.

As the door closed behind them, Alan saw that they were in some sort of video surveillance center. The far wall was covered with at least three dozen video monitors. All showed live color feeds from cameras throughout the stadium.

Three officers sat at a long table in front of the monitor wall. Martinez guided Alan to a position behind one of the seated officers. "Mr. Olsen. Take a look at monitor thirty-three, please," Martinez said. Tapping the shoulder of one of the tech officers at the table, the lieutenant said, "Rewind that recording for me, again, please."

A moment later Alan stared in amazement as the monitor showed him leaned against the wall watching the mass of fans flowing by. He saw himself turn and speak to a bearded man who had wandered over and stood beside him—the man wore a red windbreaker.

At one point, the guy took hold of Alan's arm. He remembered the guy spouting off a bunch of boring statistics on the history of the Miami Dolphins. Now that he thought about it, the guy seemed like he was trying awfully hard to keep Alan's attention.

At that moment, the seated officer froze the picture, and a set of numbers on the bottom of the image designated the individual frame.

"Now take a look at monitor thirty-four, Mr. Olsen," Martinez said. "Watch the left side of the image."

As Alan watched, he saw the exit to the men's room. "There's my son! That's Devin." He pointed to the screen.

Devin Olsen emerged from the exit and turned to his left. At that moment, the officer froze the picture. The numbers on the bottom of the image matched the frozen image on thirty-three.

"Now, play both in sync," Martinez said to the officer.

As the two images played, Devin walked away from the men's room exit and blended into the crowd. Two boys, appearing to be slightly older than Devin, followed right behind until they were out of frame. At almost the same instant, the guy beside Alan in the adjacent monitor turned and wandered away, also disappearing into the river of fans.

"I don't understand," Alan said to Martinez. "Where is my son? Where did he go?"

"Mr. Olsen, I'm sorry, but we believe he left the stadium with two other boys."

Alan took a step back. "That's impossible. He would never . . ."

"Mr. Olsen," Martinez said, motioning with his arm. "Please take a look at monitor fourteen."

Alan slowly followed the detective's gesture. He moved forward and glared at the video monitor labeled 14. It showed the parking lot somewhere outside the stadium.

As the video played, Alan swallowed hard, unable to believe what was there. A wave of nausea swept over him when he clearly saw his son playing a handheld video game while walking with the two boys who had followed Devin from the men's room. A few paces behind was the bearded man in the red windbreaker.

TRUCK STOP

TERA THRASHED IN HER sleep, her breathing rapid as she trembled in her mother's arms.

Lindsay curled behind her daughter and snuggled her. "Shh, baby. It's okay. It's okay," she whispered, stroking Tera's hair.

Soon, the girl settled into slow, rhythmic breaths as she drifted back to sleep. But Lindsay's eyes stayed wide open. She stared out the rear window of the Dodge conversion van. The fold-down seat seemed comfortable at first, but after several hours in the cold, cramped space, she ached—her limbs were stiff and sore.

Lindsay had spread an old sleeping bag on top of the makeshift bed and used a wedding ring-pattern quilted comforter for warmth. It was a wonder the child could sleep at all with the glare of the lights from the truck-stop signs and the never-ending growl of the big diesels as they came and went in the night. But it was cheaper than staying in a motel. Once the cash she had withdrawn from her checking and meager savings accounts ran out, there would be nothing left.

How could it have all wound up like this?

The cause of their flight started two weeks ago when Tera and Lindsay were grocery shopping. Suddenly, her daughter dropped a bag of fruit and gasped.

"One of them is here, Momma," Tera said, looking up at her mother. "He's here to take me." Her blue eyes welled up and spilled over, the tears leaving shiny streaks down her cheeks. "I don't want to go."

Lindsay held Tera. "You're not going anywhere, baby. No one can ever take you from me. Not ever." She rocked back and forth, holding her so close she felt both their heartbeats.

As she consoled her daughter, Lindsay caught sight of a man at the end of the aisle. He was tall, gaunt, with a shock of snow-white hair, and he appeared to be watching them. When he saw Lindsay's stare, he turned and walked away.

Lindsay had learned long ago that Tera *saw* and intuited things. In Tera's earliest years, Lindsay and her husband found it amusing—almost entertaining. Sometimes Tera would tell her mother that the kitties were at the door waiting to be fed. The door would be closed, but when Lindsay went to look, sure enough, Bogey and Bacall would be waiting for their dinner. Or Tera would stand next to the phone seconds before it would ring—many times she would announce who was calling before picking up. And from the time she could compose sentences, she talked about heaven and how she had one day looked down on earth and chosen Lindsay and Neil as her parents.

If not for Tera, they would never have joined the local church. Before Tera started showing signs of her talents, Neil and Lindsay had no interest in religion. God was never a part of their lives.

But as Tera grew, she seemed to communicate directly with God. It wasn't that Tera told them to join a church. She hadn't. It was rather that Neil and Lindsay sought answers about their remarkable daughter and hoped to find them there.

Tera's talents grew more thought-provoking as she got older, and as others began to notice, she became regarded as strange, peculiar—an oddity. About three weeks after Tera started kindergarten, Lindsay got called in for a conference.

"Tera is a lovely little girl," the teacher said. "She is certainly bright—even gifted. And her artwork is amazing. But Mrs. Jordan, we are having a little problem with her. Sometimes Tera frightens the other children."

"Frightens?"

"Well, she, um, says inappropriate things to them or tells them things that upset them."

Lindsay sat numbly. "What do you mean? What kind of *things*?"

"Like today. She asked one of the boys why his father had drowned all their puppies. William, that's the boy's name, argued that the puppies got sick and died. But Tera insisted until William ended up terribly upset and crying. His mother came in, and as you can imagine she was disturbed. She told me that their family is financially struggling right now and couldn't afford to feed a litter of pups. Her husband had done what he had to do. But they didn't want their son to know. He is too young to grasp what had happened." The teacher shook her head. "I don't understand how Tera—"

"I'm so sorry," Lindsay said. She wasn't sure what else to say or how she could explain. All she wanted to do was run home and enfold her daughter in her arms.

"And there have been some other instances," the teacher continued. "But not quite as upsetting as the latest incident. I thought you would want to know so you can talk to Tera."

"Yes, I will. I'll do that. Thank you."

"Most everyone around here knows you and Tera, but you have to realize William's family moved here recently. His mother wanted to know who Tera was. She asked for your address and phone number. Of course you know it's against policy to give out that information."

"I appreciate that," Lindsay said, hoping she would not have to confront William's mother. The woman would never understand about Tera.

Afterward, Lindsay did talk to Tera, but it was hard for her daughter to understand something that seemed to come so naturally to her. A month later, there was one more similar conference with the teacher, but that wasn't what drove Lindsay to withdraw her daughter from public school and start home schooling. She made that decision on Tera's birthday. She had sent out a birthday party invitation to every child in Tera's kindergarten class.

No one came.

Lindsay's heart broke for her baby girl. She promised to shield her from the rest of the world—a world unready and unwilling to deal with a child like Tera.

Besides becoming aware that Tera was special and had incredible gifts, Lindsay also learned to trust her daughter's insights. If Tera said someone was in that grocery store to take her away, Lindsay suspected she was telling the truth, but always in the back of Lindsay's mind was the seed of doubt—that her daughter was mentally unbalanced. Lindsay refused to give in to that thought.

After seeing the tall, gaunt man at the end of the store aisle, she had grabbed Tera's hand and left, abandoning the half-filled cart. As they were about to pass through the doors, Tera hesitated and turned to stare into the store.

Lindsay looked back in response. *He* was there, standing to the side of the checkout counter, watching.

"Hurry," Lindsay said, tugging her daughter's hand, leading her to their van.

As Lindsay had driven along the main highway that day, she checked her rearview mirror. A silver car followed. It was never close enough for her to see the driver. Something told her not to go home. She turned along a road heading in the opposite direction from her farm.

The car followed.

Lindsay made another turn toward the local Wal-Mart.

Again the car followed. Then it suddenly dropped back as the driver seemed to sense her suspicion, finally disappearing altogether.

For days after the grocery store incident, Lindsay kept a vigil at the window, anticipating seeing a silver car ramble down the dirt driveway. Then, one night Lindsay awoke from a frightening dream. In the dream she had walked to the end of the drive, taking the garbage to the roadside for pickup the next day. It was near twilight, in that nether realm just before daylight surrenders to the night. She heard it first, making her look down the road. The silver car raced toward her, then turned into the drive, leaving her behind in terror. She ran, but as often happens in dreams, Lindsay's legs didn't respond, and she fought for every sluggish step. Before she could reach the house, two men in black suits carried Tera to the car. One man threw Tera in the rear seat, her arms tied behind her back. He climbed in behind her as the other took the driver's seat.

"Momma," Tera screamed before her next cry was muffled, then silenced. The car sped off, passing Lindsay again but in the opposite direction, spraying grit and dust in her eyes. The dream came to an abrupt halt and Lindsay sat up in bed, her mouth and throat dry as if she had actually breathed in the cloud of dust. She shot to her feet and scrambled to Lindsay's room, relieved to find her daughter safe and sleeping. She crawled in next to Tera and held her through the rest of the night.

Not long after that night, Tera had stared out the window and told her that someone was coming for her. That's when Lindsay called Cotten.

She covered every window after locking them all. Neither Lindsay nor Tera left the house, living on the food stored in the pantry and freezer. She had not even taken the garbage to the roadside.

Finally, out of supplies and terrified that at any moment someone would come and rip Tera from her, Lindsay decided she could no longer wait on Cotten.

Slipping out of the house in the middle of the night with only a few hastily packed items, she and Tera had headed south. Driving straight through the next day, they stopped only for short breaks to stretch and fill up with gas. Finally, in late afternoon, Lindsay pulled into a truck stop in Brunswick, Georgia.

Now, as she lay with Tera in the back of the van, the midnight cold seeped into her and reminded Lindsay of the chill of being followed that day not so long ago. Since the incident in the supermarket, she had tried countless times to figure out who would want to take Tera. And why? If she knew, then maybe she would know how to fight for her daughter. Until then, they would stay on the run. Hopefully, Cotten would find her note and come searching for them.

The monotonous on-off cycle of the red neon truck-stop sign reminded her of what happened when she and Tera had finally arrived home the day they were followed.

"You okay, baby?" Lindsay had asked.

"He was ruby," Tera said, so low that Lindsay wasn't sure she heard right. Tera's gaze had left the window to find her mother's eyes. "That man in the store. He was ruby red. Like Pastor Albrecht."

ARRIVAL

"THIS IS IT." COTTEN pulled the rental into the dirt drive of Lindsay Jordan's farm.

"You're right," John Tyler said, sitting beside her. "Doesn't look like anyone's taken care of the place in quite a while."

Cotten had gone to Louisville to pick up John after spending the previous afternoon searching the barn and farmhouse again for additional clues to Lindsay and Tera's whereabouts. Once she realized the artwork and poetry were created by an eight-year-old girl, their lifestyle and sudden disappearance became even more of a mystery.

On the drive from the city to the farm community of Loretto, Cotten and John discussed every detail of what she had discovered. She showed him the note from Lindsay saying they could wait no longer for Cotten, and had already fled.

It took many miles before Cotten had calmed her nerves at seeing John for the first time in almost a year.

She had waited like a schoolgirl with butterflies of anticipation until she spotted him emerging from the crowd of arriving passengers. When he took off his sunglasses, she stared into those deep ocean-blue eyes, and a flood of emotion washed over her. At that moment, she felt safer than she could ever remember.

"You look wonderful," John said.

She tilted her head, taking in all of him and smiling. "Not too bad, yourself." The urge to cry with happiness welled up, and she pushed it back into the secret place deep inside where it lived. Her words felt forced as she struggled to make light conversation. "I thought you'd be decked out in your official cardinal's robes and a gold cross around your neck. Instead you show up in jeans and a polo shirt. What must the ranks of heaven think of you?"

John smiled warmly. "They're all preoccupied with much more important matters." He took her hands in his. "So, Cotten Stone, how are you?"

"I'm wonderful now that you're here. But I feel guilty pulling you away from real work and making you come to this out-of-the-way place. After all, this may turn out to be nothing but a wasted trip."

"I'm here because you're here," he said, wrapping his arms around her. "I wanted to see you, mystery or not."

She hugged him back then put her palm to his cheek. "Thank you." For a moment she felt frozen, her eyes locked on his as if she couldn't look away—didn't want to look away—deliciously drowning in the sea of blue.

When she met John seven years ago, he was teaching biblical archaeology at a small college in upstate New York. She sought out his expertise in identifying an ancient relic that was thought to be the Cup used to collect the blood of Christ at the Crucifixion. Working together they delivered it to the Vatican after stopping a plot to use the human DNA from residue found in the Cup to clone Christ. The Grail conspiracy thrust John and Cotten into the harsh limelight of notoriety.

John was called to Rome and appointed by the Holy Father as prelate of the Pontifical Commission for Sacred Archeology. He was soon consecrated a bishop.

Cotten became senior investigative correspondent for the Satellite News Network specializing in religious antiquity. Over the years, she and John embarked on a number of adventures, including uncovering a new cache of ancient scrolls in caves near the Dead Sea, and in Jerusalem they oversaw the discovery of the thirty pieces of silver that Judas Iscariot was paid to betray Christ.

Cotten and John worked together to locate a five-thousand-year-old crystal tablet some believed was inscribed by the hand of God and contained a secret to entering the Kingdom of Heaven. During that episode, John revealed to Cotten that he had been given the role of director of the Venatori, the intelligence-gathering arm of the Vatican, and arguably the oldest spy organization on earth. In taking on the duty as head of the Venatori, he was again elevated by the pope, this time being named a cardinal.

Cotten had fallen in love with John, probably from the moment they met, and although he could not act upon it, he had professed his love for her as well.

With every stolen glance at John on their ride to Loretto, she knew in her heart more than ever how much he meant to her.

As the sound of the tires on crunching dirt and gravel stopped, Cotten shut off the engine. "Why don't we start with the barn? You're going to be amazed."

John nodded and they got out. She led the way down the hard-packed dirt path. Once inside, they went from painting to painting, pausing before each. "Can you believe an eight-year-old could do this?" Cotten took John to the special painting in the back of the barn, the portrait of the man with the evil eyes and red glow. "What do you make of it?"

"Scary," John said. "I can't imagine what could have been going on in a child's mind to create something so sinister and evil."

When they had finished exploring the barn, they went inside the farmhouse. Cotten led their tour and showed him how the windows had been draped and sealed with heavy tape. She had already removed most. The smelly garbage was gone, and she had done some general cleaning and dishwashing. She pointed out the closet where the garbage had been stored. A slight odor lingered of something long dead.

"This is fascinating," he said, standing in Tera's bedroom. "Such ambiguity and contrast." He motioned to the ballerina spread and other evidence that a little girl lived there, yet she was surrounded by so much magnificent artwork. "Tera is an extraordinary child. There's no doubt that something unusual has happened here. And that they are in some sort of danger. The question is why and from whom."

"Follow me," Cotten said, leading John into the living room. Once they were seated on the couch, she pushed the play button on Lindsay's answering machine and the message from Pastor Albrecht blared from the small speaker.

"Outburst at church?" John said once the recording ended. "Wonder what caused that?"

"Good question." Cotten watched John pick up the pile of mail from the coffee table. "There's not much to go on."

"I don't know. Maybe." He opened the MasterCard statement and looked at the charges. Then he pulled his cell phone from his belt and pressed a speed dial number. A moment later, he said, "This is John. Please do me a favor and run a trace on a credit card. Charges in the last seven days." He gave the card number then waited for a moment. "Okay, call me back." Flipping his phone closed, he looked at Cotten. "Tracing Lindsay's purchases might help us establish her trail and find out where she is." John folded the statement and put it in his pocket.

"So, mister secret agent man, where would you like to begin?"

"That's easy," John said, standing. "We'll go have a chat with the good Pastor Albrecht."

THE WOODS

BENJAMIN RAY STOOD ON the bank of Stone Creek Lake at sunrise. Purple coneflowers and late-blooming white aster covered the ground under the thick maples and basswood that hid the lake up to the very edge. A morning mist lay across the water like a gossamer quilt—not a breath of air moved a leaf or caused a ripple.

A faint snap came from Ben's right. His pulse jumped as he froze. Slowly, he turned his head and looked into the eyes of a doe standing only ten feet away. For a few seconds, he wondered who the real deer in the headlights was. Even after three months of hiding in the Ozark Mountains, his nerves were still raw. He had hoped that once he started venturing out from the remote cabin on his early morning walks, he would be able to stop looking over his shoulder. But then, why would anyone come hunting for him? He was officially dead and buried.

Seeming to sense no danger from the bald, heavyset man, the deer turned and walked back into the thick brush, her coat blending with the forest as she disappeared.

A shadow in the forest. Like me, Ben thought.

He had secretly arranged for the purchase of the cabin and surrounding eighty acres a few months before the federal indictment was filed. *Always pays to plan ahead.* It was just about the time everything started falling apart. His partner referred to it as the wheels coming off the wagon—the collapse of Presidium Health Care, their chain of ninety-seven for-profit hospitals and extended-care facilities across the country. After filing for bankruptcy, investigators discovered that Ray and his partner had concealed more than a billion dollars of debt and inflated profits. Thousands of their employees lost their jobs, and many thousands more their life savings. Now his partner was sentenced to forty years for multiple counts of fraud and conspiracy, the same sentence Ben faced before "dying" of advanced coronary artery disease. The truth is, he *did* have heart disease and was getting his medication mailed to him under the name Ben Jackson from a pharmacy in Tijuana. Same name that was on his driver's license, the title to his Jeep, and the deed to the cabin. It was amazing what money could buy, including a convincing death certificate, not too hard to come by in your own medical facility, by a doctor on your payroll, and of course followed by a speedy cremation. He often wondered what was really inside his funeral urn. *Every man has his price,* Ben remembered his father used to say. It was the understatement of a lifetime.

After the first month of total isolation, Ben started venturing out for morning walks. All the family vacations in Aspen and St. Moritz had given him a great love of the mountains and forest. He and his wife of thirty years enjoyed hiking and camping. *She would like it here if she knew he was alive.* He regretted her not knowing, but this way, if he were ever caught, she could not be held as an accomplice.

Ben's cabin was roomy and comfortable. He had electricity, running water, satellite TV, a new Wrangler in the carport, and a great deal of cash hidden in a basement water heater. Actually, there were two heaters—one brand new and environmentally efficient—the other old and rusty, pushed like an afterthought into a nearby corner. Ben told the plumber he didn't need it hauled off, saying he planned to convert it into a planter. Now it contained more than two million dollars in mixed denominations.

He had spent that much just on living-room furniture in his Ocean Drive, Palm Beach, winter home, Ben thought with a chuckle as he turned away from the tranquil Stone Creek Lake and headed back. The woods were thick as he made his way along an embankment down into a rocky ravine. He remembered taking this path once before. A few hundred yards beyond the other side of the ravine, the forest opened to a serene meadow filled with the last of the blooming wildflowers and tall autumn-gold grass. At the far edge of the meadow, an old dirt logging road led past the rear of his property. From there he was only a short walk to his morning reward: fresh coffee and scrambled eggs.

A shadow in the forest.

Just as he crested the opposite side of the ravine, he heard the sound of an approaching vehicle—a rare event this deep in the woods.

A white panel van came into view along the logging road. Suddenly, it ground to a halt. The driver's door flew open and a bearded man in a red windbreaker jumped to the ground.

"I've had just about enough out of you," he yelled, sliding open the side door.

Ben hid behind the trunk of a thick maple tree and watched as the man grabbed what appeared to be a young boy from the floor of the van. He pulled him out and dropped the boy onto the side of the dirt road. He was blindfolded and his hands were bound behind his back.

"Stand the hell up," the man ordered. He yanked the boy to his feet.

Ben's impulse was to approach the man and ask him what the hell was going on. Ben was guilty of a white-collar crime, but that didn't mean he had no conscience. Still, he didn't dare risk his anonymity by getting involved. At this point all he could do was watch. *Fuck,* he thought. *What kind of man have I become?*

The driver untied the boy's hands and pushed him around to the back of the panel van. "Hurry up and pee—you've already made us late." The blindfold remained on.

Ben felt a cheap sense of relief. The guy was annoyed, but wasn't going to hurt the kid. At least not right now.

The boy fumbled with his zipper and awkwardly relieved himself. As soon as he finished and zipped up his jeans, the man forced the boy's arms behind his back and re-secured them. He guided the boy to the side of the van and shoved him in, slamming the sliding door shut. Back in the cab, the man closed the driver's door, put the van in gear, and continued on down the logging road.

Ben stepped from behind the tree and cautiously moved across the meadow to where the van had stopped—the sound of the engine already fading on the wind through the autumn leaves.

The road was rarely used—the tire marks left by the van were the only noticeable tracks. Ben glanced down at the dark spot in the dirt where the boy had urinated. *What the hell was that all about? A kidnapping? Damn, why did he have to witness it?* The earnest sense of shame clutched up in his chest. *Ben Ray, I don't even know you anymore.*

Ben put the fingertips of his right hand over his carotid, feeling a stuttering pulse. He couldn't think about what just happened. He had to get back to the safety of his cabin.

Taking several deep breaths, he concentrated on relaxing. After a few moments, he calmed down and was ready to head home. The last thing he needed was to come in contact with anyone.

When he had first moved into the cabin, he had shaved his head, cut off his mustache and goatee, and started wearing thick-rimmed glasses. He'd even called up a hint of his mother's Virginian southern accent. It was important to blend. But it wouldn't take Columbo and a few probing questions about his background to raise suspicion. He had fabricated his history and rehearsed it often, but if pressed and stretched, he was certain it would tear. As far as anyone knew locally, he was a retired banking executive from Atlanta. The simple fact was that he couldn't afford any amount of time with the authorities or anyone else who might catch on if he wanted to keep from spending the rest of his life in prison. Reporting what he had just seen on the old logging road was out of the question.

Ben massaged the back of his neck before looking around. He wondered where the road led. He had never followed it. No matter.

The van and the boy were gone.

Taking a last look around, he crossed the road and entered the woods.

Like a shadow in the forest.

VIGILANCE

"Welcome, Sister Stone," Pastor Albrecht said, extending his hand. "The Almighty is so pleased to have such a notable daughter of Loretto come and visit His holy house."

"Thank you, pastor." Cotten shook his hand as they stood in the old brick Church of the Risen Savior. "I'd like you to meet John Tyler, a friend of mine from back east."

"Brother Tyler, so nice to see you," Albrecht said. "I must say you look somewhat familiar."

"I have one of those faces, Reverend Albrecht. It's my curse in life."

"Well, I can sure think of worse crosses to bear." Albrecht motioned to the front row of pews. "Please be seated and tell me how I can be of assistance."

Cotten savored the smells of the old church—the heaviness of the dark cherry paneling, the sweetness of half-spent candles, and the fragrance of fresh-cut flowers around the sanctuary. A soft rainbow prism streamed from the stained glass windows, radiating across the pews in a transparent veil. The old wood creaked as she and John sat down. Although she had never been inside this church, she remembered watching it bathed in early morning mist as she glanced at it through the window of the county school bus.

"I'd like to talk to you about Lindsay and Tera Jordan," Cotten said. "I received—"

"How are those two sisters of God?" Albrecht said. He had remained standing as if he were about to give his next sermon.

"Well, that's just it. I received a call from Lindsay recently in which she expressed concern for the safety of her daughter. She asked me to come to Loretto and help her ease those concerns. Once I—"

"Actually," Albrecht said, "there was an unfortunate incident not too long ago that might have upset Lindsay. I sincerely hope it didn't. But you know, it occurred right here where you're sitting."

"Why don't you tell us what happened?" Cotten said.

"By all means, Sister Stone."

Albrecht opened his arms in a grand gesture Cotten knew he had rehearsed in front of a mirror a thousand times.

"As you may have heard, I am new to this congregation, having recently been relocated. It was only my second Sunday service when Lindsay and her beautiful daughter entered the church and took their seats right there." He pointed to Cotten and John. "I was in the sacristy making my final preparations for our ten-thirty service. As our small, but dedicated, choir began their opening hymn, I walked out to the middle of the sanctuary to lead the congregation in song. I recall looking down at the faces of those in the front row, and it was at that point that the young lady met my welcoming gaze. Suddenly, she emitted the most blood-curdling scream I have ever had the misfortune of hearing. I must tell you, it seemed to come from the very depths of hell."

"What was Lindsay's reaction," Cotten asked, becoming increasingly uncomfortable in the presence of Albrecht. She remembered her mother using the term *snake oil salesman*.

"Well, of course her mother tried unsuccessfully to calm the girl, but the child had quickly become hysterical. There was no soothing her. The poor creature had to be physically removed from the church by two of our larger male parishioners. It was a most unsettling and embarrassing experience for all concerned."

"Why do you think it happened?" Cotten asked.

"I have absolutely no idea, Sister Stone. Even as I recall it now, I tremble."

"Were there any other instances of an outburst like this? From Tera or anyone else?"

"No. None whatsoever. It was a one-time occurrence, I can assure you. We are all at a loss as to what could have provoked the incident."

"You've been extremely helpful, Reverend Albrecht." Cotten stood, John following her lead. "We appreciate your time."

"I really don't know what I've done to help other than describing an awkward event for that poor child. I have tried to contact Lindsay and ask if I could minister to her and her child. I've left messages, but she has not returned my call."

"Apparently they've left the area," Cotten said. "Can you think of any reason why they would feel that leaving town was necessary?"

Albrecht shook his head. "I'm afraid not, unless it's the embarrassment. Unfortunately, Tera's *fit* was the talk of the town. But I do hope that wherever they are, Lindsay can get some help for that poor child."

"Thanks again," Cotten said, shaking Albrecht's hand and turning to walk down the aisle.

As John followed, Albrecht said, "You're a mighty quiet man, Brother Tyler. But I believe there is a storm of thoughts going on in your mind. May I ask you a personal question?"

John turned and faced the minister. "Of course."

"Do you believe in the devil?"

Cotten watched as John's face hardened, his eyes darkening. His body tensed.

"Yes," he said stiffly. "I do."

"Good. Remember that Peter said, 'Be ever vigilant.'"

"Thank you for that advice, Pastor Albrecht."

As they walked down the steps to the Church of the Risen Savior and headed for the car, John said, "He just couldn't resist playing his cards."

CYBERSYS

ALAN OLSEN STOOD IN his downtown Miami office and stared out the window at Biscayne Bay in the distance. Twenty stories below, members of his staff along with others from surrounding businesses wandered across Biscayne Boulevard and over the lush carpet of grass to spend a relaxing lunch break near the water. His stomach twisted into knots as he realized that all of them were going about their normal day while Devin was still missing. Gone for four days. Disappeared in the parking lot of Dolphin Stadium as seventy-five thousand fans cheered inside.

He propped one hand on the glass and leaned on it. Even work was no distraction.

"Alan, are you sure there is nothing I can get you?" Kai Chiang said, standing behind him, massaging his shoulders.

Alan didn't turn to face her but saw her refection in the glass. Porcelain skin, black almond eyes rimmed with long lashes, and long, straight black hair that shone like onyx under light. She had joined CyberSys six months ago as his personal assistant, but their relationship quickly became physical, with all the passion and recklessness of teens in the back seat of a car. The first love affair since the death of his wife. Kai made no demands on Alan and certainly was not a clinger. She was there when he needed her, no questions, and he found he needed her more and more, especially since Devin's disappearance. To her, Alan confided his deepest thoughts, not only about business, but also about his personal life.

Kai pressed her body against his back and wrapped her arms around him, kissing his shoulder and neck. "I wish I could do something," she said.

"You are."

"You still have the two o'clock meeting. They called a few minutes ago and wanted to know if you were up to it—that they would understand if you wanted to cancel. I said I would check and get right back to them."

A long spiraling breath came from Alan. "No, I'll be fine. Maybe it will get my mind off Devin."

Kai reached beneath Alan's suit jacket and scratched his back with her long red nails, then pulled away. "I'll tell them the meeting is on."

When Alan heard the click of the door closing, he wandered to his desk and sat down. Inlaid in the desktop was the blue thunderbolt logo behind the CyberSys name. He remembered choosing the color shortly after learning of Devin's condition. If only news of Devin's whereabouts would come as fast as the idea for the design of Alan's famous corporate symbol. This waiting—the not knowing—was ripping him apart. Miami-Dade police negotiation specialists and detectives were encamped in his private conference room. If Devin had been kidnapped, they were prepared for the ransom call. After all, Alan was rich. Extremely rich. And he had received his share of threats and crank calls.

As founder and president of CyberSys, Alan had amassed a personal fortune in the hundreds of millions directing the development of high-speed encryption technology for government security systems. His programs, produced by CyberSys engineers, were used by U.S. government agencies worldwide, and his team's research into the latest quantum computing hardware was getting closer to building the first working model of the elusive super computer each day.

As yet, there had been no calls or demands, and the police had no leads, no information, nothing. Nothing but the blurry parking lot surveillance recording of a white panel truck leaving with Devin inside.

They had issued a statewide Amber Alert, but he'd had to force them to do so by calling on friends in the government. A Florida State representative happened to be his neighbor and helped put the pressure on law enforcement to issue the alert. The reason they had hesitated was their insistence that Devin had appeared to leave the stadium voluntarily. There was no physical evidence of abduction or threat on the video. Devin was playing a hand-held video game and seemed to go with the two older boys without a sign of an argument or resistance.

That was bullshit!

Yes, Devin was . . . different. He had been diagnosed with a specialized form of autism—specifically a rare type that produced prodigious skills. Devin could recite or write down complex mathematical equations—some that covered hundreds of pages. He could list every city in every telephone area code and Zip code.

It was no challenge for him to identify most classical music compositions after listening to only a few bars, and tell the date the music was written and the composer's birth date and place of birth and death. By the time he was seven, he had read more than four thousand books and could recite the contents of any page from memory. He had been called an autistic savant by his doctors. Alan simply called his son's talents a great gift.

Devin lived with extraordinary ability and disability. He was resistant to change, had difficulty expressing his needs, and had no real fear of danger. One of the most prominent symptoms of his autism was poor social interaction. Even as a baby he had stiffened when someone held him. Devin never would have voluntarily left the stadium with a stranger. That would be impossible for him.

Alan glanced across his penthouse office through a door to an adjoining room—a playroom for Devin with a small desk in the far corner—one he had set up for Devin where his son would come and spend the afternoon after school. Devin loved to play video games so Alan had his favorites installed on the CyberSys central server and placed a workstation on the boy's desk. Even now, he could easily picture his son sitting at the desk for countless hours, engrossed in war games—his favorites. Devin even had his father show him how to access and view the code engines that made the games work. He could recite any portion of the code back to Alan, to the amazement of the CyberSys senior engineers.

Devin was special, loved . . . and missing.

Once again, Alan went to the window. A cruise ship navigated Government Cut leading from the Atlantic into the Port of Miami. Traffic along the MacArthur Causeway shimmered in the South

Florida sun. The high-rises along Miami Beach formed a jagged spine along the horizon.

Life went on.

Alan was imploding. All he ever wanted was for Devin to live a normal life. He despised the label of autistic savant and everyone's quick association with the character in *Rain Man*.

There was one other label attached to his son, one that he chose not to mention to the police. The one that had inspired the color of the corporate thunderbolt logo.

Indigo.

MAGIC KINGDOM

DAYLIGHT SEEPED THROUGH THE slats in the blinds, forming a ladder of light on the van window. Lindsay thought she had only just fallen asleep. The grumbling engines of eighteen-wheelers pulling in and out of the truck stop had gone on all night, but at dawn the number rose substantially as the big rigs got on their way.

Lindsay sat up and rolled her head, stretching the tight muscles in her neck. When they left Loretto, she hadn't been certain where they were going—only that they needed to leave and not come back. Sometime during their all-night journey, she decided on what might be the safest place for Tera. She had heard an old saying that to keep something from being found, hide it in plain sight. So she had decided to take Tera to a place where she would be surrounded by thousands of kids.

"Wake up, sleepyhead," Lindsay said, sweeping Tera's hair from her face. "We've got to get this show on the road. I have a surprise for you."

"What?" Tera said, her voice soft with sleep.

"You'll see."

"My throat hurts," Tera said, sitting up.

Lindsay pressed her palm to Tera's forehead. She felt warm. *Shit, Tera had a fever.* She grabbed her purse and fumbled through it, latching on to a bottle of Tylenol. Pouring a tablet into her palm, she retrieved a half-consumed bottle of water from the drink holder.

"Okay, lazybones, swallow this, then we'll go take a shower. You'll feel better."

Later, inside the truck stop travel center, Lindsay bought some toiletry essentials she had forgotten to pack in the frenzy of leaving their farmhouse. She paid $2.00 for a shower and was given a towel.

"Can I have one more for my daughter?" Lindsay asked the clerk.

"You only paid for one shower."

"Please," Lindsay said.

The clerk stared at her for a minute, then acquiesced.

"Thanks."

The multi-showers were self-contained, each having a small but dry area to dress.

"All right, Ladybug," Lindsay said. "Off with your jammies."

Lindsay adjusted the temperature of the shower and was the first in the stall. Tera followed.

"Just like camping, isn't it, Tera?" Lindsay said, shampooing her hair. She closed her eyes to rinse. Over the rush of the cascading water she heard a sound like the rattling of the door. Lindsay vigorously washed the shampoo from her face, trying to see her surroundings.

"Tera?" She reached out to touch her daughter with one hand while wiping the water from her eyes with the other. Squinting through the foam that still dripped into her eyes, she focused on her daughter who was blowing soap bubbles from the ring she made with her thumb and forefinger.

Damn, Lindsay thought. *Paranoia runs deep.*

———

"Feeling better?" Lindsay asked through the van window as she finished filling the tank with gas.

Tera nodded. "Where are we going?"

Lindsay climbed in and turned on the ignition. "If you could go anywhere, where would that be?"

"Heaven," Tera said.

Lindsay's heart stuttered, and she felt the blood drain from her face. "No, baby," she said, her voice lacking the exhilaration it had a moment before. "I mean if we could go on a vacation, a really wonderful place, where would you want to go?"

Tera's face beamed. "Disney World."

Lindsay pulled out onto the Interstate. "Then Disney World it is."

Tera gleefully clapped her hands. "Yay, Disney World!"

The sight of Tera's excitement sent a flurry of emotions through her mother. Lindsay didn't get too many glimpses of her daughter being just a happy little girl, and so she cherished this fleeting moment.

By afternoon, they reached Orlando. It seemed like the whole area was a theme park, lit from corner to corner with neon, strobe, and animation. Every store, every gas station, motel, and restaurant along International Drive competed for tourists.

Lindsay pulled into the parking lot of a bungee jumping site. She felt Tera's forehead. It was slightly warmer than it should be, but not too hot. Maybe just the onset of a cold, Lindsay hoped. "How's your throat feel?"

"A little bit sore."

No more truck stops for now, Lindsay decided. If Tera was getting sick, she needed a good night's sleep and the comfort of a real bed. "Well, here's the deal, Ladybug. We're going to find a nice motel, take a nap, and chill out this afternoon. Then we'll go pick out a Mickey Mouse shirt and hat and get a bite to eat at some really cool restaurant. And tomorrow, when you feel better, we'll tackle the Magic Kingdom. How does that sound?"

Tera stretched to look out the windows. "I want to go now," she said.

"Me, too. But I think we'd better give your throat a chance to get better. You won't enjoy it as much if you aren't feeling up to snuff."

———

Inside the $39.99-a-night room of the Tropical Breeze Motel, the cheapest she could find, Lindsay dropped on the end of the bed.

Tera hopped up and started jumping.

"Guess you are feeling better," Lindsay said. "Hey, you're going to bust your noggin." She grabbed Tera's legs and brought her down. Lindsay tickled Tera's sides, loving the solid, uncontrolled belly laugh from her daughter.

"Who loves you, Ladybug?"

"You do," Tera said.

"That's right." She hugged Tera and kissed the top of her head. A moment of silence passed. *Nobody would ever take Tera from her. Nobody.*

"After a little nap, we'll find that Mickey shirt and hat." Lindsay pulled down the covers and they snuggled beneath.

———

Lindsay was drawn awake by a tapping on her shoulder.

"Mom. Momma."

It was Tera's soft voice, nearly a whisper.

Lindsay turned over to see her daughter staring down at her.

"Can we go now? My throat hardly hurts at all."

It was 4:48 PM on the nightstand clock. "Wow, we must have been tired. I was sleeping hard." Lindsay yawned as she sat up. "So, are you ready to do a little shopping?"

Tera's face lit up.

"Let me make one phone call first," Lindsay said, reaching for the phone. She took the paper from her pocket that had Cotten's cell number written on it. After charging the call to her room, Lindsay finally heard the ring at the other end, but was disappointed when she only reached Cotten's voice mail.

"Hi Cotten, it's Lindsay. I'm sorry I couldn't wait any longer for you. Tera and I had to leave. Hope you found my note. We're in Orlando. I decided to take Tera to Disney World where she'll blend in with all the other kids. I'm going to try to stay inside the park, but don't know how much it's going to cost or how long I can afford it. I'll call you back with specifics. Please come. I'll find some way to repay your expenses." She paused a moment wondering if

93

there were something else she should say. She glanced at Tera, then said, "Thanks, Cotten."

Lindsay put the receiver in the cradle. "Okay, then let's get going," she said getting to her feet. As Lindsay rounded the bed she noticed a motel notepad and a pencil were on the floor. Several sheets were torn off and scattered about. Tera's sketches. "So, you've been awake for a while."

"Yep," Tera said.

Lindsay stooped to pick up the papers. "What have we got here?" But before she could collect the papers, Tera burst from behind her and scooped them all up.

"One of them is a surprise for you," she said. "You had a surprise for me, and I have one for you."

"What is it?" Lindsay asked, her lips spreading into a smile.

"There are really two surprises." Tera sorted through the papers. "This one," she said, holding out a sheet to her mother. "And this one." Tera held a second paper to her heart.

"Oh, Tera," Lindsay said when she had finished reading a lovely poem her daughter had written about a mother's love. "Every word is true. I *do* love you just that way."

Tera held out the other piece of paper. Lindsay took it, stared at it, and then her gaze shifted to her daughter. She shook her head, confused and astounded. "How, Tera? How did you . . ." She was so astonished she didn't know what to say.

Lindsay set both papers on the dresser and knelt down to be at eye level with her daughter. She held Tera's face in her palms. "You are incredible, Tera Jordan. You always amaze me. And I love your double surprise." Lindsay touched the sketch. "But how do you know what she looks like?"

Tera broke into a wide grin, and her eyes sparkled like the stars in the heavens.

"Because she's my sister. My twin sister."

STORM

LEANING AGAINST THE RAILING on the front porch of his mountainside cabin, Ben Ray stared out over the thick forest. Bathed with the vibrant morning sun, the fall leaves turned the valley beyond into myriad tones of orange, red, and yellow. The weather had cooled from the previous day—the chilly autumn temperature made him shiver. From the deck, he watched the wind brush across the valley treetops like a hand through fur.

Ben had not slept well, tossing and turning for hours. When he closed his eyes, he saw the blindfolded boy, hands tied, being jerked from the van like discarded trash. When he stared into the darkness of his bedroom, he heard the edgy voice of the bearded man in the windbreaker. The scene played out over and over through the night.

Ben's reaction to the boy made no sense. After all, he was labeled as "the iceman" in the press—the CEO who had stood by and knowingly let the life savings of thousands of hardworking employees turn to vapor while he bled his company dry. He watched the falsely inflated value of the corporation's stock rise like a Roman candle, only to explode and die a quick death. And through it all, he slept soundly every night. But there was something different about what happened in the woods the previous day. Maybe it was because the boy seemed so helpless, blindfolded and standing on shaky legs beside the meadow.

Ben was not proud of what he and his partner did to their company. Happy that he was rich and not going to prison, but not proud. Maybe it was because he never saw the faces of those who went down with the corporate ship. Actually, he never saw the face of the boy in the woods, either. But he knew he was real. Alone. Helpless.

If he went looking for the kid, chances were he would find nothing, anyway. The Ozark National Forest was a big place—more than a million acres. The road might go on for miles. Maybe the van was just passing through, taking a shortcut.

But what if the boy was in real danger? Would it be worth the risk to try to find him? So far, Ben had managed to stay hidden from the outside world. He limited his trips into town for supplies and gas to once a month, usually around midmorning on a Monday when everyone was at work. No one seemed to waste time looking at a short, pudgy man minding his own business. They were too annoyed that the weekend was over.

Going to look for the boy would be outside Ben's game plan. It would take him into the unknown, and remove his ability to control his environment. That was not part of his nature. He had to be in control, or control those who were.

A casual drive along the logging road was all Ben would do—nothing more. It was a big forest, and he was still a shadow in its

97

midst. With a cautious nod, he turned away from the autumn view.

Dressed in jeans, hiking boots, and a flannel shirt, he slipped on a jacket before heading down the stairs. Backing the Wrangler out of the carport, he steered up the dirt drive, and a half-mile later he emerged on a two-lane blacktop country road that ran along the border between his property and the National Forest.

Turning east, he drove at a leisurely pace, scanning the tree line for the entrance to the logging road. He saw one other vehicle—a green Forestry Service pickup coming from the other direction. The ranger gave him a friendly wave and he returned the greeting. Ben watched the truck fade in his rearview mirror.

Soon he spotted the turnoff to the logging road. Rarely used, it resembled two parallel ruts with a high grass backbone that disappeared into the dark woods. Ben put the Jeep in four-wheel-drive before leaving the blacktop.

As he entered the forest, the sun fought to penetrate the swaying trees, creating ever-changing patches of light and dark. The woods still retained its brilliant foliage even though most of October had slipped away.

The road threaded through a valley bounded on each side by sloping bluffs and dense underbrush. After ten minutes, Ben spotted the meadow where he had first seen the white van. He stopped long enough to open his thermos and take a sip of steaming coffee while he listened to the wind and the distant call of a crow. He wondered about the deer he met yesterday along the banks of Stone Creek Lake. It was hunting season.

Closing the thermos and setting it behind the passenger's seat, he cranked the Jeep and drove on.

The road followed along the floor of the valley. Ben caught glimpses through the trees of the steep mountain slopes that bordered the road. He became aware of rushing water and soon came upon a small, swift stream flowing parallel to the road. The water swept over rocks and deadfall in the same direction he traveled, telling him that he was headed in a gradual downward grade.

After a mile or so, the road abruptly turned away from the stream. The sound of cascading water faded into the sudden rush of wind overhead. It was then that Ben realized the sky had darkened. Glancing out the window, he spied charcoal gray clouds through a break in the trees. A fast-moving mountain storm threatened.

Ben debated whether to continue on or head back. If the weather got nasty, he didn't particularly want to get caught so far from home.

Soon, a light rain fell. He'd driven about five miles, he figured, since leaving the blacktop. Through the steady drizzle, the mountains grew darker. He was just about to turn around when he spotted a tall, chainlink fence up ahead on the left. The logging road ran along the perimeter of the fence. Approaching it, he saw it was old and falling apart. The Constantine security wire that had once spiraled along the top had snapped in many places and sagged or fallen to the ground. Corroded and barely readable, a metal sign attached to the fence bore the warning: *No Trespassing. U.S. Government Property*.

Ben drove on through the light rain until he noticed a clearing on the other side of the fence, and he came to a gate. The logging road continued past the gate and disappeared into the woods beyond.

Pulling up to the gate, he looked for any evidence that the van had passed through or continued on the logging road. Because of the rain, there was no trace of any vehicle.

On the other side of the gate, a one-man guardhouse stood like a ghost from a bygone era—its wooden frame sadly in disrepair. A snarl of vines had taken over the small structure and seemed to be the only thing holding it together.

A padlock secured the gate. The rain slackened into a light mist, so Ben shut off the engine and got out for a closer look. The padlock held together the ends of a chain that coiled through the gate frame. Although the chain was old and rusted, the lock appeared fairly new.

He noticed that a couple of the clamps holding a section of the chainlink on to the metal frame had long ago fallen away. With some effort, he pushed on the mesh and produced a space big enough to slip through. He would just have a quick look around and then move on.

Walking past the old guardhouse, he followed the dirt road for a hundred yards or so until a large block-shaped structure loomed out of the drizzle. It stood in the middle of a collection of smaller buildings—perhaps five or six in all. As the details of the buildings became clearer, he saw that all were in as poor a condition as the guardhouse and fence. Most were single-story, wood-frame structures with broken windows and dark, hollow openings for doorways.

The largest of the structures was a windowless concrete building appearing to be about one hundred feet wide and towering over him at least three stories high. Paint peeled, gutters and drains slumped, and the surrounding area was thick with overgrowth.

What had once been a paved road was now dirt, with only small chunks of asphalt remaining. For the most part, weeds and brush had reclaimed it. Atop the main structure was a radar dish frozen at an odd angle in a paralysis of rust.

The building's main entrance was boarded up with plywood—heavy bolts held the panels in place. The wood bore the dark staining of long-term exposure.

Deciding to take a few more moments to explore, Ben wandered around the side of the building and came upon a door with a sign that read *Authorized Personnel Only*. He tried the knob but it didn't give. Moving on to the back of the building, he found another door labeled *Danger. High Voltage*.

Suddenly, the skies opened and the rain came down in sheets. The wind picked up, roaring across the open area and turning the raindrops into pinpoints of pain. Thunder shook the ground as a bolt of lightning struck nearby. He pulled on the door with no luck. Trying again, it finally gave way with a resistant groan. He stepped inside and shook the rain from his hair and clothes.

He left the door ajar for what little light came in from the dark sky. Thunder cracked again shaking the walls of the huge building. He had apparently entered some kind of utility room—the only entrance was the single door. Mounted on the rear wall was an electrical connection box. It had to be at least four feet wide and six feet tall. Six thick metal conduits, each about the diameter of a baseball bat, ran from the top of the box and disappeared through the ceiling. He was no electrician, but it was obvious that the building once required a tremendous amount of power.

Like the gate, the electrical box was also protected by a padlock. He examined it—a Sargent & Greenleaf high security U.S.

government padlock. Heavy duty, indestructible, and as shiny as the day it was made.

Why protect the electric service of an abandoned building with such an expensive lock? Curious, Ben glanced around. Other than the electrical box, the room appeared empty.

Then he saw it.

Mounted high over the door—barely noticeable in the murky light, the tiny red LED on the motion detector stared at him like the cold eye of a predator.

HARVEST MOON

"Was the good ole preacher boy's remark about keeping vigilant what I think it was? A warning?" Cotten steered the rental out of the church parking lot and back on to Burks Spring Road. It was getting dark fast, and shadows hung heavy over the rolling Kentucky hills as she switched on the headlights.

"That's the way I read it," John said, looking over his shoulder at the fading image of the church. "First he asks if I believe in the devil to get my mind on that track, and then he makes the *vigilant* comment. I believe that was his way of informing us who we are up against, as if that wasn't already becoming clear. He was warning us to back off."

"Puts the nail in the coffin, then. Tera must have somehow recognized Albrecht as being evil. Whatever she saw scared her pretty bad."

"If Albrecht is a member of the Nephilim, or worse, one of the original Fallen, and Tera has the ability to identify them, then they definitely want her to vanish. And that means she is in grave danger. We have to assume that they're already hunting her down. We've got to find her before they do."

Cotten's hands tightened on the wheel. "And they know we're onto them, and that we'll be searching for Lindsay and Tera, too. They'll be hell bent on stopping us."

She looked over at John who seemed puzzled and distant in thought.

"What is it?" Cotten asked. "What are you thinking?"

John laced his fingers and tapped his thumbs together. "There's something else, something more to it, I just can't put my finger on it. Tera is certainly a unique child, and it looks like she may be able to ID the Nephilim and the Fallen, but it doesn't seem like that's enough."

"What do you mean?"

"She's a little girl growing up in the middle of nowhere, so it's not like she's going to come across a huge number of them out here in the sticks. Her encounter with Albrecht could have been a coincidence. She freaks out when she sees the pastor, so what? The whole town thinks the kid is off kilter. Why would Tera be such a threat to them?"

"You may be right. Maybe that's exactly why Albrecht is way out here in Loretto in the first place, because Tera is a threat."

"Hopefully, when the Venatori office in Washington gets back to me with the credit card info, we'll know where to start."

"I'm going to give Ted a call and ask for some additional time to investigate this."

"Cotten, I can follow up from here if you need to get back to New York."

"I know, but Ted is aware that this is a personal matter. Let me call him first and clear it." She reached to the center console then hesitated. "Check and see if you're sitting on my phone. Or maybe it fell on the floor."

John leaned forward and felt beneath him, then looked down between the seat and the console, then the seat and the door side pocket. "I don't see it."

Cotten ran her hand beneath her and on both sides of her seat, then dug in her purse. "I could have sworn I left it in the cup holder on the console."

John checked around again, including the glove box.

"Must be under your seat or mine," she said. "I'll check when we stop."

"I'm serious about taking it from here," John said. "You don't have to ask for time off."

Cotten vigorously shook her head. "No, no, no. Lindsay called *me* for help. And besides, you know as well as I do that this is what I'm supposed to do with my life—it's my birthright, so to speak. Granted, it's taken long enough for me to come to terms, but I can't deny it any longer."

"Yes, it has taken a long time," John said. "A difficult road for you."

Her eyes stung at the onset of tears. "You were right—it's been quiet way too long. I knew something like this was eventually going to happen, I just didn't know when. I even started to believe that it was over—that I could begin living a normal life. No more supernatural bullshit." She turned to John. "This is never going to end, is it?"

John brushed a loose strand of Cotten's hair behind her ear. "Let's try to take it one step at a time. So far, we are only speculating. Good speculating, mind you, but no real proof, yet. So whether it's our old adversary we're dealing with here or just the active imagination of a depressed widow and her talented but high-strung daughter, our first goal is to find Lindsay and Tera. Agreed?"

Reluctantly, Cotten nodded. She managed to hold back the tears, only allowing the first of them to well up. She wiped her eyes, and that was the end of it. The urge to cry wasn't out of self-pity; it was for Lindsay, Tera, and all the friends and acquaintances she had lost along the way.

The introspection was finally broken when John said, "I hate to change the subject, but my stomach is growling. Hungry?"

Cotten reached for John's hand and held it. "Thanks for giving me a few minutes to recollect and rant. This never gets any easier for me."

"It's not an easy task you've been given. No one is expecting you to think otherwise, especially me."

She squeezed his hand. "So, you're hungry. We can go back to Lindsay's and scrounge around for something to eat. But there's not much left in her cupboards. There's a diner a mile or so from here. Want to try some country cooking?"

"Sounds perfect." John stared out the window. "What's the claim to fame in your hometown?"

"Actually, we're just about to pass it." Cotten motioned up ahead on the right. "They're closed for the evening now, but that's the entrance to Maker's Mark Distillery. They've been making Kentucky straight bourbon there for a long time. Growing up, I used to like the smell of the fermentation when I would ride my bike into town. A poor man's aromatherapy."

"So you had the potential to become a bourbon *aromaholic* from an early age?"

"Very funny. Actually, I would love an Absolut over ice right now. Probably not something I'll find at the diner."

"Did you enjoy growing up here?"

"There were great times. Many with friends like Lindsay. But once my father died, my mom and I didn't do so well. She suffered from depression after we lost the farm. We moved to Lexington and she went to work in a textile mill there. After I graduated from the University of Kentucky, I left and never looked back."

Cotten turned into the parking lot of the Goldenrod Grill. "It's not much on ambiance," she said, "but the food is good."

Before going in, Cotten searched the car again for her cell phone.

"Maybe you left it at Lindsay's," John said.

"No. Just before we went into the church I checked it to see if I had any messages or missed calls. I set it in the drink holder in the front console." She heaved out a sigh. "That's just great." Cotten closed the car door and they headed for the diner entrance.

Inside, they seated themselves in a booth. The vinyl seats were a mustard-yellow, and the tables were wood, covered with what looked like a half-inch layer of polyurethane. The menu was embedded under the polyurethane in four spaces.

"Guess the menu stays pretty much the same," John said.

The waitress brought tall plastic glasses of ice water and straws. "Let me know when you're ready to order," she said. "Just wave me down." She turned to leave, but then wheeled around and cocked her head. "Well, I'll be dipped," she said in her southern drawl. "That is you. Cotten Stone." She walked closer to the table. "It's me, Caroline. Caroline Duckett. Andy's sister. You dated my brother in eleventh grade."

"Oh, my God," Cotten said, realizing the waitress was the younger sister of a month-long, old high school flame. "Caroline." Cotten got to her feet and hugged the waitress. "I haven't seen you in forever. How's Andy?"

"He's great," she said. "Every time he sees you on TV he tells his wife about how you two dated. He thinks it makes her jealous, but I think it just pisses her off."

They all laughed and Cotten scooted back in the booth. "Caroline, this is John Tyler, a friend of mine."

"Pleased to meet you, John."

"Hey, do you know Lindsay Jordan?" Cotten asked.

"Sure. Town's not that big," she said rolling her eyes. "What a tragedy, Neil dying and all."

Cotten nodded.

"I don't think the child ever recovered from losing her father. Tera is real peculiar. Beautiful little thing, but an odd duck. She didn't fit well in school either, so Lindsay started teaching her at home. I think she has been under a lot of stress trying to do it all."

"I'm sure," Cotten said. "Have you ever been around Tera?"

"Not much. I hear she's quite an artist. Her mother said that was because Tera was—what did she call her?" Caroline tapped the pencil eraser on her chin. "I remember, an Indigo child, whatever that means. At least that's what I've heard." She shook her head. "Small towns don't have much going on, so gossip spreads like wildfire. Believe me, if you strike a match, everybody in Loretto knows it before you can blow it out. Like the *fit* Tera threw at church a few Sundays ago. Phones were ringing off the hook. That's all you heard folks talk about in here for days. Nobody's seen Lindsay or Tera much since."

"I came to visit Lindsay," Cotten said. "But it looks as if she and Tera have left town—left in a hurry."

"Wouldn't surprise me. I know they've gone away before. Always came back, though. Maybe this time, they'll get a fresh start somewhere, not in a small town."

"Let's hope," Cotten said.

———

When they left the diner, their hunger satisfied with generous portions of country-fried steak, collards, mashed potatoes, and sweet tea, John motioned toward the east. "The moon looks so much bigger out here in the country."

"That's a harvest moon, John," Cotten said, taking his arm. "I ordered it up special, just for you."

"I probably need to find a place to stay tonight," he said. "I saw a sign for the Hill House Bed and Breakfast."

"You'll do no such thing," Cotten said. "There's plenty of room at Lindsay's. Discussion closed."

"Well, I guess I'm staying at the Jordan farm tonight," he said as they got in the rental.

Cotten pulled onto the highway, still annoyed that she had lost her cell phone. Taking her mind off it, she said, "That is an amazing moon." The huge orange ball brought back memories of parking on lover's lane many years ago.

"Looks like there's some sort of glow on the horizon under the moon," John said. "Is there a factory or mill out that way?"

Cotten saw the glow in the distant night sky. As they traveled toward it, it grew brighter. Suddenly, she caught the flashing of red lights in her rearview mirror followed by the droning of a siren. She eased the car onto the shoulder as a fire truck roared past, its strobing emergency lights casting a scarlet blanket over the nearby fields. Before Cotten could pull back onto the highway, a second emergency vehicle shot by in the wake of the fire truck.

As they rounded a bend in the highway, Cotten and John spotted a collection of red and blue emergency lights up ahead. A half dozen fire and police vehicles had converged on the site. Flames bit at the black sky as the huge harvest moon hung above the scene. It seemed to grow brighter—fed by the heat of the fire.

Then it became obvious. Flames engulfed Lindsay's farm.

DEVIL OR ANGEL

ALAN SAT ON THE bathroom floor, the image of his son's face burned inside his head. For the past hour he had huddled over the toilet until he thought he would retch up his very insides. Even with nothing left to purge, his body didn't want to relent. The nausea came and went with his thoughts of Devin, like giant sickening waves rolling over him. Today it had finally gotten the best of him.

There was a knock on the bathroom door.

"Alan?"

"Kai, not now."

She opened the door and came to him. "Sweetheart, I'm only here because I care." She pulled Alan to his feet, undressed him, and helped him into the shower.

He heard the click of the door as she left him alone.

Alan stood under the hot flowing water for a long time, trying to wash away the fear and sorrow as much as the stench from throwing up.

Through a heavy fog of steam he finally got out, dried off, and slipped on a bathrobe. Then he wandered into the dark bedroom and lay on the bed, exhausted.

He felt Kai join him and pull away his robe. He realized she was naked as she straddled his thighs. She trickled warming massage oil onto his back, then closed the bottle and tossed it next to her. The air was suddenly rich with the scent of almond.

"Relax and let me work out some of the tension," she said, spreading the oil. Her thumbs pressed along either side of his spine as she slid them up his back, stretching out long lines of muscle and tendons. "This will make you feel better, I promise. We'll order something for dinner later, if you feel like it. For now, let me help you unwind."

"That feels great," Alan said, finally sensing the stress and tension abate beneath her hands. He had worried about Devin to the point of numbness, and his mind couldn't think any more. He would give in to this moment of reprieve.

The tingle and warmth, and the firm pressure of Kai's hands, were a mixed sensation. Alan wasn't sure which he wanted to respond to—the relaxing of his muscles or the mounting sexual arousal. Whichever, it was total respite from the nightmare of the kidnapping.

Kai's magical hands kneaded his shoulders, then down his upper arms, returning to his neck, then across his shoulder blades. Then the heels of her hands found his lower back, flattening out every knot and kink.

Taking her time, she finished with his back then dragged her fingers through his hair at his temples, working in circles across his scalp. Alan hadn't noticed how taut his facial muscles had been until he felt them start to relax.

"Are you an angel?" he whispered.

"I am whatever you want me to be," Kai answered.

God, she was good, Alan thought as she slipped down his legs until she sat on his ankles, her perfect ass on his heels. She dribbled a little more of the oil down each of his thighs and calves. Alan not only felt the oil warming at her touch, but he detected her heat resting on his ankles.

After massaging his legs, she feathered her fingertips up and down, from calf to upper back, a fine delicate tickle on his skin. She lightly nipped his buttock before urging him to turn over.

"Mmm, Mr. Olsen," she said, eyeing his erection. "I was supposed to relax you, not—"

"You aren't finished yet," he said rolling her beneath him.

Kai smiled and arched her neck as he kissed it. "We can both relax," he whispered, sitting up. Alan poured a nickel-sized portion of the massage oil in his palm and closed the bottle. Then gently, he eased his hand between her thighs.

Kai's breath caught in a gasp, turning into a long, audible, streaming sigh. She pushed her hips up to meet his hand.

Alan watched her face, her eyes closed, sometimes her teeth biting her bottom lip, her forehead bearing lines of strain. Her head turned from side to side, her hair shiny, sliding on the sheets like black mercury. She swallowed, followed by a low, lingering moan. He loved seeing her like this, beautiful, flushed, so vulnerable in the moment.

Kai pulled him down on her. She whimpered a cry for him to hurry.

He entered her, her legs wrapping around him, her hips rocking to his rhythm, rising higher, pressing harder against him with each thrust until finally, Kai's whole body stiffened. Before she pulsed and shuddered in the last throes of orgasm, Alan matched her ecstasy, and a moment later they lay spent, his face buried in her neck.

———

Alan woke to movement on the bed. He opened one eye and saw Kai climbing in beside him. She was still naked, her hair mussed. He perceived the light scent of soap.

"I was a little on the greasy side. But, don't think I'm complaining," she said, snuggling next to him. "I'm afraid we've ruined the sheets. I don't think the oil stains will come out."

"Screw the sheets," Alan said.

Kai laughed. "We kind of did."

Alan put his arm around her and drew her closer so her head rested on his shoulder.

"Next time I give you a *massage*, we'll spread a beach towel."

He kissed her forehead. "I needed that badly. Maybe I can regroup now."

"I know you can't stop thinking about Devin. Taking a minute or two to shut out the world will help you stay sane." She stroked the soft tuft of hair on his belly.

"I just don't get it," Alan said. "No ransom, nothing. I think I would rather have received some type of demand. At least I'd know what they want, and then I could give it to them. This is more like some pedophile or sicko who hurts kids."

"Don't think like that, Alan."

114

"I try not to, but it is a possibility."

"I've grown to love him, too," Kai said. "And his father. So far, the kidnappers don't want money, so that might eliminate one motive. It could, God forbid, be a pedophile. What else is there?"

Alan turned and kissed her again. "I haven't told anyone this, but there is one other possibility that scares the hell out of me. It could put Devin in more harm's way than he already is."

"Maybe you shouldn't tell me, either," she said.

"No, I need to talk to somebody who cares about him, who loves him."

Kai caressed his jaw.

"Let me back up so you can see the whole picture. You already know about Devin's . . . talents. They used to call people like him idiot savants. But there's nothing idiotic about him. Since he was diagnosed, I've spent years studying autism. Most recent theories indicate that in autistic savants that are extreme, like Devin, there is no communication between the left hemisphere of the brain and the right. When normal people, like us, attempt to learn things, our brains are being bombarded with other information, and it searches for connections to past experiences or ways to make generalizations, that kind of thing. So there is a lot of interference. But Devin's brain doesn't work like that. It's pure learning with no interference. That's why he has a photographic memory. There's a lot more than that— one of the newest studies also suspects a problem with mirror neurons in autistic children. But the bottom line is that Devin literally remembers everything he sees, hears, and reads."

"Interesting," Kai said. She picked up her head and looked at Alan. "But what has that got to do with what's scaring you?"

Alan used his palm to shove his hair back. "You know how Devin memorizes books the first time he reads them?"

"Yes."

"And you know he's got a thing for numbers."

"Right. And dates."

Alan continued. "Devin has seen the programming code to the operating system for Destiny, the quantum computer we're working on. And because he's seen it, I know he's memorized it, just like he memorizes all the names and numbers in a hundred telephone books."

Kai was silent for a moment. "And?"

"What if someone wanted to steal that information? You know we have the tightest security possible at CyberSys. No one is ever allowed to bring in or remove any object from the building. You can't even wear a watch or wedding ring past the detectors. And you can't remove anything, not even a paper clip or tissue."

He stared up at the ceiling. "But every time Devin comes to see me, he walks out of the building with our most valuable data right in his head. Kai, trust me when I say that there are people who would do anything to get the Destiny OS code."

"OS?"

"Operating system. You see, if we have as much success with Destiny as it appears, it will make all current encryption methods instantly archaic."

"You're talking over my head, darling."

"Sorry. Encryptions are based on mathematics. The more computational difficulty involved, the more difficult to decrypt. It's not that they are impossible to break, it's that they are impossible to break in a reasonable period of time. It would take hundreds, even thousands of years for current computers to decrypt most of the military's most securely encrypted information. Codes that deal with launching nuclear weapons, for instance. Most of the world's security networks, from financial institutions to global positioning satellites, depend on encryptions devised in this manner. The CyberSys computer itself is just hardware—a collection of lasers, ion traps, mirrors, lenses, and photodectors, all made from metal, silicone, and plastic. You need an operating program to control the hardware and interpret the computing results, just like a home PC needs Windows to make the hard drive talk to the modem or the DVD player communicate with the sound card. So if someone knows that Devin has memorized the code to the operating system, after they get what they need from him, there's no reason to keep him alive." Alan stared at her. "Kai, they'll kill my son."

"But you're the only one who knows he has memorized the code."

"That's what I hope is the case," Alan said. "That's what I pray, because if not, Devin is as good as dead."

They held each other for a while in uneasy silence. Finally, Kai scooted out of bed. "Want to order pizza?" she said, moving around to his side of the bed. She looked down on him with a coquettish arch of her brow. "Drink a little wine, watch a movie? Maybe get tipsy, skinny dip, and fuck like rabbits in the hot tub?"

———

Alan pushed the pizza box off the nightstand so he could see the phone and check the caller ID. It was Max Wolf, CyberSys' director of engineering. He pushed the talk button. "What's wrong?"

"Everything, starting with the interaction noise levels."

Alan heard the click of a cigarette lighter. "You're not supposed to be smoking in the lab."

"You want this shit to work or not?"

Alan sat up. "I want you to live long enough to see it work and not blow up my building. Now, what happened?"

"Your idea of using the nitrogen vacancies in the diamond almost worked," Wolf said. "Right up until the whole thing crapped out."

Alan visualized Wolf with his bushy, walnut-brown hair and wearing one of his hundred Hawaiian shirts, cutoffs, flip-flops, and a perpetual cigarette hanging from his mouth. Alan found it hard sometimes to be in the same room with Max—he was a brilliant scientist, but he reeked of cigarette smoke. Max Wolf had joined CyberSys right out of MIT. Within six years, he was heading up Alan's quantum computer project code-named Destiny.

"Suggestions?" Alan asked.

"It's the same old shit. Right now our qubits are turning to junk when we probe with the laser. It all boils down to bad spectral-hole-burning material. Your suggestion of diamonds with impurities was the closest we've come—but no cigar."

"Max, go home. Get some sleep. We'll all meet tomorrow and regroup. I firmly believe we'll find the right material. It's got to be out there somewhere."

"Maybe you're right, Alan," Max said. "I've had it for tonight."

"Go home, or you're fired."

"You'd just rehire me tomorrow."

Alan pushed the off button and placed the phone back on the nightstand. He turned to see Kai standing naked by the doorway holding a bottle of wine and two glasses.

She winked and gave him a seductive smile. "I'm feeling more like a devil than an angel."

CRASH

"Shit!" Ben said, looking up at the motion detector. The LED glowed bright indicating it had sensed his presence. Storm or no storm, it was time to go.

Pulling on the door, he opened it enough to slip through. The storm had turned the forest into a combat zone with almost constant strobes of lightning and booming thunder. Ben ran along the side of the building and around the corner toward the road leading to the gate.

"Hey you!" came a yell.

Ben looked over his shoulder to see the white panel van in front of one of the older wooden buildings. The guy in the red windbreaker had jumped out and was yelling for Ben to stop. The man got back in the van and put it into gear.

Ben felt his heart slamming against his chest as he ran along the asphalt road. He could see the guardhouse and gate in the distance—sheets of rain rolling across his vision. Over the sound of the storm, he heard the van coming, its engine racing.

At the gate, Ben pushed through the small opening. A coil of the old Constantine wire hanging down from the top cut across his bald head like a scalpel. The pain was intense as his foot caught in the fence and he fell into the mud. Scrambling to his feet, he jerked open the door to the Jeep and jumped in. His hand twisted the key and the engine cranked. As he turned the Wrangler around, he caught sight of his face in the rearview. Blood ran in rivulets, his head covered in red.

Ben heard the van slide to a halt behind the gate, its bumper slamming into the chain link and metal frame.

The forest boomed with thunder, and the wind whipped the trees into swirling madness as Ben raced the Jeep along the logging road. He wiped his face on the sleeve of his jacket and saw it come away bright red.

"God damn it!" he screamed, pounding the steering wheel. "I knew it, I knew it." The pressure built in his chest. The deep cut on his head hurt like hell. "This was a God damn mistake!"

The Jeep swished along the muddy road through the torrents of rain. Ben wiped the blood from his face and gritted his teeth. He felt the pain in his chest worsen. Limbs and branches whipped at the Jeep, the wipers barely keeping up with the downpour.

He passed the stream, now to his left. It rushed by angrily, swollen with the deluge running off the mountainsides.

Feeling lightheaded, Ben found it hard to steer. The road seemed to split up ahead. He didn't remember there being two roads. Which way? He would follow the one . . .

The airbag blasted Ben back into the seat as the Jeep slid off the road and crashed into the trunk of a huge oak. A second later, it deflated. Ben tried to breathe, his chest burning from the impact of the airbag and the stress on his heart. Through blurry eyes that were dimming, he saw movement in the rearview mirror.

A white van, a red windbreaker.

BLAZE

THE JORDAN FARM BURNED—flames shot skyward, jumping to the surrounding trees and fields. The ancient oak that had provided a century of shade had become a ball of fire, a freak sun that blazed in the night sky. The paintings, the poetry—all traces of Lindsay and Tera Jordan were being erased.

Cotten knew her age-old enemy had just declared war.

"What should we do?" she said, slowing down as they approached the entrance to the farm.

"Keep driving," John said.

"Do you still have any doubts about who we're dealing with?" Cotten watched the glow from the fire fade in her rearview mirror.

"None." He had turned in his seat to watch out the rear window. "Let's go a little farther, then double back and make another pass."

"Someone sure wants all the evidence gone. Especially the painting of Albrecht. Not very flattering with the wicked red glow around his body."

A state police car came from the opposite direction and passed them, lights flashing, siren screaming.

"What do you make of your friend Caroline's comment back at the diner? That Tera was an Indigo child?"

"I've heard the term," Cotten said. "SNN ran a special on gifted children about six months ago. Some of the kids were referred to as Indigos. It has something to do with their auras. Some psychics claim they can see indigo auras surrounding those kids. And it shows up using special photography."

"Kirlian photography—I think they call it."

"Right, that's it."

"So if Tera has an indigo aura, then Albrecht must have a red one. That's what she was painting—Albrecht and his aura. That might be how Tera identifies them. A red aura, how appropriate."

John's cell phone rang. "Yes," he said after flipping it open. "No, that's quite all right. What have you got?" He listened intently for a few moments. "Can you make flight arrangements for Ms. Cotten Stone and me? Yes, out of Louisville. As soon as possible. We can be at the airport in a couple of hours." Another pause, then, "Thank you." He shut the phone.

"What did they find out?" Cotten asked.

"Lindsay purchased gas in Brunswick, Georgia, four days ago. She used her card again at a motel in Orlando the next day."

Cotten thought for a minute. "Nothing after that?"

"No."

"Maybe she has headed to Disney. Think about it, John. What a perfect place to hide Tera. There are millions of kids there. She'd be hard to pick out in a crowd like that. Pretty smart, if that's the case."

"It's going to make it hard for us to find her, too."

Another state trooper flew past. Cotten pulled onto the shoulder of the road. "Ready to go back and take one more look?"

John glanced at the dashboard clock. "I think we got the message. Let's get on to the Louisville airport. Was your luggage at Lindsay's?"

"I didn't even think about that," she said, driving back onto the roadway.

"We'll pick up whatever you need at the airport or in Orlando."

"Oh, shit," Cotten said.

"It's just material things, Cotten."

She briefly looked at John. "I was thinking about the mother cat and her kittens. I hope they got away."

"I'm sure they did. Animals have an instinct when it comes to fire. They don't hang around."

John's cell phone rang again. He opened it and stared at the caller ID on the glowing LCD. Then he gave Cotten an expression of bewilderment.

"What's wrong? Who's calling you?" she asked.

"You are."

HADES WORM

"THE ONION ROUTERS ARE in place," Tor said. "They went online right after the initial flood attack last night."

Tor's face—narrow glasses, short hair, goatee, and pompous smile—filled the video screen as Rizben Mace watched from a windowless, dark-paneled office in the basement of his McLean, Virginia, home. He remembered the first time he met Tor, twenty years ago. Mace was conducting the induction ritual into the Ruby Army of a dozen of the Nephilim, offspring of Fallen Angels and mortal humans, and Tor had been one of the eight-year-olds receiving the honor. In chatting with the boy after the ceremony, Mace quickly realized that Tor stood out as being extremely bright and technically gifted. He had predicted the boy would prove himself a valuable asset sometime in the future.

When he was tasked with recruiting special Rubies for the newly conceived Hades Project, Tor was the first candidate who came to mind. He found Tor at a science and technology convention in New York. Now twenty-eight and a respected scientist, Tor chaired the consortium of two hundred universities in conceptualizing Internet2, and was giving a presentation on the development of optical transmission service beyond one hundred gigabits per second using photonic crystal fiber. When Mace offered him the position as project director, Tor could not say yes fast enough.

As Mace sipped black coffee from a DHS mug and stared at Tor's face in the video monitor, he said, "How long before the phishing e-mails go out?"

"Within the next twenty-four hours," Tor said. "Ten million will be sent in the first wave. We've developed about a thousand different packages covering everything from PayPal, eBay, major banks, credit card providers, discounts from national retailers, even Omaha Steaks and Linens 'n Things. Some are set up as customer satisfaction surveys and credit bureau alerts. Multiple languages are utilized for international targets. Each package is indiscernible from the real thing. We've had them designed to fool even the security experts at the companies we're faking. All of the components such as graphics and text are pulled in real-time right from the authentic site. It's the links that are ours. They are what sets the hook."

"The first phase of Hades is the most critical," Mace said. "I have high expectations, Tor." He could see the rows of floor-to-ceiling server banks over Tor's shoulder in the video feed. Like seeing a reflection of a mirror in a mirror, they seemed to go on forever into the stark recesses of the master Hades control center. Tor had once told Mace they could generate more computing power than NASA needed to launch the space shuttle—a thousand times more.

"Just don't be clicking on any links in any e-mails for the next few days," Tor said with a grin. "We wouldn't want your home PC infected with the Hades worm."

Mace nodded. "The onion routers will give you total secrecy?"

"Absolute. We are behind three layers of anonymity with 256-blowfish encryption between the layers."

"And you feel confident with the rootkit approach?" Mace asked.

"Completely. The minute the target clicks on any link, including unsubscribe, the rootkit embeds the worm in their system. And we can utilize cross-site scripting to get them to one of our fake sites. Doesn't matter whether it's Linux, Solaris, Unix, or Windows—even Macs. It can't be detected."

"Have you finalized the launch mechanism?"

"You'll be proud of its amazing simplicity. Just like my original proposal stated, all computers go out each day to sync their clocks with government clocks. The Worm's payload remains dormant until we shift the Atomic Clock giving Hades the launch command. All the harvested information from the targets will be placed on floating P2P servers for later retrieval. And like I said, as far as anyone is concerned, we are completely invisible. Because we're using a distributed, anonymous network, there's no way to trace IP addresses or, for that matter, anything in the header of the messages. Traffic analysis is also impossible. With the multiple layers of the onion routers, it would take a quantum computer to crack us."

"How far are we away from completing our own quantum computer?" Mace asked.

"Sooner than you think," Tor nodded. "The CyberSys guy's kid is just about finished giving us the code. But he's unpredictable. One minute he's typing away and the next he's staring at the ceiling and spouting off the names in a phone book from some city in the Midwest. So depending on his mental state, I believe we're only a few days—a week—from starting phase two. I call it information exfiltration and networking entrenching."

"Clever. So what about our retired banker friend from the cabin in the woods?"

"What a stroke of luck we had finding him. While he was unconscious, we ran his fingerprints. You'll never guess who he is."

"I give up?"

"Ben Jackson is actually Benjamin Ray."

"I thought he died of a heart attack just before the federal sentencing."

"Faked his own death. Been hiding out in the woods ever since. He's even got a bundle of cash stashed in an old water heater—did have, that is."

"You can't trust anybody these days," Mace said with a smile. "So he'll play the part of the desperate kidnapper?"

"Yep. Once we get the final chunk of code from the kid, we take them both back to the cabin. Jackson will compose a ransom note referring to Devin Olsen who happens to be tied up in the basement. An anonymous call will lead the authorities to the cabin where they'll find kidnapper and victim dead of an unfortunate gas leak. Identification confirms that Jackson is the previously departed Benjamin Ray—a man used to living like a king and who became desperate for money. That's why he snatched the kid of a multimillionaire, and it'll explain why a ransom note was never received—Jackson died before he could send it. A sad story with a sad ending."

"You're a genius, Tor."

"I know."

"Are we on track to meet all deadlines?"

"By the time we get to phase five, we will control the global GPS satellite system, time will stand still, communications world-wide will cease, airplanes will be falling from the sky, and ICBMs will be fueling up."

"And the Hades Project will live up to its name," Mace said. "Good work. Keep me informed." With a farewell nod, he switched off the video feed.

"He is such an excellent choice, Pursan." The voice came from behind him, but Mace knew who spoke. He was rarely called by his Fallen name, and hearing it reminded him of when he once belonged to the Order of Thrones, the highest tier in the celestial hierarchy. Such a loss fanned the flame of bitterness to this day, even though it was ancient history. The Hades Project would give him and all the Fallen sweet revenge.

Mace swiveled around in his chair to greet his visitor. From the far shadowy corner of the room, the Old Man stepped forward. Mace watched him move to a red velvet chair in front of the desk. He ambled stiffly as if his joints were rigid. His hair was the color of ash; his face only barely wrinkled and worn—amazing, considering his age. His clothes were black, and there was a general dark-ness about him, except for his eyes, which glinted like smoldering embers.

When the Old Man was seated, Mace said, "You're right, young Tor is perfect. You might remember, I predicted his talents many years ago at his initiation ceremony."

"You've always had good instincts." The Old Man rubbed his face. "The girl is still lost?"

"No." Mace held back a smile. "We stole Cotten Stone's cell phone from her car while she and the priest were meeting with Albrecht. We used it to intercept a message from the girl's mother. They are in Orlando. We left her credit card alone so we can track her. She has little liquid resources and only one card, so hopefully she'll keep using it. Just to punctuate Albrecht's warning, we called the priest's cell from Stone's phone and gave him a warning to back off before things got deadly."

The Old Man's face brightened. "Nice touch." But then his expression darkened. "I am intrigued by this child, this Tera Jordan." He rubbed his nose, sniffing. "It's so chilly in here, Pursan. Can't someone as important as you afford heating?"

Ignoring his visitor's sarcasm, Mace said, "I was impressed with her abilities as well. Let's hope she's nothing more than a freak and is the only one who can identify us."

"The thought of there being others is unsettling," the Old Man said, sniffing louder. "But I think the chances of that are slim."

"Really?" Mace said, inviting his guest to explain. But when the Old Man did not respond, Mace said, "Phase two of your Hades Project will soon begin. Would you like to know the technical details of what happens then?"

"Do I look like I want to know?"

Rizben chuckled. "I don't blame you." He rocked back in his chair. The Old Man was being particularly difficult today. "Can I ask you a question, since you brought up the girl?"

"Do I not always answer your inquiries?"

Mace stood and walked around his desk. "Would you like a drink?" He strolled to the glass bar.

"Nothing for me. You need something to fortify your backbone before you ask your question?"

Mace didn't answer, instead he lifted a bottle of *Pasion Azteca* tequila from the shelf under the bar and filled two shot glasses. The Old Man was right—he did need a drink to give him the balls to question his superior. Mace cowboyed one shot, foregoing the lime and salt. "You have ordered a lot of attention to this child from the beginning, sending Albrecht to Loretto, the constant surveillance, and now the chase. The level of attention to her has risen to what I think is unjustified unless she is more of a threat than you are telling me. And the most puzzling element is your hands-off policy. Why have we spent all this energy tracking, stalking, watching her? If she is such a threat because she identified Albrecht and may be able to identify all of us, including our Ruby children, why haven't we just taken her out? Be done with it. There have been plenty of opportunities—even to make it appear accidental for that matter. The kid and her mother could have perished in the fire. We could have torched their farm weeks ago. Or set up some sort of a tragic car accident. I can think of a dozen ways." Mace knocked back the last tequila shot and set the glass down. "I don't understand."

The Old Man nodded, his eyebrows pinched. "I can see why you are perplexed. Down through the eons, I have learned the hard way not to rush things and run the risk of a mistake. Every decision and move I command must be thought out—just like you have done by taking my idea and turning it into the Hades Project. And how we handle the girl must also be well-planned and executed, no knee-jerk reactions." His piercing eyes locked on Mace.

The Secretary of Homeland Security broke the burning stare, feeling the heat of the tequila in his belly and the chill in the air. "I understand, and I'm not questioning your judgment. All I want to know is what have you not told me about the child?"

The Old Man stood and went to the door. Reaching for the doorknob, he turned to Mace. His features hardened, frozen, stone-like in anger. In a reverberating voice that seemed to come from somewhere other than his physical body, he said, "I think God has played a trick on us."

SOUVENIR

AFTER CLEANING UP AND Tera taking another dose of Tylenol, Lindsay and her daughter drove to a nearby strip mall and walked down the sidewalk lined with Disney souvenir shops. Lindsay was deep in thought. What had Tera meant about the person in the sketch being her twin? Tera was an only child. But Lindsay recognized the face immediately. What kind of confusion was going on in her daughter's mind?

They entered a busy store called *Heigh Ho, Heigh Ho*. It was crammed with rows of Disney character toys and costumes, along with the excited cries of exuberant kids. The soundtrack from *Snow White and the Seven Dwarfs* played in the background. Once inside, Lindsay and Tera were totally immersed in a Disney fantasy world.

Lindsay placed the traditional Mickey Mouse ears hat on Tera's head, and they both quickly agreed on a Minnie Mouse shirt. Lindsay added a Cinderella nightshirt for Tera.

Just as Lindsay handed over her credit card to the clerk, Tera tugged on her arm. Lindsay looked away from the clerk, fixing her eyes on her daughter. Tera's face was all scrunched up.

"What's wrong?" Lindsay asked.

"The ruby people."

"What ruby people? What do you mean?"

"The ruby people are here." Tera's eyes brimmed with tears and her bottom lip quivered.

"It's okay, baby," Lindsay said, glancing around. Tourists packed every aisle—no one in particular stood out to Lindsay. "Just stay calm. Okay?"

Tera nodded, but her expression showed increasing concern. Her little eyes squeezed shut and her hands fluttered at her side.

The clerk handed Lindsay the receipt to sign.

As she did, Lindsay whispered to the clerk, "Do you have a restroom?"

"In the back on the right."

"Thanks." She took Tera's hand and led her away. "Pretend that you're looking at more things to buy," Lindsay whispered. "Don't look at anything but the stuff on the shelves."

Tera nodded again and trained her eyes on the souvenirs.

Slowly, Lindsay maneuvered through the aisles, trying hard to appear casual, as if she were still shopping. From the corner of her eye, she kept watch on the other customers. "How many?" she whispered.

"Four."

"Where?"

"Two by the front door." Tera looked around quickly. "One in the next aisle over and one at the counter."

"Okay. Keep smiling and looking at the toys. Don't let them know we see them."

Lindsay spotted a hallway in the back of the store. A sign read *Restrooms*. The restrooms were at the end along with a third door labeled *Employees Only*.

Holding Tera's hand as they came to the end of the hall, Lindsay opened the third door. It was a stock room, chock full of stacked boxes and overflowing shelves. Moving between the metal shelving, she saw a back window. Lindsay unlatched the window and raised the lower portion. Shoving on the screen, it tore away.

"Okay, princess, up you go." She helped Tera stand on a crate so she could climb through the opening. Then Lindsay balanced on the crate and snaked her way through the window. A moment later, she was clear. They were in a service alley, and they appeared to be alone.

Lindsay stooped down. "Okay, baby, here's what we're going to do. Run as fast as we can to the end of this alley, then get back to the parking lot and find the van. Are you ready?"

"Yep."

Hand in hand, they raced down the alley and soon were back on the strip mall sidewalk.

"This way," Lindsay said. Darting into the parking lot, racing through rows of parked cars, she finally spotted the van. "I see it," Lindsay said.

Just at the instant they reached the van, Tera froze. "Momma, they're coming," she screamed.

Lindsay had already pushed the remote to unlock the doors. She grabbed the passenger door handle and yanked it open. "Get in, get in!"

But Tera remained rooted to the spot. "Red, red, ruby red!" she cried.

Slamming the passenger door, Lindsay yanked on the side sliding door and shoved it open. She pushed Tera inside, stumbled in behind her, and with a hard tug, closed it. Lindsay scrambled to the driver's seat and jammed her key in the ignition switch. The engine turned over and she backed out without even looking for other traffic. She snatched the gear shift into drive and floored the accelerator. With a screech of rubber and a cloud of gray smoke, the van shot out of the parking lot.

Lindsay looked into the rearview mirror but saw no one following as they sped down the street and merged into the traffic. *Who were these ruby people? How had they found Tera and her so quickly?*

Then a pang of doubt shot through her. *What if there were no ruby people? What if no one was chasing them and it was just Tera's overactive imagination—just her daughter's mixed-up emotions? What if all she was doing was reaching out in some strange manner for attention, unable to cope with the death of her father? What if they were running from nothing but phantoms and ghosts?*

INFECTION

THE WOMAN STARED AT the computer screen. Her e-mail inbox had thirty-five messages. She could tell by the subject lines that most were spam. There seemed to be no end to the junk e-mail—Rolex replicas, sexual enhancement products, prescription drug offers, hot penny stocks. As convenient as e-mail was, she sometimes wanted to toss the PC and go back to letters and phone calls. But it was a fast way to keep in touch with her daughter at college and her mother out on the West Coast.

Delete, delete, delete. She tapped the key again and again after a quick preview of each message. Wait. Firewall update. That sounded important. How often had she been told to keep her antivirus and firewall programs up-to-date with the latest versions and security patches?

The choices read: *click here to download and update* or *click here to be reminded later.* "It can wait," she said. Dinner had to be started—her husband would be home soon. She would download the update tonight after she wrote a note to her mom. Sometimes the files took a long time to download, and afterward, the PC always required rebooting. Too much trouble for now. It would have to wait.

The woman clicked the button in the message to remind her later. Then she got up and headed for the kitchen. Her stomach was already growling and she wanted to open that new bottle of Yellow Tail shiraz and sip on it while she cooked. As she left the room, she didn't notice the LED on the front of her computer glow for a second indicating a quick burst of hard drive activity.

———

"Of course I heard about it. It's all over CERT-dot-org." The kid was a third-year information technology major working nights as a maintenance engineer at WebCorps, an Internet service provider hosting sixty-five thousand websites. The company was located in a two-level basement in downtown Cincinnati. "I'd have to be living on another planet not to have heard about it."

"Just asking." His friend, a communications major, stood behind the engineer as he used a cordless Makita to back the mounting screws out of the rack holding the Dell PowerEdge server. "It must have been quite an event to take down so many ISPs around the world."

"Happens all the time," the engineer said. "Assholes in China like to blow up our mainframes with denial of service assaults. Nothing better to do, I guess." He slid the server out of the rack and placed it on a roll-around cart.

"What do you have to do with that?" the friend asked.

"New hard drive. This one crashed a few hours ago." As he started to push the cart down the long line of computer racks, a message popped onto the service video monitor beside him. "Another patch? Jesus Christ, is that all Bill Gates has time to do, issue service patches?"

"What's it for?" his friend asked.

The engineer read the reference code. "Yet another buffer overrun issue. Not my decision to install the hotfix."

"What are you gonna do?"

"Leave it for the geniuses who work the dayshift." The engineer took the mouse on the pullout keyboard rack shelf and clicked the cursor on *download; do not install.* "There, now it's someone else's problem." He pushed the cart toward the maintenance shop. "Let's get a snack."

———

The supervisor for the Air Traffic Control Emergency Notification Grid located in the Seattle FAA center listened to air traffic controller chatter from the speaker on his desk. A large plasma display on the wall showed a live feed from Seattle-Tacoma International Airport tower's Terminal Radar Approach Control (TRACON) system. As he listened, he read the flash bulletin on his PC monitor. The Joint Interoperability Test Command at the Department of Defense had scheduled a security systems test for tonight. It requested compliance and was signed by the commander of JITC, Fort Huachuca, Arizona.

"They just did the same test a week ago," he mumbled to no one, since he was alone in his office. "Some pencil-pushing desk jockey with too much time on his hands."

The problem was that the DoD tests ate up bandwidth and always seemed to occur during peak traffic. Right now there was a freak fall blizzard moving down from Canada that had already created a thirty-minute delay across the board. This time, he would make them wait. He guided his cursor to the choice to reschedule the test, which caused the small message window to display a momentary hourglass before closing. Good riddance, he thought, and went back to watching the TRACON display.

THE SKETCH

"I JUST KNOW LINDSAY would have called my cell by now," Cotten said.

John glanced out the window of the plane to see wispy cheese-cloth clouds gliding past. Illuminated by the brilliance of the full moon, they had an almost supernatural quality that harnessed his thoughts. He imagined standing in their midst, the coolness breezing past. It seemed that would be the epitome of simplicity and peace, a sanctuary from this troubled place.

He looked at Cotten, her face drawn, and her eyes glassy. "Why don't you get a little rest before we land in Orlando?"

"I don't think I can. John, they've got my cell, and if Lindsay calls . . . They won't answer, they'll let her leave a frigging message." Cotten pushed back in the seat. "They're going to get to her first."

"There's nothing you can do right now. If you don't rest a little, you won't be thinking clearly later."

"I know, I know, but I can't stop trying to unravel this mess. And like you said, why call out the big guns to go after a little girl? Just because she painted a red aura around some country preacher?"

"That's what's gnawing at me, too," John said.

"The damn phone. It's my fault. I should have locked the car. But we were in a church parking lot—in Loretto, Kentucky. It's not like a back alley in Detroit or something."

"Quit beating yourself up. That won't change anything. You can dwell on it forever, but the facts will remain the same. Direct all that energy toward a solution—something positive."

Cotten sighed. "You are so good for me."

Even through all the rough peaks and deep valleys she'd wandered over the last several years, she still had innocence about her, John thought. Part of her charm. "Come on," he said, cradling her head with his palm. "Lean on my shoulder. Let a little peace settle over you."

Cotten yielded, leaning against him. He took her hand in his. In a few minutes he felt her relax and heard her breathing slow and even out. They were scheduled to land in forty-five minutes. He was glad she was sleeping, not only because she needed it, but because it gave him time to think . . . to think about the call from her cell.

The voice clearly sent a warning, saying that if John really cared for Cotten, he would convince her to back off. The man on the phone conceded that they could not kill her—after all, she was of their bloodline, and they did not kill their own. But they could hurt her—maim her, disfigure her, cause her immense pain and suffering. And they would, without hesitation. All John had to do to save Cotten from such consequences was make her stop looking for the mother and child. It was as simple as that. They were leaving it up to him.

John stroked the top of her hand with his thumb. She depended on him, thought he could work miracles. But he was only a man, not a miracle worker. He hadn't told her exactly what the message said—only that it was a warning to retreat.

John's ears popped as the plane began its descent. What should he do? Convince Cotten to call off the search for Lindsay and Tera? He already knew what her answer would be, but going on would put her at grave risk. John would have a hard time living with himself if something happened to her. He knew that by the time the wheels touched the tarmac he would have to decide.

———

"I'm sorry, but I don't have a reservation," Lindsay said to the clerk at the front desk of the Contemporary Hotel in Disney World. She had followed the signs as they approached the theme park and arbitrarily chose the Contemporary. At least inside the Disney property with its strict security and protection, she felt that they would be safe, and harder to find.

"Well, you're in luck," the clerk said. "We were totally booked, but a European tour group got stranded in severe weather up north. Their rooms have opened up for one night."

When asked for a credit card, Lindsay suddenly had a revelation. That's how they had tracked her, found her so fast—her credit card. "Oh, no," she stammered. "My husband would kill me if I put anything else on plastic. I've kind of run up the cards. I'll pay cash. How much?"

The clerk grimaced. "I'm sorry, but we require a card on file," he said. "Policy. But we don't charge anything to your account until you check out. Then you can choose to pay the tab in cash when you leave if you like."

A sick feeling grew inside Lindsay. One night would be all she could afford, and that was stretching it. With reluctance, Lindsay handed over her MasterCard.

———

The next morning Lindsay checked out, paying in cash for the room and day passes to the Magic Kingdom. She inquired again if anything had been put on her card. Relieved there were no charges, she arranged for the hotel to hold her bags for her to pick up later.

On the fourth floor concourse of the Contemporary, she and Tera caught the Monorail and headed into the park.

Tera wanted to see Cinderella's castle first, and that is what they did. Tera stood enchanted and wide-eyed in the middle of Main Street USA, craning her neck to look up at the blue and white castle, its spires pricking the blue sky, truly what fairy tales were made of. They wandered through the castle and learned that the top floors were originally an apartment where Walt Disney would stay during his visits. Tera was a bit disappointed that it wasn't really a castle inside even though she appeared intrigued by the beautiful mosaics on the walls depicting Cinderella's story.

Lindsay checked the dwindling cash in her wallet. "How about we have lunch, here in the castle? Wouldn't that be fun?" It was expensive, but that would be the last splurge. They would only be here for one day. She wanted it to be memorable as well as safe, and a diversion for Tera. But to Lindsay's surprise, Tera shook her head.

"It's not really Cinderella's castle, Momma," Tera said.

When Tera seemed satisfied that she had seen all there was to the castle, she and Lindsay sat on a bench and studied the park map. They decided on their first stop—It's a Small World.

It wasn't a long walk, and the sun felt good in the 72-degree temperature. The line snaked back and forth, winding through the maze-like path, but it moved much faster than Lindsay anticipated. Their wait was less than five minutes.

"Okay, Ladybug, hop in the boat," Lindsay said. It wasn't really a boat, just a theme park car with rows of seats that traveled a rail in a couple of inches of water. The boat chugged off into the dark mouth of the tunnel, and in an instant, they were surrounded by a rush of cool air and the repetitious chorus of "It's a Small World" theme music.

Tera was mesmerized, looking in every direction at the animated characters and magical scenes all around her. Her eyes sparkled with delight.

The boat glided smoothly along a meandering water path, constantly bringing new sights into view. Dolls, donning the dress of countries around the world, sang and danced, swung on glittering pink crescent moons, swayed beneath windmills, rode in gondolas, and walked beside the Taj Mahal. Room after cavernous room, hundreds and hundreds of animated dolls sang the infectious theme song. Sometimes there was a brief and subtle native influence, like the ukulele in the background as they passed the hula dancers and the Spanish guitar in the scenes from Mexico. But always clear and foremost were the words reminding everyone what

146

a small world it was. *No wonder they called this the Magic Kingdom*, Lindsay thought. It really was—a hiatus from the real world.

Lindsay watched her daughter and was glad that they had come. She hadn't been able to bring herself to tell Tera that they wouldn't be able to stay another day—it was just too much money. She knew she had already overdone it, but it was worth every cent to see her daughter so happy.

Tera squealed with amusement as the boat rounded the next turn, coming into a room revealing new characters and giant long-necked giraffes in a jungle setting.

Lindsay put her arm around her little girl and pulled her close. "Are you having a good time?"

Tera's face beamed. "This is the best ever," she said.

Lindsay thought back to their harrowing race from the strip mall parking lot the previous day. She had driven around the area for over an hour checking the rearview mirror repeatedly for signs that anyone followed. There had been none.

But even as she sat next to Tera in a place filled with joy and happiness, she couldn't shake the dull fear that still resided deep inside. Her heart beat heavy and she felt jittery and apprehensive.

Lindsay touched the back of her hand to Tera's forehead. A tad warm, or maybe not? She'd sneezed and coughed several times in the night, so Lindsay suspected Tera was simply catching a cold. She was thankful it was nothing more serious.

Turning, she glanced at the rows of people in the boat behind her. Passing through a dark tunnel, their faces were momentarily hidden. Were they tourists like her? Just there to enjoy the ride? If any of them were the ruby red people, Tera would have certainly said something long before they got on the boat.

Suddenly, Lindsay felt panic grip her. They were surrounded by thousands of strangers. She was overcome with the reality that they were sitting in this boat in the dark. If something happened, there was no place to hide, nowhere to run. Her pulse quickened as she faced forward, checking for an escape route. Cold sweat washed over her—a sour taste rose into her mouth.

The ride immediately lost all entertainment for Lindsay, and vulnerability crept its way into every corner of her body. She held Tera tighter, glancing behind once again.

Then finally, brightly painted daisies and pansies, flowers of all varieties and sizes surrounded them, announcing the end of the ride with *goodbye* inscribed on their giant heads in multiple languages.

Adios.

Ciao.

Then came the automated recording growing louder and louder. *"Please remain seated until your boat comes to a complete stop at the dock and you are asked to disembark."*

Lindsay could make out daylight ahead and her rapid breathing slowed. They had to get out of the boat. No more rides. No more dark tunnels. This had been a bad idea after all.

She quickly stepped out of the boat, pulling Tera by the arm.

"Momma, are you all right? Didn't you like the ride?"

"Yes, sweetheart. I just got a bit claustrophobic in there. Let's get outside in the sun."

Lindsay felt the world crashing down on her. There was so little cash left. No more credit card charges. Where were they going to spend the night? In the back of the van? Where was Cotten? Why hadn't she returned her call? As soon as they were outside, she would call again and beg her to come find them. If Cotten was not coming, then there was no one left.

———

John rented a car at the Orlando airport, and after a thirty-minute ride they arrived in the parking lot of the Tropical Breeze motel where Lindsay had last used her MasterCard.

"I'll just pretend that Lindsay is my sister and that I was supposed to meet her here," Cotten said. "Then we'll play it by ear, I guess."

"I don't have a better plan," John said.

John parked the car, and they went inside to the front desk.

"Welcome to Tropical Breeze," the clerk greeted. "How can I help you?"

"I'm looking for my sister. She's staying here. Lindsay Jordan," Cotten said.

The clerk scrolled down the guest list. "Jordan? Jordan . . . no I'm sorry, she checked out."

"Darn it," Cotten said, then looked at John rolling her eyes as if exasperated. "She's such a ditz." She looked back at the clerk. "You don't have any idea where she might have decided to go, do you?"

He shook his head.

"By any chance, did she leave a message for me?"

"Your name?"

"Cotten . . ."

The clerk searched a box under the counter. "No, sorry." He smiled. "I do remember that she checked out the same day she checked in. I took the call, actually. She said they had left the motel,

149

to please check them out and charge the room to her credit card on file."

Cotten frowned. "Are you sure there is no message for me? Please, would you check again?"

The clerk scanned the mailboxes behind him, then returned to the counter and fumbled through what sounded like papers. "Nope. Oh, wait a minute." His head bobbing up. "I see a note here that we have some of her belongings in lost and found. She left some stuff in the room."

"Well, isn't that just like her? We tease her all the time that she must really be a blonde," Cotten said and laughed. "I'll be glad to take it to her."

"You'll have to sign for it," the clerk said.

"Sure. It's going to give us something to rib her about."

The clerk disappeared into a backroom for a moment before reappearing with a small suitcase and a plastic bag. He ripped off a slip of paper that was taped to the bag and stapled it to another one he had removed from the suitcase. Then he pushed them across the counter to Cotten along with a pen.

Cotten signed . . . Cotten Tyler. She stared at it a moment. "Thanks," she said, forcing her eyes off the signature.

"I've got this," John said taking the items from the clerk. Outside, he opened the car door for her. "You okay?"

"Yes," she said, slipping in the front seat, taking the plastic bag from him and setting it in her lap. She heard the trunk pop and the suitcase thump inside. As John went around to the driver's side, Cotten peered inside the plastic bag. A lipstick. Two toothbrushes. Toothpaste. A hotel message pad and loose drawings. She pulled out the drawings.

"What have you got?" John asked getting in behind the steering wheel, key ready for the ignition.

"Miscellaneous," Cotten said, beginning to flip through the papers.

"So, any ideas where we go from here?" he said, starting the engine.

Abruptly, Cotten's examination of the bag halted. Frozen, she studied one of Tera's drawings, ran her finger across it, then handed it to John. "Look at this." She watched John's expression turn somber before shooting a glance back at her.

"Am I right?" she asked, knowing John would understand her question.

He nodded, looking again at the sketch. "It's definitely you."

TOR

BEN OPENED HIS EYES. His lids felt as if they were held down by bricks. Slowly he turned his head from side to side. Pain. His neck hurt, as did his chest. The airbag had slammed into him hard. His face stung—probably caused by the hot gases from the deflating airbag. He still had his clothes on but his jacket was gone. Slowly he reached and felt the top of his head. A bandage. Someone had treated his cut.

Ben tried to sit up but did not have the energy to overcome the pain. Everything hurt. He managed to prop himself on an elbow.

He was in what looked like a small dormitory. Eight single beds—four lined each side of the room—and a metal locker beside each. The room was lit by overhead florescent fixtures—only one was on.

As he took in his surroundings, he realized he was not alone. Someone lay on a bed at the other end of the room. A small boy, covered in a blanket up to his neck, his back to Ben. He appeared asleep.

Ben summoned up the strength and slowly swung his legs over the edge of the bed. Dizziness. Leaning forward, he placed his face in his hands. *This was going to be tough*, he thought. But he had to find out where he was and then try to get out before anyone recognized him.

"Twenty-eight thousand, eight hundred and forty-six."

Ben looked up. The voice had come from the boy. Soft, almost whispered.

"What?" Ben said. "Did you say something?"

"Twenty-eight thousand, eight hundred and forty-six." The boy repeated a little louder.

"I don't understand." Ben leaned forward trying to hear. "What do you mean?"

"How long you were asleep," the boy said. "Twenty-eight thousand, eight hundred and forty-six seconds."

Ben shook his head. "And how do you know this? Do you have a stopwatch or something?"

"I just know."

"You mean you counted every second I was asleep?" As he spoke, Ben looked around the room. The walls were painted gray and the floor was a dull, cream-colored linoleum. Each bed had a blanket and pillow. Plain and basic, like temporary sleeping quarters for a fire station or a military bunkhouse. He remembered seeing pictures in a magazine of the bunks for airmen who manned underground missile silos. Then he recalled the stark concrete building with the old radar dish on top. Was that where he was? But there were no ICBM silos in Northern Arkansas.

"I just know," the boy said again.

Ben studied the boy. Could this be the same kid that he saw blindfolded and pulled from the van beside the meadow?

"That's amazing," Ben said, humoring the kid. "What's the deal? What are you doing here?"

"Play games." The boy scratched his ear but did not turn around.

"Games?" Ben tried to get up. "What kind of games?"

"Show them how to play games."

"Who?" He stood on shaky legs holding his arms out to balance.

"They want me to show them how to play games."

"Okay," Ben mumbled to himself, "we've established that." Feeling that he had regained some of his strength, he walked to the end of the bed where the boy lay. A door led from the room, and Ben tried the handle. Locked.

He stared down at the kid. He was probably eight or nine. Short blond hair, round face. "What's your name?"

The boy rolled onto his back and opened his eyes. "Olsen."

"Well, hello, Olsen."

"No, Olsen is my last name." He grinned. "I'm Devin Olsen."

"Okay, Devin Olsen. Nice to meet you. My name is Ben." He sat on the end of the bed opposite Devin. "Do you know where we are?"

Devin sat up. In a matter-of-fact tone, he said, "We are in Arkansas, the twenty-fifth state. It entered the Union on June fifteenth, eighteen thirty-six. The state motto is *regnat populus,* which is Latin and means 'the people rule.' The population is—"

"Hang on, hang on," Ben said. "Where is this place?" He pointed to the floor. "This building."

Devin shrugged, looked away and began rocking. Then he ended his silence. "Arkansas," he said.

"You're a pretty smart kid. How do you know we are in Arkansas?"

Devin stopped rocking, but still didn't make eye contact. "The last stations on the radio were all Arkansas stations."

"The radio stations you listened to in the white van with the guy with the red jacket?"

"Uh-huh."

Clever kid, Ben thought.

The door opened.

"Mr. Jackson?"

Ben looked up to see a short, slim man standing in the doorway. He looked to be in his late twenties or early thirties, and was dressed in black track shoes, jeans, and a T-shirt that said, "Qubits or Cubits, they all add up." He had a narrow face with a dark goatee, wore wire-rimmed glasses, and his brown hair was cut short. He extended his hand as the door closed behind him.

"How's the head?"

Ben stood, but didn't shake the guy's hand. Just before the door closed, he caught a quick glimpse of a large, low-lit room filled with racks of electronic gear—he heard the hum of computer cooling fans. "Who are you?"

"Call me Tor." He motioned for Ben to sit back on the bed.

Remaining on his feet, Ben said, "What are you doing with this kid?" He pointed to Devin who was now sitting crossed-legged on his bed. The boy had shed the blanket, and Ben saw that he wore a yellow T-shirt and jeans. A Miami Dolphins jacket and a pair of sneakers rested on the floor beside the bed.

Tor smiled and said, "Devin is here to help us with some computer issues. Once he's done, he'll be going home."

Ben turned to the boy. "Devin, where is your home?"

"Miami." He stared up at the ceiling. "Incorporated on July twenty-eighth, eighteen ninety-six. Population at the time was four hundred and forty-four—"

"Thank you, Devin," Tor said.

The boy gave Tor a stony glare and crossed his arms.

"What's going on here?" Ben said. "Did you kidnap this kid?" If that were so, Ben figured he was caught in a huge bucket of shit.

"Mr. Jackson," Tor said, holding up Ben's driver's license, "like Devin, you are now our guest here. If you behave yourself, you will eventually be allowed to go back to your cozy little mountain cabin and continue doing whatever it is you do there. For now, I suggest you make yourself at home. You and Devin will be well cared for as long as you do as you're told." He nodded toward the boy. "I would hate to have anything happen to him because you decided to become heroic and try something stupid like attempt to escape."

Ben felt his pulse quicken. This asshole was telling him what to do. Giving him orders. In that instant, he realized that he must remain calm. As far at this prick was concerned, he was Ben Jackson, retired banker, who loved the solitude of the Ozark woods. Nothing more.

"Do you understand, Mr. Jackson?" Tor said.

Ben nodded and sat back down on the bed.

"Good decision." Tor smiled. "Now it's time to go and play our games, Devin." He waited while Devin put on his shoes, rose, and walked to the door.

As Tor opened it, Ben said, "Where is this place?"

Tor glanced around the small dormitory as if it were a museum, its walls covered with great works of art. A slow, malevolent grin stole across his lips, sending a chill through Ben.

"This, Mr. Jackson, is Hades."

SILVER TEARS

"THIS IS SO FUCKED," said Scar, the teenage boy with the long, dyed black hair. The bottom of his dark trench coat snagged the grass as he walked in six-inch platform leather boots along the dirt road near the Potomac River. He carried a flashlight to light the way in the dark Maryland woods.

"Shut the fuck up," said Crow, a bit taller than Scar, and dressed equally gothic in an all-black outfit of alchemy shirt, crossroads bandana, triple hex belt buckle, wool trench coat, and raised boots. His shaved head was hidden under his hood. The light of the lantern reflected off the silver studs and hoops of his facial piercings.

"How did you ever figure out where to find it?" Scar asked, looking over his shoulder at the moon burning orange through the trees.

"Legends, my man," Crow said. "Urban-legends-dot-com."

"Everyone says the stories are bullshit."

"Well, we're going to find out if the legend is crap or the fucking truth tonight," Crow said. "You can only witness it on Halloween.

Well, guess what, dickhead, it's Halloween. And we're gonna fucking find it tonight. Now shut the fuck up."

"So who's supposed to be buried there?" Scar asked.

"What part of shut-the-fuck-up don't you understand?"

Scar stopped and turned around to face his friend. "Hey, fuck you, man. I'm out here in the cold when I could be back at the party screwing that blonde bitch from second period, who by the way said she'd suck my dick anytime I wanted. So fuck you."

Crow looked at Scar and weakened slightly. "O-fucking-kay. You're such a prick. First, you can bang her any time. Second, tonight is Halloween. The only night in three hundred and sixty-something days a year that you can see it. So go fuck yourself. Either you want to go with me and find it or you don't. Make up your fucking mind."

Scar flashed the light in his friend's face. "Asshole."

They started walking again.

"You ever wonder if we're playing with shit that we don't need to be messing with?" Scar asked. "I mean with all the fucking spells and incantations and Satan shit?"

Crow yanked back his hood. "I fucking give up. What is it with you? All I want is some fucking quiet time so I can get into the mood of this whole fucking thing and you won't shut the fuck up."

"That's it, asshole." Scar turned and headed back along the dirt road. "You go find it by yourself." He handed his flashlight to Crow. "Fuck you."

Crow watched Scar until he was out of sight in the darkness. *Fuck him! If he wants to miss out on the greatest event in his life, he can go fuck himself.*

As the moon crested over the trees, Crow continued on, deep in thought as to what he would find hidden in the heart of the Maryland woods.

The wind ran through the forest, carrying with it the call of the great horned owl. Crow pulled the hood over his head, wanting to become part of the night and the wind. He envisioned himself a vapor, a specter, a spirit of the underworld. Quickly forgetting Scar, he slipped on through the shadows.

He had heard the legend many times—the story of the haunted fire ring, the one that could only be seen on Halloween. The story went that, in the early 1700s, a group of young village girls claimed to see and communicate with the devil. They were branded witches and burned alive in the town square. In a common unmarked grave deep within the Maryland woods, the village elders buried the children's bodies—the location marked by a ring of rocks. But the legend tells that each Halloween the girls rise up and roam the woods, crying out in torment as they search for the devil among the thick forest. Those who claim to have witnessed the apparitions say the girls' bodies are engulfed in flames.

Crow came upon a small stone marker in the weeds beside the dirt road. It was a mile marker placed there when the road was heavily traveled by the colonists hundreds of years ago. Standing beside the stone marker, he recalled the instructions from the website. Six hundred sixty-six paces due north of the marker lay the resting place of the Potomac Witches beneath the haunted fire ring.

He took in a deep breath and stepped forward, eager to become a master in the netherworld of the occult, Satan worship, and the black arts.

Mace pulled his BMW into the grove of witch hazel and black walnut trees. Other cars were already there—he was the last to arrive. As he got out, he looked at the moon shadows on the ground—silver and shimmering. *What a wonderful night. A perfect Halloween.*

The air chilled him as he slipped into his ceremonial scarlet robe and moved down a sloping path along a hillside to the circle of rocks. He smelled smoke—pungent but sweet. It drifted through the forest like wispy tentacles beckoning him to the heart of its heat.

"Good evening, Pursan," said a tall man in a flowing black robe standing beside the path. He bowed slightly.

"Urakabarameel," Mace said. "We've missed you the last few gatherings."

"I've been spending a lot of time in the Middle East. War is hell."

Mace chuckled. "That it is." He placed his hand on the other's shoulder as they walked on down the hillside. "So all that's your doing over on that side of the world?"

"I can't take complete credit. Ezekeel and Dagon have had a hand in it as well."

"Give them my regards," Mace said as they approached the circle of fire—a ring of stones about thirty feet in diameter. In the center, a cone-shaped pile of logs blazed, sending sparks into the heavens. Surrounding the fire, a dozen children stood holding hands, their faces hidden by the hoods of their black robes. Circling behind the children, a group of robed adults formed an outer ring.

"A good gathering," Urakabarameel said.

"Yes," Mace said. "Our new Ruby Army grows so quickly."

"How is your Hades Project coming along?" Urakabarameel asked.

"It's a challenge." Mace paused as one of the adults brought him a golden cup of wine and a jewel-encrusted dagger. "I'll tell you more after the initiation."

Urakabarameel nodded and took his place among the adults. Mace was handed a golden chalice of wine and a jewel-encrusted dagger before he stepped through a gap in the circle of children and said, "It is time." He glanced around at everyone. "Let us begin by calling upon Samael, the Guardian of the Gate."

In unison, the children intoned, "Samael."

A rush of wind stirred through the surrounding forest causing the branches to bow beneath the star-filled sky.

"I call upon Azazel, the Guardian of the Flame," Mace said, "the Spark in the Eye of the Great Darkness."

Again, the small voices echoed, "Azazel."

A tongue of flame swirled up and crackled as it fed on itself.

"I call upon the Light of the Air, the Son of the Dawn."

"Son of the Dawn," the children repeated.

The Old Man came to stand next to Mace, his face aglow in the heat of the flames. "The time grows close," he said. "You are our newest warriors." He spread his arms in a sweeping gesture as if gathering the children in an embrace. "The great Ruby Army will soon unite, and you will be our future vanguard. Stand proud in your purpose, for this world will belong to us. Soon we will take back from Him all that He stole from us. Now, come forward and dedicate your souls to me and the future of our new world."

Mace sipped from the chalice before saying, "In the name of your mighty sword and the flowing lifeblood that gives you the power to conquer, enter into the minds, hearts, and souls of these young soldiers, and fill them with your terrible and crushing strength."

Mace lifted his arms high as the children formed a single line. Each came and kissed the blade of the dagger, then took a sip from the chalice. Once done, they returned to their place in the fire circle and drew back their hoods.

"Oh, great Son of the Dawn, behold, the newest soldiers of your vanquishing army."

The Old Man surveyed his youthful warriors. "So be it," he said.

Each child turned to be congratulated by his or her father—a Fallen Angel.

The ceremony finished, Mace returned the dagger and cup to a nearby Fallen brother. As he did, he moved close to the Fallen's face and whispered, "We have a visitor—a young man enchanted by the lure of legends and darkness."

The Fallen brother said, "I am aware of him lurking in the distant shadows."

Mace smiled. "See that he finds what he seeks."

"Of course."

Mace nodded a thank-you before turning to walk up the slope where he saw Urakabarameel waiting. "Oh, yes," he said. "I intended to tell you more of the Hades Project." Side by side, they strolled along as Mace talked. "What we're going to do will amount to the biggest trick since the Son of the Dawn tempted Eve to eat from the Tree of Knowledge. And, as they say, a little bit of knowledge is a dangerous thing. That's the clincher to this whole idea. Men will make decisions according to what they think they see, what they believe is happening, based on their knowledge, when indeed there is nothing really there to see and nothing is really happening. Only an illusion that we create. And based upon those illusions, they will eventually turn against one another and commit the gravest of sins against God."

"How do you mean?" Urakabarameel said.

"It is probably premature for me to go into such detail, but let me give you an example. Let's say we alter GPS satellite diagnostic and control by displaying a problem or error. Upon seeing that, the human operator will make appropriate corrections. However, since the problem is contrived, when the operator makes his corrections, his response will actually create a problem. In other words, we skew a few numbers, the operator compensates and skews all GPS coordinates."

"Interesting."

"It gets better." Mace relished his position in the Fallen hierarchy and could not resist the opportunity to flaunt that he was one of the Son of the Dawn's chosen insiders. He would not miss this opportunity. "Maybe I shouldn't divulge so much," he said, "but the grandeur of the plan is magnificent, and I must share with you. Let us say that the authorities receive word that a hundred inbound airliners have been hijacked and they rush to land all planes."

Urakabarameel smiled. "Because the GPS coordinates are wrong, planes descend over the wrong areas."

"Yes. Air traffic controllers panic and instruct pilots to take drastic measures to land, resulting in numerous crashes while other planes run out of fuel and fall from the skies."

"That's quite original, Pursan, but I assume there's more to it than airplanes crashing?"

"Oh, yes. We will affect global systems such as banking, defense, communications, utilities, and finally the power grids in an equally chaotic manner. The end result will be a complete, worldwide shutdown of all resources. On the evening of the last day of Man, each individual will be at war with his neighbor. Many will take the lives of others before their own, and we will welcome their souls with open arms."

"I like it already," Urakabarameel said. "And you'll be guiding everything from within?"

"I've already started."

"Keep me informed."

"Are you heading back to the desert?" Mace asked.

Urakabarameel nodded. "Dealing with terrorists is like communicating with mongrels, but I enjoy the challenge."

As Mace arrived at his car, he waved to the departing Urakabarameel. Removing his robe, Mace glanced briefly toward the dark woods nearby, knowing the young visitor was still there. He smelled the boy's fear.

Mace got behind the wheel and started the long drive out of the forest back to the Virginia suburbs. The Ruby initiation ceremonies always invigorated him, and he smiled with the excitement of knowing the Hades Project was about to become a reality.

———

Crow watched from behind the cover of the forest as the BMW left. Soon, all the cars had gone and the night was quiet, the wind calm, and the moon spread a pewter haze over the Maryland woods.

But Crow was not calm and quiet. He had already shed the heavy trench coat as sweat soaked his body. "What the fuck?" he whispered.

Standing on shaky legs, he stumbled down the sloping hillside toward the fire ring. He had to either confirm what he had seen or find reason to laugh at his misunderstanding. He prayed for the latter. Either way, he had to know.

Smoke hung heavy in the air, almost like a cloudy sentry standing guard. Crow cautiously approached the rock circle. The fire had died away, only embers glowed faintly from the black mass of spent logs.

Crow still couldn't grasp in his mind what he had witnessed. And yet he knew it was something that went way beyond the role-playing he and Scar did with their make-believe spells and incantations. Scar was never going to believe this. No one would believe it.

Crow looked at the stones and touched one with his foot. The heat burned through his shoe. The acrid smell of smoke stung in his nostrils, and he had no doubt that he had trespassed into an evil place. The air, laden with the odor of sulfur, had moments ago been inside the bodies of those vile creatures. Now it was in his lungs. That thought convinced him that he had experienced enough.

Suddenly, the embers sprang alive with the brilliance of an exploding sun. A flame shot over Crow's head, bringing with it a blast of heat. He backed away, fearing his feet would melt into the ground.

Then he saw them.

The Potomac Witches.

They appeared before him just outside the stone ring, only a few feet away, their naked bodies consumed in fire.

He turned to run, to get as far from this place as possible. But when he did, the witches suddenly materialized in front of him, blocking his way, forcing Crow back to the fire that now raged. He felt the intense heat bite his neck. His shirt and pants burst into flames. The air filled with howling as the witches rushed forward. Their wails were matched only by his shrieks of terror. As he fell into their embrace, the metal objects piercing his skin melted and ran down his face like silver tears.

THE CODE

Ben awoke to the sound of someone whistling the national anthem. Lying on his side facing away from the other beds in the small dormitory, he turned to see who was there.

"You are supposed to stand." It was the boy, Devin Olsen, sitting on his bed at the other end of the room. He whistled another bar, then sat Indian style on the mattress.

"What?" Ben said, slowly swinging his legs over the side. He rubbed the sleep from his eyes.

"Supposed to stand at attention when you hear 'The Star Spangled Banner.'"

"You're right," Ben said, glancing at his watch. It had been about five hours since Tor had taken Devin from the room. He must have been asleep when the boy returned for he had heard nothing. "But I see that you're not standing."

"It's over. You don't have to stand when it's over." Devin held his arms outstretched as if to emphasize the obvious lack of any whistling.

168

Ben glanced at the plastic tray holding a Styrofoam plate on the floor by his bed. There was a partially eaten ham and cheese sandwich and a can of ginger ale. Tor had brought Ben lunch a few moments after taking Devin away. Ben asked where he had taken the boy, but the guy had said nothing other than to enjoy the food.

Ben was glad to see that Devin had returned and was okay. He walked over to a chair near Devin and sat. "Are you all right?"

The kid didn't look him in the eye. Instead his focus was just barely off to the left, not much, but noticeable. And the boy's face showed little expression.

Devin scratched his scalp, which was covered by a mass of unkempt blond hair. He continued staring off in space, shaking his hands near his head as if his fingers had gone numb and he was trying to bring the circulation back. Ben had seen him do that several times, like a nervous tic. The kid seemed brilliant in some areas and yet there appeared to be this odd, gaping deficit.

"Devin?" Ben waited for the boy to stop shaking his hands and pay attention. Finally, he said, "Where did Tor take you?"

"Games." He stilled his hands but didn't alter his focus.

"Can you look at me?"

The boy's eyes wandered before landing on Ben's.

"What kind of games?" Ben asked. "Video games?"

"They let me play *Titan Quest, Warlords, Prey,* and sometimes *Ghost Recon.*" He scratched his head again. "Tom Clancy's game. Heard of Tom Clancy?"

"Of course I've heard of him." He got the feeling that the kid was, in some strange way, talking down to him. "Is that it? They let you play video games?" There had to be more to it than just entertaining the kid, he thought. What was going on here?

169

"Then I type." Devin held his hands out and mimicked typing on an air keyboard.

"Type what?"

"Code."

"You mean like Morse Code?"

Devin gave Ben a look as if the question was stupid. "Destiny code."

"Okay, I give up. What is Destiny code?"

"My dad's computer. He calls it Destiny."

Ben leaned forward slightly realizing he was on the verge of getting some answers. "Who is your dad?"

"Alan Olsen."

"What does he do?"

Devin looked confused.

Ben decided to rephrase. "What is his job?"

Devin answered, still with a slack face. "Boss at CyberSys."

Now it was starting to make sense. Ben had watched the news reports covering the kidnapping of the Olsen kid. Dolphin Stadium. Autistic child. No ransom demands. No trace or clues. CyberSys was the quantum computer outfit. Ben even owned stock in the company a few years back. Made an 18 percent return, if he remembered correctly. Not too bad by his standards. Now they had everybody looking for this kid who was sitting in front of him. This was not good, Ben thought. Worse than he had thought. If the FBI managed to locate Devin, they would also find Ben Jackson, the retired banker from Atlanta, and they would start asking questions. Next thing you know, Ben Jackson becomes Ben Ray, the new federal prison inmate in cell block . . . Fuck.

Ben stood. Maybe the kid wasn't telling the truth about who he was or what he did when they took him away to play games. "How do you know the software code, Devin?"

"Memorized it when I played games in Dad's office."

Ben shook his head, incredulous. From the little he knew about computer codes, there was no way a kid, or anybody, could do such a thing. Ben grinned. "You're pulling my leg, aren't you?"

Devin glanced at Ben's legs. "Why would I do that?"

This was another discovery about Devin Olsen. He took everything literally.

"I mean wouldn't that be a lot to memorize?"

"Not really. Hundred thousand lines of Destiny code, ten thousand of the classic PC code."

"Are you telling me you memorized a hundred and ten thousand lines of software code? That's impossible."

"No, it's easy. Like memorizing books."

"How many books have you memorized?" Ben wondered if the kid was just playing with his head.

Devin shrugged. "Six thousand, four hundred, twenty-eight. Last one I read was *The Language of God*."

Ben had never heard of it. "Okay, if you're telling me the truth, what's the first line on page . . . thirty-three?"

Without hesitation, Devin answered. "*If you started this book as a skeptic . . .*"

Ben stared at the kid as if he had just revealed where Ben had hidden his *Playboy* magazines when he was a teen. He had no way of confirming that those were the first words on page 33 of the book, but Devin's amazing confidence convinced Ben that the answer was probably correct.

"Let's say I believe that you have memorized the code to your father's Destiny computer. Wouldn't it take a long, long time to type it all out? I mean, how fast can you type?"

"I don't know. World's record is held by Barbara Blackburn in the town of Salem, the state capital of Oregon. Population three million, four hundred twenty-one thousand. Barbara Blackburn can maintain one hundred and fifty words per minute. That's thirty-seven thousand, five hundred keystrokes. Her top speed was two hundred and twelve on a modified keyboard. It's in the *Guinness Book of World Records*."

Ben's head reeled. They had kidnapped this eight-year-old to steal memorized computer code. He was obviously some sort of genius or prodigy. The big question was what they intended to do with him once they had what they needed.

Devin shook his hands again.

"Devin, do you have any idea why Tor needs the code?"

"Don't know."

Ben was an impatient man, but for some reason he sympathized with the kid. What must it be like to be in Devin's head? What was locked inside this eight-year-old? And these assholes had no conscience. He cringed at the thought of what they would do once they got all they needed from Devin. But still, it would take a while for him to type a hundred and ten thousand lines of code, even at *Guinness* speed. At least the lengthy process of typing the code would give Ben some time to figure out how to escape, and take the kid with him.

There was the question of what they intended to do with Ben Jackson. He didn't have anything to offer like Devin—no value.

Ben's *destiny* was bleak. It would help if he knew the timeline. How much code was left? And what if they only needed a portion?

"Devin, do you have a lot of code left to type for Tor?"

"Lots."

"How much is lots? How long will it take you?"

Devin shrugged.

Ben felt his gut tighten. "A couple of days?"

Again, Devin shrugged.

"Maybe less?"

Devin stared blankly.

Ben let out a long sigh. Once they had the Destiny code, they would most likely have no further need for Devin. And, Ben thought, there was no reason to delay his own demise. That could come at any minute. He was amazed they hadn't done away with him already. Why were they keeping him alive? "Then I'd better think of something fast to save us both—the handwriting is on the wall."

Devin's head jerked up and his gaze spun from one wall to another.

"No, no, there is no writing on any wall. It's just an expression."

Ben paced. "Devin, while I figure out how we can escape, we have to keep our plans a secret from those cutthroats. Understand?"

"Yep," Devin said, dragging his finger across his neck like a pirate slicing a captive's throat.

ARTIFACT

"Secretary Mace, you have such a magnificent collection," the woman said. In her elegant evening gown, she moved gracefully from one display case to the next in the grand study of Mace's home. The low, indirect lighting contrasted with the soft glow of the displays, making them appear like jeweled islands in a sea of dark mahogany and Persian rugs. She stopped at a case containing Egyptian artifacts. Whispering to her husband standing beside her, she pointed to a bracelet arranged on scarlet velvet.

"That one is a favorite of mine," Mace said, watching her reaction. As other dinner guests joined him, he took a sip of champagne from his crystal flute and continued, "The ancient Egyptians adopted the scarab or dung beetle as a symbol of the sun god because they were used to seeing the insect rolling a ball of dung on the ground. The action suggested to them the invisible force that rolled the sun across the dome of the sky."

"It's stunning," the woman said. "Darling, buy it for me." She elbowed her husband who pretended to go for his wallet.

The group chuckled as Mace beamed, proud of the collection that had taken him so many years to amass. "The gold, by the way, is encrusted with lapis lazuli."

"And this one, Secretary Mace?" another female guest asked, pointing to a different case. "Tell us about it."

"Aztec." The group followed him and gathered around the multicolored vase, radiant in the delicate wash of strategically aimed spotlights. "The face on the front is the god Tlaloc. Those are coiled serpents around his eyes. The vase symbolized the water that brought forth the bounty of their crops."

"It looks frightening," the woman said, bending for a closer inspection.

"In many ways, they were a brutal people, and their art reflects it." Mace smiled with the knowledge that many of the Brotherhood of the Nephilim were once Aztec priests and warriors.

"Secretary Mace?" A man in a tuxedo gestured to an elaborate crystal box about the size of a toaster oven in its own display case. "Your collection has so many amazing pieces, yet the most breathtaking display contains what looks like a small piece of black wood. What's so special about this one?"

Inside the crystal box, atop white satin, was an object the size of an eyebrow pencil. It was so black that there seemed to be no detail to it, nor did light reflect from its surface.

"That is my prized possession," Mace said.

"A little piece of wood, Mr. Secretary?" the first woman said. "More than your five-thousand-year-old beetle bracelet?"

Her remark brought a grin from Mace and laughs from his dinner guests. "I never thought of the Egyptians as Beatles fans. From now on, I'll refer to that piece as Ringo's bracelet." This brought a bigger laugh.

"So is this really wood?" a male guest asked.

"You're close. It started out as wood. What you see is actually crystallized sap. But the wood it originated from is what makes it so unique."

"You're keeping us in suspense, Mr. Secretary," a guest said. "Please tell everyone what it is."

Mace set his flute down on a side table and stood over the display. He withdrew a set of keys from his pocket and unlocked the case. "The story is a captivating mixture of biblical history and legend. Let me ask you all, would everyone be impressed if I told you I owned a unicorn?"

There were collective nods.

"In many ways, what you're looking at is just as rare as the mythical unicorn." He opened the display case and touched the top of the crystal box with his fingertips, almost like he was caressing the skin of a lover. "For those familiar with the book of Genesis in the Bible, God instructed Noah to build a vessel in preparation for the coming Great Flood. Noah was to construct the vessel out of resin-wood and pitch. Down through the centuries, many men have searched for the final resting place of the Ark. A number of years ago, a group of explorers located what they believed was the remains of the Ark on the snow-covered slopes of Mount Ararat in Eastern Turkey. A few remnants of the crystallized sap from those resin-wood planks detailed in Genesis were found preserved. So what you see is a small piece of Noah's Ark that survived the Great Flood over five thousand years ago."

Mace watched the always predictable expressions of surprise on his guest's faces each time he revealed the identity of the tiny black object.

"You're serious?" the man said, staring at Mace. "The real Noah's Ark?"

"Yes." Mace moved around to the opposite side of the display so he could face his friends. "This particular piece, along with a handful of others, once rested in the Baghdad Museum, brought there by the expedition that discovered the Ark. The Baghdad Museum was a remarkable depository of antiquity. You might recall that in April of two thousand and three, right after the collapse of Saddam Hussein's regime, the museum was ransacked. It was a despicable act of looting comparable in scale to the sack of Constantinople and the burning of the library at Alexandria. Those like me who treasure the antiquity of mankind were devastated. It was only shortly before the start of the Iraq War that I came into possession of this artifact."

"If it was part of the museum's collection, how did you get it?" another guest asked.

Mace had practiced this little spiel he was about to give in front of his bathroom mirror, testing facial expressions that would make his lie convincing. As rehearsed, his appearance became melancholic. "Despite the immense fortunes amassed by Saddam Hussein," he said, "little of his money went to the preservation of the region's heritage—not even his own country's archaeological treasures. Most went to his personal palaces and extravagant lifestyle. So to raise funds for the museum, from time to time the curator would hold an auction. Actually it was more like a raffle. It would cost each patron a million dollars to buy a lottery ticket." It was at this point he allowed his face to brighten. "This was the prize and I won."

Mace evaluated his audience. Not a single questioning raised eyebrow. He forced back a smile.

"Were the other stolen pieces of the Ark recovered?" a male guest asked.

"No," Mace said. "In reality, the thieves may not have even realized what those pieces were. They could have easily been overlooked among the thousands of other more notable artwork, sculpture, and such that were taken. The ransacking was chaotic beyond belief. Sadly, this may be the only remaining piece from Noah's Ark in existence."

"Amazing," a male guest said. "You're lucky that you got it before that terrible event."

"Mr. Secretary, you have an urgent call."

The group turned in unison as a young man in a black suit stood nearby holding a cordless phone in his outstretched hand.

"If you all will excuse me for a moment," Mace said. He closed the display case, locking the crystal box and artifact inside before taking the phone. Not until he was in the privacy of an adjacent hallway did he hold the phone to his ear and say, "Mace, here."

"It's Tor."

"Is this going to upset me?"

"Yes."

MOTNEES

"How could an eight-year-old kid that you've never met draw a detailed portrait of you?" John asked, staring at the sketch.

"There's got to be a logical explanation," Cotten said. She watched the dribble of traffic come and go in the Tropical Breeze motel parking lot as she and John sat in the rental car.

"I'm sure you're right," he said. "After all, we're a bit on edge right now and tend to read too much into everything." He scratched his day-old beard. "Tera must have seen a picture of you."

"Of course, that's it," Cotten said. "In the scrapbook. I found a picture of Lindsay and me back in high school. It was with the note she left me saying they were on the run."

"But that was an old picture. The sketch isn't of a high school girl. It's the way you look now. Unless, of course, you haven't changed a bit."

"I'd like to make that claim, but it was seventeen or eighteen years ago." Cotten gave him a challenging glance, daring him to comment on her age.

He seemed to pick up on her body language, and he held up a hand in defense. "I can't imagine you being more beautiful than you are today."

A grin flickered across her face. "Right answer," she said, taking his hand in hers. The playfulness drained from her eyes. "You're right, the portrait isn't based on my high school picture. But Tera could have seen me on TV. After the Russian incident, I was all over the press."

Cotten turned to look out the window as a thought bubbled up inside. "But there's something way too coincidental going on here." She squeezed his hand, then let go and looked at him. "I think she left the sketch behind on purpose in case we came along. I think she meant for me to find it. Like some kind of message."

"Which is?"

"No idea. But we're not going to find out sitting here."

"Well, that's another problem we need to discuss."

"What problem?"

"The call. The one that came from your cell phone back in Kentucky."

"You said it was a warning to back off. So what else is new? How many times have the Nephilim used that old, worn-out line?" She shrugged. "We've heard it before. You and I know that they won't kill me. It's against their covenant that protects the offspring of the Fallen. John, my father was Furmiel, Angel of the Eleventh Hour. If he hadn't repented and become mortal, I would not have been born. I *am* Nephilim—at least half of me. So they won't kill me."

"But they can hurt you," John said. "That was the warning, Cotten. Back off or they *will* hurt you. Badly." He took her hand

and held it with both of his. "Maim, disfigure, take you to the edge of death—a place filled with constant pain. Is finding a kid who had a run-in with a backwoods preacher worth the risk?"

"It's not just that, John. You know it's bigger than that." Cotten leaned her head back on the headrest and stared through the windshield. "Something happened when I touched Tera's picture. Something so odd, so intense. It was a special connection, like I was in touch with my own mortality, my own soul. My perfect reflection." She turned and looked into his eyes. "This goes way beyond sketches, paintings, poems, and red auras around Pastor Albrecht. I'm compelled to find her." She stopped short of revealing who she thought Tera was. John would think she'd finally lost it.

John took the sketch and studied it for a moment before setting it on the dash. "You said 'my reflection.' Are you talking about Motnees, your twin?"

Cotten nodded. *God, he knows me so well*, she thought. There was not another person in the world who knew so much about her—knew everything about her, the good, and the not so good. "Her name sounds so silly, now. But that's what I called her. Her angel name. Even though she died at birth, her spirit still came to me when I was a child. I've told you how she would appear in my room and comfort me when I was sick—speak to me in our made-up twin-talk. When I touched Tera's picture back at the farm, it was exactly the same memories that flooded back, the strong bond, the incredible connection. I could almost hear her calling me."

"In Enochian, the language of angels—your twin-talk?"

Cotten felt tears well up. "Yes." It took a moment to gather her composure. "If Tera is the incarnation of Motnees, it scares the hell out of me."

"Why would you be afraid of her? I don't understand."

"No, not her. I'm afraid of what it means. Why would she come back after so many years? We may not yet know the reason, but her presence surely means something terrible is about to happen. She must be a profound threat to the Fallen. That's why they are pursuing her so fiercely. Tera must have a key role in confronting them, and they must suspect it. They'll never give up until they have hunted her down."

"I don't want anything to happen to you."

"I know," she said, leaning against him, feeling the security that his closeness always brought.

He stroked her hair. "But, I can see I'm not going to get anywhere trying to talk you out of this. If the connection is that strong, then there must be something to it. We won't know until we find Tera. If we just understood why they wanted to find her so badly. What threat could a child have against the Forces of Evil?"

Suddenly, Cotten sat up in her seat. She looked at John, her eyes wide with surprise. "My God, we're so stupid."

"I don't understand."

"We want to know why they fear her? John, they've got my cell phone."

"Of course," he said, shaking his head.

Cotten smiled. "We'll call and ask."

DEGRADE

"What do you mean it's not working?" Mace said. He had left his dinner guests to take the call from Tor. With the phone to his ear, he walked out onto the river stone patio of his home overlooking the Virginia countryside.

"It's what I suspected all along," Tor said. "The thodium has degraded from thousands of years of exposure in the freezing Turkish mountains."

"So you're telling me that it's not going to work?"

"I didn't say that. Only that it's not 100 percent reliable. I'll need more time to isolate a workable sample from what you gave me."

"How much time?"

"Too soon to estimate."

"What about using the artifact I've got here?"

"It's all from the same place. I can try it, but no guarantees that it will work any better."

"What's the alternative?"

"Unless you can find me a pure source of thodium, we're back to the drawing board."

Mace rubbed his chin. "How's it going with the kid?"

"Slow. He's totally unpredictable."

"And our banker friend?"

"He and the kid are getting chummy. But Jackson, aka Benjamin Ray, doesn't have much luck with the kid either. Sometimes I think we should have hacked into the CyberSys mainframe rather than dragging the code out of an eight-year-old—especially this one."

"It would have been the chicken and the egg routine if you had. You need a quantum computer to hack in and you need to hack in to steal the OS to run the quantum computer. The kid has got to be the easier of the two."

"Then you come up here in Hicksville and try your luck."

"I don't have the patience for such matters. Just keep at it. In the meantime, I'll have someone bring you the other thodium artifact. They'll fly to Little Rock and drive it out to you."

"That's fine, but like I said, no guarantees it will work any better than what you already gave me."

"I don't need guarantees, just results."

"Have whoever's delivering the artifact call my cell when they get into town. This place is a bitch to find, so I'd rather go meet him. And for that matter, he's not staying. The place is already getting too crowded with the Olsen boy and the banker. I designed this system and I can run it myself."

"Fine, just keep at it, and get the rest of the code from the kid."

Mace pushed the off button on the cordless phone. He hadn't counted on the thodium being degraded. That could present a big problem in his timetable. Where would he find other sources? The answer was buried somewhere in the story of the Great Flood, of that he felt certain.

Mace paced the patio, trying to recall the many facts of the Flood kept hidden or lost down through the ages. There were details of the event not documented in the Scriptures, thanks to the Fallen's influence over the arrogance and egos of the men who approved and assembled the Bible. Many ancient writings, scrolls, and books were left out because they didn't conform to the teachings of the Church or because the Son of the Dawn chose to have them eliminated. Selective inspiration, he called it.

One fact dealt with the construction of the Ark. Mace knew that in Genesis, the wood used to construct the Ark was called gopher wood or resin wood—an obscure, Pre-Deluvian material that by design was not well defined—and did not exist anywhere in the world today. In reality, the wood used to construct the Ark was lumber originally cut from the Tree of Life east of the Garden of Eden. After the flood, the Ark was disassembled, and the wood carried by Noah's descendants to faraway lands as they repopulated the world. But it was the sap the wood excreted that held the key. Once it crystallized, it transformed into a material of unusual powers and properties—fitting for a material that originated in the Garden. The crystallized resin of the Tree is what Tor called thodium, the power behind the Hades computer.

The Tree was now gone forever, having given up its last limb and branch to the Ark five thousand years ago. But the fact that the wood was dispersed to Noah's descendants meant that other objects may have eventually been made from the wood and may still exist.

The small remains of the Ark on Mount Ararat had been so easy for Mace to obtain—the ransacking of the Baghdad museum a convenient diversion for stealing them. The task ahead of finding other objects from the Ark would not be so unproblematic. He'd have to consult with the Son of the Dawn and delve into his leader's eons of wisdom and in-depth knowledge of the Bible and other ancient documents. Somewhere, a pure source of thodium waited. Now it was a matter of finding it before the Hades Project was discovered and the future of the Ruby Army was compromised.

With a sense of renewed determination, Mace walked back into the grand study where his guests awaited and said, "Ladies and gentlemen, let's have dessert."

THODIUM

Max Wolf looked into the camera as the Satellite News Network reporter said, "Dr. Wolf, please let Mr. Olsen know that all our prayers are with him in the swift recovery of his son, Devin."

"Thank you," Max said. "I'll pass that on to him." He and the reporter, along with the SNN remote location crew, were gathered in the shade of palm trees across Biscayne Boulevard from Cyber-Sys headquarters in downtown Miami. A weather front had moved through South Florida the previous night. Now the air was cool and crisp under a pristine blue sky as the late fall breeze rustled the palm fronds and mixed with the hum of afternoon traffic.

The reporter had wanted to hold the interview inside the company's labs but corporate security regulations forbade cameras being brought into the restricted research areas, so they settled on the lush tropical park nearby with the CyberSys building and its dynamic cobalt blue thunderbolt logo in the background.

"Without getting too technical, can you explain for our viewers just exactly what Project Destiny is?"

Max said, "Destiny is the codename for what we hope will be the world's first fully functional quantum computer."

"And what is a quantum computer?"

"Perhaps a way to visualize it is to compare it to the classical PC that we're all used to seeing. Imagine the PC as the venerable space shuttle *Enterprise* and a quantum computer as the fictional Starship *Enterprise*. One travels at tens of thousands of miles per hour, the other travels at close to the speed of light—in the movies at least. So one of the biggest differences in the two computers is the speed of performing computations."

"That's quite a strong comparison, Dr. Wolf, and a huge leap in technology."

"Speed is everything in quantum computing," Max said. "For example, some modern simulations that are currently taking IBM's Blue Gene supercomputer years to do would only take a quantum computer a matter of seconds."

"Impressive," the editor said. "Now, many in our audience are familiar with CyberSys and the fact that you are a leader in both the development of high-speed encryption technology and quantum computing research. Tell us, what is the main obstacle standing in your way to creating a working Destiny system?"

"In a word," Max said, "decoherence. In a quantum computer, all data is stored in what's called a qubit—basically one bit of information per atom. In the process of computing, we need the qubits to interact with each other, but not interact with their surroundings, which can induce noise and other undesirable results. We must keep the computer in a coherent state—the slightest interaction with the external world causes the system to decohere, thus creating our biggest enemy, decoherence and the corruption of our computations."

"How close are you to finding a solution?"

"We still have a ways to go. The problem is storing the qubits. We've tried using just about everything. Gone through virtually all known atoms—even something as exotic as nitrogen vacancies in diamonds—to find the perfect storage material. Nothing works well enough to avoid some level of decoherence."

"So if you've tried every material there is, then can we conclude that it is impossible to build a real quantum computer?"

"Well," Max said with a smile, "what I meant was every known substance that we can get our hands on. Only ninety-two elements exist in nature, but scientists have discovered additional ones from time to time under specialized testing conditions. A recent discovery that we think would produce positive results is an element called thodium, a previously unknown atom high up the periodic table."

"How do you know it would work?"

"So far, it's a theory based on quantities of one or two atoms created in particle accelerator tests."

"Not enough for your needs?"

"No. We can't produce enough to positively confirm its compatibility, and unfortunately we are unaware of any natural source. At this point, the natural existence of the element is hypothetical."

"I must admit, I'm not familiar with thodium."

"Like a handful of other elements that are either theoretical or extremely rare," Max said, "thodium is usually confined to the footnotes of science journals."

The reporter nodded. "I remember a couple from back in college. Never knew why we bothered studying something so scarce that the total amount in existence would fit into a thimble."

"You're probably thinking of astatine or francium. It's estimated that there is only one ounce of astatine in the entire world, and scientists tell us that there are about five hundred grams of francium in all of nature."

"Can you describe thodium?"

"Technically, it is a specific form of crystallized resin. Our simulations show that it exhibits all the characteristics needed to avoid decoherence in the storage of qubits. If the theories are correct, thodium would be a perfect spectral hole-burning material. With it we could address individual thodium atoms using our lasers and read out their states with no problem. We theorize that thodium atoms interact strongly with each other, allowing us to perform fast quantum logic gates. And we believe that it possesses an atomic transition of two hyperfine energy levels that are so wonderfully insulated from the surrounding environment that a qubit could live there effectively forever, undisturbed by noise or decoherence."

"So all you have to do is round up a batch of thodium and you can build the first fully functional Destiny system?"

"Theoretically, yes."

The cameraman signaled that the segment time was almost up.

"This has been fascinating, Dr. Wolf. I know our viewers can't wait for news from CyberSys that you've solved the problem of decoherence and built the first working Destiny quantum computer. When you do, we hope you'll invite us back to cover the story."

"Of course," Max said.

"One more question, Dr. Wolf."

Max nodded.

"If someone could build such a powerful computer as your Project Destiny, how would it affect us all?"

"It would render useless all cryptographic systems in use today." As an afterthought, Max added, "And strike fear into the hearts of every security agency in the world."

GAME ROOM

THE DOOR OPENED AND Tor walked into the small dormitory. Sitting on the edge of his bed, Devin immediately started shaking his hands as if he were trying to air dry them. Ben leaned against the wall at the other end of the room and watched.

"Devin, it's time to go play your games," Tor said.

"Play, play, play, play." Devin repeated the words at machine gun speed.

"You know how much you like playing, Devin." Tor stood beside the boy. "We just installed the latest version of *Company of Heroes*. You love that one, remember?"

"*Company of Heroes, Company of Heroes.*" His chant switched to the game title.

"You're making things difficult, Devin," Tor said.

"Ben go, Ben go, Ben go."

"I think he wants me to tag along," Ben said, thankful that the kid was following their plan. He hoped Devin would remember everything.

"Mr. Jackson doesn't play video games, Devin," Tor said.

Devin put his hands in his lap and rocked—his focus just barely to the left of Tor.

"What harm could it do?" Ben said, trying not to be too pushy. "Maybe he'll be more cooperative."

Tor turned and looked at Ben. "Maybe." He hesitated a moment as if giving the idea some thought. Turning back to Devin, he said, "Did you hear that? Your new buddy is going to join us and watch you play. Now will you come, Devin?"

Devin stopped rocking and stood.

"Things are getting better already," Tor said. He walked to the door and opened it. "Right this way, gentlemen."

Ben fell in behind Devin as the three left the dormitory. They entered the much larger room Ben had only glimpsed earlier. The first thing he noticed was the frigid air—cold enough to see his breath. He assumed this was to keep the rows of computer equipment from overheating. He and Devin followed Tor past twenty-five rows of six-foot metal racks as they made their way to the other end of the room. Ben estimated each row ran for more than fifty feet. He found the overwhelming hum from the electronics to be unsettling. Thousands of tiny, multicolored LEDs blinked back from the dark rows of equipment like alien eyes. Ben noticed no one else as they walked along, but felt that Tor could not be the only one here. And he had seen the man in the red windbreaker in the woods and just before his crash. This was much too big an operation for just one person.

He stole a couple of glances at the ceiling confirming the placement of the jet nozzles—just like the ones in the data storage vaults of his hospitals many years ago before the banning of CFCs.

But the regulations did exempt certain critical users such as the military. If that were the case here, and the Halon tanks were still armed, then his plan just might work.

At the other end of the room, Tor led Ben and Devin up a flight of metal stairs to a second level of what Ben guessed were once offices—each with a large window overlooking the electronics room.

In the short time that they had walked from the dormitory, Ben's teeth had begun to chatter. "Do you have to keep it so cold?" he asked.

"Those mainframes would melt down in no time if we didn't," Tor said. "Besides, you get used to it."

"Maybe *you* do," Ben said.

Motioning the two into the first office, Tor closed the door and flipped on the overhead florescent lights. It was significantly warmer in the office, for which Ben was grateful. Casually, he glanced at the light fixture. Right beside it was a Halon nozzle.

Inside the room was a desk and chair set up against one wall with a PC, keyboard, monitor, and joystick. A couple of other folding chairs were against the opposite wall.

"There you go, Devin. The latest version of *Company of Heroes*. Have a seat. You've got the usual thirty minutes to blow up some bad guys. Then I'll be back to get you started from where we left off yesterday." He patted the back of the chair and Devin sat.

Within a moment, the sound of WWII tanks and planes filled the room as Devin moved through a virtual burned-out battlefield somewhere in the European Theater.

"Sit, Mr. Jackson," Tor said, motioning to a handful of metal chairs along the wall. "I'll be back soon."

As he started to leave, his cell phone rang. "Yes." Tor listened for a moment. "Okay, you're only about twenty minutes from here. Stay on the county road that runs along the edge of the Ozark National Forest. The main entrance to the old military base will be on your right. It looks all closed up. Don't worry. Just wait for me at the gate and I'll meet you there." He listened again for a moment. "Any problems getting the thodium through security?" A final pause. "Good. See you then."

Tor pushed the walky-talky button on his phone.

"Yeah?" came a male voice.

"Come up to the game room and watch the kid and Mr. Jackson. I've got to go meet the courier."

"Right," the voice replied.

Ben heard the clank of footfalls on the metal stairs. The bearded man in the red windbreaker appeared. Tor spoke to him in a hushed voice, then headed down the stairs. The man grabbed one of the chairs from the game room and placed it just outside the office, its back to the observation window.

"Can't stand the sound of those games," he said, closing the door behind him.

Ben heard a clunk and knew the door had automatically locked. He stared at the back of the man's head until he was sure the guy had mentally drifted away.

"Devin," he said softly. "Don't turn around. Keep playing your game. We need to change our plan."

The boy continued to manipulate the joystick and keyboard. Ben wondered if he had heard him.

"Devin, did you hear me?"

Devin stopped for a second and shook his hands. Then he went back to blowing up tanks.

Ben walked over behind the boy. Placing his hands on Devin's shoulders, he said, "Okay, here's what I want you to do."

TRACER

"THAT'S CORRECT," JOHN SAID into his cell phone. He gave Cotten's number to the Venatori section chief at the Vatican Embassy in Washington, D.C. "It's a Nextel Motorola iDEN equipped with AccuTracking." While he spoke, he nodded to Cotten.

They sat on a bench under a massive mossy oak along the banks of Lake Eola in downtown Orlando. A huge circular fountain that reminded Cotten of a UFO dominated the center of the lake, spraying plumes of mist into the warm, Central Florida sun. Mothers with strollers, inline skaters, and tourists moved along the park paths surrounding the twenty-three-acre lake.

"We're ready to make the call. Get back to me as soon as you have a location. Thanks." John snapped his phone shut and turned to Cotten. "We're all set."

"I'm nervous," she said, shifting her gaze back to the fountain in the center of the lake. "I'm not sure what to say."

"Just what we discussed. Ask them why they want to harm Tera. See if they would like to meet and discuss."

"It sounds so easy now." She wrung her hands. "But when I get on the line, I know I'm going to fall apart."

An elderly couple walked by conversing in Spanish. Once they were out of earshot, John said, "Okay, let's do it."

Reluctantly, Cotten took his phone. She opened it and stared at the keypad. Who would answer? Man or woman? They would see the caller ID and know it was from John. She had to show confidence in her voice. No hesitation. No stammering. John had told her to be in command and control.

She gripped the phone firmly and dialed her cell phone number. Bringing the phone to her ear, she listened while she looked into John's eyes, thankful that he was with her.

One ring. Two rings. Three rings.

Hi, this is Cotten. I can't answer your call right now, but leave a message and I'll get back to you real soon.

Beep.

She held the phone close to her mouth and said. "What do you want with Tera Jordan? She's just a child. Leave her alone. Leave her mother alone. They have done nothing to you. If you want a confrontation . . ."

John shook his head.

"Why don't we meet?" Cotten continued, holding her voice steady. "Call this number. I'll talk to you. Stop harassing Tera. Leave her alone!" Her voice rose in pitch with the last words. She took a deep breath, closed the phone, and scrunched her mouth. "Bad?"

"No," John said. "You got your message across. We knew they wouldn't answer anyway. No surprise there. Now relax and let's see what happens." He stood. "Let's get some lunch."

Cotten handed him back his cell. Would they return her call? She gave it as good a chance as meeting the aliens from the UFO fountain in the middle of Lake Eola.

———

"They're going to let us stay for free, Ladybug," Lindsay said as she and Tera stood at the door to room 14 of the Dos Palmas Motel, a few miles south of Key Largo. "Isn't that the best news?"

Tera shrugged. "I guess."

Lindsay stuck the key in the lock and opened the door. They stepped inside and she flipped on a light switch. A lamp glowed on a bedside table. The room was small and worn—way overdue for new paint, furniture, and carpet. The refrigerator was compact, half the size of the one at home, and the oven and stove combo was also a midget version. It would do. The guy at the front office said they were in the process of renovation, but Lindsay saw no evidence of tools or workmen anywhere on the grounds of the out-of-the-way, rickety old motel in the Florida Keys.

The deal she had made with the manager was a free efficiency in return for housekeeping, running the laundry, and a bit of bookkeeping in the front office. The job was seven days a week, but the motel had only twenty units. The manager had assured her she would be done by mid-afternoon each day. Probably a lie, she thought as she put away their meager belongings into the dresser drawers. She supposed a lot of people came down here to disappear just like she had.

Tera plopped onto the bed and used the remote to turn on the TV. The image was snowy. "What's wrong with the picture?" she asked.

"You have to adjust the rabbit ears, sweetie," Lindsay said, pointing to the two metal wands sticking up from the back of the set.

She had never expected to live like this, but at least she and Tera were safe. They didn't have to register or use her credit card. She had given fake names and she hadn't been asked for any ID. She'd be paid a small, off-the-books cash compensation—considerably less than minimum wage—enough for food at least. They would get by.

While Tera played with the rabbit ears, trying to get a decent picture, Lindsay stood by a window overlooking Florida Bay. Across the shuffleboard courts, through the palm trees, she could see the gentle lapping waves. Suddenly, she felt empty and spent. Her life had come down to a tiny, grimy room in a 1950s motel. She was no different than the burnouts, the dead-enders, the baby-boomers still stuck in the sixties who found refuge in this part of the Sunshine State. She had a gifted daughter who just might be going crazy, and there was no word from Cotten Stone.

Lindsay felt alone, abandoned, helpless. Trying to mask her sobs so Tera would not hear, she covered her mouth and cried.

———

Cotten and John had just finished their sandwiches at the Terrace Restaurant beside Lake Eola when his cell phone rang.

"Well, here we go," he said, pulling it from his belt clip. "This is Tyler."

Cotten had been watching a few of the swan-shaped paddle boats cruise around the edge of the lake as she sipped her tea. Listening to

John's conversation, she tensed in anticipation of what the GPS location tracer had found.

"Really?" His eyebrows rose. "You're absolutely certain? All right, I appreciate the extra effort confirming it."

"Well?"

John closed the phone and shook his head. He stared out over the lake for a moment then turned to her. "You're not going to believe this one."

"Try me," Cotten said, feeling like she was about to explode.

"They had no problem tracing the location of your phone. But the result was so . . . unusual, that they ran it three more times." He leaned forward as if his words would be heard by everyone in the restaurant. "Your cell phone is in Washington."

"Yes?"

"In the White House."

HALON

Ben pressed down on Devin's shoulders to get his attention as the boy continued using a joystick to wreak havoc across the virtual French countryside.

"Remember how we were going to get into the security system and make the fire alarms go off tonight?"

"Fire, fire, fire," Devin said, never losing a beat with the game.

"No, no, shhh. Don't talk. Just listen." He leaned over Devin like he was closely watching the action of the game. "We have to change our plan. I want you to make the alarms go off in three minutes—in 180 seconds."

Ben looked back to check on their guard. The man had resituated his chair and now faced them. His eyes were fastened on Ben.

Ben waved at the guy in a friendly manner and returned to his position over Devin's shoulders. He hoped he could get the kid to understand without giving away his hand. They needed to take advantage of Tor's absence.

"Okay, Devin," he said softly, patting the boy's back as if he were congratulating him for some win in the game. "Make the alarms go off in one hundred eighty seconds. Then set off the Halon five seconds later. But—and this is very important," he said resting his hands on the boy's shoulders, "make the gas go off only in this room. Can you do that?"

Devin nodded. He paused the game and opened the control panel to change the game's settings. At the same time, he opened another window displaying the facility's internal security configuration settings.

As he did, Ben checked his watch and positioned himself to make certain he blocked Red Windbreaker's view of the computer screen. Ben wasn't a computer whiz and couldn't tell what adjustments Devin made. He could only hope.

"Devin," Ben said in nearly a whisper, "as soon as you hear the alarms, be ready to run to the door. That guy is going to come in to get us. When he does, the Halon gas will go off. I'll take care of him while you run out of the room. You've got to get out fast or you won't be able to breathe. The gas replaces all the oxygen in the air. Understood?"

The boy had already gone back to the game. He nodded as he blew up a German tank.

Ben prayed the kid understood and would do as he asked. But Devin was unpredictable, and other than the kid nodding, Ben didn't see any convincing indications that Devin did comprehend. He couldn't force an eyeball-to-eyeball conversation with Devin while under the guard's scrutiny. All he had to go on was the kid nodding his head. Ben clapped the boy's shoulders as if in reference to a move Devin had made in the game. Then he whispered, "Once you're out of the room, run down the steps and find a door to the outside of the building. The system should unlock all the doors automatically. Get out and head for the woods. Don't stop. Don't wait for me. Just keep running. Do you understand?"

Devin nodded again.

Ben stood behind Devin until there were eighteen seconds left. "Okay. I'm going to go sit down. Remember, when the alarms go off, get ready to run."

Ben walked back to his chair. He nodded and smiled at Red Windbreaker as he did. *I hope you like a chair in the face, asshole.*

Casually glancing at his watch, he dropped into the folding chair and stretched his arm across the back of the one next to him. Slowly, he gripped the top.

Five seconds.

Ben felt his pulse race. Sweat poured from under his arms. This was it. The boldest move he would ever make. Much more so than standing in the courtroom and denying with a blank expression that he did anything wrong when he hid billions of dollars in debt and wiped out thousands of employees' retirement funds. Much more so than faking his own death. This would be the most important moment of his life—saving an eight-year-old boy from certain death. The closest thing to redemption that he—

The alarms screamed and strobe lights flashed around the computer mainframe room below while revolving red emergency lights swept the walls with a scarlet wash.

Devin froze in his seat, frantically whimpering and waving his hands near his ears, shaking his head.

"Devin, get up!" Ben yelled, then grabbed the boy and yanked him to his feet.

Devin blinked repetitively and dropped his hands by his sides.

"When the door opens, run," Ben said. "Ready?" Ben grabbed the metal chair by its back and held it up, prepared to swing at Red Windbreaker.

As the man opened the door, the Halon discharged from the nozzle overhead, its ear-splitting hiss resembling the launch of a rocket. The normally colorless Halon formed a white cloud as the sudden release of pressure cooled the gas when it came in contact with the moisture in the air.

Ben swung the chair full force. It struck the man in the face and chest, sending him flying against the window.

Devin was still rooted to the same spot.

"Run! Devin, run!" Ben screamed. As he pulled the chair back for a second swing, he felt the first stab of the heart attack. Its sledgehammer force hit him so hard that he doubled over. Straining to stand, he saw Windbreaker stagger forward through the Halon fog, blood flowing down his face, his arms flailing at the air.

Ben shoved Devin toward the door. "Run, damn it!"

As the man took a step toward him, Ben swung the chair again, slamming it into his assailant with all his strength. He heard the unmistakable sound of bones cracking. A grunt from Red Windbreaker told Ben he had struck a devastating blow.

Just as quickly, the pain in Ben's chest exploded. He sank to his knees, knowing that he too had been dealt a fatal blow. The sound of the screaming alarms seemed to fade. As the lack of oxygen blurred his vision, he remembered standing on the bank of

Stone Creek Lake at sunrise. A morning mist lay across the slate-flat water. Beside him stood the doe, her eyes calm and tranquil. In them he caught a glimpse of his redemption as he faded like a shadow in the forest

THE CARLYLE

"GENERAL," THE PRESIDENT SAID as he looked across the table at the head of Central Command, "I appreciate the frankness in your report on the war on terrorism. Your detailed analysis was both enlightening and thought provoking."

The president, along with his cabinet and a number of visiting military officers, sat in the Cabinet Room of the White House as the forty-five-minute meeting came to an end.

"And Madam Secretary," he said turning to the Secretary of State, "I trust that you will deliver my message to the prime minister in no uncertain terms?"

She nodded affirmatively.

The president leaned forward and looked down his side of the table at Mace. "Secretary Mace, thank you for the in-depth follow-up report on the recent Internet global cyber attack. I think I can speak for everyone that we are relieved at the news that there was so little damage to this country's networks and virtual infrastructure."

"You're welcome, sir," Mace said, knowing most of his report had been carefully fabricated to diminish the recent flood attack and hide the widespread propagation of the Hades Worm. If the president and his advisors had seen Tor's latest progress report, they would have called for an emergency meeting of the National Security Council.

Everyone in the Cabinet Room stood as the president rose and strode out. While most of the attendees remained to chat, Mace went into the corridor and pulled the cell phone from his suit jacket pocket. It had started vibrating ten minutes before the end of the meeting.

Knowing that the press secretary was still in the Cabinet Room, Mace walked down the hall and ducked inside the man's empty office.

"Yes?" he said, just above a whisper.

"Do you still have Stone's cell phone?" It was Mace's key advisor inside the Department of Homeland Security.

"Yes," Mace said, watching the hall in case the press secretary headed his way.

"Dump it! The surveillance division of the Venatori just ran a real-time GPS locator trace on it."

Mace snapped the phone shut with enough force to send it in for warranty service. He stepped into the hallway and walked toward the corridor leading to the cloak room in the first floor, West Wing lobby. Entering the large walk-in closet, he pulled his heavy overcoat from the hanger and slipped it on. He knew he had to get rid of Stone's phone, but doing so would mean losing all contact with Lindsay Jordan and her daughter in the event they left any more messages. Without their voicemail messages, there would be little he could do to track their whereabouts. He had no choice. The phone was a direct link to him.

"Rizben, can you grab mine while you're at it?" It was his single adversary in the cabinet, National Security Advisor Philip Miller.

Mace turned to Miller, knowing in an instant that he had found his dumping ground. "Sure, Phil. Which one is it?"

"The navy one, two down from where yours was hanging."

Mace turned his back to Miller. As he pulled the presidential advisor's coat from the rack, he reached inside his own and grabbed Cotten Stone's cell. In one swift motion, he dropped it into the deep side pocket of Miller's heavy woolen coat.

"Here you go." Mace handed the overcoat to his colleague. "Stay warm out there."

————

"Ted, I want to see Tera Jordan's face all over SNN," Cotten said into John's phone. "Give her so much air time that whoever is hunting her and Lindsay will see it and start pissing blood."

"Jesus, Cotten," Ted Casselman said. "Calm down."

Cotten and John were speeding down the Bee Line Expressway on their way to the Orlando International Airport.

"I don't want to calm down." She realized she was close to yelling.

"I've got a good bit of sway around here," Ted said, "but I don't know how much I can do outside of the normal channels."

"Ted, I don't ask for much." She heard John give a nervous cough. "But whoever stole my phone—whoever threatened my life—

whoever burnt down Lindsay's farm—is in Washington. The Venatori trace placed my cell in the White House, for Christ's sake. How much more newsworthy do you want?"

Cotten glanced at John who was trying to maneuver through the heavy traffic. She held her palm over the phone. "How much longer?"

He pointed to the sign indicating the off ramp to the airport. "Just got to drop the car off. We'll make our flight with a few minutes to spare."

"Ted, we'll be landing in Washington at 3:47. Get a crew and remote truck ready to meet me at curbside."

"We can't go live with this, you know that," Ted said.

"Not asking you to. We'll tape it, and I'll send you a final edit as soon as we get back to the local affiliate."

"A White House connection could be big, Cotten, or it could burn your ass to dust."

"Just have the crew ready. Once John has the Venatori run the trace on the phone again and we know the exact location, I'm going to find out who's at the bottom of this."

———

The constant hum of Interstate 395 a block away drifted along South 28th Street in Arlington as National Security Advisor Philip Miller emerged from the Carlyle Restaurant. Beside him was his wife—two FBI agents had been waiting outside for the couple. The Millers were heading home after dining on jambalaya pasta and Hong Kong–style sea bass. The temperature had dropped below freezing, and Miller was wrapped tightly in his heavy overcoat.

As his Lincoln Town Car pulled up to the curb, the bright floodlights mounted atop a Sony DVCAM came to life, bathing the sidewalk in white light.

"Dr. Miller."

The National Security Advisor turned toward the camera light.

Cotten approached Miller with a mic in her extended hand. "Do you have a moment to answer questions this evening?"

An agent stepped between them, but Miller held up his hand indicating there was no threat. "Hello, Ms. Stone," Miller said. "It's good to see you back safe and sound from your Russian adventure. If your question concerns what I think of the excellent cuisine here at Carlyle, I can assure you that Mrs. Miller and I enjoyed every bite, especially the vanilla bean crème brulee." He started to turn toward his car, obviously wanting his action to signal the end of the impromptu interview.

"Actually, I was wondering why you are trying to harm an eight-year-old child."

Miller had motioned his wife toward the car, but he turned to stare at Cotten. "Excuse me?"

"Tera Jordan? And her mother, Lindsay? Do their names sound familiar?"

Miller faced Cotten. "I have no idea what you're talking about."

"So you're denying responsibility for burning down their farm in Kentucky?"

He shook his head. "I can honestly say that I've never been to the great state of Kentucky. What's this all about?" He stiffened and crossed his arms. "And can we please turn off the camera?"

"So you did not have my cell phone stolen from my car in Loretto, Kentucky, then used it to call Cardinal John Tyler, a Vatican diplomat, and convey to him that I was to back off in my search for Tera and Lindsay Jordan or else?" Despite the rage building to a boiling point inside her, Cotten worked at remaining calm and steady. "What exactly did you mean by 'or else' when you threatened me, Dr. Miller?"

"Ms. Stone." His words had the subtleness of a leaking steam pipe. "I have never threatened you. I don't even know you except by reputation. I had nothing to do with any fires on any Kentucky farms. I don't know anybody named Tera Lindsay."

"Tera Jordan," she said.

"Whatever." He flipped his hand in a patronizing manner. "And I absolutely did not steal your cell phone. This is ridiculous. Now, if you will excuse me . . ."

Cotten nodded to her producer, standing a few feet away. The woman punched a number into a phone she held.

"Dr. Miller," Cotten said. "She is dialing my number right now."

There were five seconds of silence on the freezing sidewalk outside Carlyle Restaurant as the hum of the traffic filled the void.

Miller shrugged. "What does that mean?"

Cotten listened for the ring of her cell, but only silence followed. She dropped the mic away from Miller. They'd screwed up somehow. They'd traced the phone here to the Carlyle, and Miller was the obvious White House connection. How could they have been wrong?

ESCAPE

DEVIN STOOD IN THE doorway, coughing and rocking from side to side—his hands covering his ears to block out the horrific sound of the alarms. Reacting to the strobes, he blinked repeatedly. His overloaded senses induced a state of panic and he panted, causing his nose and throat to dry out and hurt.

With a heavy thud, he saw Ben kick the door, slamming it shut. Devin heard the familiar clunk of the lock, leaving him alone outside on the second floor open hallway. He froze, his body stiffening, his hands still clamped over his ears. Finally, he spun around and raced to the head of the metal stairs. The blare of the siren and the pulse of the lights herded his focus to a single compulsive need to get away.

Devin scrambled down the stairs, each footstep clanging, echoing in the icy-cold mainframe room. He ran from wall to wall, searching for a way out, an escape from the terrible shriek and flashing lights.

Finally, he spotted a door at the end of the last row of electronics racks. It was ajar, automatically unlocked to allow an emergency escape from the building. Devin heaved it wide open and burst into the sunshine. The sirens dampened without the echo inside the building.

He didn't stop to look back, but followed Ben's last orders and ran as hard as he could, avoiding the dirt road and heading across a wide expanse of fields toward the far-off timberline.

Finally, within the shadows of the forest, Devin took his hands from his ears—the sound of his blood drumming in his head was louder than the alarms he left behind. His heartbeat thudded in his chest, his neck, his temples, his calves—and his lungs stung with each frenzied gulp of air. A muscle cramp in his side made him stagger. Exhausted, depleted, and confused, he plunged deeper into the cover of the woods. Soon, he could go no farther, and he collapsed.

Devin sprawled face down, and his nose filled with the dank odor of humid soil and decomposing vegetation hidden beneath the brittle crust of recently fallen leaves. He sputtered and spit a scrap of debris from his lips.

Once his breathing became calm, Devin crawled up beside a tree and propped himself against the rough-barked trunk. For over an hour, he sat and counted the autumn leaves—something he never saw in South Florida—stacking them in heaps of one hundred each. Small mounds, vibrant with the blends of gold, and red, and orange encircled him.

Devin's stomach growled and he became aware that he was hungry. He stood and turned in a circle, as if searching for a landmark or clue as to which way to go. But there were no landmarks, nothing familiar, only endless dark woods. Choosing a direction opposite from the one he had come, he started walking.

Hours passed, and the forest grew denser, thickening with coarse underbrush, brambles, and spent berry bushes with needle-like thorns that pricked and snared his jeans.

As the sun went down, Devin succumbed to his weariness. He chose a place between the sturdy trunks of two trees and cleared himself a spot on the ground. A thorn caught his thumb, ripping a stinging thin line in his flesh. Devin let out a hollow-sounding yowl, then put the tip of his thumb in his mouth and sucked away the tiny beads of blood.

Finally, he curled on his side, frantically shaking his left hand next to his ear. Devin's belly grumbled with hunger, and gooseflesh broke out on his skin as the temperature dropped. He drew into a tight ball, stilling his left hand and tucking it under his chin. He turned his head so he could see a small swatch of sky above. When the heavens darkened he found some solace counting the stars, whimpering until he drifted into sleep.

Devin woke with the first stab of light through the trees. He became so cold during the night that he gathered the leaves around him and brushed as many over him as he could. He needed to pee, but it was too cold and too dark to get up. But he couldn't control his bladder. He'd been off the bathroom routine for days now. Devin felt the warmth of his urine on his legs as it seeped beneath him. There was some comfort in the warmth at first, but it quickly transformed to cold moisture that permeated his body to the bone.

Devin sat up, the leaves cascading off like molting feathers. The earth was steeped in fog so thick that he could see the fine droplets of water in the air. It was still so cold, and he was still so hungry. Devin huddled, his hands rubbing his upper arms. He had to pee again, but held it, thinking of the cold. Finally, he could wait no longer.

Devin got up and walked several yards from his makeshift forest bed. As he reached for his fly, he heard a loud pop. A sudden stab of pain struck beneath his right collarbone, searing all the way through to his back. Stunned, he saw a perfectly round hole, about the diameter of a pencil, in his shirt at his upper right chest. A small red stain rimmed it that started to soak the front right side of his shirt.

He heard voices nearby and looked up for a moment. Shouts of profanity rang over the crunch and swish of the brush being trampled.

Devin cupped his hand over the hole in the fabric and stared at the rim of his palm that was spidering with streaks of blood. Perplexed, he gawked at the sight for a moment before his knees buckled.

———

Alan burst through the glass lobby doors on Stone Creek Medical Center, Kai trailing a few feet behind. The room's tile floor, a glossy gray, seemed to stretch for acres between him and the information desk.

"Devin Olsen," he told the lady in the pink volunteer uniform.

Kai came beside him entwining her arm with his. She held his hand and they laced fingers.

"Room four-o-six," the woman said after looking at a clipboard. "Pediatrics."

Alan turned away from the volunteer and scanned the lobby, quickly spotting the elevators.

Kai picked up the slack in his manners. "Thank you," she said, then matched Alan's stride.

He repeatedly punched the up button until the elevator door finally slid open.

The ride to the fourth floor was silent, Kai leaning her head on Alan's shoulder, stroking his arm. He stared at their reflection in the stainless steel. He was lucky in so many ways. Thank God his son was going to be all right. The bullet had passed straight through his shoulder, miraculously missing all vital organs and bone. Alan had plenty of questions for the police, but first he just wanted to see his son.

The doors opened. Rooms 400 through 418 were to the right. Alan glanced down the corridor and immediately knew which door belonged to Devin's room. A uniformed police officer sat in a chair beside it.

"I'm Alan Olsen," he said as he approached.

The man stood. "Detective Zimmer is inside."

Alan nodded a thank-you and entered Devin's room. Kai fell behind, their arms stretched apart, but hands still linked.

At Alan's arrival, the man sitting in the corner of the room rose to his feet.

"Alan Olsen," Alan said, raising his hand to whom he assumed was Detective Zimmer.

"Can I speak to you outside?" Zimmer asked.

Alan's eyes fired at the man. *What was the cop thinking?* This was the first time Alan would see his son since the kidnapping.

Kai extended her arm across Alan's chest and placed her hand over his heart, a silent signal of support as well as a reminder of keeping in control. Her simple gesture soothed him, and instead of responding to the detective, Alan moved to Devin's bedside.

Asleep, he appeared so pale and small in the whiteness of the tightly drawn sheets and grayscale-colored, sterile hospital room. Alan brushed the hair from his son's face.

"Hey, sport," he said. "Dad's here."

Slowly, Devin opened his eyes. He blinked twice, each time pinching his face and eyes.

"It's okay, Devin. It's me," Alan said, leaning close. He scooted a metal frame chair under him so he could sit beside his son. That's when he noticed the restraints. He touched Devin's hand. *Jesus, why had they done this?*

Devin's eyes closed, and he slipped back into sleep.

Alan stood and looked at Kai. "Stay with him. I'll be back in a minute."

"Mr. Olsen," Zimmer said. "We need to talk."

"Just give me one fucking minute, will you?" Alan whispered. He stalked out of the room and headed to the nurses' station.

"I want the restraints off my son," he said to the nurse at the desk. "You can't do that to him. You don't understand."

"I'm sorry sir, you are . . . ?"

"My son is in 406, and his hands are tied down. I want the restraints off."

"Devin is sedated, Mr. Olsen, because sometimes he thrashes and rips out the IV lines." She looked at Alan. "The name is Mr. Olsen, right?"

Alan nodded. "If he's sedated, then why the hell do you need the restraints?" Alan shoved his fingers through his hair.

"It's for his own safety, sir."

"No, no, no," Alan said shifting. "Devin is autistic. Didn't anybody tell you that?" She was shaking her head.

"Who is the idiot who gave the orders?" As soon as he asked, he knew it didn't matter at this point. "Look, Devin has some little quirky things he does . . . has to do . . . like shaking his hands beside his head. Preventing him from doing that will cause an unbearable amount of frustration. What if you had an excruciating itch and somebody bound your hands so you couldn't scratch. What would that do to you after hours of being tied down? It's the same thing. You need to talk to somebody right now, because I'm going back in there and cut off the restraints. You do whatever you have to do to keep the IV lines in, but tying him down is not going to be an option. Have I made my point?"

"I'll see what I can do," the nurse said.

"Good." Alan marched back to Devin's room, already fishing his pocket knife out of his pants. If he had flown on a commercial airliner rather than the CyberSys corporate jet, the knife would be in his luggage.

Detective Zimmer waited outside Devin's room. "I didn't mean to rush you."

Alan passed him without acknowledging the comment and went inside. Kai nodded and smiled. Devin was still sleeping peacefully. Without saying anything, Alan cut the restraints. "There you go, sport," he whispered. Turning to Kai, he said, "If he wakes, come get me. I'll just be in the hall."

Kai took Alan's hand, brought it to her lips and kissed it. "Don't worry."

Alan backed out of the room and pulled the door partway closed. "Okay," he said to Zimmer. "Talk."

"Mr. Olsen, we've found Devin's kidnapper."

MILLER

COTTEN WAS STUNNED AND reeled back. She had been so sure they would nail Miller on camera. But there was no ringing cell phone.

As embarrassment rushed through her, she was ready to apologize and grovel on her knees if she had to. Suddenly, Cotten saw Miller's expression change from belligerence to puzzlement, and his right hand dropped to the side of his overcoat.

"What's in your pocket, Mr. Miller?" she asked, barely able to get the words out of her dry mouth.

Shock rolled over his face. The National Security Advisor looked down at his overcoat. Hesitantly, he reached into the pocket and removed a vibrating cell phone. With a look of confusion, he held it out as if it were a snake about to strike.

"Aren't you going to answer," Cotten said.

"I have no idea how this got in my overcoat," Miller said, staring at the phone in his hand.

"Either you do and you're lying," said Cotten, "or someone in the White House found out we ran a GPS location trace on it and planted it in your coat to distract us.

"Mr. Miller, we didn't do this blindly. We obtained a list of everyone in the White House at the time of the trace. The second trace identified the Carlyle as the phone's current location. Next, we had our crew check out every patron. That little birthday celebration going on inside was staged by SNN so we could take photos of everyone in the restaurant without arousing suspicion. We uploaded them to our research department, and guess what? You're the only face who was on the White House list. What other conclusion should I draw?"

Miller looked around the sidewalk as if to gauge the reaction of the others there.

"Before we broadcast this as a feature story, would you like to discuss it in private with me?"

He glanced at his watch. Then he motioned to the restaurant's entrance. "Perhaps I've got a couple of seconds for you, Ms. Stone."

Moments later, Cotten and Miller were alone in the manager's office of the restaurant. The SNN crew waited outside in the remote truck while the two FBI agents and Miller's wife occupied a booth in the hastily closed restaurant.

"First, I'm impressed with your attention to detail to narrow it down to me," Miller said. "But I don't care whether you believe me or not. The fact is I'm not lying." He leaned forward in the chair. "What I do care about is that the phone was in my coat in the first place. That means someone intentionally put it there." He stared at

Cotten, who stood on the opposite side of the desk. "We're talking about a group of people with the highest security clearances in the country, starting with the president on down." He scored his bottom lip. "The entire cabinet, along with two members of the Joint Chiefs and the head of Central Command were present at the same meeting I attended. Not to mention the vice president and the White House senior support staff. Then there's all the other staff wandering about, right down to the cook."

"Anyone there for the first time or out of the ordinary?" Cotten asked.

"I wouldn't know other than those present at the meeting." Miller stared off into space as he seemed to be picturing who was in attendance. Finally, he said, "At least not in the cabinet meeting. Even the generals had all been there several times."

"You mentioned the support staff? Anyone new to the White House? Someone you never saw before?"

"I didn't notice any unfamiliar faces. Aside from the Oval Office, the Cabinet Room where we were is the inner sanctum of executive power. Nobody gets in there that doesn't belong. It's impossible. I can't speak for those not in the Cabinet Room who might have found access to the cloakroom. But I suspect that type of opportunity is unrealistic."

Cotten dropped down into a chair in front of the desk, not wanting to believe that someone high up the political food chain could be connected to the Brotherhood of the Nephilim, or worse, one of the Fallen Angels.

Trying to think of an alternative, Cotten asked, "Could someone have put the phone in your coat before you arrived for the meeting?"

Miller shrugged. "I went in late today, driving directly from my home to the White House. I have two people that work for me—a housekeeper and a secretary. The housekeeper was sick, and it was my secretary's day off. That leaves my wife and my dog. Both are loyal to me beyond reproach." He smiled.

"I believe you," Cotten said, returning the smile, "about their loyalty, that is." She removed her small notepad from her pocket and scribbled on it. "That doesn't change the fact that you had my phone—the one stolen from me in Loretto, Kentucky, while I was investigating the disappearance of a mother and her daughter. The same phone that was used to threaten my life." Cotten tapped the end of the pen on the pad. "It looks like we're at a stalemate here."

Miller folded his arms on the desk. In a hushed voice, he said, "What the hell is this all about?"

———

Thirty minutes later, Cotten and Miller, along with his wife and the agents, emerged from the Carlyle. Cotten stood on the sidewalk and watched the National Security Advisor assist his wife into the back of the Lincoln Town Car. As he followed his wife into the car, Miller turned and gave Cotten a reassuring nod. A moment later, the car sped off into the Virginia night.

Walking the half block to the waiting SNN remote truck, Cotten realized that if what Miller had told her turned out to be true, it would rock the nation to its core.

RACKY-SACKY

THE CORRIDOR OF THE hospital was cold and colorless. Only gray, white, and a rare blotch of muted green stretched in all directions. *A person could get sick in here just from the chill and the boring decor,* Alan thought.

"Your son is a lucky boy," Detective Zimmer said.

"Seems so," Alan responded. "Obviously, I haven't seen the doctor yet, but I did talk to him on the phone. Devin's going to be fine." Alan glanced at the officer who still sat outside the room, then back at Zimmer. "I think I need a little more explanation as to what happened. You say you've caught the bastard? I hope he burns in hell."

"Your wish might be happening as we speak. The guy is dead," Zimmer said. "We found him this morning."

Alan stared at Zimmer. "Who? Why did he do it? Please tell me it wasn't some sicko, some child molester. Since there was no ransom demand, all I've been able to think about was . . . I know the doctor said Devin showed no obvious signs of any type of sexual abuse. But shit, you can't tell what the guy might have done to my son."

"Mr. Olsen, you can relax," Zimmer said. "It wasn't anything like that. Why don't we go have a seat in the waiting room?"

"No, I want to be here if Devin wakes."

"I understand. Then let me start with a question and we'll go from there. Do you recall the recent financial scandal surrounding Presidium Health Care, the for-profit health care conglomerate?"

"Of course," Alan said. "What's that got to do with anything?"

"And remember one of PHC's big guns under investigation was Benjamin Ray?"

"Right," Alan said, nodding in frustration. "His partner is already in prison. I read where Ray died before he could be sentenced."

"That's the way it seemed. Apparently Mr. Ray had enough money to have his death falsified—from death certificate to cremation. Ray didn't die. He was hiding out in a remote cabin near the Ozark National Forest using the name, Ben Jackson. Trouble is he was running short of cash. The government managed to strike a deal with the foreign banks to seize his funds so they could return the money to the stock holders. Ray was caught in a desperate situation and decided to try his hand at kidnapping for ransom. He fingered you as a rich guy with an only child. I don't think he had any plans of hurting your son—he's a white-collar criminal, not a murderer—but he was counting on getting enough money from this one shot at you to live on for the rest of his life."

"But there were no demands. I didn't get any calls or a ransom note."

"He simply hadn't sent it yet. Who knows why the hold up. Maybe he was just waiting for the heat to die down. Apparently he was holding Devin in his cabin. That's where we found Ray—collapsed on the floor of his basement beside a few of your son's belongings. Ironically, it looks like he died from a heart attack—the same thing he faked just before his sentencing date in court. A real quirk of fate, wouldn't you agree?" Zimmer paused a moment when Alan didn't laugh, then went on. "There was a ransom note addressed to you demanding two-and-a-half million dollars. From the *prelims*, it appears that Ray croaked before he could send the note."

"Christ," Alan said, rubbing his face. "I'd have paid that and more, no questions asked."

"I'm sure you would have, Mr. Olsen. But before he could pull it off, he dropped dead and Devin wandered off into the woods. Kind of ended in a sweet payback, don't you think?"

"Except for the fact that Devin was shot."

"No, of course I didn't mean that. But still, how lucky it happened the way it did. The hunters who shot Devin could have panicked and left him, but they didn't. It was foggy out there, and we believe an accident. Actually, the fog was a blessing in a way. If Devin had been two hundred yards away instead of thirty, the bullet from that 30.30 would have ripped his shoulder apart. He would have probably bled to death before they got him out of the woods. But being so close, it passed straight through. I'll tell you, those guys were pretty shaken when they got here. They called 9-1-1 on the way in and told dispatch they were on their way to the medical center. It's up to the county prosecutor, but at this point,

227

I don't see any charges being filed. Can't speak for the FBI, but they'll probably see it the same way."

"Sure, right," Alan said. "I understand it was an accident."

"Alan?" Kai's voice came from Devin's room.

"Excuse me." Alan left Zimmer in the hall.

"Somebody is awake," Kai said in a sing-song voice. She stroked Devin's head. "Your dad is here, sweetheart."

Alan kissed his son's forehead. "How you feeling, big guy?"

Devin blinked several times and looked off to the side.

"He hasn't said anything to anyone," Zimmer said, coming in behind Alan. "Noncommunicative. Does he talk?"

"Of course he talks," Kai said sharply. "He's autistic, not mute."

Zimmer shrugged and held up his hands. "I don't know much about that autism thing. No intention to offend."

"It's okay," Alan said. He motioned to Zimmer and moved to the open door. He spoke quietly, keeping his voice below the level of the hum of the monitors hooked to Devin. "Even the experts don't understand it. Devin does talk. He's extremely bright in specific areas. His language is delayed, but not his . . . It's difficult to explain. His brain is wired differently."

"Maybe you can get him to talk to us," Zimmer said. "We need to ask him some questions."

"Well, that's uncertain," Alan said. "Social skills, reactions to strangers, relationships, are all unpredictable—other than the fact that they are poorly developed most of the time."

"We could use his help to wrap this thing up."

"We can try," Alan said, "But there's no guarantee he can tell you anything useful. Right now I'm exhausted and I just want to spend a little quiet quality time with my son. Mind if we give it a go tomorrow?"

"No problem," Zimmer said. "But the Feds will have some questions, too. They should be here soon. I know they were on their way in. A word of warning—I don't think they are as sensitive as us locals." Zimmer arched his brows. "Just my humble opinion. Anyway, I'll be dismissing the officer outside now that you're here. But I'll be back in the morning."

"Fine," Alan said.

Alan shook Zimmer's hand, then returned to the bedside and gazed down at Devin. "So, sport, you've been on quite an adventure. Feel like talking about it?"

Devin shook his head. His eyes darted to the door, then around the room as if taking attendance. He looked back at his dad. "Juice," he said.

"You want some apple juice?" Kai asked.

Devin shook his head.

"Orange?" Kai asked.

Again Devin gestured a negative response. "100 percent vegetable juice. Ingredients, from concentrate, tomato concentrate, reconstituted vegetable juice blend, water and concentrated juices of carrots, celery, beets, parsley, lettuce, watercress, spinach, salt, vitamin C—ascorbic acid, flavoring, citric acid—"

"V-8 juice," Alan said, recognizing the ingredients his son spouted. He'd heard it a million times. Devin memorized everything he ever read, even down to the labels on food products. *Kid wonder*, Alan thought. He wished he could understand his son's mind. "I don't think they have V-8," he said, smiling at the boy. "We might have to settle for plain tomato juice."

Devin seemed to disapprove, but nodded.

A rap at the door drew their attention to a dark silhouette in the doorway. "Mr. Olsen? I'm Agent Roselli, FBI."

"I'll speak to you outside, if you don't mind," Alan said. "In the waiting room."

The agent backed out of the doorway.

"Looks like more visitors for your dad," Kai said to Devin. "But we'll be just fine, won't we Dev?"

Alan gave Kai a peck on the cheek, tousled his son's hair, then joined Agent Roselli.

———

"Boom-a-racky-sacky," Devin said to Kai after his father left.

"Oh, no," Kai said. "You know I'm no good at that."

"Boom-a-racky-sacky," Devin said, breaking into a full-fledged smile.

This was a game he often liked to play. Alan had taught him the game, which was a revised version of a college drinking game. Kai knew Devin especially enjoyed playing with her because it was such an easy win for him. One of them would start counting, beginning with the number one, and they would alternate each number. Beginning with three and every multiple of three thereafter or any number with a three in it, instead of saying the number, they would say boom-a-racky. For the number seven and its multiples and numbers with a seven in it, they would say boom-a-sacky. For multiples of both three and seven or with any three and seven combination, they would say boom-a-racky-sacky. Because of frequent playing, Kai was okay up until about 252, but after that she quickly fell off. Alan usually got out a calculator after about 1225.

Devin allowed it, just so he could keep playing. When he played with Kai, he appeared to simply like the win.

"All right," Kai said. "One."

"Two," Devin said.

"Boom-a-racky," Kai said.

"Four."

"Five."

"Boom-a-racky."

"Boom-a-sacky," Kai said. She sighed. "Were you scared out there in the woods alone? It must have been awful."

"Eight," Devin said.

"Boom-a-racky." She brushed back Devin's hair from his forehead. "I'm glad you're home again. Knowing how you can't sit still, you must have been terribly bored."

"Ten. I played games. Games. Games. Games." Devin jolted his hands in the air.

Kai grabbed his arms and pulled them down. "Whoa, Devin, you're going to pull out your IVs."

"Boom-a-racky-sacky. Boom-a-racky-sacky. Boom-a-racky-sacky."

"Okay, Devin, okay. Take it easy," Kai said. "Eleven. Were the games fun? What kind of games? Were you good at them?"

"Boom-a-racky. *Company of Heroes*. Code. *Company of Heroes*."

"Boom-a-racky. Were you good at the *Company of Heroes* game, Devin?"

"Boom-a-sacky." Devin simulated the sound effects and began moving phantom video game controls.

"Boom-a-racky," Kai said. "And what about the code? Were you good at that, too? Tell me more about that, Devin."

"Sixteen. Devin is smart."

"How is Devin smart? Did you finish the code game?"

"Play, Kai. Play."

"I'll play after you tell me more about the code. Was it the Destiny code game?"

"Say boom-a-sacky. Devin is smart. Say it, Kai. Play the game."

"Boom-a-sacky," Kai said. "Tell me how smart you are."

Devin's voice rose as if agitated. "Racky sacky, racky sacky, boom, boom, boom."

Kai heaved out a frustrated gush of air. "I *am* playing, Devin. Eighteen. I mean boom-a-racky."

"Nineteen. Racky sacky, boom, sacky, racky, boom."

"Stop it Devin. Just tell me about the code."

"Boom, boom, boom, racky. Play the game."

"Twenty," Kai huffed. "Fucking twenty, okay. Now explain to me how you are so smart. Did you finish the code game?"

Devin tossed his head from side to side in rhythm to his chanting of the name of the game. "Boom-a-racky-sacky. Boom-a-racky-sacky. Boom-a-racky-sacky. That's the name of the game, not racky sacky, boom, boom. That's how Devin is smart."

He shook his hands near his ears and Kai ignored it.

Her face suddenly paled. Kai grabbed Devin's wrists to still them. "You mean you mixed it up? Scrambled the code?"

Devin's face bloomed with pride. "Devin is smart."

Kai dropped Devin's wrists and picked up her purse from the floor, digging through it. Finally, she lifted her cell phone and flipped it open. Moving to the window, she kept her back to Devin and pressed speed dial.

BOOK OF EMZARA

MACE STOOD BACK AND waited until the group of Asian tourists moved away from the front of James Smithson's memorial inside the Castle of the Smithsonian Institute. The guard had told him they were the last group to come through and he would have about ten minutes of privacy until closing. He was intrigued by the substantial collection at the Institute and came often to meditate among the relics of the ages. As he stood in reverence to the founder of the Smithsonian, he heard a voice.

"He was the illegitimate son of the Duke of Northumberland and Elizabeth Hungerford."

Mace turned to see the Old Man standing behind him.

"Some of the best men in history were bastards," Mace said. "This one died in Genoa, but Alexander Graham Bell brought his body here." Mace looked into the eyes of his mentor, hoping to soften the blow of the bad news he had delivered earlier when he requested the meeting. News that not only had the boy escaped before giving Tor the complete operating system code for the Hades computer but that the kid may have scrambled parts of it. Then there was the fact that the banker and Tor's assistant were both dead. Finally, the second thodium artifact sent to Tor was only slightly more reliable than the degraded original. "It's a shame Smithson didn't bother to add objects made from thodium to his vast collection here."

"That would have made it too easy, Pursan." The Old Man came to stand beside Mace. "Has Tor located the child?"

"He spent the day searching the woods but no sign of the boy. I had him take Jackson's body to the banker's cabin along with some of the boy's belongings."

"Tor must make sure there is no trace of either one of them at the Hades facility," the Old Man said. "If the authorities do come around, they must find nothing more than a collection of run-down buildings on an abandoned radar installation."

"We have all the paperwork in place showing that one of the buildings is being used by an Internet data storage company operating out of the Midwest. They have a long-term lease on file with the Department of the Interior to rent the property. All the documentation is in order in case Tor must prove he has a permit to be there." Mace watched the stoic expression on the aged face of the Old Man. "These problems can all be dealt with. The bigger issue is where we will get a non-degraded source of thodium. All we have had to work with were some raw pieces of planks left of the Ark. Even extracting the crystallized sap from the wood has been a task."

The Old Man smiled—the all-knowing expression that often annoyed Mace. "Then we must find out if there were other objects made from the Tree."

Mace thought hard, trying to recall his Biblical history, but nothing came to mind. "But if there were, wouldn't they have vanished in the Great Flood?"

"Maybe there was something taken aboard Noah's barge. Certainly if there was an object made from the Tree of Life, it would have extraordinary sacrosanct value to Noah. Such an article would not have been left behind. And then of course, the obvious—the lumber of the Ark was distributed and used in the new world for building houses and furniture and producing tools. It could be worth the effort to track the family lineage. Who knows what may have been passed on from generation to generation?"

"Mr. Secretary," a young FBI agent said, approaching Mace. "We need to leave in five minutes."

Mace gave him a be-right-there wave and waited until the man walked back to the entrance to the shrine of the Smithsonian's founder. "How can we find out what might have survived?"

"There are a number of ancient writings dealing with Noah and his clan—documents that were ultimately rejected by the Church at the First Council of Nicaea. The reason given was that some would have been contradictory to Church teachings at the time and possibly taken the faith in a different direction. Instead, they were destroyed or hidden away from the eyes of the world."

"Which should we be seeking?" asked Mace.

"One comes to mind—the Book of Emzara."

"Which is?"

"Pursan," the Old Man said in a condescending tone. "I would have thought you to be more versed in these matters."

"Ancient scriptures are not a topic that interests me."

"In order for the Hades Project to succeed, ancient writings like the Book of Emzara will be the key." He looked harshly at Mace. "Emzara was Noah's wife. She is not named in Genesis, but the Book of Jubilees identifies her. In Jewish tradition she is called Naamah, but I prefer the later. Emzara was the designated scribe of their ordeal, and she kept good records of the event, including a manifest of the Ark's inventory. Maybe she chronicled the family history after the Flood. The Book of Emzara may lead us to your alternative thodium source."

"Mr. Secretary," the agent said, walking toward Mace.

"Coming." He waited until the man had retreated. "Where is this Book of Emzara?"

"Among a collection of other sought-after remnants of religious antiquity."

In an instant, Mace realized he knew the location.

As they turned to leave, the Old Man said, "There is one other thread that needs tying up—the matter of your fellow cabinet member."

Mace smiled. "It's being taken care of even as we speak."

THE NEWS

LINDSAY FLUFFED THE PILLOWS, trying to make them look a little more attractive in their yellowed cases. This was the third room she'd cleaned this morning and it was only 8:00 AM. The majority of the guests were either fishermen who got up before dawn or long-haul truckers who left the do-not-disturb signs on their doors most of the time.

She smoothed the wrinkles from the bedspread and stepped back. It was the best she could do. The material was faded, like the walls and carpet in every room of the Dos Palmas Motel. She knew the linens were clean because she had laundered them all herself. The management didn't provide bleach, just a generic brand of detergent. She'd been told that bleach would shorten the life of the linens, gradually eating them up, but maybe putting some of the sheets and towels out of their misery would be a good thing. She bought bleach at the Winn-Dixie supermarket nearby and kept it in her room, taking it with her when she did the motel laundry as well as her own.

While she worked, Tera sat on the floor with a baggie of Cheerios and leaned back against the foot of the bed.

"Get up," Lindsay said, her face grimacing at the thought of what lay hidden in the depths of the carpet. She grabbed a fresh but threadbare towel off the cleaning cart parked outside the room. "Sit on this," she said, tossing it to Tera.

Tera spread the towel and plopped down, Cheerios in one hand and the TV remote in the other.

Lindsay moved on to clean the bathroom. She heard Tera change the channel on the television. "I hope you're watching something educational," she said. "If we were home, this would be *school* time."

Lindsay scrubbed the tub, but the glossy finish on the porcelain was long gone, and no matter how clean she got it, it still appeared dull and drab. A lock of her hair fell in her face and she used the back of her forearm to sweep it away. *When was this ever going to end?* She wanted normalcy in her life. Lindsay sat back on her heels with her rubber-gloved hands in her lap. She couldn't recall the last time her life had been normal. It had to have been before Tera was born. It was hard to remember what that had been like.

She leaned over the tub again and sprinkled more cleanser as if it might make a difference.

And where was her friend, Cotten? She hadn't even responded to the message Lindsay had left. After getting no return call from Cotten the first time, Lindsay didn't bother to call back, assuming that she would become a nuisance to her old friend. And after all, they hadn't seen each other in years. What had she thought, that Cotten Stone, famous television journalist, would drop everything and come running? "Stupid, Lindsay. Just plain stupid," she said aloud. "You and Tera are in this by yourselves."

"Momma," Tera called.

Lindsay had a hard time finding her voice. It wanted to crack with the threat of tears, and she didn't want Tera to hear that.

"Yes," she finally managed to say. Lindsay scrubbed the dull porcelain in circles. She exerted more and more pressure, as if that helped her fight back the urge to cry. In a moment, when her daughter hadn't responded, she stopped and listened. "Tera?"

No answer. Lindsay chucked the sponge in the tub and got to her feet. "Tera?" Slowly, she emerged from the bathroom, peering around the door.

Tera stood in front of the television, her gaze fastened on the screen, the bag of Cheerios open, a small sea of oat circles on the floor.

"What is it?" Lindsay asked, snapping off the gloves and dropping them on the dresser.

Tera touched the television screen with her index finger.

Lindsay's attention moved from her daughter to the story on the morning news, only catching the tail end. "And so what could have been a tragedy ends on a happy note," the reporter was saying. A video of a man embracing a boy filled the screen. "Devin Olsen is safe and home again." There was a pause. "In other news—"

"We have to go see him," Tera said.

Lindsay had seen several reports in the newspapers and on television about the boy's disappearance, and was happy to hear that he was found and safe. She certainly felt for his dad and understood how helpless the man must have been. And the boy was autistic on top of it all. Most stories of missing children with disabilities didn't have happy endings. Why did Tera have such an interest? "Why do we have to go see him, Tera?"

"I know him," Tera said.

"No, you don't sweetie. He's from Miami, not Loretto."

"No," Tera said. "I mean from before."

"Before what?" Lindsay took both her daughter's hands in hers. "We've never met that little boy," she said.

"Not you, Momma. Me."

Lindsay pulled Tera near the bed and had her sit on the end. She cradled her daughter's face in her palms. "That's impossible," she said.

Tera smiled with a knowledge that seemed to go beyond her years. "You weren't with me then."

"Where, Ladybug? Where did you go without me? Where did you meet him?"

"Before I was born. In heaven."

EXFILTRATION

Tor looked at his watch. Five minutes to go. Mace would be calling for an update, and he wanted to be ready.

"It's freezing in here," he said to himself, rubbing the end of his nose to warm it. He had lowered the temperature to fifty degrees earlier in the day. Icing down the building was necessary to prepare for the enormous flood of information that would start pouring into the system over the next twenty-four hours as the Hades Worm—hiding dormant deep inside millions of computers around the world—was triggered as each system went out and synchronized to the international atomic clock.

Although the data from individually infected systems would trickle out information about the users, the computers, and the affected business enterprise networks, the overall amount of data would be enormous. The mainframes in the Hades facility would be working at maximum capacity, and overheated processors were the last thing he needed.

It seemed like everything was getting on his nerves as the pressure of the phase-two deadline loomed. First off, he was now alone at the old military base in the middle of the Arkansas backwoods since his assistant was killed when the kid escaped. Burying the body in the rocky terrain had taken half a day away from his work, which hadn't been going that well in the first place. The frigging quantum computer still wasn't as stable as he would like. Even if every phase of the Hades Project went flawlessly, if the computer didn't maintain stability using the degraded thodium sample, he would never be able to crack the government encryption codes. And to add to the aggravation, Mace was calling two, three, sometimes four times a day.

Tor much preferred to talk to Kai—in many ways. It amazed him that Mace was vain enough to believe that the Chinese beauty was attracted to him—and dedicated to his cause. Mace didn't understand that Kai Chiang always fucked the highest bidder. Years ago, Tor had once been the guy with the biggest payoff. How the hell did Mace think Kai found her way into Mace's life, anyway? Tor had been a stepping stone—he'd known it and really hadn't given a rat's ass. She'd been a wild ride for a short time—no investments, no commitments. Suited him just fine. Tor knew the bitch would sell out anybody—just like she was doing to Alan Olsen. One day she'd hock Rizben Mace for the next stone to step on.

As if on cue, the phone rang.

"Are we on schedule?" Mace asked.

Tor looked at his watch again. "Thirty seconds to midnight GMT."

Starting at 12:00 AM GMT and each hour following, as the next time zone clicked over to midnight, the Hades Worm would come alive and start identifying servers on each affected network. Once the servers were identified, an attempt would be made to log in, using null password authentication—searching for any usernames with blank passwords. If the worm resided on a computer where the user had administrative privileges, it would hijack the user's credentials and complete the login.

Once the Worm accessed the system with borrowed administrative privileges, it would act as the authorized user and instruct the compromised computer to start looking for other hosts across the network. Utilizing basic ping requests, which would appear as benign traffic, it would try to connect to specific domain names followed by their respective dot com, net, org, edu, gov, and mil extensions. Each of these specific hosts held pieces of the virus. As each ping hit the host, the reply back to the compromised computer would include more and more pieces of the virus.

Tor knew that the great part of using these common ping packets was their ability to hold hidden data in unused sections of the packet header. Virus hunters would never think to look at the headers to reveal the pieces of the Hades Project code. Like a cyber scavenger hunt, the compromised computer would eventually bring all the pieces together to assemble and execute a rootkit program, with the sole mission of giving the Hades Project complete control and backdoor access to the compromised computer.

A novice hacker would have had the worm connect to the host computer via IP addresses instead of host domain names. In that scenario, once the authorities took down that IP address, the game would be over. But Tor had designed the worm to look for host computers via domain names. The domain name address could point to as many different IP addresses as there were that hosted mirrored versions of the virus. Even better, Interpol and the FBI would be chasing IP addresses all day while new IP addresses are assigned to the sole domain name. Since Tor had already hacked into and hidden the virus on host servers all over the world, the authorities should give up the hunt after dealing with the headaches from hosting providers in multiple countries. By the time they got to the end of the trail, phase two of the Hades Project would be old news.

"Are we poised to begin phase three?" Mace asked.

I've told the bastard a thousand times already, Tor thought. That's the way he would like to answer Mace, but he knew better. It didn't matter that Tor was Nephilim, the offspring of a Fallen Angel and human—which made him a Ruby—Mace would have him out on his ear or worse if he showed insubordination. "Yes, we're on schedule," Tor said. "Remember, Rizben, we're creating millions of zombie computers out there. It'll take time to distribute the rootkits. As soon as we do, phase three will begin immediately."

Tor liked to call phase three "ID Recon"—the identification of specific, main targets in order to manipulate their systems. The final success would depend on a predictable human reaction causing a domino effect of catastrophic proportions.

Mace said, "We're only going to get one shot at this. The reaction we're predicting must be correct."

"I just do the geek stuff. You're the one who calculates how people will think. I take no ownership in that part."

Tor reviewed the main targets in his head. The GPS Satellite diagnostic and control systems; Air Traffic Control Emergency Notification Grid; SWIFT Global Banking network; Defense Information

Systems Agency Network and its Global Information Grid; the U.S. Power Grid Network and corresponding foreign networks; the maintenance channel for Safety Parameters Display System that monitor and control nuclear power plants; eighty supervisory control and data acquisition networks that included electricity, natural gas, water, sewage, railroads, and telecommunications; and the mother of all targets—the AT&T Global Satellite Communications monitoring station.

He glanced at the monitor displaying the operating system interface to the Hades quantum computer. *The little shit thought he was so smart,* Tor thought, picturing Devin Olsen typing away in the game room, trying to trick him by mixing things up. But Devin wasn't the one with doctorates in theoretical physics and mechanical engineering. Tor was. After the call from Kai warning him that the kid had tried to be clever, it only took Tor a few hours to straighten out and complete the code. Who's the clever boy now?

One last time, Tor looked at his watch. A few seconds to go.

The screen was blank. He could feel his heart beating heavily in his chest. Despite the chill, he started sweating. His grip on the phone tightened. He heard Mace's breathing on the other end.

Midnight.

Tor held his breath. This was it. No second chance.

Suddenly, the Hades Project's master control monitor blinked. A line of text appeared on the bottom of the monitor.

XOCSSOV.MOLDAVID.echo.YORK.0022039

He leaned forward. Almost immediately, a second line appeared under the first, moving the original line up.

XOCSSOV.LANCAST.echo.ABBY.0022048

Before the second line could finish, a third appeared at the bottom and then a fourth. As each appeared, the previous lines moved up the screen. Then, like a floodgate opening, the lines came rushing in by the dozens, hundreds, and then thousands. The progress of a line appearing and pushing the previous text up became a blur.

Tor smiled.

"Rizben?"

"Yes," Mace said.

"Welcome to Hades."

BLUES

LINDSAY TOSSED THEIR BELONGINGS in the back of the van and took a last look at the Dos Palmas Motel before climbing in the driver's seat.

"Are we coming back?" Tera asked, buckling up.

"I don't know yet." Lindsay started the engine and twisted around to watch as she backed out of the parking space.

"Then why are we taking all of our stuff?"

"Because we might not come back."

"But you have the room key," Tera said, pointing at the jangling key ring.

Lindsay checked both directions, then pulled out and headed north on U.S. 1, the Overseas Highway.

"You need to buckle up, too," Tera said. "Are we spending the night in Miami?"

"Maybe," Lindsay answered.

"Won't they miss you at work tomorrow, if we do? You'll get into trouble."

Lindsay sighed with exasperation. "Yes, Tera, you're right. Listen, here's the deal. You said you wanted to go see this Devin Olsen boy, so that's where we're going. I don't know what will happen after that. Maybe you know the answer, because I don't." She stared at her daughter. "You always seem to mysteriously know more about everything than you tell me, anyway." She immediately regretted her words.

Tera turned away and stared out the side window.

They rode in silence for miles. Lindsay knew she was on edge and had snapped at Tera without real reason more than once that day. Tera was just being a kid, wondering what was going on. Lately, both of their lives had been so unpredictable. Tera simply wanted to find out what she could count on—what to anticipate in her immediate future. Who else would she ask but her mother? Children felt safe with routine and structure, two elements sorely missing from their lives.

Lindsay rubbed her forehead. Tera deserved better than her less-than-stellar parenting skills of late. She latched her seatbelt and then reached across the center console for Tera's hand. "I'm sorry, Ladybug. I love you."

"I love you, too."

"Want to stop at Shell World? You can pick out a pretty shell."

Tera's small face brightened.

———

At Shell World, Tera spent nearly half an hour searching for just the right shell, finally choosing a conch. Tera said it was so beautiful, admiring its shiny gloss surface on the inside. The man at the register told her how conchs had been used long ago in the islands to announce weddings, and Tera had been intrigued. He took one from under the counter and blew through the man-made hole on the top, creating a most exotic bellowing horn sound. She told her mother that she loved it and wanted to carry the conch out in her hands—no bag.

Once they got back on the highway, Tera drew several sketches of her conch shell, but complained that she wasn't happy with them because of the unsteadiness of the pencil in the moving van.

Almost two hours later U.S. 1 merged with Biscayne Boulevard in downtown Miami. With the radio blaring, Lindsay and Tera were singing the chorus of "You're the One That I Want" along with Olivia Newton John and John Travolta. They were in the middle of belting out "Ooo, ooo, ooo," when the CyberSys building appeared ahead on the left. Lindsay's voice dropped off and questions rolled around in her head. *What on earth was she going to say when they walked into the building? How would she explain why they had come?*

The song ended with Tera gazing at her mother, her enthusiasm for singing also lost.

Lindsay parked the car in a nearby lot. "You know, they might not let us in," she said, putting the keys in her purse. "Devin's father doesn't know us. Nobody does." She brushed Tera's hair back with her fingers. "I'm sure Devin's daddy loves him just like I love you. And he just got Devin back from a bad experience. He'll be cautious and protective of Devin, and want to keep him safe, like I want to protect you. He probably won't understand why we're here." *I don't understand why we're here.* Lindsay leaned close to Tera. "And I'm not really sure, either, Ladybug."

"Don't worry. I'll tell his daddy that Devin is like me."

"What do you mean, sweetheart?"

"He's blue."

It took a moment for the word *blue* to register with Lindsay. "You mean Indigo? You believe Devin is an Indigo child? You think he has special gifts like you?"

Tera nodded vigorously. "Yes, yes." She smiled, her eyes twinkling. "Devin is very special. Like me."

Lindsay steepled her fingers and tapped them to her lips before speaking. "Devin is special, sweetie, but not in the same way you are. He has something called autism. It kind of makes him think different and feel things different."

"Like me," Tera said.

"No, not like you."

"He doesn't draw," Tera said. "But he does other things."

Lindsay wondered what it was that an autistic kid could do that Tera would think of as a special gift.

"Devin knows things like I do. He will remember when I picked you and when he picked his dad," Tera said.

"What?"

"We all got to pick."

Lindsay shook her head in confusion.

"We looked down and picked our moms and dads. I picked you and daddy. Devin picked his dad and his mom. All of the Indigos get to choose."

"Tera, we talked once when you asked about babies—where they come from. Remember that? I told you how—"

"I don't remember being a baby inside you. I don't remember being one year old."

"Of course you don't. Nobody remembers when they were babies."

"But I remember before I was a baby. I remember Devin and all the others and my sister—my twin—she was already here."

Lindsay pressed her spine against the seat and leaned back, staring up at the sagging headliner. "You can't go around talking like that, Tera. People will think you're—"

"Devin won't. He was there. There are a lot of us. He'll remember."

"Us?"

"Blues. You know, Indigos."

Lindsay sat quietly. How in the hell was she going to walk up to Alan Olsen and tell him her daughter wants to talk to his son, recent kidnap victim, because they were someplace together before they were born? What the shit had she been thinking? *Who's the crazy one, Lindsay Jordan? Who drove all the way to Miami with such a bizarre notion?*

"You'll see, Momma. I promise. Please believe me. I know why they took Devin."

"What do you mean?"

"They needed the numbers in Devin's head."

"Okay, look," Lindsay said. "If Mr. Olsen agrees to see us, it's probably better we don't talk about the kidnapping or you knowing Devin before you were born and all that stuff. It might scare him away." She swept a wisp of Tera's hair from her face. "Just follow along with whatever I say. Do you understand?"

Tera nodded. "Okay."

Lindsay unbuckled their seatbelts, then drew Tera into her arms and held her close, feeling herself slightly sway back and forth like she had done years ago while holding Tera when she was an infant. Lindsay breathed in the sweet bouquet of Tera's hair and felt the softness of her daughter's skin against hers. She wished she could just absorb Tera, enfold her precious child and protect her from the world forever.

"I love you, baby," Lindsay murmured. She finally released Tera and looked deep into her blue eyes. "Let's go meet Devin's dad."

SECRETS

"ZILCH," TED CASSELMAN SAID. "You got nada."

"That's not exactly true," Cotten said. She sat alone in one of the sales department's office cubicles at the Washington SNN studios. Ted had made her promise to call him at home in New York as soon as she finished the interview with Miller. It was 12:30 AM.

"Then let me recap," he said. "You arrange this elaborate confrontation with the National Security Advisor of the United States, bring in a dozen of my Washington staff to stage a fake birthday party—with me paying them overtime, I might add—utilize one of our remote trucks, call in a producer, tie up enough video gear to shoot Steven Spielberg's next movie, and you come up with nothing but egg on your face." He paused. "What part of that is not exactly true?"

"You're exaggerating the facts. And I did come away with something. Miller told me he thinks he knows who planted the phone in his coat."

"Of course he told you that, Cotten. It was getting late and he wanted to go home. He would have said he suspected the Easter Bunny if you'd have pressed him hard enough."

"He said it was someone in the White House, in the Cabinet." She heard Ted give out an exasperated breath.

"Look, I love you like my own daughter. I trust you explicitly. I've come to know that your instincts are like a razor. And I know your secrets—secrets that go beyond . . ."

She heard the faint scratching sound from the stubble as he rubbed his face, and pictured him sitting on the side of his bed in the dark, trying not to awaken his wife. Cotten hated so much to disappoint Ted.

"But this time," he said, "you're pissing in the tall grass with the big dogs. The friggin' presidential cabinet, for Christ's sake. Do you have any idea what kind of position you could be putting the network in if this thing goes south?"

"I understand there's a lot at stake," Cotten said.

"A lot at stake? Cotten, forget losing your job. Hell, how about me losing mine. What about the credibility of the network?" He paused again. "Sometimes, you tend to forget that there are a whole bunch of folks I have to answer to, and they have a whole bunch over them called the board of directors. And the board answers to the stock holders. And none of them give a flying fuck about your instincts or your . . . secrets. Remember that a reporter is only as good as her last story. Don't you understand that?"

He stopped as if knowing it would be futile to try to reason with her. There was silence for a full minute. Then Ted said, "Miller gave you a name, didn't he? Who does he suspect planted the phone?"

"I promised I wouldn't reveal the name until he has some sort of concrete proof."

"How can I give you any support if I don't know what I'm dealing with here? Is it the cook or the president? And for that matter, why in God's name would someone in the White House want to steal your cell phone, burn down a farm in Kentucky, and threaten your life? It just doesn't make any sense, Cotten."

"From what I've learned about Lindsay and her daughter, Tera, I think this goes way beyond the theft of a cell phone."

"Fine, so rather than Watergate, now we got Loretto-gate. Come on, Cotten. How stupid does that sound?"

"I asked you to trust me with the Grail Conspiracy, and I was right, wasn't I?"

She heard him grunt.

"I asked you to trust me when you agreed to the live London broadcast just before we opened the time capsule and found the crystal tablet. Remember how many lives that saved? I was right that time, too, wasn't I?"

Another grunt followed by a heavy sigh.

"You said my instincts were second to none, right?"

Silence.

"That you know my secrets, my—"

"All right, already," Ted said. "Enough. There's no winning an argument with you. I never have, and I never will." He paused as if in reflection. "And thinking back, I thank God that I didn't win all our arguments. But this time, I need something to go on—some direction—something that will help me justify the expenses and time. Who does Miller suspect?"

Cotten listened to the sound fragments coming from through-out the building—the SNN graveyard shift. She heard a faint ringing of a phone, a distant conversation, someone's radio playing soft jazz, a chuckle. But beyond the solace and calm, somewhere out in the night, the Fallen and the Nephilim were amassing their forces. All the signs pointed to yet another attempt to strike at the one thing God treasured most—his prized creation—man. They had tried it with the attempt to clone Christ and create the Anti-Christ. They had caused a global suicide epidemic that resulted in the deaths of thousands, perhaps millions. And now, they were raising their evil heads again. She knew it because one fact over-shadowed all others. God had sent her a message—he had given her back her sister, Motnees—Tera. There could be only one rea-son—it would take them both to stop the Forces of Darkness. She had to find Tera before they did. As with any battle, there could be only one winner.

"Cotten? Are you there?" Ted asked. "What's the name?"

"It's the Secretary of Homeland Security," she said. "Rizben Mace."

THE SHELL

LINDSAY GRIPPED TERA'S HAND—her daughter's palm was warm, but hers was clammy. They walked through the double plate-glass doors into the lobby of the twenty-story CyberSys building. Inlaid in the marble floor was the corporate logo with its blue thunderbolt.

"Look," Tera said, pointing at the symbol. "Just like mine."

Lindsay stared at the logo, then at her daughter, with a feeling that things were spiraling out of control.

They stopped in front of the security desk.

"We'd like to see Mr. Olsen," Lindsay said.

"Do you have an appointment?" the Wackenhut guard asked.

"No," Lindsay answered. "But it's very important. It's about his son."

The guard's countenance told Lindsay that he thought she was one of the many kooks who loitered about downtown Miami. "What's your name?" he asked.

"Lindsay Jordan." She nodded to Tera. "This is my daughter, Tera."

Without taking his glare off Lindsay, he picked up the phone and made a call, talking quietly into the receiver. Almost as soon as he hung up, several security officers, clad in the same white and green Wackenhut uniforms, appeared and marched toward her.

"Please," Lindsay said, holding her hand up, anticipating that security was about to escort them out of the building or worse. "We mean no harm. I think we have some information Mr. Olsen would want to know. Please, just give us a minute to speak to him."

"Excuse me, Miss," a man in a navy blue suit said following behind the guards. He made his way to Lindsay.

She assumed he was not part of the security team, but rather a personal assistant or PR man for CyberSys.

"Mr. Olsen wishes everyone to know that he appreciates the outpouring of sympathy to his recent situation and is truly thankful for their support. But he is not seeing anyone at this time. I'm sure you can understand and respect his privacy."

Lindsay squeezed Tera's hand, knowing that this was doomed from the start—the meeting with Alan Olsen was not going to happen. "Of course," she said. "It's just that I believe Mr. Olsen will want to know what we have to tell him. It's about the kidnapping of his son. If I can just speak to Mr. Olsen for a moment and explain."

"I am certain that you mean well, but if you have any pertinent information, you should contact the FBI." The man reached in his pocket and thumbed through his wallet. "Here," he said, holding out a card. "Call this number and ask for—"

"I have something for Devin," Tera said, speaking up. "It's a present." She held out the conch shell.

"That's very nice." The man reached to take the shell. "I'll be happy to see—"

But before he could take it, a commotion came from the direction of the elevators—stiff leather-soled shoes on the marble floor echoed throughout the lobby. A man holding the hand of a boy emerged from the elevator surrounded by a handful of uniformed guards. They marched across the lobby toward the front entrance.

Lindsay knew it had to be Alan Olsen and his son. One of the guards she had been speaking with took her arm and pulled her and Tera aside.

"Step this way, please," he said.

Suddenly, Tera bolted toward the group and darted up to the boy before anyone could stop her.

Upon seeing the girl charge toward them, two of the guards attempted to block her, but Tera had already scooted her way between them to Devin.

The group halted as Tera reached out her hand to the boy. In it she held the conch shell. Everyone stood in silence as the boy broke into a broad smile.

Tera lifted the shell to Devin's ear.

Lindsay pulled away from the guards and ran to her daughter's side. A calm fell over the lobby as each person stood rooted in place, mesmerized by what was happening as Devin listened to the sound of the shell.

He cupped his hand over Tera's, pressing the shell closer.

Then Tera whispered, "Hi, Devin, remember me?"

Devin's face brightened. In a small voice, he said, "Hello, Motnees."

BALL LIGHTNING

COTTEN LEFT JOHN AT the Vatican Embassy so he could catch up on the latest Venatori intelligence briefings. It started to rain, and she heard distant thunder as she headed up Wisconsin Avenue and turned east on O Street in Georgetown. National Security Advisor Philip Miller had given her directions to his two-story townhouse, saying he had the proof she needed to confront Rizben Mace.

As she approached the Victorian home, she saw a black SUV parked in front. Miller had mentioned that there were two FBI agents on duty outside whenever he was home.

Cotten pulled into a curbside space and switched off the engine. The rain was pounding harder now—the underbelly of the furious clouds swollen and menacing.

She got out and opened her umbrella. Seeing that the passenger's side door was opening on the agent's vehicle, she held up her hand. No need for them both to get soaked. The door closed again, and she stood by as the window came down a few inches.

"Ms. Stone, can I see some ID?" the agent asked as the downpour intensified. "Formality. Sorry, especially in this weather." His last words were buried in an ear-splitting crack of thunder.

Cotten pulled her press credentials from her inside coat pocket and passed them through the window.

The agent shined a flashlight on them and then back out the window to her face. He returned the ID to Cotten. "Try to stay dry. Dr. Miller is expecting you."

She ran along the front walk and up the entrance steps. At the door, she huddled beneath the portico and rang the bell.

A moment later, Mrs. Miller opened the door. "Ms. Stone. Good to see you again," Mrs. Miller said as she motioned Cotten in.

"Thanks," Cotten said, closing the umbrella and trying not to drip water on the hardwood floors. "You have a wonderful home."

"Thank you." Mrs. Miller took Cotten's coat and hung it on a brass coat rack. "It was built in seventeen-ninety. We've completely refurbished it from floor to ceiling and tried to maintain its heritage. It's been the home to three presidential cabinet members and two ambassadors over the years."

"Ms. Stone." Philip Miller came across the living room, his hand outstretched. "Nasty night out there."

"And getting worse," Cotten said, shaking his hand. Her statement was punctuated by another thunderbolt. "Thanks for cooperating. I have to apologize again for accosting you and your wife on the sidewalks of Arlington."

"You were just doing your job," he said. "And I'm grateful that you believed me." He gestured that she sit on one of two couches facing each other in the middle of the living room. Burning logs crackled and hissed in the fireplace a few feet away.

"Can I get you something warm to drink?" Mrs. Miller asked. "Coffee, tea?"

"Tea would be great."

"Philip?" Mrs. Miller asked.

"Tea would be fine for me, too."

Cotten watched his wife disappear down a hall. Once she was gone, Cotten said, "I know this is awkward for you, working so closely with Secretary Mace. But I believe that identifying the person who has been stalking my friend and her daughter is more important than you can possibly imagine."

"Not awkward at all," Miller said. "It's time he paid his dues."

"Really?" she said. "So you two don't get along."

"We behave in public. But I have good reason for my distaste. I made a bid for governor of Arkansas a number of years ago. Rizben backed my opponent with an amazing amount of funding and support. He wound up buying the candidate and the election as far as I'm concerned. And one of the biggest campaign issues was converting old military bases into private research centers. The argument was that it would create jobs and increase the tax base. All it really did was filter money back to Rizben, I'm sure. He was heavily invested in some of those research outfits that expressed interest in the plan. There were a lot of other ways those facilities could have been utilized for public good. There was plenty of name calling and mud slinging. Consequently, there's still a lot of animosity between us. So rather than me confronting Rizben, I'd prefer to turn over what I've found and let you do it through the media. I have no problem throwing him under the bus."

"Did he actually convert any of the old military installations into commercial projects?"

"One, maybe. The whole matter seemed to fade away after the election. I guess I had called too much attention to it, and it became a hot potato. Like I say, there is no love lost." He reached in his pocket and took out a miniature cassette tape. "This will do the job."

"What is it?" Cotten asked.

"Recordings of phone conversations from a wiretap—another reason it has to go through you. You do protect your sources?"

"Absolutely."

Miller waved the tape. "This can never be connected back to me, but what I've got here is irrefutable proof that Rizben ordered the torching of the Jordan farm. What it doesn't explain is why."

"You don't have to worry about that," Cotten said. "Figuring that out is my job, and I guarantee it will never be linked to you in any way. You have my word."

"Good. And there seems to be something else. I'm not sure what it's all about, maybe you'll figure that out, too. Let me ask you, does the word thodium mean anything to you?"

Cotten was about to say no when intense white light flooded through the windows as lightning struck right outside. The explosive crack of thunder was instantaneous, telling Cotten the house was probably struck.

"My God," Miller said, standing.

Loud popping and sizzling caused them both to turn toward the fireplace. The blaze increased in brilliance as the fingers of flames leaped out into the room. Then a brilliant blue sphere about the size of a baseball emerged from the fire and floated a few feet above the hearth.

The globe sparked radial tentacles as it moved in a slow, random, zigzag. Behind it trailed a comet-like tail of white light.

Before either of them could react, the sphere shot from the fireplace hitting Miller square in the forehead.

Miller screamed and clawed at his face, his hair on fire. Then he collapsed onto the floor.

Cotten grabbed a pillow from the couch and smothered the fire.

"Oh, my God," Mrs. Miller said. The tray of teacups and saucers slipped from her hands and crashed. "Philip. Philip." She rushed to his side.

Cotten knelt next to him and pressed her fingertips to Miller's neck, searching for a pulse in his carotid.

Nothing.

"Do something," Mrs. Miller screamed.

"Call 9-1-1," Cotten said. "Go!" At the same time, she jumped up and raced to the front door. Pulling it open, she stood on the front steps and waved her arms at the agents in the black SUV. When she was sure they had seen her and were coming, she ran back to Miller, knelt, and started CPR. The odor of singed hair and burnt skin filled her nostrils as she leaned over him and pumped his chest.

"What the hell?" the first agent said, running into the room. He had a gun in his hand but holstered it as he activated his radio and broadcast an alert for assistance.

"Step away from Dr. Miller," the second agent ordered Cotten.

She ignored him and continued applying CPR.

"They're coming," Mrs. Miller shouted as she ran back into the room. "The ambulance is on the way."

"Ms. Stone," the agent said, "I need you to stand and step away."

Cotten reluctantly got to her feet and moved back as the agent took over applying the CPR.

"What happened?" the other agent asked Mrs. Miller.

"I left my husband and Ms. Stone talking while I went to get them some tea. I heard a loud explosion outside. A second later, my husband screamed. When I rushed back into the living room, Philip was lying on the floor and Ms. Stone was kneeling beside him."

Over the sound of the rain and thunder, Cotten heard the faint droning of a siren.

The agent looked at Cotten. "What happened to him?"

"We were talking when lightning must have struck the house. A bolt of lightning or an electrical discharge or something that looked like a glowing blue ball came into the house through the fireplace. By the time we both saw it, Dr. Miller was struck in the head. He collapsed. His hair caught fire and I put it out." She pointed to the blackened pillow on the floor.

There was a commotion at the front door as the EMTs entered and moved toward Miller's body. Cotten heard the static squawk of their radios and the crackle of plastic and paper as one paramedic opened his kit and peeled back the wrappings of needles and tubes while the other EMT cut Miller's shirt open.

She was sure they would do all they could to revive their patient, but in her gut, Cotten knew it was to no avail. This was more than a freak accident. This was another message directed at her. She was getting too close. Back off.

As she watched the medical technicians work on Philip Miller, she noticed that his shoes were blown off and parts of his clothes burned. There was only a single red spot on his forehead. One of the buttons on Miller's shirt had melted into his chest.

Mrs. Miller stood beside them, sobbing, her hand over her mouth. The shock had to be so great that she wasn't even able to process what had happened, Cotten thought.

When the paramedic lifted Miller's hand to start an IV, she saw him quickly drop it.

"What the—" he said.

The flesh of Miller's right hand was fused to the melted cassette tape.

INDIGOS

ALAN, DEVIN, LINDSAY, AND Tera stepped out onto the twentieth floor of CyberSys.

"That will be all," Alan said, leaving the guards behind.

Lindsay was impressed by the sleekness of the décor— all glass, aluminum, and mirror-finished stainless steel, and not a single fingerprint or smudge anywhere that she could see.

Tera took Devin's hand as Alan led them to his private office.

As they entered, Lindsay saw a woman standing beside the desk looking at a computer screen. She whipped around, seemingly startled. "Alan," she said, "I was just tidying up. I thought you were going to be out for a while."

"We were," he said. "But something came up. Kai, this is Lindsay Jordan and her daughter, Tera." He turned to Lindsay. "Kai Chiang is my personal assistant."

Kai leaned toward Alan and kissed him on the cheek as if she wanted to force a more elaborate introduction.

"Well, she's more than just an assistant," Alan said. "Kai and I—"

"I'm pleased to meet you," Kai said. "We try not to be too obvious. Affairs in the workplace usually don't breed good morale."

Tera snuggled against her mother's side.

"Why don't we all sit down," Alan said, motioning to the leather couches and matching oversized chairs.

Lindsay took one of the chairs, and Tera sat in her lap. Kai and Alan occupied a couch while Devin plopped onto the floor at his father's feet.

"So, what's this all about?" Kai asked.

Alan stretched his arm along the rim of the couch behind Kai's shoulders. "Ms. Jordan says she has some information regarding the kidnapping."

Tera squeezed her mother's hand.

"Really," Kai said. She glared at Lindsay. "You are aware that the case is closed—the kidnapper was identified?"

Lindsay nodded. "Yes, I saw that on TV, but I hope you will hear me out."

Devin put the shell to his ear, looked across at Tera, and smiled.

Alan's delight in seeing the way his son responded to Tera was obvious.

Kai slid her hand onto Alan's knee and eyed Lindsay. "You understand that Mr. Olsen and his son have both been through quite an ordeal. We are trying to get back to normalcy and wouldn't want anything to interfere with that."

"No, of course not," Lindsay said.

Kai continued. "And Devin is a special child. We can't let him be exploited."

"Then you will probably be more open to what I am going to tell you," Lindsay said. "Like Devin, Tera is also special."

Kai leaned forward. "I don't think you understand," she said condescendingly. She lowered the volume of her voice to almost a whisper, as if that would keep Devin from hearing her. "Devin is an autistic savant."

"Indigo," Tera said.

"Shh," Lindsay whispered through her daughter's golden hair. "Remember what we talked about?"

"Indigo, Indigo, Indigo," Devin said.

Lindsay brushed Tera's bangs back. "Well, I wasn't going to start with that, but . . . have you ever heard of Indigo children?" she said to Alan.

Devin waved one hand beside his ear.

"I've done considerable research on my son's condition," Alan said. "And yes, one of the things I've run across is the mention of a connection between some kids with autism and what they are calling Indigo children. Same thing with exceedingly gifted kids—and ADD and ADHD kids for that matter. So, yes, I've looked into that a little. I know they are given the name Indigo because of the supposed deep blue aura surrounding their bodies and that they have certain unexplained talents. But I have to confess that I dropped the ball and didn't pursue it much further—other than it inspiring me in choosing the color for the CyberSys thunderbolt logo, that is. I thought the whole concept was fascinating."

It's way more than fascinating, Lindsay thought. *It's downright scary.*

"And I certainly saw several characteristics in my son, but I think I just got sick of labels for Devin. To me, labeling is really

269

the equivalent of name calling, only on a socially acceptable level. I finally had enough. Devin is Devin."

"I agree," Lindsay said sympathetically. She knew too well what it was like to protect a child from the rest of the world's misconceptions. The heartaches. "Maybe during some of that research, you read about a recent wave of these—forgive the label—Indigo children being born. They believe there have always been Indigos, but not many. Then in the late 1970s, there was a major wave of births, but nothing compared to the Indigos being born just before and since the year 2000. I believe they are really wise old souls who are here to lead us through terrible times. To prepare us for enlightenment, some say. These children have *metagifts*. Tera is an Indigo. I can't see their auras, but Tera can. When she saw Devin on the television, she immediately recognized him as one of her own."

Kai rolled her eyes. "Alan, I think we should thank Ms. Jordan for her visit and—"

"No, please, Mr. Olsen. Let me finish. I promise you will be glad you listened."

Alan rested his forearms on his thighs and tapped his fingertips together. "Would you mind if Devin and Tera go to the playroom? It adjoins my office. I had it especially built for Devin. It's pretty much self-contained—bathroom, refrigerator, toys, games. There's no other way in or out other than through here. They'll be safe, and I'll feel more comfortable with our conversation."

Lindsay checked Tera's expression. "Okay with you, Ladybug?"

Tera nodded.

"Kai would you show the kids the playroom and maybe rustle up a snack for them?" Alan said.

From Kai's sour expression, Lindsay could tell that Alan's suggestion didn't sit well with his *special assistant*. But Kai agreed and led the children away.

"She's just trying to be protective," Alan said, nodding toward the closing door. "I am interested in what you have to say, and I don't mean to rush you, but I'm afraid I have little time this morning."

"Thanks for your patience," Lindsay said. "I feel like I'm being a scatterbrain, but there's so much to tell."

Alan nodded, and gestured for her to continue.

Lindsay took a deep breath. "Tera has some unique gifts. She is an artist, a poet, and above all a spiritual child. All Indigos know who they are spiritually. I'm convinced they have some kind of heavenly connection. And I know how you must be feeling right now. I've been coming to terms with all this, bit by bit, for eight years."

"But this Indigo thing," Alan said. "Like I told you, I entertained it for a short time. But in the end I realized that Devin is an autistic savant, no more, no less, and that's enough burden for him to bear."

"I don't know his specialty, but I understand that savant's have immense gifts. He doesn't have to be a poet or an artist, or a virtuoso. Devin does have some special talents, right?"

Alan stared at the floor. "Yes, if you mean his ability with numbers and dates. He memorizes anything he's ever read." He looked up, seemingly pleased at his next thought. "Devin can read two pages at a time—one with his left eye, one with his right." His expression faded. "Ms. Jordan, you've given me plenty to think about, but I don't see what any of this has to do with Devin's kidnapping. So why don't we call it a day."

Lindsay knew his next words would be to politely ask her to leave. It was hard to believe he had listened to her this long. She had to do something. She couldn't stop now.

Alan started to stand. "I thank you for all your concern about my son, but—"

Lindsay didn't move. "I didn't want to come here." Her voice trembled with its rising volume. "But Tera was so insistent, so beside herself, I had to bring her. I am convinced there is a link between Tera and Devin that will lead to uncovering more about Devin's kidnapping."

Alan shifted. "Devin was kidnapped for money, pure and simple greed."

"But I read there was never any ransom note. Did you ever pay anything to anybody?"

"No. But the authorities found a note. It just hadn't been sent yet."

"Why would someone kidnap a child for money and wait so long to make a ransom demand? It doesn't make sense. I think . . . Tera thinks there's another reason someone would want to kidnap your son."

Alan fidgeted, his face blanched, and she knew she had pricked a nerve.

"All right, Ms. Jordan, what does your daughter think is the reason?"

"Tera said the kidnappers wanted to steal information your son had memorized—numbers he has in his head."

THE MOTIVE

Alan stared at Lindsay, his expression packed with shock. He seemed to be calculating if he should let her into his confidence. She could tell he was considering what she said about the motive for Devin's kidnapping.

"Your daughter has come up with an interesting theory," Alan said. He continued to stare at her, and she knew there was a debate raging in his head.

Finally, he said, "Yes, there is another possibility. Your daughter is correct—Devin may have been kidnapped to obtain information. The numbers in his head."

"What kind of numbers?" Lindsay asked.

He rubbed his hands together. "My company, CyberSys, is on the verge of completing the world's first working quantum computer. It will revolutionize the speed of data processing and the power of encryption—the ramifications to global security and safety are enormous. But we're not the only ones trying to develop a quantum computer. There are a few others. As you can imagine, the race to be first to market is highly competitive. Obtaining confidential computer codes and information that might help someone beat us to the punch would be worth millions, perhaps billions of dollars."

"So Devin could have been kidnapped to extort that from you?"

Alan nodded. "That's what made your daughter's observation startle me—that they want to steal something from Devin's memory. They wouldn't need me for that. Because of his extraordinary ability to memorize and recall copious amounts of information, Devin has everything they want right inside his head. I've tried to press Devin for details of what happened, but he's shut the door on the whole episode. The police think it was all about money—some white-collar criminal faked his own death, then snatched Devin for ransom. The information that Devin carries around in his brain is worth more than any ransom.

"The police didn't have any luck getting my son to reveal what happened, either. I was hoping it would come out little by little once Devin felt he was safely at home. But all he has told me is that while he was being held, he spent the time playing games. And yet, the authorities didn't find a computer at the kidnapper's cabin—not even a PlayStation or Nintendo."

"That doesn't make sense," Lindsay said.

Alan nodded. "No, the more I think about it, the more it isn't logical."

"Listen, I don't know much about computers or industrial espionage, but I do know that Tera and Devin are somehow tied together with what's going on here. Mr. Olsen, Tera and I have been on the run. Someone is after my daughter. I think the reason Tera was so distressed and adamant about coming to see Devin is that she realizes they have the same enemy—what she calls the red people, the Rubies. I think there is more to this than we can figure out by ourselves. But I have a suggestion."

Leaning forward, his forearms resting on his legs, he said, "I'm listening."

"If in your gut you think there's more to it than just ransom money, then we need to do something. I have a friend who might be able to help. She's an investigative correspondent with years of experience. You have nothing to lose if I ask her to help. You might know her from television. Cotten Stone?"

"Sure," Alan said. "SNN. The Grail thing—I've followed her adventures with interest—gutsy lady."

"Right. If we can get her involved, maybe even ask her to come to Miami, I believe she can help unravel all this."

"I don't quite see her connection with Devin and Tera."

"She's an expert on solving mysteries that are out of the ordinary." She studied Alan's face as she waited for a response. "It would cost you nothing to at least talk to her."

He stretched back in deep thought. Finally, he rose, walked to his desk, and pressed a button on his phone.

"Yes, Mr. Olsen," a woman's voice came through the speaker.

"Call the Satellite News Network's offices in New York and see if you can get in touch with one of their correspondents. Her name is Cotten Stone. When you get her on the line, put her through."

"Will do," the woman said.

Alan sat in the desk chair and swiveled so he looked out the window. "It seems like a long shot to me, but I would do just about anything to find the son-of-a-bitch who's really responsible for taking my son."

"I don't blame you," Lindsay said. "There are many questions I need answered about Tera and the people who have been tracking us down. I truly believe Cotten can help us both."

Kai came back into the room. "The kids are getting along fine. I made them sandwiches and cut up some strawberries. That okay with you, Ms. Jordan?"

"Perfect. Tera loves strawberries. And please, call me Lindsay."

Kai stood behind Alan's chair and massaged his shoulders. "Want to fill me in on what I missed?"

Alan stilled her hands with his before turning around. "Remember I told you that I had this fear that Devin could have been kidnapped for the Destiny code?"

"Right, but—"

"Maybe he was."

Kai shook her head as if feeling pity for Alan. "Oh, babe, don't torture yourself anymore than you already have. There's no evidence that was the motive at all. We know who kidnapped Devin. Benjamin Ray. He was desperate for money and just didn't get the ransom note off before he had a heart attack. You shouldn't let someone stir you up over something that has no basis." She looked at Lindsay. "No offense, Ms. Jordan, but the police have already told us what happened. And Devin hasn't said it was anything else."

"I'm not sure," Alan said. "But I don't think we'll find out from Devin. I think we have to take some action on our own."

"You . . . we have your son back," Kai said. "That's all that matters."

Alan turned his attention to Lindsay. "I think you and Tera should stay here for now. If the threat to your daughter is as real as you say, the security at CyberSys will keep you safe. There's a conference room down the hall. It has a couch with a foldout bed and a private bathroom. No four-star accommodation, but—"

"That would be wonderful," Lindsay said. "I don't know how we can ever—"

"Alan, she's a total stranger. Are you sure this is wise?"

Alan glanced toward the playroom. He could see Devin and Tera through the window sitting side-by-side, engrossed in watching cartoons on TV. "Yes," he said, "I'm sure."

The phone on his desk buzzed.

"Mr. Olsen," came a voice through the speaker. "I have Cotten Stone on the line."

BAD NEWS

Lindsay stood at the CyberSys conference room window overlooking the Port of Miami. She had been up a few hours and tried to be as quiet as possible so Tera could sleep in. Now she heard a stirring and looked around to see her daughter sitting up on the foldout sofa bed. "Good morning, Ladybug," she said. "Did you sleep well?"

Tera shook her head, rubbing her eyes. "This bed is so lumpy."

"But we're thankful for Mr. Olsen letting us stay here, safe and sound, aren't we?"

"I guess so."

Lindsay sat on the edge of the bed and wrapped her arms around her daughter. "I realize this is tough. You miss home. So do I." She stroked Tera's arms. "I know we'll be able to go back to Kentucky soon—I just know it. Mr. Olsen is going to help us. And you heard the great news. My friend Cotten is coming to see you. She'll help us, too."

Tera smiled at her mother. "My sister, Momma."

Lindsay studied Tera's eyes. There was no hint of fantasy, only pure expression of what her daughter thought was fact. "So, things could be worse, right, princess?"

"I don't like Kai."

"Why not, sweetheart?"

"She's not nice to Devin."

"What do you mean?"

Tera shrugged. "I just don't like her," she said, scrunching up her face and shaking her head.

"Let's just keep our feelings about Kai to ourselves. Okay?" She tickled Tera's ribs. "Are you ready for some breakfast?"

A wide grin bloomed on Tera's face. "Pancakes," she said, clapping her hands.

"Well, I don't know about that, but Mr. Olsen said there's a fully stocked kitchen down the hall. Let's get you dressed and go check it out."

Tera hopped from the bed and scampered to her bag on the floor. She pulled out a pair of jeans and a bright orange T-shirt, then darted off for the bathroom.

Lindsay watched her daughter disappear behind the door before returning to the window. How had all this happened? She and Tera were just Kentucky farm folks. Nothing special, and yet, somehow they were submerged in an ocean of madness. People with ruby red glowing bodies that only Tera could see were trying to harm them. Yet she had absolutely no proof any of it was true. Some things were best left unsaid. Indigos and Rubies were enough. Alan Olsen never would have believed that her daughter was able to pick her parents before she was born or that she knew

Devin in Heaven. And this whole thing about Cotten being her twin sister. In her heart, Lindsay believed it all. But in her mind, in her intellect, she struggled. And so would Alan.

It was a miracle that he had given them the time of day, much less a safe place to stay. He must want to do whatever it takes to find who had kidnapped Devin.

Besides them being Indigos, what was the big link between Tera and Devin? Lindsay prayed they would find the answer so she and Tera could go home and have a normal life. That's all she wanted.

That's all she ever wanted.

She heard a soft knock at the door and went to open it.

"Good morning," Alan said. "I hope you guys are hungry." He held a large takeout food bag in each hand.

"Mr. Olsen, you really didn't have to do that. We'd have found something in the office kitchen."

"God only knows what's in there." Alan smiled, holding up the bags. "I've brought fresh fruit, bacon, eggs, bagels, even waffles and pancakes."

"Pancakes!" Tera squealed as she ran across the room and wrapped her arms around him.

"I take it that's what she wants," he said.

"Her favorite," Lindsay said, trying to ease her daughter's bear hug on Alan.

"Then she'll love these," Alan said. "They're from Devin's favorite restaurant a few blocks away." He cocked his thumb toward the hall. "Let's head for the kitchen and start eating before they get cold."

"Is Devin here?" Tera asked.

"He's waiting for you."

Tera sprinted off ahead of them.

"I can't thank you enough, Mr. Olsen," Lindsay said.

As they followed in Tera's wake, Alan said, "First of all, it's Alan, not Mr. Olsen. And second, you already have thanked me. You know, Tera is all Devin has talked about since we left you guys last night. He is the calmest, most coherent, most . . . normal I've ever seen him. I don't know what it is about your daughter, but she has a profound effect on my son. And for that, I'm eternally grateful."

Lindsay took one of the bags from Alan. "Tera thinks the world of him, too."

"Okay then," Alan said as they entered the kitchen. "Who wants pancakes?"

———

Kai stood with her arms crossed, staring out Alan's office window. Lindsay sat on the couch in front of his desk and leafed through a copy of *Newsweek*. Her daughter and Devin were in the playroom watching TV.

It was almost noon, and Alan had passed the last thirty minutes in silence reviewing a stack of financial statements. His phone rang. When he pushed the button, a woman's voice came through the speaker. "Mr. Olsen, Cotten Stone and Cardinal Tyler are here."

"Show them in," Alan said. He glanced at Lindsay. "This should make you feel better."

Lindsay closed her eyes, relieved. "I just know Cotten can help us. I'm sure of it."

Alan peered into the playroom. The television was on, but Tera and Devin ignored it, choosing instead to draw on sheets of chart paper that Alan had taken off the easel in the conference room. "It's so amazing to see how the two of them connect."

"Tera desperately needed a friend," Lindsay said. "They are good for each other."

"I agree."

Kai turned from the window as the office door opened. Lindsay thought she noted harshness in the woman's expression. Perhaps it was just the glare from the window that caused Kai to narrow her eyes and tighten her face.

Lindsay stood as Cotten came into the office. She smiled at the sight of her old friend. Moving to her, she opened her arms. "Cotten, thank you so much for coming."

"Lindsay," Cotten said, hugging her. "It's been too long." She pulled back at arm's length. "I'm so sorry about Neil. I know it's been hard on you both. And now with all this craziness. I just wish I could have gotten to you sooner."

"But you're here now," Lindsay said, hugging her again. "That's all that matters."

Finally, they broke their embrace and Lindsay said, "Cotten, I'd like you to meet Alan Olsen, president of CyberSys."

Alan was already moving toward them. He shook Cotten's hand. "It's a pleasure, Ms. Stone. I'm a big fan."

"Thank you for taking care of my friend and her daughter."

"Of course," he said.

Lindsay said, "And this is Kai Chiang, Mr. Olsen's . . . personal assistant."

"It's okay, Lindsay," Kai said. "Alan is my significant other," she announced, but didn't bother to leave her spot by the window.

Cotten nodded to Kai, then turned. "This is my friend, Cardinal John Tyler."

"Cardinal Tyler." Alan said. "It's indeed an honor to meet you. I still remember following the amazing Grail conspiracy story in the news. That must have been such an adventure."

"Kept us on our toes," John said. He acknowledged Kai with a nod. "Nice to meet you both as well."

"Why don't we all make ourselves comfortable," Alan said, gesturing toward the couches.

Cotten and John sat with Lindsay while Alan waited for Kai to join him on the opposite couch.

As she sat, Kai said, "So, Ms. Stone, your friend *insisted* that you come here to help her solve the mystery of the connection with her daughter and Alan's son. Alan and Devin have been through a hard time recently with the kidnapping and all, and we—"

Alan patted Kai's leg. "We're all under quite a bit of stress right now, so please forgive Kai. She just wants us to get through this as quickly as possible and move on with our lives."

"Alan, you don't have to apologize for me," Kai said, placing her hand on his.

"I understand your concerns," Cotten said. "And I thank you both for helping Lindsay and Tera. Unfortunately, I don't believe we will get to the root of what is going on too quickly." Cotten took in a deep breath. "Lindsay and Tera are definitely in danger. It's not imagined. Not only are they being hunted, but those who are doing the hunting are extremely dangerous . . . people."

Kai leaned back into the couch with a huff.

Cotten turned to Lindsay. "I went to Loretto to find you, but you were already gone. I visited your farm and it revived a lot of fond memories. I took some time wandering around. I saw Tera's paintings, drawings, read her poems. It's clear that your daughter has special gifts, not just talent." Cotten swallowed, then said, "Lindsay . . . I'm sorry to be the bearer of bad news. I hate to tell you. It's so awful. Everything is gone. Someone set fire to your home and burned it to the ground. The house, the barn, the big oak, all of Tera's beautiful work, destroyed."

"Oh, no," Lindsay said, the color in her cheeks bleaching. She hid her face in her hands, shaking her head, whispering, "No, no, no." Finally, she looked up. "That's all we had." Her voice was pinched from holding back tears.

"Who would have done that?" Alan asked.

"While I was in Kentucky," Cotten said, "My cell phone was stolen. That's the reason I was not getting your messages, Lindsay. The person who stole it used my cell to call Cardinal Tyler and threaten my life. I was told to back off trying to find Lindsay and Tera. They also said that burning down Lindsay's farm was a warning of worse things to come."

"Sounds like a teenage prank," Kai said.

"It wasn't a prank," John said. "Cotten's phone has a GPS auto tracking system built in, and we were able to track the phone to Washington, D.C."

"Alan, this is just plain nuts," Kai said. "I don't see what this has to do with Devin or the kidnapping."

Cotten looked at Kai and then Alan. She was fighting a losing battle with Kai. It would be better to direct everything to Alan. "The phone was tracked to someone in the White House."

Alan sat up straight. "Are you serious? That's unbelievable. Do you know who?"

"Yes," John said.

"Yesterday evening," Cotten said, "I met with Dr. Philip Miller, the National Security Advisor. He was about to give me a tape recording of phone conversations that would prove beyond a doubt who stole my phone, who ordered Lindsay's farm destroyed, who threatened my life, and who is trying to find and kill Lindsay and Tera."

"You have the tape?" Kai said, her voice rising in pitch.

"No," John said. "Dr. Miller was killed in a freak accident just as he was about to hand over the evidence to Cotten. The tape was destroyed."

Kai exhaled. "There you are, Alan. Just another bit of conjecture, guesswork, rumors. I think we've heard enough."

"Dr. Miller had already disclosed to me the identity of the person on the tape," Cotten said.

"Who is it, Ms. Stone?" Alan asked.

"The Secretary of Homeland Security, Rizben Mace."

The hush that descended on the room was suddenly interrupted by a piercing scream coming from the playroom.

"It's Tera," Lindsay said, springing to her feet.

Alan raced right behind Lindsay across the office into the playroom.

Devin sat on the floor shaking his hands beside his head and rocking.

Lindsay rushed to Tera, sweeping her daughter into her arms. "Baby, what is it? What's wrong?"

RED ALERT

Tera stopped screaming and pointed to the TV screen. "He's red! Momma, he's one of the Ruby people."

Everyone focused on the image of a man speaking at what appeared to be a news conference. Across the top of the image was the banner, *The Tragic Death of Dr. Philip Miller*. Underneath the speaker was the graphic text title, *Rizben Mace, Secretary of Homeland Security*.

"My God," Alan said. "She's pointing to Rizben Mace. And she says he's—"

"Red. A Ruby," John said. He turned to Cotten. "That goes along with Miller's suspicions connecting Mace to the theft of your phone."

Unlike the others, Cotten was not looking at the television. Her eyes were transfixed on Tera. The others were talking, but to Cotten their voices were background noise like wind through distant trees. Nor could she see anything other than Tera as cascades of lights swirled about her, blinding Cotten to anything else. She felt as if she gazed through a tunnel of dazzling white light with Tera in the center.

"Cotten?" John said. "Are you okay?"

Lindsay had her arms wrapped around her daughter. She let go as the child met Cotten's stare. A slow, wide, smile grew on Tera's face. "Hello," she said in nearly a whisper.

"Hi," Cotten said, feeling an avalanche of emotion roll over her. "Motnees," Cotten said softly, going to her knees.

Tera came to her, touching Cotten's tear-streaked face. "I knew you would come," she said. "I told Momma you would."

Cotten enfolded the girl in her arms. For a moment, she recalled childhood memories of Motnees appearing in her room at night. They would talk for hours about the things of life that Cotten now realized were, at the time, beyond her years.

Finally, she held Tera at arm's length. "The time is near, isn't it?" she said quietly.

Tera nodded. "Devin is blue, like me . . . Indigo. But the bad people are red—Rubies."

At that instant, Cotten understood the danger, the urgency, and the risk. The final conflict was about to happen. Only one force could win. Good or evil. Indigos or Rubies.

———

After the scene in the playroom, everyone including Tera and Devin returned to Alan's office.

"So what is a Ruby?" Alan asked when everyone was seated.

"Before I explain, let me give you some background," Cotten said. "I was recently in Moscow. You may have heard about the presidential assassination attempt on the news."

"It was a brave thing you did," Alan said.

"Thank you," Cotten said. "It was just before I was to leave for home that I received an urgent call from Lindsay. She told me that Tera was in danger—that someone was coming to take her daughter from her."

Tera nodded as she sat on her mother's lap. "Rubies."

Lindsay hugged her. "Hush, sweetie."

"It's all right, Lindsay," Cotten said. "In reality, Tera may know more about this than anyone." She looked back at Alan. "You mentioned when you called me that you don't believe your son was kidnapped for ransom. You said it may have been industrial espionage—that Devin had memorized vital computer code for your Destiny project and the kidnappers needed to have him recreate it for them. Is that right?"

"Yes," Alan said. "It just makes more sense to me than the ransom theory."

"Then, we need to find a connection," Cotten said. "And we think it's what Tera calls Rubies."

"This is ridiculous," Kai said. "There is no connection. Alan, this is a total waste of time."

"Please, Kai," Alan said. "If you're right, then we'll all be out of here by lunch." He looked back at Cotten. "So you believe that Rizben Mace is a—"

"Mace, Mace, Rizben Mace," Devin said, one hand jiggling chest high.

Alan spoke to his son. "Devin, let the adults—"

Devin looked up at the ceiling. "Forever, Kai. Love, Kai."

"What's he talking about?" Kai said. "Alan, can't you shut him up?"

Then both of Devin's hands waved vigorously on each side of his head. "Return path. Kai at Cybermailserv. Received from mxm-0-one dot corp to rmace at dhs dot gov."

Kai stood and stepped away, her face reddening.

In a monotone, Devin continued, "Rizben, I can't take it any more. I need you, I need you, I need you. Forever, Kai."

"What is he saying?" Cotten asked.

"E-mail. Devin's repeating e-mail that he's read," said Alan, his eyes slowly settling on Kai as he began to understand.

"This is bullshit," Kai said. "I can't believe—"

"Return path," Devin said. "Rizben Mace at dhs dot gov. Received from zzp-0-six dot corp to kaic at cybermailserv dot com. Tor working on the little bastard. Hades project almost complete, but the element is unstable. Found a way to fake the kidnapping. It won't be long now. I need you, too. RM."

Devin stopped rocking, his hands dropped to his lap, and like everyone else in the room his eyes were trained on Kai.

THE TRUTH

"He's making this shit up, Alan," Kai said. "He doesn't know what he's talking about." Kai inched away from Devin.

For a moment, Alan was speechless, trying to process what he had just heard. This guy, this Rizben Mace, was Kai's lover? And the Hades Project had to be a quantum computer that he was building. Kai knew who had kidnapped Devin all along. She was a part of it. He shook his head. "You're right," Alan said. "My son doesn't know what he's talking about. He's simply reciting something he's seen, like any of the thousands of texts he's ever read. But this time it's your e-mail, Kai. Devin can't make things up. He doesn't know how."

"Fucking little retard," Kai said. "Snooping around where he doesn't belong. He gives me the creeps."

Alan moved within inches of her, backing her against the wall. His jaw clenched and the tendons in his neck stood out. "All along, you've been feeding Rizben Mace inside information about my company and our product. But you couldn't give him the Destiny code because you didn't know how to get access to it. So you allowed Devin to be taken from me." His fists were balled at his sides. "Jesus Christ, Kai, who are you? We loved you. I trusted you. And all this time—" Alan drove his fingers through his hair as he looked around at everyone in the room. "Fuck." He shot his gaze back at Kai. "Fuck you!"

After a long silence, Lindsay said, "Why don't I take the kids to the playroom?" She gathered Devin and Tera up and led them away, closing the door behind them.

Kai tossed back her jet hair and smoothed her red, silk brocade dress about her hips. "All right. It's true. But it's nothing personal, Alan. I'm not in love with Rizben Mace. That was just to get him off. It was something I knew he wanted to believe." She raised an eyebrow at Alan. "I don't love him or anyone else for that matter. It's a job. That's all. After this one, there will be another. As they say, every woman has her price."

"Funny you should say that, because I don't think you calculated the price *you* are going to pay," Alan said. "I intend to have you arrested for conspiring to kidnap my son and for industrial espionage. The Destiny code is worth millions, and my son is priceless. You're going to have a tough time working your next job from inside a federal prison. I'll do whatever it takes to put you away for life."

"And what proof do you have?" Kai said. "The word of your little carnival freak reciting some e-mail that's long been deleted? The cops already told you who kidnapped Devin and why. I'll walk away from this free and clear."

"You'll deal with the FBI first," Alan said, stabbing the air with his finger. "You can count on that."

Cotten stood, and Alan turned to her. "I'm sorry you had to see this, Ms. Stone. I apologize for any embarrassment to you and Cardinal Tyler. This is a private matter, a disgrace." He turned back to Kai. "You're a disgrace. You disgust me."

"You don't have a clue who you are working for, do you, Kai?" Cotten said.

"I'm freelance. I work for myself."

Cotten laughed. "Wow, you are in denial."

Kai's almond black eyes flashed. "What are you talking about? I was recruited by Tor, a friend of mine, to work for Rizben Mace."

"You've been duped by the best," Cotten said. "Mace is a big fish in an even bigger ocean of brimstone."

"What are you talking about?" Alan said.

"Before you call the FBI, you may want to ask yourself what is really going on here," Cotten said.

Alan turned from Kai. "I think I already know, but why don't you tell me anyway."

"It's obvious that you've been betrayed. Kai risked your son's life. She helped steal the secrets to your Destiny computer. That much we can surmise. Correct?"

Alan crossed his arms and nodded. "What are you getting at?"

"Rather than asking why Kai did it, which is obvious, ask yourself why Rizben Mace, the Secretary of Homeland Security, wants the operating system code to your quantum computer."

"Well," Alan said, "Maybe he's got an investment in our competition."

"And who is your competition?" Cotten asked.

Alan rubbed his chin. "Because the technology is still in its infancy, most of our competitors are research facilities and universities."

"So you think a research facility or university would be a likely candidate to kidnap your son and plant Kai in your organization to steal your secrets?"

"Well . . ." Alan said.

Cotten said, "If it's not research facilities and universities, then who else could it be? And for what purpose?"

"I just assumed that it would be the competition . . ."

"According to what I've found out about CyberSys, you are the ones on the cutting edge. You have competitors, but at this point no real competition," Cotten said. "So why don't we go ahead and rule that out?"

"I'm a business man, Ms. Stone," Alan said. "That's the way I look at everything."

"What if it were terrorists?" John said.

"Terrorists?" Alan said. "I guess it could be. But there would have to be a lot of capital and talent. It's a possibility."

John said, "Do you know of any other country that has the technology you do?"

"Maybe the Chinese," Alan said. "But I think that information would be leaked or evident. It's a very small community of groups trying to build a quantum computer. Although many are trying to do so, we're way out front in actually developing one. And our specific progress is only known in a small circle inside CyberSys. Me, Max . . ."

Alan looked at Kai.

Kai raised both hands. "You're way off," she said. "I don't work for the fucking Chinese. For God's sake, I'm fifth-generation American. And I'm sure Rizben doesn't, either. He told me he reports to some old guy who wants this quantum computer so he can sell it—for profit. Millions and millions. They're not terrorists. It's all about the money."

She really doesn't have any idea, Cotten thought. *And the old guy Rizben reports to*—Cotten knew who that was. How was she going to lead Alan to this conclusion without him thinking she was totally deranged?

"So we know the lynchpin is Rizben Mace," Cotten said. "If he's not your competition, or a terrorist, or working for another government trying to steal your Destiny computer, then who is he? Who does he work for?"

"I don't know," Alan said.

Cotten glanced around the room. "Think about it, Mr. Olsen. Tera already answered that question."

NEGOTIATION

COTTEN REALIZED SHE WAS stepping into risky territory. But it had to be done.

"Mr. Olsen, you said you were a fan of mine. I assume that means you've followed my career?"

"That's correct," Alan said.

"So you are familiar with the kind of reporting I've been involved in. If you remember the Grail Conspiracy story, you will recall that someone was attempting to take the DNA from the Holy Grail and clone Christ—a creation of the Anti-Christ in a sort of blasphemous Second Coming. And then several years ago, there was a rash of suicides around the world that were suspected to be demonic possessions."

"Yes," Alan said. "I remember both very well."

"I am convinced for many reasons that we are up against the same group that orchestrated both those events—the same group Tera calls Rubies, and she has identified Mace as a Ruby. He's not just some industrial thief. He's not doing it for money as Kai thinks. He kidnapped Devin to gain the technology to build this Hades Project mentioned in the e-mail. He tried to kill Tera for one reason—because she can identify him and members of the group he works with."

Alan clasped his hands behind his head and stretched his neck down, eyes closed. "You're asking me to take some big leaps here with all this Ruby talk. I understand the Indigo stuff because I've done the research, because I know my son, but now you're talking about something else altogether."

"You're right, it will be a huge leap," Cotten said. "But whether you take the leap or not doesn't change the fact that both groups exist. The Indigos are being brought into this world for a purpose—to do the good work of God. The Rubies are here for just the opposite reason."

"I'm sorry, Ms. Stone, but I'm not a religious man. I don't know if I can make the leap you are asking," Alan said, now looking up.

"Okay," John said. "We would be remiss if we didn't tell you what we think, but you don't have to buy into everything. All you need to do is understand that Rizben Mace is building a quantum computer to be used for a terrible purpose. Will you give us that much?"

Alan nodded. "For now."

Cotten suddenly turned to look at Kai. "You know she holds the answers. And she's a working girl."

Alan slowly turned to her as if experiencing a revelation. "Maybe you can help me make the leap Ms. Stone wants. What's your price, Kai?"

"Always negotiable," Kai said, smiling.

"Not really," Alan said. "I can call the FBI, or as Cotten suggests, you can cooperate."

"If I tell you what I know, I want some guarantees," Kai said.

"Like what?" Alan asked.

"When this is over I want to walk away. But I have expensive tastes, you know that. My lifestyle would demand a great deal of compensation." With a flick of her hand, she flipped her hair over her right shoulder and dropped down into one of the large, leather chairs. She crossed her legs, and the hem of her dress rode up mid-thigh.

Alan worked his jaw, the muscles distending and relaxing. "Perhaps it could be arranged. But it will be a one-shot deal, Kai. When you are out of my life, if you try to come back, it will be with an FBI escort."

Kai rolled her eyes and gave a quick chuckle. "Fair enough."

"All right, then," Cotten said. "Let's go back over one of those e-mails that Devin told us about. I have some questions. Do you mind, Mr. Olsen?"

"Call me Alan," he said. "And no, I don't mind."

"Hades Project. What is that?"

Kai re-crossed her legs. "It's what Rizben calls some plan he has for the computer."

"Details," Alan said.

"I don't know any—just that he and Tor had spent a lot of time mapping out a plan."

"That's another question I had," said Cotten. "Who is Tor?"

"He's the computer geek—the guy who designed the Hades Plan and the computer. Rizben doesn't know that much about computers. He relies on Tor. Tor's the one who tried to get the

Destiny code from Devin—and, like I told you a minute ago, Tor recruited me." She blinked slowly at Alan, almost flirtatiously. "My mission was to establish a relationship with you. At first we thought I could get the Destiny code, but that didn't work out, so all I did was relay updates on your progress and any other scraps of information I came across."

"You told them all about Devin, didn't you?" Alan said.

Kai nodded nonchalantly. "And when you were taking Devin to the football game. It was a big break for Rizben. He had tried to find a way to get to Devin, but that wasn't an easy task. The ballgame fit the bill—crowds, confusion, and no Code Adam. We knew Devin would fall for a chance to try a new video game."

"Damn you," Alan said, his face looking as if he had a bad taste in his mouth.

"You're paying for the truth," Kai said. "You let me know when you don't want to hear it." She smiled at Alan, only one side of her mouth turned up and one brow arched.

"Where is this Tor?" Cotten asked.

"He's at the Hades facility," Kai said.

"Where is that?" Alan said.

"No clue. All I know is that it's in some remote location."

"You don't know much," Cotten said. "I think Alan is overpaying you."

"I have a question," Alan said. "There was something in the e-mail about an element not working. What element was he talking about?"

"Some weird shit they needed for the computer. They had some, but it was unreliable, didn't work all the time. Sodium. Podium. Something like—"

Alan's head shot up.

"Thodium?" Cotten said.

"Yeah, that's it," Kai said.

Alan turned to Cotten. "How do you know about thodium?"

Cotten said, "Miller asked me if the word *thodium* meant anything to me."

Alan had already crossed the room and punched the button on his phone. "Get Max Wolf up here."

CUBITS OR QUBITS

"THIS MACE GUY HAS a source of thodium," Alan told Max after he had explained what had led up to this moment.

"Could be he's found a way to create more than a few atoms at a time, but I doubt it," Max said.

"You want to know where he got the thodium?" Kai said. "Heavens, Alan, for the price you'll be paying me, all you had to do was ask."

"Spit it out, Kai," Alan said. "If you've got information, give it. Can you do that?"

"Well, I have to admit, it is entertaining to see all the gyrations," Kai said. "But all right, I get your point." She clasped her hands, steepled her fingers, and pointed them at Alan. "I don't think you're going to believe me, though."

"Try me," Alan said.

"Rizben has a collection of archaeological artifacts. He's a collector. Anyway, from what he told me, in his collection he had a fragment of Noah's Ark. How he got it from the Baghdad Museum into his collection is a long story, and it doesn't really matter, so I won't go into that . . . unless of course you want me to take the time."

Cotten could see that Kai's over-politeness was grating on Alan. She stepped in. "No, we don't need all the background."

Kai sank back in the cushions. "Rizben said that the Ark was built from lumber that came from some tree mentioned in the Bible—in Genesis—you know the one?"

"The Tree of Knowledge or the Tree of Life?" John said.

"The second one," Kai said. "The Tree of Life. And this particular wood secreted a sap, or resin I think he called it. After a long time, that resin crystallizes into the stuff he needs for the computer—thodium. He managed to extract the thodium from some splinters of Noah's Ark. I thought it was pretty wild, actually. Tree of Life. Fucking Noah's Ark." Kai glanced at Alan. "You never were any good at hiding your feelings. I can tell from your face you don't believe me."

"You're right," Alan said. "I don't believe you."

"Maybe she's telling the truth," John said. "In one translation of the Bible, God tells Noah to build the Ark out of gopher wood. In another translation God says to use resin wood."

The door to the playroom opened and Lindsay came out carrying a sheet of chart paper against her chest, the blank side showing.

"I found this from when the kids were drawing before. I don't know, but I think it might be important."

"What is it?" Cotten said.

"Tera said she drew this as Devin described it to her. She says it's a sketch of the man who was holding Devin."

"Turn it around," Alan said.

Lindsay flipped the paper around so everyone could see the image.

"It's certainly not Ben Ray," Cotten said.

"No, that's Tor," Kai said. "Wow, she's a really good artist."

"Thanks, Lindsay," Alan said, sounding disappointed. "It is important, but we've already identified—"

John suddenly got to his feet. "Wait a minute," he said walking closer to the sketch of the young goateed man in glasses and tee shirt. "Look at this," he said, touching the T-shirt. "It says 'Cubits or Qubits, they all add up.'"

"What does it mean?" Cotten asked.

John turned around. "Isn't qubits with a Q a computer term?"

Max said, "It's short for a quantum bit, a unit of quantum information stored in a quantum computer."

Alan said, "'Qubits and cubits' is an interesting play on words."

John said, "Looks like Kai is being honest about where Mace got the thodium. It's too much of a coincidence for this guy, Tor, to be wearing a T-shirt that says cubits or qubits. The shirt suggests there's a connection between the two. Cubits, spelled with a C, is an ancient measurement of length. God gave Noah the dimensions of the Ark in cubits—three hundred cubits long, by fifty cubits wide, by thirty cubits high."

"What did you say?" Max's eyes blinked rapidly. "Can you repeat that?"

"Three hundred cubits, by fifty cubits, by thirty cubits."

Max thrust his arms in the air. "Holy shit!"

THE LEAP

"What is it, Max?" John said.

Max had both hands on his head in amazement. "Those measurements, the dimensions of the Ark, are exactly the same as the dimensions of the thodium crystal we intend to use in the Destiny computer—three hundred atoms by fifty atoms by thirty. Each one of those atoms holds a qubit of information. Destiny will hold four hundred fifty-thousand qubits."

Alan's face was solemn, and he stared blankly.

"You all right, Alan?" Cotten asked.

"Yeah, yeah," he said nodding. "I'm fine." Alan met John's gaze. "You told me I didn't have to buy into everything . . . and I didn't. But now . . . I don't know. There's just too much for me to ignore. I don't like it. I've always considered myself grounded in certainty—scientific facts. But we just made the leap from science into something else. Something foreign to me."

John put his hand on Alan's shoulder. "The perceived gap between science and religion is not as wide as it seems once you've made the leap. Trust me, Alan. I've seen it happen more times than I can count, so don't rush it."

"It's not a matter of rushing anything, I just feel like I've been blindsided. When I got up this morning, I never expected anything like this." He ran his hand over his face. "So, where can we get a piece of Noah's Ark?"

"Kai said Mace got it from the Baghdad Museum," John said. "That's obviously out. Who knows where any of the artifacts from the Ark are now—the museum was ransacked right after the invasion. And you know what's funny? When those pieces of the Ark were first discovered, there was very little news about it. I think that, mostly, no one believed it. It was regarded as a hoax by a majority of the scientific world. Like the Ossuary of James. I recall that just before the Iraq War, there were some tests being scheduled to authenticate the fragments—at least date them and things like that. Then of course, the museum was wrecked, so nothing ever came about."

"Do you think there might be remains of the Ark somewhere?" Cotten asked. "Could we track them down?"

"Forget it," Kai said. "Rizben likes to tell the tale that he bought his fragments at a museum auction, but in reality, he's the mastermind behind the ransacking. He has all the pieces of the Ark."

"Dead end," Max said.

"The only way to stop Mace and his Hades Project is to beat him to the punch," Alan said. "It will take another quantum computer. Destiny."

"Isn't there some other source of thodium?" Cotten asked.

Max shook his head. "We haven't been able to find one."

John said, "Lumber from the Ark would have been quite valuable after the Flood waters receded. They would need it for building, for fire, tools, many different uses. There might be some structure, some item still in existence. Or maybe there were other objects made from the Tree."

"How would we find out?" Cotten asked. "Where would we even start? Does it say anything about other items in Genesis?"

"No," John said. "We won't find the answer in the Bible this time. But there are other sources."

"Like the Dead Sea Scrolls?" Alan said.

"You're close," John said. "There is a church called St. Mary of Zion that houses thousands of ancient Gnostic texts, scrolls, codices, and gospels. What we might be looking for is what's called the Book of Emzara. Many years ago, I remember reading that it was among the documents in the treasury church of Saint Mary of Zion. You don't hear much about the church's depository other than the suspicion that the Ark of the Covenant is hidden there. Or at least a lot of people believe that's where it is. There's no real proof."

"Like *Raiders of the Lost Ark*?" Kai said.

John smiled at her. "Exactly."

"So who is Emzara?" Cotten asked.

"Noah's wife," John said.

"And where's the church?" Max asked.

John pointed out Alan's office window toward the east. "Axum, Ethiopia."

AXUM

THE TWIN TURBOPROPS ROARED when the Ethiopian Airlines DHC-6 swung around for its approach to the small airfield in Axum. Cotten and John occupied the first two of the six passenger seats. The flight from the capital city of Addis Ababa had been turbulent because of a bad weather front that swept in earlier from the Red Sea.

The late afternoon light cast long shadows as Cotten stared down at the countryside surrounding the old city. Jagged peaks formed from the remnants of ancient volcanoes dotted the highland landscape, while a few dirt roads stretched across parched farmland.

She was anxious—not comfortable flying on any airplane, much less one so small. Gripping the armrests, she glanced at John across the narrow aisle. "I hate landing," she said.

The tires bit into the dusty landing strip, and the plane vibrated as the pilot applied the brakes and reversed the engines. Soon, the plane slowed enough to turn and taxi toward the small terminal.

Once the aircraft was parked and the engines wound down, the passengers were allowed to disembark. Clutching a small carryall each, Cotten and John made their way across the open field to the terminal and on through the building to the gravel parking lot.

A short, potbellied black man came toward them. He was wearing a threadbare three-piece suit, a New York Yankees baseball cap, and sandals. With a heavy accent, he said, "Your Eminence, it is with my extreme honor to be in person and greet a prince of the Roman Church." He grasped John's hand, dropped to one knee, and held it to his forehead.

John blessed the man with the sign of the cross.

"We welcome your presence," the man said, getting to his feet. "I am Berhanu, your guide." He shook John's hand and then Cotten's. "And it is also the huge pleasure to meet a famous person, as you are." He looked back to John. "Many funds were wired ahead to be paying my services and also your rooms at the African Hotel. How long are you to stay?"

"Just tonight," John said. "We leave on the return flight to the capital tomorrow morning."

Berhanu pointed to a vintage Land Rover parked a few yards away. Its color was a combination of faded orange and lime green among patches of rust and Bondo. The side window was spiderwebbed with cracks spreading from a bullet hole.

"Someone use your car for target practice?" Cotten asked as they approached it.

"Oh, no. They were definitely trying to kill me." Berhanu laughed as he held the side door open for her. "Fortunately, they were not shooting good. War is always close by in Ethiopia."

Cotten got in the back seat while John joined Berhanu in the front, and they drove from the airfield toward town.

The ride was noisy, and Cotten had to lean forward to be heard. "Did they tell you why we are in Axum?"

"Yes," Berhanu said. "You wish that to visit the holy church of the St. Mary of Zion." He crossed himself.

"Right," John said. "An arrangement has been made for us to meet with the guardian monk."

"And I am your person who translates all that he speaks."

"Can we go directly there now, Berhanu?" Cotten asked. "I know it's late in the day, but we are anxious to speak with him."

"I am driver for you," Berhanu said. "If you wish straight away, then I take you."

Cotten watched as they passed small shops and open food markets lining the dirt roads. The thick dust, like the poverty, was everywhere. Young boys swarmed the car with outstretched hands, trailing behind the Land Rover, begging for handouts or a few birr. The buildings were old and in disrepair—she saw only dirt roads and ill-kept paths connecting the neighborhoods. Piles of trash and garbage dotted the landscape. Cotten felt something close to guilt or shame for having money in her pocket and the lifestyle she enjoyed with her job at SNN.

"Berhanu, do you live here in Axum?" Cotten asked.

"Yes. I was birthed here and am the worker for the Ministry of Culture. My job is to keep watching out with an open eye for the treasures of Axum." He turned the Land Rover onto a potholed road and motioned to the right. "What you see there are all that's remaining of the palace of the Queen of Sheba. She was married to King Solomon."

A hundred yards down the side of a gently sloping hill, Cotten made out the remains of low walls forming the ruins of an ancient building.

About a mile farther along the bumpy road, Berhanu said, "And there is the destination for which you are arriving." He motioned to a spacious walled compound on their left. It contained two churches, the larger one appeared old, and the smaller a much more recent design with a domed roof and a bell tower in the shape of an obelisk.

"Which is St. Mary of Zion?" Cotten asked.

"Both," Berhanu said. "The ancient church dates to the seventeenth century. It was the building for which the great Emperor Fasilidas made."

"And the new one?" John said.

"The treasury church became built about thirty-five years previous from today."

"Is it true that the Ark of the Covenant is kept inside?" Cotten asked.

"Quite, yes," Berhanu said.

"And have you seen it?" John asked.

"No, no." With a swift, jabbing motion, he crossed himself again and glanced up at the inside roof of the Land Rover as if seeking forgiveness for even thinking himself worthy. "The guardian monk is the all who sees what is inside the treasury church. He alone can look upon the blessed Ark."

"Have you met the monk?" John asked.

He shook his head. "The guardian monk lives in seclusion. He received his calling before my birth, so he is never seen by my eyes."

Berhanu pulled the Land Rover up to the front gate of the church of St. Mary of Zion. "And now we arrived."

Getting out, Cotten looked at the older of the two churches. It reminded her of a castle with its tall, grand turrets and imposing battlements ringing the tops of the walls.

Moving through the gate, they approached the large double latticed doors and entered the old building. Within its dimly lit interior, Cotten saw murals covering almost all the walls and ceiling including one depicting the life of Mary and another series showing the Crucifixion and Resurrection. There seemed to be a perpetual veil of candle and incense smoke creating a milky, soft glow to everything. From the far recesses of the church beyond the altar came the scraping of feet on stone. A figure appeared. He must have heard them enter.

Cotten watched the man, stooped and leaning on a prayer staff, shuffle toward her. Dressed in a long flowing white robe, he was old and bearded. When he finally stood before her, he spoke at length in Tigrigna, the local language. His voice was meek, reminding her of an un-oiled door hinge. She noticed he was toothless. When he finished, Cotten and John turned in unison to Berhanu.

Berhanu, who kept his eyes cast downward in the presence of the holy man, conversed briefly with the monk, and then looked to Cotten and John. "He asked who you are, and I told him you are the visitors he agreed to see. He says he has pleasure in meeting you and has wishes to serve you."

"Tell him we are pleased as well," Cotten said.

Berhanu again looked at the floor as he translated.

Introductions complete, the monk slowly extended his hand to John. Then he turned to Cotten and did the same. As she grasped it, Cotten smelled the faint but unmistakable scent of frankincense. "It is an honor, Father," she said.

The guardian monk stiffened. His eyes met hers, and although they were clouded with cataracts and sunken with age, he focused intently.

As a trace of a smile crossed his lips, Cotten felt uneasiness rush through her, and tried to release his hand. He kept his grip firm.

The monk spoke barely above a whisper before he let go of her hand.

John glanced at Berhanu.

The guide shrugged, his jaw agape. "I'm sorry, but I did not understand." He looked perplexed and frustrated. "It was in a speaking foreign to my ears."

Cotten stared at the monk in amazement. He had spoken in Enochian, the language of heaven, the tongue of the angels—a language she clearly understood, which meant he understood who she was, her legacy and her destiny.

And his words filled her with wonder.

BEYOND THE VEIL

"What did he say?" John asked. They stood in the back of the sanctuary of St. Mary of Zion church. The guardian monk had opened a door leading out through a walled garden to the smaller treasury church.

"That he knew my father," Cotten said, still dazed from having the monk speak to her in Enochian. "That my father was pleased I had come here, and that there are things inside that I should see."

"That's impossible," John whispered. "How would he have known you father?"

Cotten shook her head and shrugged. "I don't know—"

"I'm afraid that we can go not beyond this door," Berhanu said, holding his hand up to John. "The holy monk speaks that it is forbidden. Only Miss Stone may be proceeding into the treasury church."

John turned to meet Cotten's gaze. "You don't have to go alone if you're uncomfortable. Let's just tell him what we need—give him a list."

"I want to go," Cotten said. "After what he said, I'm compelled."

"Are you sure?" John touched her arm.

She closed her eyes and relished his touch for a moment. "Yes. Maybe I'll learn something about my father—if nothing else, that he's finally at peace."

The guardian monk spoke again to Cotten.

John gave her a questioning look.

"He said he will show me the Book of Emzara—that it will reveal all we seek."

"I don't feel good about this," John said.

"I'm a big girl." She smiled. "Let me go get what we need and be done with it."

With obvious reluctance, John stepped back. "I'll be waiting right here."

As she followed the monk through the church door, she glanced over her shoulder at John before the door closed with a sense of finality.

Cotten realized that twilight had quickly embraced the countryside. The pale moonlight and the glow from the town combined with the African star-filled sky, now cloudless after the passing weather system. The treasury church was a short walk along a path through a thick stand of trees. The building loomed out of the darkness, a boxy stone structure about fifty feet square. A tall brick wall topped with iron fencing surrounded it.

The monk unlocked a barred metal gate and led Cotten a few yards farther to the treasury entrance—an imposing wooden door on which was painted a portrait of St. Mary surrounded by saints and angels, Joseph, and the infant Jesus. He inserted a key into the lock and pulled the massive door open.

As Cotten followed him, she was struck by the intense fragrance of candle smoke and incense. Around the perimeter of the large room hung hundreds of candle lanterns suspended from heavy wooden beams by chains of varying lengths—each flame encased behind red glass lenses. The room glowed with a shimmering ruby red light that constantly moved like sunbeams through water.

Shelves lined the walls, reminding Cotten of what her mother called pigeonholes and cubbies. Each varied in size and held books, scrolls, piles of paper and parchment, and other small objects. There were thousands.

In the middle of the room stood a marble altar on which sat a collection of what appeared to be hundreds of antique objects—crowns, crosses, daggers, ancient books bound in thick leather and encrusted with jewels, and many more items Cotten could not fully identify through the smoky haze.

As she stood mesmerized by the uniqueness of her surroundings, a hot breeze brushed past her, causing her to wonder where it came from in the closed building. In the distance, through the haze, Cotten saw a thin veil of gauze-like cloth hanging from ceiling to floor—the breeze had moved it just enough for her to distinguish it from the smoke.

In English, the guardian monk said, "Do you wish to go beyond the veil and cast your eyes upon the Ark of the Covenant?"

Stunned, Cotten spun around. "You speak English?"

"I speak many languages."

A chill enveloped her. A shudder moved through her like the first tremors of an earthquake. *Maybe coming alone was a bad decision.* Feeling lightheaded, Cotten braced herself against a wooden bookcase. Her sight narrowed like looking through a tunnel. Darkness squeezed in, blurring her peripheral vision.

"Something wrong?" the monk asked, his form becoming less distinct as he drifted in and out of the smoke.

She pressed her fingertips to her temples. "No. I'm fine." A buzzing sound filled her ears, and the violent thumping of her heart slammed against her sternum.

"I asked if you wish to look upon the Holy Ark."

"No," Cotten said, fighting to keep her equilibrium. "I'm here regarding a different Ark—Noah's Ark. And the Book of his wife, Emzara. I need to see . . ."

She fought to focus her thoughts. *Keep talking. Keep your mind on task.* "We have to search the Book of Emzara for any reference to objects that could have been forged or shaped from the Tree of Life. I need to know if there is a manifest."

She looked at the monk and saw a twisted smile on his face. When he spoke it came to her ears as an echo.

"Since you do not desire to look upon the Holy Ark, it is all the more reason that you must. For within it lies your destiny. Let it reveal the secrets concerning your father, Furmiel."

Mindlessly, remarkably lacking any self-will, Cotten followed him until they stood before the thin veil of cloth—a slightly transparent barrier protecting what she guessed was the Holy of Holies, the Ark of the Covenant.

Cotten noticed light coming from the other side. More candles, intensely red, lit the chamber behind the sheer material.

Using the tip of his prayer staff, the monk separated a seam of the veil. Holding it aside, he motioned for Cotten to proceed.

Like the main sanctuary, this one also had dozens of hanging candle lanterns, their ruby light glittering. In the middle of the chamber, a long canopy of silky gauze hung from the ceiling and flared at the bottom. The monk moved to the canopy and slipped his hand into a space dividing two seams. Reverently he pulled back the material, exposing a golden chest resting upon a low marble stand.

Cotten gasped as her eyes filled with the reflection of the flickering candlelight. It was as if the object had trapped the stars. The golden sides were embossed with the image of a spreading tree, and atop the chest were two kneeling cherubs. They faced each other, and their outstretched wingtips met in the center. The air thickened and her breathing became labored. Beads of sweat gathered and dribbled down her back and between her breasts—her legs wobbled.

"Come forward," the monk whispered. "Bear witness to the wonder."

Cotten stepped within inches of the golden chest. She extended her hand and held it over the relic, somehow feeling its energy flow into her. Like the faint tingle of electricity, it stimulated her skin.

The monk grasped the hinged top of the Ark, swinging open the lid with its shimmering cherubs. Like the outside, the interior was lined with gold. Cotten leaned over and gazed inside. What she saw made her reel backward, and she realized in that instant that she had made a terrible mistake.

ASHES

When Cotten gazed into the Ark of the Covenant, she did not see the expected tablets of the Ten Commandments. Instead, she stared into the eternal fires of Hell.

The sickening odor of sulfur replaced the aromatic incense, and a blast of blistering wind slammed her onto the floor. Like a magician's flash paper, the silky gauze canopy that enclosed the Ark erupted into flames. An instant later, the ashes of the loosely woven fabric floated through the air like black leaves from a diseased tree.

Screams of tormented souls filled the church, a sound resembling the scraping of giant metal machines colliding. Cotten pressed her palms to her ears to block out the piercing noise. Spinning in wide arcs above her, the ruby candle lanterns blazed like exploding stars.

As if glaring into a blast furnace, the glow from the Ark intensified until the priceless artifact melted into a molten mass.

Squinting, Cotten realized that the guardian monk had transformed. Standing over her was a gray-haired man—old, but not stooped or bearded or toothless. The wrinkles in his face were not folds of weary flesh, but rather finely chiseled lines, and his eyes raged with fire deep within the dark irises.

He was dressed in a suit the color of raven feathers. In his hand he held a book—its cover and bindings ancient and worn like an old leather glove, its pages starting to crumble into tiny pieces and rain down.

"Is this what you seek?" he asked.

His words cut through the screams and cries coming from the depths of the Ark, even though Cotten had covered her ears. She tried to focus on the book, but the maddening effect of the spinning candle lanterns made her dizzy.

"The Book of Emzara." He extended it to her.

Like fighting against a raging river current, she tried with all her strength to take the book. As her fingertips touched its surface, it ignited just as the gauze canopy had done—a momentary flash before it vaporized. She watched its ashes drift away, and knew the source of the answers she sought had just vanished forever.

"Go home, daughter of Furmiel. Your task has ended—you are too late, and too weak."

As quickly as the tumult began, it was over. The vision of the Old Man faded, becoming part of the smoke-filled room.

Cotten lay breathless on the church floor as the heat receded, the voices of the damned died away, and the frantic motion of the lanterns stilled. Slowly, she rose to her knees, then stood on shaky legs—the odor of incineration everywhere.

In the middle of the floor, the remains of the Ark of the Covenant had become a pool of smelted gold. As she stumbled away from the Holy of Holies, she saw that piles of ashes filled the thousands of pigeonholes. Upon the altar, the ancient relics were nothing but unrecognizable heaps of cremation. A pall of gray haze settled over the interior of the church while Cotten made her way to the entrance. Pulling on the heavy door, she stumbled into the clear African night. Breathing deeply, she tried to clear her lungs of the stench, her mouth of the bitter taste, and her head of the terrible cries.

Looking up through a cloud of confusion and blurry eyes, she saw a man rushing toward her, and she suddenly fell into the arms of John Tyler.

———

"Where am I?" Cotten asked, looking at John's face. She lay on a bed in a sparsely furnished room—the only light was a lamp on a bedside table.

"A room at the African Hotel," John said, sitting on the side of the bed. "You passed out, and Berhanu and I brought you here. I wanted to take you to a medical clinic, but he said the closest one is across the border in Asmara, about seventy miles away."

Cotten slowly sat up, swinging her legs over the edge of the bed. As if a great revelation came flooding over her, she said, "The church, the Ark of the Covenant, all those priceless objects and documents, all burned to ash."

John gave her a confused look. "Burned?" He shook his head. "What are you talking about?"

THE ARCHIVES

"COTTEN, NOTHING BURNED DOWN." John handed her a wet cloth. "Here, use this to wipe your face. It'll make you feel better."

"Where is the guardian monk?" she asked, taking the cloth.

"At the monastery, I assume. He followed you out of the church and said you were overcome from the smoke of the candles. He suggested we take you someplace to rest."

Cotten recalled the transformation of the monk, his taunting her with the Book of Emzara, and his warning to go home. She put her face in her hands. He hadn't been the guardian monk at all—the man who led her into the treasury church was evil incarnate, her mortal enemy, the Son of the Dawn—Lucifer. He had lured her inside to terrorize her with a dramatic display of his power and to let her know that he had the secrets to the Book of Emzara, and that she never would—that she could never defeat him. Now she also understood what he had meant when he said he knew her father, Furmiel, the Angel of the Eleventh Hour. He referred to knowing her father before he had repented—eons ago when Furmiel and Lucifer were both a part of the legion of the Fallen Angels. Lucifer abhorred Furmiel—the only Fallen Angel to ever beg for God's forgiveness. Most of all, Lucifer hated Cotten—the living reminder of Furmiel's betrayal.

"If this is all of my needs for this tonight, I will be gone home to my family," Berhanu said.

It was the first time that Cotten had noticed the guide sitting in a chair nearby.

Berhanu glanced at his watch. "Will there be more of my services?"

"No, nothing else," John said.

Berhanu bowed, and John walked him to the door. The guide stepped into the hall, but then turned, his palms together like he was praying. "I hope with sincerity that Cotten Stone will feel much fine and have a pleasant trip back to America."

"Thank you, Berhanu," John said, blessing him. "We wish you and your family well."

John closed the door and returned to Cotten's bedside. "I'm sorry you had to go through this for no reason."

Cotten stared at him.

"The monk told us that as he retrieved the Book of Emzara from a pile of ancient scrolls, it literally disintegrated to dust in his hands. He said he offered to search through other books in the church library, but that's when you became dizzy and wanted to leave."

Cotten slowly shook her head.

"He said that when you first entered the church, you asked to see the Ark of the Covenant, but he had to refuse. No one is allowed to see it but the guardian monk. He told us you demanded to look see it."

"I did see it, John. He showed it to me." She whispered, "I witnessed it melt and burn . . ."

"You saw what burn? What are you talking about?"

Where to begin? she thought.

But she knew where to start.

From the moment she had looked into the eyes of the Beast.

———

They sat in the waiting area of the Bole International Airport in Addis Ababa, Ethiopia. Their British Airlines flight to Rome was about to board.

"Then it's obvious that the Book of Emzara is extremely important to the Fallen Ones," John said. "We can assume that an item made from the Tree is noted in that book, either in narrative or on a manifest. The big questions are—do any of those objects still exist, and if so, what and where?"

"And they already have the book," Cotten said, "which means they have a head start in searching for what might be the only source of thodium left in the world."

She still experienced the effects from the incident in the treasury church the night before. She was unsteady and lethargic, even after a restful sleep in the African Hotel. A native breakfast of *injeera*—a baked flatbread similar to pizza—covered with local meats and cheese—helped her regain some of her energy before she and John flew back to the Ethiopian capital.

"You're right," John said. "Why else would the Fallen stage such an elaborate illusion?"

"Even if we identify a possible object from the Ark, what are the chances that it is still around after five thousand years?" She rubbed her forehead—a dull headache had persisted through the night and refused to go away. The faint odor of sulfur still lingered in her nostrils even though she had taken a long, steamy shower. "… not to mention that we'll never find another copy of the Emzara text."

"Our chances are better than you might expect. I'm convinced that a copy survives somewhere. I've got the Venatori research division looking in two places—the Coptic Museum in Cairo where the Nag Hammadi Library is housed and also in the Secret Archives of the Vatican where they should find transcripts that originated from the First Council of Nicaea. In both cases, early Christian Gnostic texts had references to Noah and Emzara. Maybe we'll get lucky."

"I've heard the term, Gnostic," Cotten said, "but I don't know what that means." She watched a group of tourists wander by, their conversation washed in a heavy French accent.

"Gnostics were religious groups that existed in the first couple of centuries AD. They considered themselves Christians, but tended to base their beliefs outside the mainstream. The term is Greek for a type of understanding or consciousness gained from personal transcendental experience. The Gnostic Gospels are ancient texts that contain details on the life of Christ not included in the New Testament—texts such as the Gospels of Mary Magdalene, Philip, Sophia, Thomas, and others. But they also include transcripts from the writings of Old Testament characters such as Adam to his third son, Seth, including a prediction of the Great Deluge. There are a few partial documents that refer to Noah and

Emzara. Some are no more than fragments of crumbling papyrus, but at this point, it may be all we've got."

"So even though some of the texts from the Council of Nicaea were lost or destroyed, there's still documentation on them?"

"There were many books of supposed prophets floating around up until the year 312 when the Council bishops took it upon themselves to decide which were keepers and which ones were tossed. But someone was always in the background taking notes during every proceeding. I believe many of those notes are still around."

"So they picked and chose what fell into step with the Church teachings and threw out the rest?"

"Pretty much. One of the most notable is the account of the raising of Lazarus, which was removed from Mark's gospel on the instructions of the Council bishops. They felt that the way he wrote it had overtones of a mystical cult. It still wound up in Luke and John."

"Are you kidding? The whole Bible has mystical overtones," Cotten said.

John smiled. "I wouldn't go that far."

"Sorry, Your Eminence," she said, grinning. "Didn't mean to ruffle the cardinal's feathers."

"Mystical overtones or not, the problem we're going to face is that the Vatican archives are huge. There are more than thirty miles of shelves, the majority covered with books and boxes of still uncatalogued records and documents—tens of thousands of documents gathered by the Venatori and other Vatican secret agents, envoys, and diplomats spanning more than a thousand years. Many secrets that were determined by the church fathers to be buried would take lifetimes to find—if they exist at all."

John's cell phone rang, and he pulled it from his belt clip. Looking at the caller ID, he said, "It's the Archives prefect." He listened intently for a moment before snapping the phone shut. With a smile he turned to Cotten and winked. "You must be living right."

———

The black S550 Mercedes slipped through the *Porta Sant'Anna* entrance to Vatican City. It sped past the Vatican Bank and the Apostolic Palace. Turning right, it pulled up in front of a gated courtyard about fifty feet beyond the Vatican Library. The driver and front-seat passenger, both Venatori agents, got out and held open the rear doors for Cotten and John. Two members of the Swiss Guard stood beside the gate and saluted as John motioned Cotten into the courtyard. A dozen paces beyond was the nondescript, easily overlooked entrance to the Secret Archives.

Inside, Cotten was surprised to see what resembled a hotel check-in desk staffed by two young Italian men.

In a thick accent, one of the men said, "Your Eminence Cardinal Tyler, welcome. It is always a pleasure to have you visit us." He turned to Cotten. "Ms. Stone, it is an honor to meet the person who recovered for all mankind, the Cup of Christ." Then he stepped around the desk, shook both their hands, and said, "This way, please. They are waiting for you."

The young man led them through the ground-floor library and *sala di studio* where a handful of scholars worked.

"They limit the number of researchers who are allowed in here to about two hundred a year," John said to Cotten. "And the approval process to get in can take an eternity as well. If you're permitted to do archives research, you must stay seated in this room and request what you need to the assistants. Everything is brought to you."

Cotten saw two rows of antique desks, each one about six feet long.

"It wasn't that long ago that they added electrical outlets at the desks for laptops," John said. "Wireless will take a miracle."

Leaving the studio of the scholars, they headed for a tiny European-style elevator, the kind that barely held three people at a time. As they stepped inside, Cotten felt it bounce as the cables stretched.

"Below us is what they refer to as the Bunker," John said. "It's the manuscript depository where the bulk of the archives are housed. But we're heading up to the *piani nobili*, the rooms that contained the original secret archives. The Borghese Pope Paul the Fifth established the archives in 1610. He had a somewhat inflated ego and decided to have his name chiseled dead center over the main entrance to Saint Peter's Basilica. Today, it would be the equivalent of Tony Blair painting 'Tony's Place' over the entrance to Number Ten Downing Street."

Cotten shook her head in incredulity. *Above all else, the popes were mere mortals after all*, she thought.

They got off the elevator and headed into a long, narrow room with lofty ceilings covered with colorful murals of celebrated papal events. An enormous portrait dominated one wall.

"Speaking of the devil," John said with a chuckle and pointed to the painting. "Paul the Fifth, ego and all."

A series of *armadi*—wooden closets—lined the room. Cotten saw two priests, both wearing black cassocks, standing beside one— the door agape. All the other closets were closed and padlocked. In front of the open closet stood a table covered with dark and yellowed parchments.

As Cotten and John approached, one of the priests said, "Your Eminence, we have located the records of the First Council of Nicaea."

"And you've found a transcript of the Book of Emzara?" John asked.

"We have, Eminence," the second priest said.

"Is there a list of items carried on the Ark?" Cotten said.

"Yes," the first priest said.

Cotten felt her pulse quicken with excitement. Perhaps they were not chasing a lost cause after all.

"And," the priest added, "we have come across something extraordinarily puzzling, and much, much more."

GHOST OF GALILEO

COTTEN STOOD IN THE Meridian Room, the uppermost chamber of the *Torre Dei Venti*, the Tower of the Winds. Constructed high above the Vatican's Secret Archives, the room had remained virtually unchanged since the sixteenth century. She stared at frescoes by Nicolo Circignani depicting events in the life of Christ and Saint Paul. Her heart beat quicker knowing she stood in the same spot where Galileo had argued with church curia that the earth revolved around the sun and not vice versa. But more importantly, she pondered the riddle found in the Book of Emzara.

She heard footsteps and turned to see John coming up the circular set of metal steps. He held a small stack of papers.

"Standing in this place is such a rush," she said as he approached.

"It does tend to humble you."

"So what have you found?"

"I ran the Greek and Latin translations by three of our best linguistic scholars. They all came to the same conclusions."

"Which are?"

"There is one curious item in Emzara's list of what was brought aboard Noah's Ark, one amazing revelation on what the Ark was constructed from, and for you and me, the answer to a nagging question."

"Read it to me," she said.

John looked at the papers for a moment. "Emzara overhears God talking to her husband. She writes, 'And God said to Noah, You are righteous and holy. And God said, preserve that which is righteous. Protect all that is created from the seed of Adam and the blood of the Tree of Life. For I will make a covenant with you and your sons. I will set my bow in the clouds as a sign of my covenant. I will never again destroy by water that which man has made. Not from the clouds but from the seed of Adam will come the thunderbolt. And it will be there on the day when my vengeance will once again destroy that which violates my land. And God said, Fear not, for they will know that I am the Lord Thy God, and I will show them the sign.'"

"What is the thunderbolt?"

"Not sure." John shuffled through the pages. "The actual inventory—the manifest if you will—is very close to the list in Genesis. Seven pairs of all the clean animals and two pairs each of the unclean."

"Clean? Unclean?"

"Probably indicated the different types of animals they were allowed to eat or not eat." John glanced at the notes again. "Emzara also mentions that they gathered together clothing, food, seeds, grain, bedding, nails, a couple of oxen carts, farm tools, and finally the mysterious reference to the thunderbolt, something made by

Tubal Cain from the blood of the tree of life—the item that has stumped everyone."

"Then whatever the thunderbolt is," Cotten said, "it's got to be the object we're looking for, right?"

"That's the best guess. It's the only item on her list that mentions who made it—Tubal Cain, the great, great, grandson of Adam. He was a blacksmith and his specialty was weapons. Thunderbolt must refer to a weapon forged by Tubal Cain from the hardened sap of the Tree of Life."

"So what's the revelation?"

"That the Ark was constructed from the actual Tree that grew east of the Garden. This confirms what Kai confessed was the source of the thodium being used in the Hades Project—crystallized resin from the Ark. Genesis says that God commanded Noah to construct the Ark from resin wood. So far, no one has ever positively identified what resin wood is. This nails it."

"And there's the reference to the signs God would leave us," Cotten said. "They've been there all along—the signature thunderbolt on all of Tera's artwork. Even the CyberSys logo. How could we have missed those obvious connections?"

"How many times have I told you the answer to everything is right in the Bible?"

"Even the qubits and cubits conversion—the dimensions of the Ark and the exact dimensions of the storage qubits needed for the quantum computers. Maybe I should start listening to you more often," she said smiling.

John spread his hands in an "I told you so" gesture.

"So if the thunderbolt is a weapon—" Cotten heard a commotion coming from the base of the spiraling metal steps. She and

John turned as murmuring voices were followed by the muffled sound of footfalls on the metal.

A man came up the steps. At first, Cotten saw his snowy hair, thick and wavy. Then the pale face with the wire-rimmed glasses, the white cassock—a gold chain and crucifix hanging from his neck. Finally, the famous red shoes.

"I'm grateful there are few stairs in the Vatican like those," he said in a slightly winded German accent. "Perhaps that's why I don't make the trip up here too often."

"Your Holiness," John said. He dropped to one knee and kissed the ring on the outstretched hand of the pontiff.

The pope motioned for him to rise. "John, I have been told by reliable sources that you and Ms. Stone are hoping the ghost of Galileo will help you solve your five-thousand-year-old mystery."

Cotten stepped forward. "Galileo's ghost hasn't granted us an audience, Your Holiness, but it is an honor to finally meet you." She took his hand in both of hers.

"Ms. Stone, the honor is all mine. In this very building, perhaps no more than a few hundred paces from where we stand, rests the single most important religious relic of the past two thousand years—the Cup of Christ, the Holy Grail. And it is here solely because of you. Not only did you recover it—twice, I might add—and present it to the Church, but you did so after stopping what would have been a great and terrible tragedy."

Crossing his arms, the pope stood back and stared up with a look of wonder at the ceiling of the Meridian Room. "Do you see the mural of Christ calming the sea?"

Cotten and John gazed in the direction he indicated.

"Look in the top right-hand corner, in the middle of the portrait of the elderly gentleman puffing his cheeks. There is a small opening approximately the side of a coin." The pontiff then pointed to the marble floor of the Meridian Room where the signs of the zodiac were etched and a meridian line cut down the middle. "Each March twenty-first, the sun shines through that tiny hole and strikes the vernal equinox line here on the floor. It was designed by the first official Vatican astronomer, a brilliant priest by the name of Ignazio Danti in the 1500s." He gestured to the symbols at his feet. "I have stood on this spot and witnessed it. Quite moving." The pope smiled at them both. "So now you want to know what is the meaning of the reference to thunderbolt in the Book of Emzara?"

"Your Holiness," Cotten said, "it is imperative that we find the object known as the thunderbolt."

"We are afraid that if we don't find it first, it will fall into the hands of the Nephilim," John said. "And from what we have learned, they plan to use it to bring about global chaos."

The pope silenced them with an upturned palm. "Like the others, I, too, was confounded by the *thunderbolt,* in the Book of Emzara. And so I did what I do whenever I seek understanding. I handed over my question to God and trusted He would answer. And so He has." He fixed his eyes on Cotten. "Part of the answer came to me by remembering who you are and what you have done. Ms. Stone, the Cup of Christ once held the blood of Jesus Christ collected at the Crucifixion. Correct?"

Cotten nodded.

He looked to John. "What caused the blood to flow from Our Savior into the Cup?"

"A Roman centurion pierced Christ's side with a lance," John said, appearing to think out each word as he spoke. "According to the Scriptures, out poured a mixture of blood and water."

The pope gripped the cross that hung at his chest and set his eyes on Cotten's. "You have come full circle, Cotten Stone. What you seek is in the Hapsburg museum."

THE LEGEND

COTTEN WATCHED OUT THE window of the Gulfstream G150 as it streaked across the amethyst-colored evening sky on a course over the Adriatic Sea from Rome to Vienna. The Vatican City crest sparkled on the jet's gleaming white skin. She was tired, but could not sleep. Though she had long accepted her destiny in this world, it still weighed heavily, especially when everything always seemed to spiral back to who she was—the daughter of a Fallen Angel, the product of a pact between her repentant father and God.

She heard the pope's words again in her head. "The revelation given to me about the *thunderbolt* began with my recollection of who you are." He went on to tell her that the spear forged by Tubal Cain was carried on the Ark by Noah, and it is the same spear that was later used to pierce the side of Christ. Blood flowed from the wound, and His blood filled the Cup. The pope reminded Cotten that she had held the Cup in her hands, and now she searched for the object that caused it to fill with the blood of Jesus Christ—thereby coming full circle in her quest. His exact words still rang in her mind. "The thunderbolt you seek is the Holy Lance, known to the world as the Spear of Destiny."

Cotten turned away from the darkening sky. She and John sat in side-by-side leather seats, a narrow aisle separating them. In front of John was a curly maple-top desk on which rested a thick red folder, its cover inscribed with the words: *For the Eyes of the Director*. Beneath the inscription was the seal of the Venatori—a round emblem showing a raging lion and a longsword with the motto: *Umbrae Manium, Arma Dei*—Shadows of Ghosts, Armor of God. The folder contained John's daily security briefing.

At the other end of the short desk, in a seat facing them, was Carlo Zanini, a thirty-five-year-old Italian priest who had joined the Venatori to work in their research division as an expert on medieval mythology and Old Testament history.

Under a tousled mop of thick black hair, Zanini stared at an open laptop screen through thick, horn-rimmed glasses. He scrolled down a series of data files and finally chose one with the click of the mouse. Once it opened, he said, "The Spear has an amazing history, just as His Holiness told you. The Book of Emzara refers to it as Thunderbolt and claims it was forged from the blood of the Tree of Life by Tubal Cain, a blacksmith and seventh generation grandson of Adam. No doubt the blood refers to the hardened sap from the Tree that grew in the Garden. As we've already learned from Emzara's text, God instructed Noah to carry the Thunderbolt aboard the Ark to be preserved and protected for use at some future time. It is the only article other than the actual Ark itself to be made from the Tree—the vessel was constructed from timbers cut from the Tree." Zanini opened another document as he pushed the heavy glasses up his noble Roman nose.

"So the next time it shows up is at the Crucifixion?" Cotten asked as she made a note on a yellow legal pad.

"Actually, no," Zanini said. "We were able to find a reference in the Nag Hammadi Library scrolls in Cairo that mentioned Joshua holding up the Thunderbolt Spear as he signaled his soldiers to shout a 'great shout' which brought down the walls of Jericho. Also in the Cairo library, our researchers found a text stating that the Thunderbolt Spear was hurled at young David by King Saul in a fit of jealousy.

"The Spear passed through the hands of Ehud, the second judge of the Israelites, and Ahab, the King of Israel. That was around 852 BC. Eventually it wound up in the possession of Pompey who later gave it to Julius Caesar. Caesar presented the Thunderbolt Spear to a Roman commander in recognition of years of devoted service. That commander was the grandfather of a soldier named Gaius Cassius. Many years later, in the hands of the grandson, the true legend of the Thunderbolt Spear began."

Zanini read off the laptop's LCD for a moment, then said, "On April fifth in 33 AD, Annas, the advisor to the Sanhedrin, and Caiaphas, the Jewish High Priest, conspired to have Jesus crucified and his body mutilated to prove to the masses that he was not the Messiah but only a mortal man, and a heretic. It was on a Friday, and the Sabbath began at sundown.

"Jewish law decreed that no man should be executed on the Sabbath. As the day wore on, and Jesus hadn't died, Annas and Caiaphas started to panic, since time was running out. They wanted to make sure Christ didn't expire after sunset, so they petitioned Pontius Pilate to let them send their own temple guard out to Golgotha—the Place of the Skull—and make sure Jesus and the other two men crucified that day died before sundown. The Roman soldiers on duty turned their backs in disgust at the brutality of the temple guards as they clubbed and crushed the skulls and limbs of the two thieves, Gestas and Dismas.

"Now, remember the grandson, Gaisus Cassius? This was years later, and he was the senior Roman officer on duty that day. He saw that Jesus had expired, and decided that rather than let the Jews disfigure the body, he would confirm Jesus was already dead, thus avoiding the mutilation.

"The story goes that Gaisus was a veteran warrior, but he was getting old and his eyesight failing. It was also said that he carried Caesar's gift to his grandfather with him at all times. So with the lance in hand, he rode his horse up to the cross on which Jesus hung and thrust it into Christ's right side between the fourth and fifth ribs. This was a Roman battlefield practice that when they wanted to prove that a wounded enemy was truly dead, they pierced him with a spear or sword. The logic was that blood would not flow from a dead body. To everyone's surprise, out flowed blood and water from Christ's wound. As the blood ran down the shaft of the Spear, Gaisus got some in his eyes. In that instant, his failing sight was completely restored. Thus we have the first evidence of the Spear's power."

"I thought the Roman Centurion was called Longinus?" John said.

Zanini nodded. "That's correct, Eminence. After he had his sight restored, he became known throughout the region as Longinus

337

The Spearman. Soon after that, he left the military and converted to Christianity, spending the rest of his life preaching the teachings of Christ until he was martyred in Cappadocia in the first century. We know him today as Saint Longinus."

"Immortalized by Lorenzo Bernini with his bronze statue in Saint Peter's Basilica of Longinus holding the Spear," John added.

"Okay," Cotten said. "But how did the Spear wind up in a display case in the Hapsburg Museum in Vienna?" She stood, took an aluminum carafe of coffee from its holder and refreshed John's and Zanini's cups before topping off her own.

Zanini said, "From here on out, the Spear leaves a rather bloody trail. It starts with the Celtic warrior queen, Boadicea, who tried to form an alliance with the Romans, but she demanded too much control for their liking. Rather than come under their domination, she called up an army of twenty thousand Celts and declared war on Rome. Longinus, along with his prized possession, had recently traveled to Britain as a military consultant. She asked him for advice, but being a loyal former centurion, he refused. Boadicea threw him in her castle's dungeon, and since she had heard all about the Spear's legendary power, she claimed it for her own. With it, she and her army massacred more than seventy thousand Roman settlers, soldiers, and their families. She sacked and burned three cities, including London. It was called Londonium at the time. It's said that on the battlefield, with the Spear in hand, Boadicea was invincible.

"By the time Nero finally sent enough reinforcements to defeat the queen's army, the bloodshed from her rampage was already enormous. Boadicea escaped during the final battle but accidentally left the Spear behind. The Romans captured it, and from that point it went underground for more than two hundred years."

Cotten gave Zanini an anxious *keep going* motion with her hand as he took a sip of coffee.

"Is she always this impatient?" he asked John.

"This is mild," John said with a shrug.

Setting his cup down, Zanini said, "In 286 AD, the Spear of Longinus, now called the Holy Lance, popped up in the possession of Maurice, a devout Coptic Christian and the commanding officer of a Roman legion stationed in Thebes in the northern part of Egypt. A dispute erupted when Maximian issued an order to his legions to take an oath naming him a god. The Roman soldiers under the command of Maurice were predominately Christian, and they refused. In a rage, Maximian had over six thousand soldiers executed for insubordination, including Maurice, and he ordered the Lance be brought to him. It all backfired on Maximian because Maurice was viewed as a martyr and later became Saint Maurice."

"Paybacks are hell," Cotten said, lifting her coffee mug in a toasting gesture.

"The influence of the Spear is undeniable," Zanini said. "This was approximately the time that its legacy was defined. Legend says that 'Whosoever possesses the Holy Lance and understands the powers it serves, holds in his hand the destiny of the world.'"

"Who got it next?" John asked.

"The next time we hear of it, the Holy Lance is in the possession of the illegitimate son of a Roman general and an innkeeper's daughter. The boy grew up to be one of the most powerful historical figures of all time, the Roman Emperor Constantine the Great."

"Did Maximian give it to him?" Cotten asked.

"Indirectly," Zanini said. "Constantine married Maximian's daughter. The emperor presented it to the couple as a wedding present. Constantine eventually converted to Christianity. With the Spear in hand, he declared himself to be the 'thirteenth Apostle' and proclaimed Christianity as the official religion of the Holy Roman Empire. As emperor, he established Constantinople—today's Istanbul.

"In 443, Attila the Hun laid siege to the city and said he would spare Constantinople in return for two things from then emperor Theodosius—six thousand pounds of gold, and the Holy Lance. Theodosius paid. Nine years later, Attila reached the gates of Rome but had to withdraw out of disgust because famine and disease ravaged the city. The legend says that when the Roman officers surrendered the city, Attila threw the Holy Lance at their feet in disgust and left.

"It came back to bite him in 451 when King Theodoric assembled the Visigothic army and joined up with the Romans and other tribes to defeat the Huns during the invasion of Gaul. But Theodoric was killed." Zanini smiled up at Cotten. "And the story is that he died within moments of the Holy Lance slipping from his hand."

"Is that really true?" Cotten asked.

Zanini arched both brows. "Legends all have some nugget of truth embedded." He took a sip of his coffee before studying the document on the computer screen, then continuing with the history. "The next owner was the Burgundian prince Sigismund who was a descendent of Theodoric. He didn't have it long, though. He was killed by his brother-in-law, King Clovis of the Franks. The Lance stayed in the family until the mid-700s when one of Clovis' descendants, Charles Martel, carried it into victorious battle to prevent Islam from spreading across Europe. Martel passed the Lance to his grandson, who became the second giant historical figure to possess the Spear of Longinus."

"Charlemagne," John said.

Zanini nodded. "In the course of changing the face of the world, it was said that the Holy Lance never left his side.

"Seventy-five years later we again see reference to the Lance when the German King Henry I received it as a gift from King Rudolph of Burgundy. Relying on the power of the Holy Lance, Rudolph defeated the Hungarian Magyars in 933. After his death, the Lance passed to Otto I and then on to Otto II and Otto III. Around the year 1000, a nail claimed to be from the Crucifixion of Jesus was inserted into the blade of the Lance, making it a double-powered relic.

"A hundred or so years later, the German King Henry IV had the Holy Lance fitted with a silver sleeve bearing the inscription *Clavus Dominicus,* meaning Nail of Our Lord, and it was about this time that the wooden shaft of the spear disappeared, leaving only the actual spear point remaining."

The phone on John's armrest chirped. "Yes?" A few seconds later, he hung up. "The pilot says we're forty-five minutes out of Vienna International Airport."

"Is there a lot left to the story, father?" Cotten asked Zanini as she sank back into the thick leather. "So far, it's been fascinating."

"We haven't even gotten to the best part," the Italian priest said with a smile. "Through a string of family bloodlines, the Lance

341

head, minus the shaft, eventually came into the possession of the House of Hohenstaufen, who were the descendants of the Saxon dynasty, and finally to the Roman Emperor Fredrick Barbarossa. He called for the Third Crusade to free Jerusalem from the Muslims, and carried the Holy Lance into battle. On June tenth in 1130, he fell from his horse into the Saleph River, broke his neck and drowned seconds after accidentally dropping the Lance.

"From there, the Lance went through a series of European kings including Frederick II who made the Holy Lance a central focal point of his monarchy, and used it as he led the Crusades. At one point, he allowed Saint Francis of Assisi to carry it on an errand of mercy.

"The Lance continued through the hands of three Hohenstaufen emperors. In 1424 Sigismund of Luxembourg sold the Lance to the town council of Nuremberg. It stayed on display there until 1806 when Napoleon came looking for it. German authorities smuggled it to Austria just ahead of the French troops so Emperor Bonaparte could not have it.

"In 1913, Kaiser Wilhelm tried to get his hands on the Holy Lance before declaring war. He petitioned the Hapsburg Emperor, Franz Joseph, in Vienna for use of the Spear, but was denied.

"The Holy Lance sat in a display case inside the Hapsburg Museum for years until along came the third giant historical figure to finally possess it—Adolf Hitler. His fascination with it probably began from his love of Richard Wagner's opera, *Parsifal*. The Spear played a major role in the work."

"Now we're into an area where I've done some research," John said. "Hitler annexed Austria, then ordered his SS troops to seize the Holy Lance, right?"

"Yes, Eminence," Zanini said. "Under Hitler's orders, the relic was transported on a heavily guarded express train to Nuremberg where he could have access to it whenever he wanted. It was kept in a fortified bunker beneath Saint Katherine's church. The vault was built in secret and at a huge expense to protect the relic from Allied bombs. Hitler hoped to rebuild the Holy Roman Empire with himself as supreme Emperor, and he believed he needed the Lance to do so.

"And in an ironic twist, on the afternoon of April 30, 1945, the Holy Lance was discovered and fell into the hands of American forces almost at the exact moment that Adolf Hitler committed suicide."

"Here's what I don't understand," Cotten said. "If the Lance is so powerful, why is it that some of its owners succeeded at using it while others, like Hitler, failed?"

"Just a theory," John said, "but I believe that success or failure is determined by what's in the heart of the person who possesses it."

The three seemed to ponder John's statement for a moment. Then Zanini said, "Here's another strange twist. While Adolf Hitler waited for so many years between his first sight of the Lance and the day he finally possessed it, Heinrich Himmler was so captivated by it that he had an exact replica made in 1935—three years before his Fuhrer marched into Austria."

"What happened to the replica?" Cotten asked.

Zanini shrugged. "No one knows for sure."

"So after the American forces captured the Holy Lance, its new owner was Harry Truman?" John asked.

"Technically," Zanini said. "Although he never actually touched it, while he had control over it, he introduced the world to the most destructive power in history—the atomic bomb."

"When was the Lance returned to Vienna?" Cotten asked.

"There was a bit of a debate about that between the U.S. and the Soviets. It seems that Stalin wanted to claim it after the Red Army raised their flag on the roof of the Reichstag in Berlin. But, in the end, Truman and Stalin agreed to let a U.S and Soviet delegation deliver the relic to the Austrian government, who then gave it back to the museum. That's where it's been ever since."

The phone in John's armrest chirped again. "Yes," he said, then listened for a moment. Replacing the phone, he turned to Cotten then back to Zanini. "That was the Vatican ambassador to Austria. The director of the Hapsburg Museum has agreed to the direct request from the Holy Father and will allow us to take the Spear from Vienna and transport it to CyberSys headquarters in Miami. Alan Olsen and our friends are scheduled to land about an hour behind us."

Cotten sighed out loud. "Once we have the Spear of Destiny, the threat of the Hades Project could be over in a matter of days."

THE COLLECTION

THE CURATOR OF THE Kunsthistorisches Museum, which housed the enormous Hapsburg Dynasty art and antiquities collection, waited patiently near the display case containing the Holy Lance. He glanced at his watch. 7:56 PM.

Nearby stood two museum guards holding assault rifles and wearing protective vests and helmets. Two more guards waited in an armored truck parked outside the museum, ready to transport the precious cargo to a restricted hangar at the Vienna Schwechat International Airport. There it would be loaded aboard a private jet and flown directly to Miami.

For the third time, the curator adjusted the position of a rolling cart on which rested a silver Anvil Ion case the size of a large attaché. Also on the cart was a black Kevlar outer sleeve that would fit snuggly over the case once the relic was securely inside. The Anvil Iron's lid lay open—the interior filled with thick foam padding. A precise cutout in the shape of the Lance head awaited the treasured relic.

The curator would not remove the Holy Lance from the display until Cardinal Tyler and Cotten Stone had arrived to witness the event. Once properly packed and ready for transport, there would then be numerous papers and forms to sign and exchange, starting with a guarantee from the Holy See that the Vatican's insurance would cover loss or damage in the amount of $20 million.

There was a letter of authenticity from the museum stating that the ancient artifact referred to as the Holy Lance was the same object presented to the Hapsburg Collection on January 4, 1946, by U.S. Army General Mark Clark, who did so at the direct order of Supreme Allied Commander Dwight D. Eisenhower.

Another document specified the dimensions and location of the tiny sample to be extracted by CyberSys from the Lance's surface—in a place hidden beneath the gold and silver outer sheaths. That way, it would not be visible to any museum visitors after the relic was returned to its home in Vienna.

The curator looked at his watch again. 7:59 PM. That's when he heard the galloping horse.

———

"The official name is the Kunsthistorisches Museum," Zanini said from the front passenger seat of the Mercedes as he spoke over his shoulder to Cotten and John. "That means art history museum. But everyone refers to it as the Hapsburg Museum because it contains the royal family's collection spanning centuries." He turned to the driver, a young Austrian Venatori agent. "If you look up the word 'opulence' in the dictionary, you'll probably see the name Hapsburg in the definition."

The driver gave Zanini a courteous nod as he steered the performance sedan past the Karlsplatz Plaza near the center of Vienna, a few blocks from their destination.

"Are you sure we aren't going to run into any snags or red tape problems?" Cotten asked Zanini.

"No, all is set. Just a few forms to sign—pure formalities," Zanini said. "The security firm supplying the armored car is already there and ready to go. I have been in contact with the crew of the CyberSys corporate jet. All flight plans and government documentation have been filed and cleared. They are fueled and ready. Mr. Olsen, his son, and Max Wolf, his director of engineering, are there. Lindsay Jordan and her daughter are with them, relaxing onboard and anxiously awaiting our arrival with the relic. I'm told they all had a pleasant flight over from the U.S. We should be at the private hangar and airborne in the CyberSys jet within an hour of leaving the museum. Customs and Immigration formalities were resolved in advance through the Vatican embassy."

"Good work," John said. He turned to Cotten. "We're almost there."

"I know there was some hesitancy about allowing Lindsay and Tera to come along, but think about it from her point of view," Cotten said. "I wouldn't want to sit by like a bystander in some corporate conference room when I knew someone was out to harm my daughter. I'd have insisted to be right here as things were happening, too."

"Absolutely," John said. "It didn't take much persuading. I think Alan understood completely."

The curator spun around at the sound of horse hooves cracking like gunshots on the marble floor. The two guards snapped around just as quickly. The three men stared with open-mouthed shock as what appeared to be an armor-clad Greek warrior, sword in hand, charged across the gallery on the back of a giant gray steed.

Even from a distance, the curator saw that the warrior's teeth were clenched and his eyes aflame. The warhorse's breathing resounded throughout the museum like an accelerating steam locomotive. The warrior raised his muscular arm, his razor-edged weapon ready for the kill. With a gasp, the curator realized his identity—the Greek cavalryman depicted on the Greco-Hellenistic frieze from the Ephesus section of the museum.

"What is this?" the curator whispered, dropping back against the wall. In some nightmarish manner, beyond his comprehension, the two-thousand-year-old stone carving had come to life. The curator was witnessing a third century BC warrior from the epic battle between the Galatians and the Greeks barreling down on him. As real as his own skin, he saw the horseman's flesh glistening with sweat. This was no illusion, and the warrior looked hell bent on killing him.

The sound of automatic weapons filled the gallery as the two guards opened fire on the charging warrior. But the bullets ricocheted off the surface of the soldier and his mount—their forms seeming as impenetrable as the stone from which the frieze was carved.

From his right came a shriek so piercing and feral it could have come from a wild cat. A woman rushed toward him, her hair a squirming and slithering mass of snakes. Rubens' Medusa.

Another female rushed across the floor at the curator—blue tunic, bare breasts, bronze war helmet—Minerva.

The walls sprang alive with Roman soldiers, Greek warriors, gods and goddesses, emperors, kings, pouncing tigers, clawing bears—all with burning eyes, screaming mouths, and flashing teeth.

The Greek warrior on his battle steed swung his sword and sliced off the head of a guard with the ease of a gardener snipping a rose from its stem. The second guard dropped to the floor, his body riddled with arrows that rained from the same executioners' bows that ended the life of Saint Sebastian in Mantegna's masterpiece—their shafts piercing the guard's body armor as if it were paper.

The curator screamed when Medusa's coiling knot of snakes struck his face and neck. As he went down, the metallic flashes of daggers and swords, the meaty odor of blood, and the sound of flesh ripping and bones crunching saturated his senses.

With his cheek flat on the cold marble floor, the dying curator's eyes took in what was left of the guards—heaps of tendons and entrails, pools of blood spreading across the marble like spilled red ink.

Then, from out of nowhere, the face of an elderly gentleman stared down at him.

The curator's eyes fluttered as the Old Man went to stand over the case containing the Holy Lance. The curator tried to speak, but only a thin wheeze gurgled in his throat.

He saw the Old Man open the display and firmly grasp the Holy Lance. The echo of the Old Man's retreating footfalls faded as the curator drew his final, shallow breath. His last vision was of the army of antiquities melting back into their canvases and carvings.

CRIME SCENE

A POLICE CAR, BLUE lights flashing, raced past the Mercedes. Cotten saw the emblem of the *Bundespolize* on the side and the word *Polizei* on the back.

"Federal police," the Austrian Venatori agent said as he stared in the rearview mirror. "Here comes more." A second and third car raced by.

Cotten glanced at John. "I've got a really bad feeling about this."

"I know, I know," he said.

"Federal police?" she said. "They're not rushing to a traffic accident or other routine crime."

As the agent steered their car into the wide, park-like area between the Naturhistorisches Museum and the Kunsthistorisches Museum, Cotten saw that it already contained many emergency vehicles. The classical statues and sculptured hedges in front of the majestic buildings were awash in red and blue. A group of men in military-style gear gathered near a large black van parked at the front entrance of the art museum. Probably the Austrian equivalent of a SWAT team, Cotten assumed. A couple of news trucks were also pulling up—one bore the SNN logo on the side.

The Venatori agent brought the car to a stop and got out. "Wait here," he said before walking toward the police perimeter. He spoke at length to one of the officers. Soon, he led what appeared to be a high-ranking officer back toward the Mercedes.

Cotten, John, and Zanini gathered in front of the car.

"Your Eminence," the agent said. "This is Oberkommissar Heinz Gruber. He is in charge of the emergency response team. Oberkommissar, this is His Eminence, Cardinal John Tyler, director of the Venatori."

"A pleasure," Gruber said in fairly good English.

After shaking Gruber's hand, John turned to Cotten. "Oberkommissar, may I present Cotten Stone, Senior Investigative Correspondent for the Satellite News Network. And this is Father Carlo Zanini, Vatican historian and advisor to the Venatori."

Gruber said to John, "I understand you were coming here tonight to meet with the museum curator to take possession of a valuable religious artifact?"

"That's correct," John said.

Gruber looked at each one of them. Then he said, "The Holy Lance, correct?"

"Yes," Cotten said. His question shot a pang through her, feeling colder than the freezing Vienna night. Even without hearing the details, she knew they were too late. Just as in Axum, the Fallen had arrived before them.

"I must inform you that the artifact is missing," Gruber said. "Not only has it been stolen, but whoever took it is responsible for the vicious murders of the curator and two security guards."

"What happened?" Cotten asked.

Gruber gave her a grave expression. "What was done here to-night was heinous. These are the most brutal and savage murders I have seen in my twenty years in the National Police Force. The scene is too grisly to attempt to describe." He shook his head. "I am close to being physically ill at recalling what I just saw inside the museum."

Cotten turned away from Gruber, not wanting him to see the tears of frustration in her eyes. The battle was never-ending.

John nodded at Gruber. "Have a copy of the official report sent to my attention."

"By all means, Your Eminence," the Oberkommissar said.

"In the meantime, if there is anything I can do to help with the investigation, please contact me through the Vatican embassy."

Gruber rubbed his face as if trying to wipe away what he had witnessed in the museum. "Short of telling me who did this hor-rific act of brutality," he said, "I cannot think of anything." He ex-tended his hand and shook John's. "I will be in touch if I have any questions." After a courteous bow, he turned and walked briskly toward the cluster of police cars and gathering media vehicles.

Cotten pulled John aside, leaving the agent and Zanini by the car. A few paces away, she said, "We *know* who did this. But if we tell the Austrian authorities, they'll have us locked up in the loony bin."

"Worst case scenario is that the Fallen have a portable version of the computer like Max's, which means they could be slicing the thodium sample out of the Lance right now."

She glanced over at the SNN remote truck. "Max said that miniaturizing the computer down to a portable size was a big deal—that even the major research universities hadn't accomplished it yet—only CyberSys. What if the Fallen still have to get the relic to their Hades facility? If that's the case, there may still be time to stop them or find out the location. We need to put some roadblocks in their way."

"What have you got in mind?" John asked.

"Let me have your phone," she said.

John pulled it from his belt clip.

Cotten punched in a number. A moment later, she said, "This is Cotten Stone. I'm calling from Austria and I need to speak to Ted Casselman."

THE REPORT

THE PRESIDENT OF THE Russian Federation stood in his bathrobe and channel surfed. He had just stepped out of the shower and wanted to catch the news on a few of his favorite English-speaking stations before breakfast. As he towel-dried his hair with his left hand, he used the other to click the remote—his arm still in a sling from the bullet wound. Pausing a moment on the BBC World News, he moved next to the Satellite News Network's headline news channel. He liked the SNN early morning female anchors because they were young, blonde, and always showed more cleavage than their Russian counterparts.

When he saw his favorite SNN newscaster, he smiled approvingly. Appearing to be in her mid-twenties, she was saying, ". . . brutal and bizarre incident took place in Vienna last night and has made headlines across Europe this morning. It seems a religious object dating back to the Crucifixion of Christ was stolen from the famed Kunsthistorisches Museum, home of the Hapsburg Dynasty art collection. The robbers left behind virtually no evidence of how they gained access to the building, but during the robbery, the curator and two museum guards were viciously attacked and killed. With details from the scene, we go to SNN Senior Investigative Correspondent Cotten Stone, in Vienna."

The image switched from the blond to a shot of Cotten with a microphone in hand standing in front of the museum. Behind her, the building was silhouetted with the early morning dawn. A mass of police vehicles still cluttered the grounds.

"Just after the museum closed last evening," Cotten said, "a robbery took place that claimed the lives of three men—the museum curator and two guards. Their bodies were found by police who were called after automatic weapons fire was heard coming from inside the building."

The video switched from Cotten to show slow, panning shots of the interior of the museum—ornate, decorative, and opulent.

"The police SWAT team swarmed the museum but found that the robbers had made a quick exit, leaving behind absolutely no clues. What the authorities discovered were the badly mutilated bodies of the three men. Unconfirmed reports describe a scene of extremely violent attacks in which at least one man was decapitated and another shot with more than fifty arrows. We learned that the curator may have died from multiple venomous snake bites to the head and neck."

The video changed to a close-up of a police officer. Beneath his image was the inserted text: *Oberkommissar Heinz Gruber, Austrian National Police.*

"It was without a doubt the bloodiest murder scene I've witnessed in my years as a law enforcement officer."

"Do you have any leads to the identity of the killers, Ober kommissar?"

"None whatsoever." He shook his head in disgust, then turned as if being called away. "Excuse me," he said.

The image returned to the establishing shot of Cotten in front of the building. "So what was stolen? What was so valuable to warrant such vicious killings? An ancient relic known as the Holy Lance was the only object determined to be missing so far."

A file shot of the Lance taken from an SNN historical documentary series filled the screen. The camera slowly moved from the tip of the spear head down its length as Cotten said, "The Holy Lance, also know as the Spear of Destiny, is attributed to being the object used to pierce the side of Jesus Christ as he hung on the Cross more than two thousand years ago. Among the powerful historical figures that once possessed the Holy Lance were Constantine, Charlemagne, and Adolf Hitler. The legend of the Lance says that whoever possesses it holds in his hand the destiny of the world.

"One theory is that it might be sought after in the highly competitive race to develop the first functioning quantum computer—a device that could render all security and encryption codes around the world useless. Some historians theorize that the Lance is actually made from a rare element called thodium, the extremely rare material needed for storage of data in a quantum computer. If this is true, then the stakes are extraordinarily high, and the Holy Lance might just be one of the most valuable objects in existence today—certainly for the handful of facilities developing the latest computing technology.

"I've been told that inspections at all borders throughout Europe are being stepped up to help intercept and recover the artifact before it reaches its final destination.

"The Austrian National Police are forming a task force to track down the missing artifact and locate the person or persons responsible for the deaths of these three men. They've assured me they will stop at nothing to solve this heinous crime. For now, this is Cotten Stone, SNN, Vienna."

The blonde anchor said, "Thanks, Cotten. Stay tuned to SNN for the latest developments in the theft of the Holy Lance, or you can visit us online at satellitenews-dot-org for up-to-the-minute news."

The president pushed the mute button on the remote before walking to his bedside table. He picked up the phone receiver and waited until his personal secretary answered. In Russian, he said, "Call the Satellite News Network's Moscow office. Tell them I need to speak with Cotten Stone immediately."

ANOMALY

The Satellite News Network anchor looked into the camera and read from the teleprompter. "The Time and Frequency Division of The National Institute of Standards and Technology reported today that a strange, never-before-seen anomaly occurred at midnight, Greenwich Mean Time, last night. For a few seconds, the atomic clock—the one maintained by the NIST and used to synchronize virtually all the computers, GPS, and satellite systems in the world shifted the current date into the future by exactly six hundred and sixty-six years. Before any action could be taken to correct the time shift, the system appeared to fix itself as the atomic clock jumped back to the accurate time."

The video showed an exterior shot of the NIST facility in Boulder, Colorado. A woman identified as an NIST spokesperson said, "Our engineers are working to identify the cause of the strange time-shift anomaly. So far, we believe that it was just a glitch in a new version of software recently installed. We want to assure everyone that the problem is being fully investigated, and we have no reason to believe it will occur again or affect the many systems that rely on us for proper time synchronization."

The image changed back to the anchor. "Thousands of extremely critical systems rely on the atomic clock for synchronization, including those used by air traffic controllers, global positioning systems, military protocols, and others. An error in the atomic clock could have serious global consequences if not corrected immediately—everything from cell phones to atomic reactors to ICBM launch coordinates. Some organizations are suggesting that the time shift of six hundred and sixty-six years, or the number six-six-six, has biblical or satanic overtones. Are they right? I guess we'll just have to wait and see. And coming up next, the latest sports scores."

———

Cotten stood in the main cabin of the CyberSys corporate jet and stared at the TV monitor. They had reached cruising altitude on their flight from Vienna back to Miami. "Was anyone else watching just now?"

Alan and John were deep in conversation. Lindsay sat next to Tera as she and Devin played a board game. Max Wolf was engrossed in a project on his laptop.

Everyone glanced at Cotten.

"What did you see?" John asked.

"A report on an anomaly in the atomic clock?"

"What's that?" asked Lindsay. "The atomic clock, I mean?"

"Among other things," Max said, looking up from his computer, "atomic clocks are the basis of the GPS or global positioning system. Each of the GPS satellites has an on-board atomic clock.

They all synchronize with each other and the main clock at NIST to make sure everyone is marching to the same beat, so to speak."

"So what's wrong, Cotten?" Lindsay asked.

Cotten turned to face the group. "The report said something strange occurred last night. For a few seconds, the NIST clock shifted exactly six hundred and sixty-six years into the future."

Max shoved back his thick brown hair. "Did they say what caused it?"

"Possibly a software glitch," Cotten said.

"Well, that could be, I suppose." Max went back to his laptop.

"Six-six-six," John said. He got up and walked toward Cotten. "Interesting choice of numbers."

"Why do you say that?," Alan asked as he followed behind.

"Six-six-six is commonly known as the mark of the beast," John said. "In the book of Revelation—the Apocalypse—it says, 'Here is wisdom. Let him that hath understanding count the number of the beast—for it is the number of a man—and his number is six hundred and sixty-six.'"

"I remember that from the movie, *The Omen*," Lindsay said. "It was on the boy's head."

"Right," Cotten said. "It might be nothing more than a coincidence, but now that we know about the Hades Project from Kai, this could have something to do with it. Max, you told us in Miami that it would take a global event to trigger the launch of the virus. Could this be it?"

Max shrugged. "Maybe. The launch could be done with an unusual event that everyone assumes would never happen, like an outrageous time shift. All clocks, including the atomic clock, are set to GPS time. To alter the clocks would mean that someone working on the inside would first have to drop a virus on the government server and alter the system. Everyday, millions of computers call home by synchronizing to the atomic clock. If a computer had the Hades worm buried on it, when it saw the date change, it might be the launch event.

"No one believes that the government's main servers can be altered. So the momentary time shift in the atomic clock would be considered just a wild anomaly. But like I said, it would have to be done by someone working inside."

"How hard would it be for the Secretary of Homeland Security to plant someone inside a government facility?" Cotten asked.

The realization seemed to hit everyone at once.

"Not very hard," Alan said.

John said, "So, let's say Mace did manage to plant someone inside NIST and they were able to infect the system. And let's say the time-shift anomaly was the trigger mechanism for the millions of computers infected with the worm. What do you think would happen next?"

Max said, "If it were me doing it, I would have the virus fool or eliminate the redundancy checks on the system." He thought for a moment. "Or even better, just fool the humans at the controls—like an air traffic controller—into thinking there's a problem when in fact everything is fine. Basic human behavior says that the operator would react to what he sees as a critical issue and make a correction. In reality, his correction actually creates a real problem."

"Like what?" Cotten said.

"Let's say he thinks a commercial airliner is a thousand feet higher than it really is," Alan said. "There's a good chance that when the plane attempts to land, it would plow right into the ground."

"Or some guy at a nuclear reactor sees a sudden and significant drop in core temperature," Max said, "and overcompensates. Next thing you know, he's shooting fuel rods on a direct course to China, and the property value around the reactor drops for a few thousand years."

"But wouldn't there be backup checks?" John said. "Safety procedures in place?"

"Sure," Max said. "But since they are all seeing the same fake problem, they all confirm that the correction is appropriate. Then when real problems start popping up, everyone overcompensates again. The house of cards starts coming down."

"How about communications?" Alan said.

"They would be highly disrupted," Max said. "Once an operator is fooled into correcting a non-existent problem in the GPS system, the subsequent effects will not only stop time, but stop most digital cell phone and RF communications. Almost every cell phone switching site utilizes GPS signals for instant conversation hand-off and decryption between sites."

"So if you have an emergency, you can't call anyone to report it?" Cotten said.

"Exactly," Max said. "Once I caused enough havoc, the very last thing I'd do is finally target the power grids. The operator sees a huge jump in line usage and starts rolling brownouts, which create blackouts. No electricity, no traffic signals, no emergency vehicles getting through. Can't call the police or fire department. Can't call anyone for that matter. Everyone becomes an isolated individual fearing for his life."

"Can't pump fuel," Alan said. "No money from dead ATMs, no natural gas or water flowing. Traffic comes to a standstill with no signal lights."

"How quickly could this happen?" Lindsay asked, hugging Tera tightly.

Max shrugged. "Days, maybe hours. Depends on how fast the human operators react to the fictitious problems and start causing really tragic corrections."

"What about the military?" Cotten asked.

"Christ," Max said, rubbing his forehead. "I didn't even think about that. There's the Global Information Grid, part of the Defense Information Systems Agency Network. Reliance on the GIG is so critical that if it were to be taken down, it would send military operations into the Stone Age. Cross network infrastructure would be compromised, and the Hades worm could gain access to the Cheyenne Mountain Operations Center and the North American Air Defense, not to mention their counterparts in other countries. The military systems are triggered to display launch preparations from Russian and Chinese nuclear missile silos. To take this to the highest level, if fake launches were displayed, and there was no way to communicate for confirmation, the U.S. Nuclear Security Council would have no choice but to authorize a nuclear response."

"I think we're starting to see why the name Hades was chosen," John said. "We're potentially facing a global threat with catastrophic implications."

"Hell on earth," Cotten said.

"And it may already have been triggered," Max said.

"With the possibility that we have only hours to stop it," Cotten said.

The intercom phone rang, and Alan picked it up. He listened for a moment before holding it out to Cotten. "You have a call."

"Who knows I'm here?" she said, reaching to take the handset from Alan.

Alan handed her the phone. "Apparently the Kremlin. It's the president of Russia."

CONFERENCE CALL

"HELLO, MR. PRESIDENT," COTTEN said. "This is such a pleasant surprise." She eased down into a nearby seat. "How is your arm healing?" Cotten listened intently for a moment. "That's great news. Yes, my wounds have healed up just fine. Thank you for asking."

John and Alan had taken their seats as everyone on the corporate jet stopped what they were doing to watch Cotten.

"To what do I owe the honor of this call, sir?" Cotten asked. She listened. "Actually, I'm onboard a private jet. We took off from Vienna about twenty minutes ago and are en route to London to refuel and then on to the U.S." She glanced around the cabin as if taking a head count. "Yes, Cardinal Tyler is with me, along with Alan Olsen, the president of CyberSys, and his director of engineering, Max Wolf. A few other friends and family are with us."

Again, Cotten listened before replying, "Mr. President, with your permission, I would like to place you on speakerphone. Would that be acceptable?"

Cotten gestured to Alan who took the phone, pushed the conference button, and placed the receiver back on the communications console.

"Mr. President, you're now on speaker," Cotten said.

The heavily accented voice of the President of the Russian Federation filled the cabin. "What I was saying was that the brutal murders committed during the theft of the Holy Lance seemed out of proportion to me. And I was asking Ms. Stone why she thought these men died such a violent death for something that is admittedly valuable, but not as priceless as other items in the collection."

"We're not entirely sure, Mr. President," Cotten said. "But we have some theories."

"After all," the president said, "the crown jewels of the Hapsburg Empire are there, along with works of some of the greatest artists of the past thousand years. If I were the thief, I certainly would have taken them before the spear." He laughed. "No offense, Your Eminence," he said. "I know how precious the Holy Lance is to the Church."

"None taken, Mr. President," John said.

"I watched your news reports, Ms. Stone," the president said. "Now I want to hear the details on which you base your theories."

Cotten shrugged.

"Go for it," John whispered.

"Mr. President, our theories are based as much on scientific fact as they are on legend. The Holy Lance has a history traceable back to the Garden of Eden. We think it was forged by the third-generation great grandson of Adam—a blacksmith named Tubal Cain. He produced the Lance from the hardened, crystallized sap of the Tree of Life, and Noah used lumber from the same tree to construct the Ark. We have found ancient writings that show that God commanded Noah to carry the Lance aboard the Ark because it would be used in some future event. We think that future event is about to happen. The Lance is made of hardened sap from the Tree of Life, a rare material now known as thodium. It's needed for storing data in a fully functional quantum computer—a critical element in the final development of the computer.

"The reason we think the Lance was stolen is because there is a group building a quantum computer called the Hades Project, and will use it to break the security framework of the world's resources. Their goal is to bring down governments, militaries, financial institutions, power grids, and international communications. The result will be chaos, anarchy, global war, and maybe the end of civilization."

Cotten breathed deeply, wondering if what she had just said sounded as incredulous and ridiculous as she thought it might.

Seconds drifted by—ten, twenty, thirty.

Finally, she said, "Mr. President?"

Silence.

Cotten was about to ask Alan if he thought they had lost the connection when the Russian president said, "I am still here."

"Mr. President, I hope you don't think—"

"Cardinal Tyler," the president said, "do you believe everything that Cotten Stone has told me?"

"Yes, Mr. President. Not only do I trust her instincts, but I have been a part of this since it first came to light. And I think if we don't stop the Hades Project, the outcome could be even worse than she described."

There was the sound of paper rustling.

"Mr. Olsen," the Russian said. "I am looking at your dossier as we speak. As an expert in the field of . . . encryption and advanced, high speed data processing, do you believe what Ms. Stone has just told me?"

"Mr. President, I do. After meeting with Cotten and Cardinal Tyler, and based upon the recent events in Washington concerning the death of National Security Advisor Philip Miller, I have no hesitation in believing her."

There was another long silence with the additional sound of pages of paper being turned.

"Mr. Wolf, the same question, please," the president said.

"I believe that we're on the verge of a global event that could bring down all order and security as we know it," Max said.

The president could be heard conversing in Russian with someone. Then he said, "Ms. Stone, as you Americans say, there is good news and bad. But in this instance, I have bad news, good news, and really good news." He seemed to smile through the phone at his cleverness.

"Please share it with us," John said. "We could use some good news right now."

"The good news is, Ms. Stone, that in the process of you saving this old Russian's life, you stood within a few inches of the Holy Lance."

Cotten could not understand what he meant as she racked her memory of the night in the tunnel dodging bullets.

"And the really good news?" John asked.

"The object stolen from the museum in Vienna is a worthless fake," the president said.

There was a collective gasp in the jet's passenger cabin. Finally, Cotten said, "Are you positive, sir?"

"Absolutely. The stolen object is a replica produced by an over-zealous Heinrich Himmler in 1935. The *Reichsführer* of the SS was quite obsessed with the occult. While impatiently waiting for Hitler to invade Austria and take possession of the Holy Lance, he had a replica made. The man was insane in so many ways—this should come as no big surprise."

"How did the replica get into the museum?" John asked.

"The switch took place at the orders of Joseph Stalin when the Allies returned the Lance to the Hapsburg Museum at the end of the war."

"Is this common knowledge?" Cotten said.

"No," the president said. "It's one of those little secrets, what's the American word—tidbits—that gets passed to each Russian president. The tsar's escape tunnel is another tidbit. Somewhat like that third secret of Fatima that each new pope gets to learn, Your Eminence."

"I understand, Mr. President," John said.

"You said that I stood within inches of the Holy Lance when I was in Moscow. You're telling me the authentic Lance is there somewhere in the maze of underground passageways?"

"Actually, no. Stalin considered the Holy Lance his prized possession and kept it hidden away for almost eight years. Then in a private ceremony held in 1953, he chose to honor Vladimir Lenin by placing the Holy Lance inside the sarcophagus under Lenin's body. That same night, after dinner with Nikita Khrushchev and a few other party members, he collapsed in his bedroom and died.

While you and I were in Lenin's Tomb, you passed within inches of the relic."

"And it's still there?" Cotten asked.

"Yes." He paused, speaking in Russian to someone with him. "Mr. Olsen? I assume that you are prepared to counteract this so-called Hades Project threat by using technology of your own?"

"Yes, sir. We have a miniaturized version of our Destiny quantum computer onboard along with the mechanical apparatus necessary to extract a sample of thodium. All we need is the Holy Lance. Once the system is up and running, we can go online, find and hack into the Hades machine, and shut it down."

"Then I would recommend you alter your flight plan immediately. I will arrange for your plane to be given priority clearance through Russian airspace. Once you have landed in Moscow, you will be flown by military helicopter to the Kremlin. We will get you your thodium sample, Mr. Olsen, and we will wait with anxious anticipation as you rid the world of this Hades threat. Is that acceptable?"

"More than acceptable, Mr. President," Alan said.

"Are there any other questions?" the Russian asked.

Cotten spoke up. "You told us you also had bad news."

"You're right, Ms. Stone. Do you remember the Chechen rebels who tried to assassinate me?"

"Of course, Mr. President. How could I forget?"

"The bad news is, they were not Chechen, and they were not trying to kill me. They were trying to kill you."

THE BEGINNING

"COTTEN, WAKE UP," JOHN said, shaking her arm. "We've got a problem."

She had finally dozed off soon after Alan informed his flight crew of their new destination—Sheremetyevo International Airport outside Moscow. He told everyone the flight would take about five and a half hours. Finally overcome from so much flying time and the fatigue from the last few weeks, Cotten had dropped into one of the plush leather seats and fallen asleep. Now she shook her head, trying to clear the dark place she had gone in her dreams.

"What is it?" she asked.

"The pilot says there have been a large number of plane hijackings reported across Europe, and the ATC centers are diverting traffic to alternative destinations."

"Hijackings?" She stared up at him in confusion. "Who's hijacking what?" She glanced out the window but saw only darkness. "Do you think this has anything to do with the Hades threat?"

"Not sure," John said. "Maybe. It could be these aren't true hijackings, even though planes are squawking hijack codes. It could be part of the Hades chaos that Max predicted."

Cotten stood and glanced around the cabin. Lindsay, Tera, and Devin were all asleep. Max was at his usual place at a table up front, working with his laptop. She noticed that while she slept, he had brought out a few other computer cases—a great deal of electronics hardware was scattered around the cabin on tables and in seats.

"So what do we do?" she asked.

"Because we've been given a presidential priority clearance, we may be able to proceed according to our revised flight plan. But the pilot says that there's a lot of confusion and disruption in communications. My guess is this may be the beginning of what we expected."

"If it is, it sure didn't take them long," Cotten said. "Come on, I've got a question for Max." She walked to the front of the cabin, John following, and waited for the director of engineering to look up from his work.

"Cotten, how was your nap?" he said.

"Sporadic. Max, something's been bothering me since we had the conference call with the Russian president. If the object that was taken in Vienna was a replica, and not made from thodium, how are they going to proceed with the Hades Project? If this is the beginning of their assault, how are they carrying if off?"

"Good question," Max said. "My guess is, they have another sample of thodium, but maybe it's not enough to do the job. After all, we have simulated thodium in partical accelerators, but only a few atoms at a time. Or what they've got could be damaged or contaminated. If their sample was indeed from the Ark, think of how long it was exposed to the elements of nature. It could have degraded. We don't know enough about thodium to predict the long-term effects. Objects that date back that far are subject to all kinds of external forces. Or maybe it's not really thodium but something with similar characteristics that we haven't thought of." He scratched his head. "Still, they did go to a lot of trouble stealing the Holy Lance from the museum, thinking it was the real thing, so that means that whatever they've been using isn't good enough. They stole the Lance because they need a good, solid sample." He smiled a wicked grin. "Someone's in for a big surprise when they go to slice up Himmler's replica and discover it's probably nothing but a piece of iron."

Cotten turned to John. "That presents a bigger problem."

"Which is?" he said.

"When they discover the Lance is a replica, they'll become desperate. All the focus of the Fallen and the Nephilim will be directed at finding another thodium source. They've started this thing, and they can't back down. By now, they know we've changed course and are headed for Moscow. It's only a matter of time before they figure out why. We have to get to Red Square first."

MIDAIR COLLISION

"WHERE ARE WE?" COTTEN asked, looking out the window of the CyberSys jet into the night.

"Over Belarus, I think," Alan said. "The capital city is Minsk—it should be off our left wing. We're roughly four hundred miles out of Moscow."

"I think I see the city lights," Cotten said. "I'm also seeing what looks like some fires," Cotten said, growing more nervous. "A couple of big ones."

Alan went to a control panel and dimmed the interior cabin lights.

Everyone found a window.

"You're right, Cotten," Lindsay said. "Some are pretty big."

"Is our navigation system working?" John asked Alan.

"Our instruments are working fine, but our pilot told me we can't synchronize or communicate with anything outside the plane. There's no contact with Russian air traffic control. After our conference call with the president I warned the guys up front this might happen. They'll get us to Moscow, but where we land is the big question."

"I see lights from two aircraft in the distance," John said. "Looks like passenger jets. It's hard to tell in the dark."

"Where," Alan asked.

John pointed.

"Oh, Jesus," Alan said.

Lindsay gasped.

Cotten backed away from the window, her hand to her mouth. She saw the planes collide and immediately burst into blinding fireballs. Wreckage streamed down like misguided fireworks—chunks of burning debris leaving swirling tentacles of smoke as they dropped into the darkness.

"What is it, Momma?" Tera rushed to her mother's side.

Lindsay took her daughter into her arms. "Everything's okay."

Cotten glanced around the cabin, which had become disturbingly quiet. Only the muffled roar of the jets filled the dimly lit space. Everyone had slipped into the closest seat, each staring unfocused at some distant spot. All she heard was the soft grunts of Devin rocking.

Finally, John said, "God help us."

MIG-29

"THERE'S ANOTHER PLANE!" TERA called, bringing everyone out of their stupor.

"Where, sweetheart?" Lindsay said.

Tera had her nose to the window. Cotten saw the girl's breath pluming on the glass.

"A military jet," John said.

Cotten stared into the dark Russian sky at the jet fighter, so close she could see the glow from the instrument panel on the front of the pilot's faceplate.

"It's a MiG-29," Max said, moving to a window. "My cousin built a model kit of one not long ago. I think NATO calls them Fulcrums."

The cockpit door opened, and the CyberSys copilot emerged. "Mr. Olsen, the Russian pilot wants us to follow him."

"How did you manage to communicate?" Alan asked.

"Most RF is down, but there are still a few radio frequencies that are hot," the pilot said. "The fighter pilot held up a small white-board with a frequency written on it. When he lit it with a flash-light, we knew where to find him."

"Where is he going to take us?" Alan said.

"All three of Moscow's international airports are shut down," the copilot said. "He wants us to go to Zhukovsky Airfield near a town called Ramenskoye. The airfield is used by the Gromov Flight Research Institute—a training and testing facility."

"Thank you," Alan said. "Do whatever it takes to get us on the ground safely."

As the copilot returned to the cockpit, Cotten said, "So where is this place?"

"About forty-six kilometers from Moscow," Max said, calling up the info on his laptop from a CD atlas.

"Look, Momma, he's going in front of us," Tera said.

Cotten saw the MiG-29 accelerate and disappear beyond the nose of the CyberSys jet. She turned to Max. "What do you need to do to get ready before we land? Is there anything we can do to help?"

"Actually, I have prepared all the gear for transport." Max pointed to two suitcase-size containers sitting on a table across the aisle. "One is the portable Destiny computer processor and interface, and the other is the spectral hole burner."

"You're going to burn holes in things?" Tera said, standing nearby. She smiled with wide-eyed wonder.

"In a way," Max said. "Once we get the Holy Lance, we'll be storing one or two qubits of information per atom in the crystallized thodium that it's made from. Then we'll address the individual atoms by tuning the laser frequency—"

"Max, please," Alan said, holding up his hand. "A simple yes would have done just fine."

"Sorry." Max looked at Tera and smiled. "Yes." Then he went back to typing data into his laptop.

"If we're forty-six kilometers from Moscow—how far is that in miles?" Cotten asked.

"Twenty-six and a half." Max glanced up at Alan with a "how's that for a direct answer?" expression.

Cotten nodded a thank-you.

"I see a lot more fires," Lindsay said from a window seat.

"They picked a perfect name for what they're doing," Cotten said.

"Tor said it." The voice came from Devin, who had hardly spoken since they left Vienna.

The group turned in his direction as Alan said, "Said what, Devin? Tor said what?"

"Welcome to Hades."

———

Cotten heard the sound of the jet engines change pitch. The plane's nose seemed to angle as the aircraft banked to the left. The fasten seat belts light came on, and a chime sounded in the cabin.

"We're on final approach," Alan said, hanging up the intercom phone to the cockpit. "Get situated and belt yourselves in. This may not be a normal landing."

"What do you mean?" Lindsay asked with anxiety in her voice.

"Don't worry," Alan said, dropping into a seat next to Devin. "We just don't know what the conditions are on the ground yet."

"I see the runway," Cotten said. She watched the dark countryside slowly move toward the plane as they descended. The glow from Moscow city lights dotted the horizon. There were also a handful of fires. "What do you think is causing the fires?" she said.

"Could be anything," Max answered. "Gas leaks, vehicular collisions, electrical fires—point is no one can call to report them, so no one can come put them out."

"They *are* going to create hell on earth," Cotten whispered.

From out of the blackness of the night, the MiG-29 appeared alongside. It quickly distanced itself to give the private jet room to land. As Cotten gripped the ends of the armrests, she saw the runway lights pass underneath. The corporate jet seemed to float weightlessly for a moment, then it dropped down and its tires bit into the concrete. It bounced once, then with a roar, the pilot slowed the plane using the jets and applied the brakes. It continued down the long runway until a complex of buildings appeared on the left. A number of military and emergency vehicles lined the runway, and they drove beside the jet until it taxied off the main runway.

"Everybody okay?" Alan asked, glancing around the cabin as the engines wound down.

The cockpit door opened, and the pilot emerged, the copilot right behind him. The pilot said, "Mr. Olsen, the Russians want us all off the plane immediately."

"But I was planning on leaving Devin and Tera here with Lindsay and you," he said.

"Sorry, sir. There's a helicopter waiting to transport all of us to Moscow."

"All right." Alan motioned to the table with Max's cases. "Give Max a hand with his stuff." Looking around the cabin, he said, "Grab only what's essential."

The pilot unlatched the side door and swung it open. A ground crew was already rolling a set of steps up to the side of the plane.

When Cotten looked out the window, she saw soldiers gathering at the base of the stairs. She and John moved forward behind Lindsay and Tera. "Why do they want us all in Moscow?" she asked the pilot as she got to the door.

"What they told us is because there's growing disorder in the city, the government felt we would be safer remaining together," he said. "If we got separated, they were concerned that we might not be able to find each other again."

The group assembled at the bottom of the steps. In English, a Russian officer said, "Follow me."

A few hundred yards away, a large military helicopter sat with its rotors spinning, its turboshaft engines hissing. The side door stood open with two soldiers beside the aircraft ready to help the passengers onboard.

They heaved the children up first, followed by Lindsay and Cotten. John and Alan boarded next—Max stood by, directing the hoisting of the delicate computer cases into the cabin.

Quickly, they were seated and strapped in. Then Cotten heard the turbines spin up and transform from a whine into a roar. At the same time, the rotors accelerated until the helicopter vibrated, straining to become airborne.

"You're about to come full circle," Cotten whispered as she stared into the darkness.

AMBUSH

THE MIL MI-17 RUSSIAN turboshaft helicopter swooped in over the Moscow River from the southeast. Seated inside, Cotten saw the onion domes of St. Basil's Cathedral slip beneath the aircraft, followed by sprawling Red Square. At 150 mph, the trip from the airfield had taken only seven minutes, but it had been unnerving.

The night was lit from the glow of city lights, but she also saw sporadic fires, a few city-block-sized blazes, and what appeared to be the crash site of a huge airplane—small explosions were still bursting around it. Most streets were clogged and at a standstill, with emergency vehicles trapped in the mass of stalled traffic. As the news of the growing chaos spread, Cotten figured thousands must be trying to leave the city.

Along with the CyberSys group, sixteen armed Russian soldiers were inside the cabin of the Mil Mi-17, having already been on-board when they left the Gromov Flight Research Institute.

The helicopter settled onto the great expanse of cobblestones outside the walls of the Kremlin. The door slid open, and the soldiers were the first out. The last two turned and assisted Cotten, John, and Max, and helped with the two Destiny computer cases.

The officer in command turned to Cotten and said, "I am Captain Markov. We have received word that an international situation has developed and is escalating. The president cannot meet with you, but has ordered that we take you and Cardinal Tyler directly to retrieve the artifact. We will split up with half my men escorting Mr. Wolf and his gear to a secure crisis room inside the Kremlin. There he can set up his computer and prepare for when we deliver the artifact. Any questions?"

Cotten looked at John and Max before nodding to Markov. "Okay, Captain." She turned to Alan who was about to step down from inside the helicopter. "There's no reason for you to go with us, Alan. Stay with Lindsay and the children in case they have to evacuate you guys out of here. We'll retrieve the Spear. Once Max has everything up and running, and it's safe, we'll have them bring everyone inside."

Alan looked at Max. "She's right, boss," Max said. "Stay with your son."

Alan glanced at Devin, then at Lindsay and Tera. "Fine," Alan said. He shook their hands before stepping back into the cabin of the helicopter, its blades rotating slowly overhead. "Good luck."

"Okay," Markov said. "Follow me."

They had landed near the State Historical Museum on the north end of Red Square, a few hundred yards from Lenin's Tomb. The boxy mausoleum had been built on the outside wall of the Kremlin. As everyone came around the nose of the helicopter and were about to split into two groups, Cotten noticed a large formation of what appeared to be soldiers amassed outside the mausoleum. Unlike the green military uniforms of the Russian Federation Army soldiers with her, these men were dressed in black, similar to the dark, commando, full-body-armor outfits worn by the rebels who had attacked her and the president in the tsar's tunnel. Cotten also noticed an odd visual distortion like waves of heat rising off a highway in the summer sun. The black soldiers seemed to drift in and out of focus as the waves undulated.

Once everyone cleared the aircraft and were walking across the open space of Red Square, the black soldiers opened fire with bursts of automatic weapons. Their guns were silenced, so the muzzle flashes appeared like hundreds of tiny sparks in the night.

A few of Captain Markov's men dropped onto the cobblestones, unmoving. Markov yelled, "Get back to the helicopter—run!"

John grabbed Cotten's arm as they retreated to the protection of the aircraft.

She heard bullets striking the street and the metal skin of the chopper. As the Russians gathered behind the protection of the aircraft and started returning fire, Cotten, John, and Max ran to the open side door.

"What's going on?" Lindsay called. "Who is shooting at us?"

"Stay down!" Cotten ordered her.

"We've got to get out of here!" Alan shouted.

Cotten heard the turbines spinning up and felt the rotors start to increase speed. The pilot yelled back to them in Russian. His words needed no translation. He had to take off to save his aircraft. And they must jump back on board.

"We can't leave without the Lance," Cotten yelled over the sound of the gunfire and the screaming turbines.

"What choice do we have?" John said. "They've got the entrance to the Tomb blocked."

Cotten went to the rear of the aircraft and cautiously peered around it. She saw that the St. Nicholas Tower gate entrance to the Kremlin was only a couple of hundred feet away. "We've got to make it to the gate," she yelled to Captain Markov while pointing in the direction of the Kremlin wall.

He nodded that he understood and relayed the order to his men. He motioned for two soldiers to bring the computer cases and follow him—the rest would give cover fire while he and the Americans raced across the short distance to the gate. Motioning to Cotten, he said, "Okay, we are ready."

"Thank you," Cotten said.

"What are you doing?" Max said. "We need to get out of here. The helicopter is leaving."

"We can't leave, Max," Cotten said. "If we do, they win and there will be no place for us to go. This is it. And unless you're going to give me a crash course in running that Destiny device, we need you with us."

The helicopter rumbled, and the downdraft from its blades made it nearly impossible to hear. Max looked at Alan then at John. Finally, he yelled to Cotten, "What the hell. Lead the way."

As the Mil Mi-17 started to rise off the cobblestones with the force of a hurricane, Cotten thought she heard Lindsay scream for them to come back. But the words were lost in the roar of the aircraft.

Markov's men opened fire on the black figures blocking the Tomb while he led the small group toward the tower gate entrance.

"How are we going to get into the Tomb?" John yelled to Cotten once they passed under the majestic tower into the safety of the Kremlin walls.

Never slowing, she called over her shoulder, "Ivan the Terrible's praying seat."

———

Tor stared at the monitor displaying the operating system interface to the Hades quantum computer. Things were holding together amazingly well, even with the degraded thodium. He held the Holy Lance replica in his hand and figured he'd hang it on the wall of his bedroom. That's about all it was worth.

Mace hadn't warned him about the Son of the Dawn delivering it personally. That was something he never wanted to experience again. Out of all the Ruby ceremonies and rituals Tor had attended, the Son of the Dawn had been a distant figure. Few Ruby children or Nephilim adults ever approached him.

And yet, he came to Tor, showing up out of nowhere like an apparition. It truly scared the shit out of him as he was concentrating deeply on his work and suddenly heard that distinctive voice from behind. Having spent so many days and nights in the old military facility alone, he almost came out of his skin.

And then when he had to give the Son of the Dawn the bad news—that the Lance was a fake—he thought he might shit himself. The only redeeming part was when Tor was told it was not his fault.

Tor felt sorry for Mace. Rizben would take the brunt of the punishment. He'd already heard the news headlines. The Secretary of Homeland Security resigns citing personal reasons. In a way,

Mace had it coming, Tor thought. The guy was cocky, self-centered, and basically an asshole. Of course, being a Fallen Angel, the worst that could happen was he would be sent to some shithole assignment. Serves him right for acting like a prick.

Tor even regretted turning Mace on to Kai. She was a bitch but the most amazing woman he'd ever met. A free spirit and a free agent. He wondered what she was doing now that Mace was out of the picture.

He glanced back at the monitor. Not bad for a piece-of-shit sample of thodium. It was still holding together—barely.

That's when the intrusion alarms went off.

VLADIMIR

ONCE INSIDE THE KREMLIN walls, Markov asked Cotten, "Where do you want me to take you?" They moved briskly along the sidewalk in front of the arsenal building.

"Cardinal Tyler and I must get into Assumption Cathedral," she said. "Mr. Wolf and his electronics gear can go on to your crisis center."

At the corner of the two-story arsenal building, Markov stopped and relayed the orders to the two men carrying the computer cases. He pointed to the right. "Mr. Wolf, follow these men to the Grand Kremlin Palace." Then Markov led Cotten and John to the left, passing in front of the State Kremlin Palace and on to the churches surrounding Cathedral Square.

Running past the front of the Church of the Twelve Apostles, the three turned right and headed for the entrance to the Assumption Cathedral. Climbing the steps to the southern portal, Cotten looked up at the huge paintings of the two archangels guarding each side of the door. "We could sure use their help," she said, pointing to the angels.

Markov nodded in agreement.

The iron mesh gates stood open, but the great wood and metal double doors were closed and locked. Captain Markov pulled on the handles, but there was no give from the three-hundred-year-old entry. "We will have to get someone to come and unlock the church," he said to Cotten.

"Captain, there's no time. Please get us inside, even if it means breaking down the doors."

Markov stared at her as if she had asked him to urinate on the Russian Federation flag.

"Captain," John said. "You mentioned there was some sort of escalating international situation going on. I can assure you that whatever it is will be mild compared to what's in store for us all if Ms. Stone does not gain access to this church. Captain Markov, I am a cardinal in the Roman Catholic Church and director of the Vatican's equivalent to your Federal Security Service—your old KGB. Please believe me when I tell you that what is happening tonight all over the globe is the beginning of a tragic series of events that could culminate in a possible—"

"Captain Markov, shoot the locks!" Cotten demanded.

The soldier stared at her for a moment before turning toward the entrance of Assumption Cathedral and pulling back the bolt on his automatic assault rifle. A second later, he fired a burst of rounds into the lock of the four-inch-thick wood doors—splinters and shards of metal flying everywhere. Stepping forward, he kicked in the door with a crunch of splitting wood. Looking over his shoulder, he said, "This way."

Rushing into the cavernous cathedral, Cotten felt overwhelmed by the memories of the rebel attack. Only a handful of lights were on, giving her the same feeling of eerie, otherworldliness that surrounded her that fateful night such a short time ago. As they moved across the marble floor, her eyes lingered briefly on the spot where her crew had fallen, murdered. Even in the dim light, the damage to the artwork that ringed the columns was evident.

Markov stopped. "Now where?"

Cotten pointed to the structure that housed Ivan the Terrible's praying seat.

"Let's go," he said, and hurried across the floor of the cathedral to the miniature building.

Standing beside it, Cotten motioned to the narrow space behind it and the wall. She squeezed through and opened the gate that led inside. Dark stains on the floor marked where the murdered PSS agent died. The Tsar's chair had been returned to its original position. Cotten pushed it aside, exposing the trapdoor. Lifting it open, she said, "Through here."

"Wait," Markov said. "I'll go first, just in case anyone is waiting to ambush us again."

Cotten watched him drop down into the hole. John went next. Just before it was her turn, Cotten stopped and listened, swearing that she heard the faintest of footsteps. If the black soldiers were coming, this was not the place to stand and fight. From here on there was only one way out. As she turned to climb down, she thought she saw two small figures dashing through the dark shadows.

"There's a light switch on the wall next to the platform," Cotten called down to Markov as she closed the trapdoor behind her.

A second later, the bulb flicked on. "Keep going to the bottom. Follow the tunnel and always bear to the left."

As they approached the end of the first light string, the group stopped. "There's another light switch on the wall," Cotten said. But before Markov could flip it on, she held up her hand for silence. The slight thump of the trapdoor closing again echoed through the tunnel. "We're being followed," she said, and nodded for Markov to turn on the next set of lights.

The passage widened just as Cotten remembered. They moved past the openings to many tunnels and drainage pipes, some appearing as if they had not been disturbed for hundreds of years.

Ahead was the set of stone stairs angling up the wall, leading to the storeroom entrance. She made her way in front of Markov. Grudgingly, it opened. "Come on," she said after flipping on the storeroom light. Moving across the room, she grabbed the handle of the door on the opposite wall and pushed, swinging it open into the dark marble hallway.

"We are very close to the entrance where the rebels were shooting at us," Markov said. "Come behind me." With his gun at the ready, he led Cotten and John down the hall and into the main chamber of the Tomb.

As Cotten remembered, it was coal black and softly lit—the walls bore large lightning bolt designs. In the center sat the long, glass-enclosed sarcophagus. Only this time, there was a major difference.

It was empty.

Cotten's heart sank as she stared at the place where Lenin's body had lain. The side of the glass enclosure was swung up and over, resting on the top of the structure.

"Where is . . ." Markov stood rooted at the sight of the empty sarcophagus.

"I don't believe this," Cotten said. She moved cautiously to the enclosure and extended her hand inside, running it along the satin-like material where the body of Vladimir Lenin had been in repose since 1924. There was no Holy Lance. Only the small, white pillow remained—a slight indention marked where Lenin's head rested.

"Is this what you seek?"

They turned at the sound of the voice.

"Dear God," Markov whispered, taking a step backward. He looked spellbound by the sight of the man standing in the corner of the mausoleum.

John's mouth dropped open, his eyes wide in disbelief.

For a moment, Cotten thought her heart had stopped. The air became hot and suffocating. She doubted her own senses as she watched the man walk toward her, the Spear of Destiny held tightly to his chest.

The man was almost completely bald, and his eyes were small and dark. He donned a mustache and goatee. His suit was black, his shirt white with a dark tie. And he spoke with a thick Russian accent. She knew who it was.

The mausoleum remained so hushed that Cotten could hear the blood rushing in her ears.

Then Markov whispered, "Comrade Lenin? Is it really you?"

"It's an illusion, Captain," Cotten said, trying to maintain control over her senses. To John, she said, "He is the Beast. Remember Axum?"

At the sound of her voice, John seemed to shake off the shock. "He took the form of the guardian monk, and now he tries to trick us again."

"You are quite observant, priest," *Lenin* said, his body surrounded in a pale ruby aura. "I can take any form that suits me."

The air in the Tomb became sweltering. "Give me the Holy Lance," Cotten said, summing up as much courage as she could.

"Did you not learn your lesson, daughter of Furmiel? I told you in the treasury church to go home. Why didn't you take my advice and save yourself so much disappointment?"

"Give her the relic," John said. "We have come face-to-face before. You lost that time, and you will lose here, too. You can't win against God. I can exorcise you, just as I did before."

Lenin held up his hand. "Do not speak again, priest. Your God is not my god." He tauntingly extended the Spear of Destiny. "Whoever possesses this Holy Lance and understands the powers it serves, holds in his hand the destiny of the world." *Lenin* proudly held it high. "Now I am the power it serves. I will determine the destiny of the world." He took a step toward Cotten. "Daughter of Furmiel, you have failed."

"No," John said. He made the sign of the cross and lifted the gold crucifix he wore around his neck. "In the name of Jesus Christ, our Lord. Behold the Cross of the Lord, flee bands of enemies. May Thy mercy descend upon—"

"We cast you out." The voice came from the hall leading from the storeroom and tunnel.

Cotten and John turned to see two figures emerge. Their bodies were clothed in cloud-like white robes giving off an indigo blue radiance that filled the room. Cotten suddenly remembered the painting of the two archangels guarding the southern portal entrance to the cathedral. *Could these be the same figures?*

One came forward to stand before the apparition of Lenin. "How you have fallen from heaven, O Lucifer, morning star, son of the dawn." The archangel stretched forth her hand and took the Spear of Destiny. "Begone from this place, you and your vile black army. For God has cast you into the abyss."

The apparition of Lenin staggered.

As the archangel took hold of the Spear, the form of Vladimir Lenin collapsed onto the floor. It became rigid and waxen as Cotten remembered when first seeing it. She looked at the angel. "Who are you?"

The archangel gave the Spear to Cotten. "Be not afraid, daughter of Furmiel, for destiny lies in your hands." The archangel turned and rejoined her companion. Then the light surged in brilliance, causing Cotten, John, and Markov to cover their faces.

When she opened her eyes, Cotten saw that the two angels were gone. Her heart raced—her body was drenched in sweat. She stared at the Spear of Destiny gripped in her hand. The relic seemed to tingle as she looked at John. "Are you all right?"

Before he could answer, voices came from the hall, calling her name. Cotten could not believe what she saw. Tera and Devin ran toward her. She bent and took them in her arms, tears streaming down her face.

Right behind them were Alan and Lindsay, along with a half dozen Russian soldiers. All were winded.

"How did you . . . ?" Cotten asked.

"Tera and Devin jumped from the helicopter just as it took off," Lindsay said. "You were already running toward the gate. So we jumped out, too."

"We tried to get the pilot to come back," Alan said. "But he was in the air, and there were bullets flying everywhere."

"The children followed you as if they knew exactly where to go," Lindsay said. "What happened here?" She glared at the body of Vladimir Lenin on the floor.

Cotten smiled as she hugged Tera and Devin, feeling as if they were two angels in her arms. She stood and handed the Holy Lance to Alan. "Go and stop this madness." Turning to Markov, she said, "Captain, please take him to Mr. Wolf."

She looked at John and spoke softly as she wrapped her arms around him. "Do you think the children . . . were they the ones?"

"Maybe they have revealed to us who they really are," he whispered through her hair.

"Then maybe this battle is finally over."

FINISHED

THE CHILL WAS WHAT Mace noticed first. Sure, it was winter in D.C., but this cold, freezing air that stung his nostrils and burned in his lungs was not because of the season. It was a cold that smoldered like heat—an unnatural, aberrant phenomenon that could only mean one thing.

He stuffed his hands in his pockets and wheezed out a cough as he turned the corner. The ice storm that encapsulated the Nation's Capital suspended in time and motion even the smallest twig within a glistening, clear cast. The ice crystals on the sidewalk crunched beneath his shoes. Now, at dusk, the city mystically twinkled in radiant prisms with the last vestiges of the sun bouncing off the shards of ice.

Mace paused at the granite lion appearing to be locked inside its own hoarfrost tomb. The statue and its twin posed silently, guarding the building's entrance. Mace took the three levels of steps one at a time, safeguarding his balance on the slippery surface. The building was closed, as was everything since the Hades

Project got into full swing. He slid his key inside the lock, and the heavy wooden door whined open.

Inside he glanced at the elevator, but decided against it. The power could go off at any minute. *Wouldn't that be a hell of a note, to be stuck in the god damn elevator?* The Old Man would never listen to such an excuse.

Mace gripped the brass banister and stared up at the winding stairs. Seven flights to the enclosed courtyard seemed eternally distant. He re-wrapped his neck with the black wool muffler and started up, listening to the creak of the steps as he climbed.

By the fourth flight he could hear his every breath wheeze on the outflow. It seemed colder in here than outside—the fucking heat was off, and by his own god damn doing. He found humor in that, and a spontaneous laugh rasped from his chest.

Finally, at the seventh floor landing, Mace waited, catching his ragged breath. The bastard knew he would have to climb all seven flights, and that's why he demanded they meet here. It would have been just as easy to meet in the comfort of Mace's living room. Tea by the fire. But this wasn't going to be a pleasant meeting, and he knew it would be freezing in the courtyard.

Mace's footsteps echoed as he approached the door to the courtyard. Opening it, a gust of arctic cold burst through, making his eyes sting and water. He sniffed up the congestion that dripped from his nose.

"You are on time, Pursan," the Old Man said, speaking from the center of the courtyard. The crescent moon cast skeleton shadows of the leafless trees across the stone floor.

"Did you think I would be late? Have I ever been?" Mace asked.

The wind whipped through the Old Man's ashen hair, blowing it back, but came in the opposite direction at Mace, and threads of his hair thrashed against his face. He used a gloved hand to push it back to no avail.

"You know why I have summoned you, Pursan?" The powerful voice rumbled across the space between them. He paused and smiled. "Of course you do."

Mace's fingertips were numb, even with the protection of the gloves, and his nose and cheeks had also lost feeling, along with his toes.

"It is over. You have failed me. A sad disappointment. I gave you such power, such position. But you were not appreciative, nor heedful. You were once a favored general in my legion. What has become of you?" He turned his back on Mace and seemed to be absorbed by the night. "What should I do, Pursan? What do you suggest?"

"I will make it up to you," Mace choked out.

The Old Man looked back, his face illuminated by the faint light—stony, pale, chiseled—eyes that penetrated. "You cannot make it up to me."

"Please," Mace said. "I have served you well, with only this single failure. We can regroup, build stronger weapons. The Hades Project was just the first idea. The next one will—"

"Stop. Can you not see even a second into the future? We have been tricked from the beginning. As I suspected, the young girl is a soldier of God. She is Furmiel's other twin daughter, and one day will lead God's army against us. That is her heritage. She was sent in disguise so that we might not identify her. Now she stands at Cotten Stone's side."

"How was I to know?"

"Because I gave you that responsibility, Pursan. You were to stop her. Must I tend to every minute detail? It is so exhausting. That is why I depended on you." He glanced down at the circle and pentagram carved into the stone floor of the courtyard. "And the other child, the boy—he, too, has our enemy's blessing. He will lead the army with the girl. Together they will rise to power. In time, they will command the Indigo army and wage war on the Rubies. That is their destiny. Ironic, isn't it, that the CyberSys quantum computer is called Destiny?"

Numbness crept up Mace's legs. "All I ask is just one more chance."

The Old Man raised his hand, and a blast of icy air roared through the courtyard. "I am finished with you."

THE OAK

THE SOUND OF THE backhoe's grinding metal gears was stiff competition for conversation.

Lindsay stood with Alan where her house had once been, while they watched Devin and Tera pilfer a pile of building materials for items they could use to build their fort.

"They don't seem fazed at all by everything they went through," Lindsay said.

"No, they don't. That's the beauty of being a kid," Alan said.

"Lucky for them they can't imagine what the world would be like today if Max hadn't been able to get the Destiny computer up and running, and start shutting down the Hades worm. I really think we'd have been thrown back to the Dark Ages if he hadn't. The kids wouldn't be searching for scraps to build a fort, we'd be scrounging for survival."

"Worse than that. We'd all be killing each other."

"I gotta say, it was so gracious of the Russians to return the Holy Lance to the Vienna museum. The presentation by the

Russian president with Cotten and John standing beside him was amazing."

"Now that it's the real thing, I'll bet they put the relic under much tighter security this time around."

"Look at them," Lindsay said, gesturing toward Devin and Tera. "They are such innocents, yet they've touched billions of lives."

Alan smiled. "Speaking of innocent, I guess poor Ben Ray's name has been redeemed. In the end, his family has something good to hang on to. He sacrificed his life for Devin's. Little by little Devin is revealing everything that happened—it's a bit disjointed—but I'm putting the pieces together. I have to remember to listen to my son and fill in the blanks for him. I almost missed the radio station numbers he kept repeating. And that was what helped the FBI zero in on the location of the Hades facility. Between Max doing his thing and them storming the facility in Arkansas, we are waking up today on a safer planet." Alan grinned as Tera tossed Devin a piece of particle board. "I didn't know little girls were into building forts." Alan said.

"Cotten and I had one. Actually it was more of a tree house. It was in the big oak that used to be right over there," she said, pointing to a charred trunk. "Such a magnificent tree. What a shame."

"I wish we could bring everything you had back to the way it was before the fire, but under the circumstances, all we can do is leave something behind—a memorial of some sort."

"What you are doing for us is very special," Lindsay said.

"It gives me great pleasure. There should be something here in memory of what happened. Once they're built, the Jordan Apartments will at least carry on your name."

"I suppose," Lindsay said. "No, I'm sorry, you're right. I'm so lost, Alan. Thank God you're here or else I would have nowhere to turn."

"I know you hate to see your homestead buried under. It has to be painful. But you and Tera, Devin and I, have to go underground. If our kids are easy to locate, the Rubies will hunt them down and hurt them. I'll find a place—I've got the money and resources to take us out of sight. I understand that you don't like to accept handouts, but you have to realize this is not a handout. This is a necessity if we're going to survive."

Lindsay bowed her head in thought. "Okay."

"I've had Max step in for me so I can spend some time getting you on your feet."

"I guess it won't be so hard," Lindsay said. "I don't have many friends and neither does Tera. We can start anew, anywhere in the world, I suppose. Living in a hut in Sumatra is better than being afraid that Tera is going to be hurt."

"Good," Alan said.

"That brings Kai to mind. What do you suppose she is doing now in her new life?"

"You mean who is she fleecing next?"

"You couldn't see because you were on the phone, but I was watching her when you were speaking to security. When she heard you tell them to escort her out of the building, I thought fire would shoot out of her ears."

"She'll get over it," he said.

The sound of a diesel engine coming up the drive made them turn.

A huge flatbed trailer threw clouds of dust and ash into the air.

"What is this?" Lindsay said.

"Something to mark the spot where your farm once stood. A living reminder of what happened here after you and Tera are gone."

Lindsay's hand went to her mouth when she saw the truck's payload. Chained to the deck was a huge sprawling oak.

———

The sky looked polished, spit-shined blue, not even a tiny puff of a cloud. The sun shone through the car window, along with the heater keeping it toasty inside, considerably different from the 23 degrees outside. Cotten had one hand on the steering wheel and the other on the console where John's hand was wrapped around hers.

"I wish we'd had time to look at Christmas lights," she said as she drove into the Louisville International Airport parking garage.

"Guess it wasn't high on our list."

"No," Cotten said. "Still, it seems we never have time to just catch up. Time alone. I know I should be grateful you had business in New York and were able to fly out here for a couple of days to bring in the New Year, and it meant a lot to Lindsay and Tera."

"I'm glad I came, too. I'd like a little time together—even better than looking at holiday lights." John glanced at his watch. "Unfortunately, there are only a few moments left before I have to check in," he said.

"I don't want you to go," Cotten blurted, twisting in the seat so she faced him. She heard the slight crack in her voice and was certain he did, too.

"I'll miss you, as I always do," he said. "You're a special lady."

Cotten hung her head and wiped a tear from her cheek. "I promised I wouldn't do this," she said. "I'm sorry." She fumbled for her purse, took out a tissue, and dabbed her nose. "Okay," she said, looking up and tossing back her hair. "Glad I got that over with and out of the way."

He smiled at her. "You don't always have to be such a tough cookie."

"You know what I think?"

"No, what?"

"Timing is everything," Cotten said confidently.

"What do you mean?"

"What if we'd met years ago, before you decided to do the priest thing?"

John smoothed her hair back. "But we didn't, and we can't change that."

"I know." Her voice was shallow and quaking.

"We are lucky people, you and I. Blessed really, that we did meet."

"Why does this have to be so damn hard?" She felt the tears swell again. "You bring out the worst in me. Nobody likes a gal on a crying jag. And it makes my mascara run. I must be a real sight."

John laughed, then held her face with both his hands. "You're beautiful. Even when you cry."

Cotten stared into his deep blue eyes, the bluest she had ever known. "I didn't really mean it. You don't bring out the worst in me. You're the best thing that ever happened to me." She glanced at the clock on the instrument panel and heaved out a loud sigh. "You better get going or you'll miss your flight. I'd walk you in, but I'd really make a fool of myself blubbering away as you disappear down the concourse." She said it almost whimsically, then hesitated before she spoke again. This time her voice was strangled and serious. "I just can't watch you walk away."

"It's okay," he said, then opened the door. "Pop the trunk for me."

Cotten pressed the button and heard the lock spring. She got out and walked to the back of the car watching him take out his bags.

"John," she said.

He folded his garment bag over his arm and looked up at her.

She knew her mouth was open, ready to speak, but she didn't dare say the words.

John put down the bag, draping it over his suitcase, then folded her in his arms.

"Me, too, Cotten Stone. Me, too."

If you enjoyed *The Hades Project*, read on for an except of the next Cotten Stone Mystery.

Black Needles

COMING FALL 2008 FROM MIDNIGHT INK

SUBWAY

Jeff Calderon knew he was dying as he shoved the token in the slot before stumbling through the turnstile and down the steps to the subway platform. The rumble of the train, even though muffled by the clotted blood in his ears, sent a spear of searing pain shooting through his skull.

Calderon braced his head with both hands until the train finally came to a stop, its doors sliding open with a hiss. He wasn't sure how long his legs would hold him. The raging 105-degree fever seemed to be melting his bones into what felt like a slurry of molten marrow. He snatched a gulp of air, and it howled through his airways like wind in a chimney.

Get on the train. Move. Get on the train.

Laboring, Calderon trapped himself in the flow of boarding passengers, their bodies pushing him along.

There were no seats available, only a spot for his hand to grip a pole. Just as he wrapped his fingers around it, a deep croupy cough clutched up in his chest. With his free hand, he covered his lips with a handkerchief, and the coppery taste of blood-streaked mucus sprayed the inside of his mouth. The flecks of phlegm bloomed like miniature scarlet geraniums, seeping through the threads of the white cloth.

The train lurched, and Calderon rocked sideways, bumping a young man with an earphone crammed in his ear and an iPod clipped to his belt.

"What the—?" The young guy stared at the handkerchief. He let go of the pole and stepped back. "What's the matter with you, man?"

Like dominoes, the passengers' attention turned to focus on Calderon. They retreated from him, crowding into the opposite ends of the subway car.

"Oh my God," a woman said, using her hands like a surgical mask.

Calderon wiped his face, breaking loose the crusts of dried blood and spittle from the corners of his mouth. He didn't blame the passengers for staring or for feeling disgust alongside their horror. They had good reason.

His eyes burned and his skin hurt to touch. The five ibuprofen tablets he choked down an hour ago hadn't seemed to dent the pain or the fever. Probably made the bleeding worse. He felt a warm, thick trickle drip from his nose and again heard gasps. He wiped away the blood with the back of his hand, smearing it across his cheek.

The train pulled into the next station, and all the passengers except Calderon fought their way through the open doors.

The first incoming passenger froze in the doorway before backing out and stretching his arms like a gate. "Stop!" he yelled. "Nobody get on the train."

"What's going on?" a man said, forcing his way past. "Get outta my way." But then, as his eyes landed on the sole occupant of the car, he bolted back. "Holy shit."

The doors slid closed, and Calderon watched the faces staring at him through the window. In a moment the train was in the darkness of the tunnel, and he closed his eyes. He wheezed a shallow breath and again was overcome by a strangling cough. He tried to stifle it and keep the cough shallow. Over the last twenty-four hours he had learned that each time he coughed it irritated his airways even more, bringing about a fit of uncontrollable spasmodic hacking. He kept his mouth closed, coughing as if in a theater and not wanting to disturb anyone. His cheeks flared with the gush of air from his lungs, but the force behind the cough burst through. A jet of blood and mucus spewed out splattering the pole, and a fine pink cloud floated in the air. After several minutes his lungs rested. Time was running out.

The next stop would be his last. He was almost there. This time when the doors opened, Calderon nearly fell out onto the platform. He saw the expressions of those who looked at him in total revulsion. He lowered his head and kept his eyes cast on the concrete. Halfway up the stairs, he grabbed the railing, doubting he could go on. He stopped and leaned against the wall for a moment before continuing up to the sidewalk.

The fever had him shivering, and he thought about what a paradox that was. His body was burning up and what he felt, except for the scorching in his eyes, was a bottomless chill.

Only half a block to go.

He approached the front entrance to his final destination.

The crowd on the street seemed to part like the Red Sea when God divided it to save the Israelites from the Egyptians. But he knew this was not the work of God. It was the result of the terror that took hold of the pedestrians at the sight of a nearly fleshless skeleton of a man whose eye sockets were soot black and every orifice leaked blood and body fluids.

Calderon pushed through the revolving doors into the lobby of the Satellite News Network. Then all his remaining strength caved in and his knees buckled. He collapsed face down on the marble floor.

An SNN security officer was first at his side. Squatting, he pressed the button on his shoulder-mounted mic and said, "Code red. Dial 9-1-1." Slowly, he maneuvered Calderon onto his side. "Jesus Christ!" He reared back at the sight.

Calderon opened one eye. He felt the strings of mucus that glued his lips together stretch as he spoke.

"Cotten Stone. I must speak to Cotten Stone."

LAST WORDS

"How long will you be in New York?" Cotten Stone asked before taking a sip of tea. She sat in a booth of the small coffee shop a half block from the world headquarters and studios of the Satellite News Network. Across from her was John Tyler, her closest friend, confidant, and the unfulfilled love of her life. Cardinal John Tyler was director of the Venatori, the ultra-covert intelligence agency of the Vatican.

"Just a few days," he answered.

Cotten smiled over the rim of her cup. They had met ten years previous when she was a rookie reporter for SNN and John was a priest and biblical historian on a leave-of-absence from the priesthood. Over the years, they had taken part in many headline-grabbing adventures together.

As she sipped her tea, she said, "Then while you're here we might be able to squeeze in some time to catch up. I mean I don't want to interrupt your schedule or anything. I just thought . . ."

"My schedule is flexible. And there's no way you could be interrupting. I've looked forward to this trip especially because I thought we could spend a little time together. You're good for me, Cotten Stone."

She closed her eyes and shook her head. "How do you always do that—make me feel like I'm the first thing on your mind?" She set her cup down. "Wait, don't answer. I don't want an explanation. It might take the magic out of it."

"Magic, huh? Is that what it is?"

"Yep. Nobody else in my entire life has ever made me feel that I was special like you do."

"Well, maybe I make you feel that way because you *are* a special lady."

"Damn," she said, wrapping her hands around the bowl of the cup.

"What?" John said.

"You know exactly what. The priest thing."

John reached across and took her hands in his. "But we've learned to deal with it."

He was right. But it didn't stop her from wishing he weren't a priest and that they could just fall into each other's arms. She tilted her head. "Know what else?"

"No. What?" he said.

"Those red robes cardinals wear aren't all that flattering. I like you better like this, in a polo shirt and jeans."

"It's casual Friday at the Vatican," John said with a chuckle. "So what would you like to do for the rest of this afternoon—"

Cotten's cell rang. *Bad timing.* "Hold that thought." Groping in her purse, she dug the phone out and flipped it open. "Cotten Stone."

She listened for a minute before snapping the phone closed. Plowing her fingers though her hair, she said, "Never fails. It just doesn't work out for us, does it? I've been called back to SNN. Some guy just staggered into the lobby and collapsed. Says he needs to talk to me." She gathered up her purse. "I wonder what this is all about?" As she slipped out of the booth, she said, "John, I'm so sorry. I really thought we could spend the afternoon together. I told them to only call me in an emergency. They said I'd better get there right away. The guy's in pretty bad shape."

"No problem. I'll settle up here and give you a call later. I'm meeting with the assistant director of the FBI this afternoon. Maybe dinner?"

"That would be perfect." Cotten paused next to him. "It's so good to be with you, John Tyler. But it wasn't long enough. You promise to call me later?"

"You bet," he said. "Now go. Find out why this guy's dying to see you."

———

Cotten barreled through the Satellite News Network's revolving doors. A bevy of SNN employees had gathered around a man lying on the floor.

News director, Ted Casselman, Cotten's boss, mentor, and friend ushered her through the crowd.

"Who is he?" she asked, catching the first glimpse of the man.

"No idea," Ted said. "Security says he's got no ID."

"Has he said anything?"

"Not a word since he asked for you. Ambulance is on its way."

Cotten glared down at the man sprawled on the floor. "What's the matter with him? Jesus, he looks so—"

"Stone." The raspy voice was barely heard over the commotion in the lobby.

Cotten started to kneel but Ted tugged on her arm. "Don't get too close. We have no idea what's wrong with him."

An SNN cameraman suddenly appeared. "Okay?" he said to Ted.

Ted gave his consent with a nod. "I'm going to get this on tape," he said to Cotten.

The cameraman moved closer, flipped on the camera-mounted flood light and focused.

The man muttered something followed by a flow of frothy blood foaming from his mouth.

"I didn't understand you," Cotten said, ignoring Ted and going to her knees.

The fast-approaching sound of sirens heralded the arrival of NYC Fire and Rescue.

He tried to speak with no success. Cotten lifted his head. He coughed, and crimson-lined bubbles swelled and burst out his nostrils. A thin thread of glistening red mucus dangled from his bottom lip.

She heard the sirens build to a crescendo before suddenly going quiet on the street outside. "What did you say?" she asked him.

"Step aside! Move back!" Harsh voices shouted from the direction of the lobby doors as the paramedics rushed toward her.

She bent close to the man's face. His glazed-over eyes finally found their target and latched on to hers.

"Tell me," Cotten said.

"Black needles," he barely scratched out before closing his eyes.

DOA

AFTER THE EXCITEMENT SETTLED down, employees began filing out of the SNN lobby to return to work. Through the glass doors, Cotten and Ted watched the medics load the sick man into the ambulance.

"What did he say to you?" Ted asked.

Cotten threaded her tea-colored hair behind one ear and shrugged. "He was delirious. Mumbled something about dirty needles, black needles, I think. Probably a junkie."

"We need to evaluate our building's security procedures," Ted said, looking over his shoulder at maintenance cleaning up the area where the man had collapsed. He and Cotten walked across the marble floor inlayed with the gold satellite dish and SNN world globe logo. Entering the elevators, Ted pushed the eighth-floor button. "How's John?"

"He's great. In town for a meeting with some people from the FBI and the State Department." She watched the digital floor indicator click off the levels as the elevator climbed to the eighth floor where the network had its news department, video edit suites, and archives.

Cotten shifted her gaze to Ted's reflection in the polished bronze walls of the elevator, thinking how much she appreciated and respected him. He was a constant source of unequivocal support—in the best and worst times of her career. And she'd had her share of major screw-ups. But when she did, Ted was there to remind her that it was okay to make mistakes, just don't make them again. His recent second heart attack forced him to slow down his work schedule and Cotten worried about him. But Ted didn't like anyone fussing over him. Even with the health issues, he still made a strong, commanding figure as news director.

Ted caught her watching him in the reflection. "It's hard for you, isn't it?"

"What?"

"John coming in and out of your life."

"It's that obvious?" Cotten looked away.

"Want my typical fatherly advice?"

"Do I have a choice?"

"Enjoy the time you have together. After my close calls with the Grim Reaper, I've learned to live in the moment, not in the next one. Everything else is a waste of time."

The elevator came to stop and the doors opened.

Ted put his arm around Cotten's shoulders and gave a comforting tug. "Live in the moment," he said, then let her exit first. "We've had enough excitement for one day, kiddo."

"You're right. That guy was in bad shape. Hope he makes it." She glanced around the newsroom at the reporters and editors moving like worker bees in the heart of the hive. "Talk to you later, Ted."

He waved as they parted, and Cotten headed for her office. But something kept nagging like an unscratchable itch—why had the guy in the lobby asked for her?

———

Three hours later, a young intern fresh out of journalism school came to Cotten's door. "Here's the first draft of the Shroud of Turin piece, Ms. Stone."

"Thanks, Tracy." She motioned the girl in. "Do me a favor."

"Sure. I'd be glad to."

"You heard about the commotion in the lobby earlier?"

"Yeah. Sounded like the poor guy was really bad off."

"See if you can find out which hospital they transported him to and the status of his condition."

"Do you have his name?"

"No," Cotten answered. "He had no ID."

"Okay, I'll see what I can come up with," Tracy said. She spun on her heels and scurried away.

Cotten glanced at her phone for the umpteenth time just in case the message light was blinking and John had called while she was on the line. She swiveled her chair and peered out her window at Central Park West. This was her favorite time of year—particularly with the leaves turning and the brisk air she enjoyed during her walk to work each morning. Only when the elements would become unbearable later in the season did she give up her sidewalk commute and take a cab.

She scanned the Shroud story—a report of a new test on pollen traces found in the Shroud of Turin. The pollen was identified as a type of thistle plant called *Gundelia tournefortii,* which was thought to have been used to fashion the Crown of Thorns worn by Jesus Christ at the Crucifixion. The plant is found primarily in Israel around Jerusalem.

After reading the script, Cotten wrote "possible second segment" across the top. She hosted a weekly, in-depth, science- and religion-based program called *Relics* that explored the facts and myths of ancient objects. This might make a good filler piece, she thought. Her prime story for the next show was the debunking of the bones thought to belong to Joan of Arc.

She did some line edits on the Shroud story, then a little more research on the Internet. But no matter what she tried to do to distract her, two things remained on her mind for the rest of the afternoon—John Tyler and the man in the lobby.

She was about to pack it in for the day when there came a knock. The new intern stood in her doorway. "Come in, Tracy. Have a seat."

The girl smiled broadly.

"What's up?" Cotten asked.

After hesitating, she said, "I don't want this to come off as a major suck-up, Ms. Stone, but I just needed to say what an honor it is to be able to work with you."

"Well, thank you," Cotten said. "You just made my day. Have a seat. And Tracy, call me Cotten."

She smiled again and dropped into a chair. "Did you know we studied you in broadcasting—there's a course on how ancient religious objects have changed our lives. It's a lot about the impact of your reporting work. When I found out SNN had accepted me into the internship program, I hoped I would just get to meet you, but better yet, to work with you."

"You're awfully sweet, Tracy, and I appreciate the kind words. We work as a team at SNN, and it's only with everyone giving their all that we make those worthy accomplishments happen."

"Well, I'm just proud to be a part of it."

"So, what did you find out about our mystery man?"

Tracy unfolded a piece of paper and handed it to Cotten. "He died en route to the hospital. This is the name of the ER physician I spoke to."

"Did they determine cause of death?"

"That's what's so weird. The doctor said that they brought the guy in but there was some kind of mix-up. Somebody released the body to a mortuary before the coroner picked it up to do the autopsy."

Cotten rolled her eyes. "How does this kind of crap happen? Typical of the right hand not knowing, blah, blah, blah. Incompetence at its best. I guess they'll get it straight in the end."

"I don't think so," Tracy said. "Nobody could find the documentation identifying the funeral home."

Joe Moore (Florida) spent twenty-five years in the television post-production industry where he received two regional Emmy® awards for individual achievement in audio mixing. As a freelance writer, Joe reviewed fiction for *The Fort Lauderdale Sun-Sentinel*, *The Tampa Tribune*, and *The Jacksonville Florida Times Union*. He is a member of the International Thriller Writers, the Authors Guild, and Mystery Writers of America.

Lynn Sholes (Florida) is a special assignment teacher for the Broward County School District in South Florida. Writing as Lynn Armistead McKee, she penned six historical novels set in pre-Columbian Florida. As Lynn Sholes, she has changed genres and is writing mystery/thrillers. Lynn is a member of Mystery Writers of America, International Thriller Writers, Florida Writers Association, the Authors Guild, Sisters in Crime, and the National Council of Teachers of English.